THE ROUND TOWER

The
Round Tower

CATHERINE COOKSON

MACDONALD AND JANE'S · LONDON

First impression, 1968
Second impression, 1968
Third impression, 1972
Fourth impression, 1974
Fifth impression, 1976

Copyright © Catherine Cookson, 1968

ISBN 0 356 02320 6

Published in Great Britain by
Macdonald and Jane's Publishers Limited
Paulton House, 8 Shepherdess Walk
London, N.1

Printed in Great Britain by
REDWOOD BURN LIMITED
Trowbridge & Esher

To John Foster White
My publisher for many years
and always my friend

BOWER PLACE

Bower Place

The four heads were almost wedged together as they looked out of the small open window of the fitting shop and leered at the uniformed schoolgirls walking down the public pathway that ran between the railings cutting off Affleck and Tate's Engineering Works, on one side, and the firm's playing fields on the other.

"There's a new one there the day; I haven't seen her afore."

"Coo! haven't you? Why, that's God-Almighty's daughter."

"No kiddin'."

"Aye, it is. They usually send the Bentley to the Convent for her."

"They're not gona let on the day."

"Let them get by and when they think we're not gona say nowt I bet yer life they'll squint round."

"There! What did I tell you."

As one of the four girls slanted her glance backwards towards the men, the tallest of them shouted, "What yer gona be when yer grow up? . . . Oh! a tart, are you?" He shook his head, "Eeh! that's nice. Let me know when you're done an' I'll come an' have a nibble at yer." When the girl's head jerked upwards, the man's voice, louder now, called, "How about a bit of homework first?"

"Never mind bloody homework, see to the dayshift!" The voice brought the heads from the window, and three of the men returned sheepishly to their benches, but the fourth one who had been doing most of the talking rubbed his greasy hands through his hair and remarked nonchalantly, "Oh, aye."

"None of your lip, Taggart; don't come the smart Aleck with me. Now get back to your bench, and bloody quick."

As the man moved away he said as if to himself, "All right, Gussie?" then, "Oh, pardon –" he looked sideways –"or should I say Mr. Cotton?"

Angus Cotton let out a string of oaths, then went to close the window. The girls, farther along the path now, were looking back, and he stared at them for a second before banging the window closed. He now glanced round at the bowed heads of the ten men of whom he was in charge, then walked to the end of the shop where, on a bench, lay a large sheet of paper on which was a square and a compass, and his teeth began grating together as he continued to work out measurements on the paper.

About five minutes later he took a rough sketch to a bench to the right of him, where stood an oldish man. "Can you follow that, Danny?" he asked. "Or will I take it along to the drawing-office and have it polished up?"

Danny Fuller surveyed the drawing, then said, "I'll have a shot." His casual reply meant that his hand would make the work as accurate as any machine could. He was studying the drawing when he said, "There'll be trouble if you don't do something with that big head. Every day they're at those lasses. One of these times they'll go home and tell their folks what's been said in passin', and then there'll be sparks flying. Taggart comes out with some red rivets I'm tellin' you. An' if I was you I'd make it me business to be in the shop around this time when they're leaving school, 'cos I'm tellin' you, lad, they come out with things. The day was nothin'."

"I don't suppose they say anythin' that those daisies haven't heard afore.'

"They're at the Convent, lad."

Angus Cotton turned a humorous glance on the old

12

man. "And you think that's any protection the day? Their real education can start when they turn the telly on."

"Oh, I don't suppose those lassies are allowed to look at the telly much."

Angus now thrust out his hand and pushed Danny, saying, "You're fifty years behind it, Danny. I bet you if you heard them talkin' among themselves your last three hairs would rise." He flicked the thin fringe of white hair hanging over the collar of the old man's coat, then returned to his bench.

But as he worked he thought, "He's right about Taggart. I'll bloody well have to sew his mouth up if it's the last thing I do; it's stretching too wide for peace." Yet he knew he'd have to get Taggart for something else other than chatting up the lasses. The fellows in this shop had always chatted the lasses. Any lass that came along that path expected it, and some could give as much as they got, but, as Danny said, those were Convent school kids.

It was thirty minutes later when Mr. Wilton caused an uneasy stir by marching through the shop, calling, "Cotton! Cotton!"

"Aye. You want me?" Angus came from under a machine, straightened his back and stood wiping his hands on a rag as he looked into the infuriated face of a man who had to be reckoned with in Affleck and Tate. Mr. Jonathan Ratcliffe might be the manager but it was his second in command whom the employees had to answer to usually. But Angus never let Wilton, or anybody else for that matter, think he could intimidate him. As he waited for the assistant manager to speak he said again, "You want me?"

Mr. Wilton now seemed to find difficulty in getting out his words. "What's been going on here?" He flung his head from one side to the other, swallowed deeply, then added, "Can't you control these louts?"

"Control these . . .?" Angus didn't repeat the word. There was only one lout in this shop, and even he wouldn't

13

thank anybody for putting a name to him. He said stiffly, "I don't know what you're gettin' at."

"You'll know soon enough when the boss is finished with you. He's at white heat; he's had two parents phone him within the last ten minutes because their daughters cannot pass down the Cut without filth being strewn over them."

"Oh . . . Oh!" Angus nodded his head.

"You know then?"

"I know nowt about filth; I know the lads have a crack now and again.'

"A crack? What are you talking about, man? These are schoolgirls from the Convent, and one, for your information, happens to be Mr. Ratcliffe's daughter."

Angus felt his body stiffen. He hadn't noticed Van there; she never came this way.

"You'd better get along, and sharp; he wants to see you. And there'll be some sweeping out of this shop if I have anything to do with it."

Angus turned a cool eye on Mr. Wilton. He liked Wilton as much as he did God-Almighty Ratcliffe. Perhaps he liked Wilton less because he had more to do with him. He walked past him now and took off his overall and hung it on a nail; then, looking into the narrow, pale face of the assistant manager, he said, "There are lots of places looking out for sweepings these days, Mr. Wilton. One should bear that in mind."

He heard a sound that could have been a chuckle coming from the direction of Danny Fuller's bench; then he went out of the shop, through the sheds, across the car park and into the building that housed the offices.

He took the lift to the third floor and stepped out into the panelled hall, looked about him for a second, then crossed to a door which bore the name "Jonathan Ratcliffe" on a gilt-lettered board. He didn't bother to knock on the door because he knew he would have to pass the secretary before he could get into the holy of holies.

Miss Morley raised her eyes and looked at the burly shock-haired workman. She didn't ask what his business was, she knew. "Wait a minute," she said stiffly.

As she went towards a far door Mr. Wilton came panting into the room, and he checked her, saying, "I'll see to this," and went swiftly through the door, closing it after him, and Miss Morley turned and favoured this Angus Cotton with a glance that told him plainly what she thought about him and all his kin: Dirty-mouthed individuals.

It was on the point of his tongue to say, "Now look here you, get this straight," when the door opened and Mr. Wilton said crisply, "This way, Cotton."

Angus was a second before moving, and then his step was slow, and as he passed Mr. Wilton he looked him straight in the face before turning his attention to the man sitting behind the big black desk at the end of the long room.

Although this was only the second time that Angus had been in the boss's office, he guessed he knew more about this man than did any of the thousand employees in the firm.

He had been eight years old when his mother first went to work at the Ratcliffes' house, as a daily. That was all they could afford in those days, because although Jonathan Ratcliffe was a draughtsman and earning good money, both he and his missus thought big, and spent big. As his mother said, they knew what they were doing right from the start, for the guests they wined and dined were always people of influence. And it had paid off. Oh aye, it had paid off for Mr. Ratcliffe, for he was the big noise of the town now. All you needed was a little bit of brain, a good bit of influence and a cart load of luck, not to mention the art of sucking up. It was the sucking up that had pushed him over Mr. Brett's head. If anybody should be sitting in that chair now it was Mr. Brett, and everybody in the place knew it, but Mr. Brett was still in the drawing office.

"Remember the last time you were in this office, Cotton?"

Neither the tone nor the words startled him as they were meant to.

"I remember, sir."

"You were then doing rough work in number one shop, and out of regard for your mother's long service with my family I wanted to help her, so I didn't only have you transferred to number three, I put you in charge of number three,"

Angus drew in a deep breath that pushed out his waistcoat, and he let it out again before he said, "You put me in number three, sir, on the recommendation of Mr. Brett, who had seen some of my drawings and thought I should be given a chance to develop."

Jonathan Ratcliffe brought his fist firmly down on the blotting pad, and he thrust his face forward slightly as he said below his breath, "Mr. Brett's recommendations would have counted as nothing unless I gave the word; surely you have the sense to understand that. And let me tell you, I was criticised from a number of quarters for going over other recommendations and pushing you up. Such chances don't often come the way of men from the floor in number one, not at your age anyway, and with your slight experience . . . ."

"Did you have me here, sir, just to tell me this? Because if you did then I've got me answers ready for you. The first is, I'm doing a good job along there, a damn fine one, Mr. Brett says . . . ."

"Be quiet! How dare you! You're forgetting yourself, Cotton. You take advantage because of your mother. But since you ask, no, I didn't bring you here to remind you why you were promoted but to tell you that in my opinion – no matter what Mr. Brett might say – you are not making a damn fine job of running number three because you cannot control the men under you. It is coming to something when parents demand to speak to me on the phone because their daughters are insulted every time they pass the works: schoolgirls having filth hurled at them, bar-room chatter, obscenities, and you allow it to happen."

"I allow nothing of the sort."

"You were present."

"I was WHAT!"

"One of the girls said so, she even described you. Big, fair hair . . . ."

"Well, she's a bloody liar, that's all I can say."

"Will you moderate your language, Cotton. I think you forget who you are, and where you are."

"I don't forget either, sir; an' I say, if she says I was there she's a bloody liar. I heard the lads at the window and I went and stopped them and shut the window . . . . But anyway –" he lifted his hand airily – "what's all the fuss about? You know yourself, sir, that all along the east side of the building where the Cut is the men have always chipped the lasses."

"These are not lasses, these are Convent school girls, young ladies."

"Huh!" Angus's head jerked backwards, and the sound infuriated Jonathan Ratcliffe further. The one desire he had at the moment was to get rid of this fellow for good and all, to say, "Get out! You're finished." But there were two simple reasons why he couldn't put his desire into action. The Union was one, and the second had even much more bearing, his wife. If he were to sack young Cotton they would lose Emily's services. Now, when they had the money to employ four servants, even with the wages they demanded to-day, they were quite impossible to come by. Helps came and went by the week in the house; only Emily was constant. Even if her blunt manner was as big a trial to his wife as was her son's I'm-as-good-as-you attitude, nothing must happen to cause Emily to give in her notice. That would be disastrous; especially at the present time with Susan's wedding in the offing and the Braintrees likely to drop in at any time.

He made a great effort to mollify his tone, but he could not look at the fellow as he said, "Well, I'll overlook it this time – not that the parents concerned will, I can assure you – but should it occur again," he now raised his eyes without lifting his head, "I will be forced to take very strong measures. By the way, who are the men concerned?"

"Does it matter?"

"Of course it matters." He was barking again.

"Roland, Weekes, Naylor . . . and Taggart."

"I'll get Mr. Wilton to deal with them, but," his finger wagged now accompanying each word, "I'm holding you responsible, Cotton. Remember that. That's what you're paid for, responsibility. That's all.

He watched the big figure turn slowly about, and when the door closed on him he drew his lips tightly in between his teeth and muttered to himself, "Insolent swine! . . . Trash."

Jonathan Ratcliffe left his office at six o'clock. Miss Morley was still working, as was Mr. Wilton, but the rest of the works seemed entirely deserted. There were only three cars standing in the car park and it was with a sense of deep irritation that he noticed a man with his head under the bonnet of a Volkswagen. As he unlocked his car door he asked, "Something wrong, Arthur?"

Arthur Brett straightened himself and smiled grimly, saying, "Third time in a week it's packed up on me. I'll have to get the garage to come and fetch it."

There was nothing for Jonathan Ratcliffe but to say, "Well, hop in."

As he drove his Bentley through the gates that the watchman held open for him, he remarked casually, "You want to change it."

"Yes . . . yes, I know that."

"Well, can't you?" He cast a swift glance towards the man whom he had lived next door to for the past eighteen years, the man who made him feel uneasy when in his presence, the man whose head he had jumped over, which jump had enabled him to take another two jumps into dead men's shoes, men who had died apparently long before their time. Well, as he had told himself often before, some were destined to move upwards and some to remain stationary. Arthur Brett had remained stationary because he had no push, no initiative; he was a plodder. What was more, he'd never had to strive for anything in his young days, he'd had it on a plate from when he was born. It wasn't good to have things too easy when you were young, not if you wanted to go places.

When he stopped at the traffic lights he stared ahead as he said, "I've been having trouble with Cotton."

"You mean Angus?"

"Who else? There's only one Cotton on the books as far as I know."

"What's he done?"

"Spewing filth from the shop window at the Convent school girls."

"Angus! I can't believe it. He's a rough customer, but his roughness doesn't take that form, I'd lay my life."

"He's your golden-headed boy, isn't he Arthur?"

"No, he's no golden-headed boy of mine, but he's got ideas. Given the chance, he'll do things. Pity he hadn't had more schooling though. But he's no fool . . . . No, he's no fool." His voice had sunk on the last words and there was a silence as they drove along the embankment, round the park and up Brampton Hill, until Jonathan Ratcliffe said, "The trouble is he can't control the fellows under him. Apparently, they are at this every day."

"You can't hold him responsible for that."

"Oh, can't I?" Jonathan cast a glance sideways. "That I can. If his men are hanging out of the windows, they're not working. I'm going to put a stop to it."

19

Halfway up the hill the car turned right down a wooded lane and came to a stop at the end of a line of larches, and as Arthur Brett went to get out of the car he said, "Thanks, Jonathan." Then standing on the kerb he bent down and, looking through the window, said slyly, "Whatever you do to Angus will react on Emily; I don't think Jane would be pleased if Emily went, do you?"

For answer Jonathan slammed in the gears and drove past the remaining larches, past the blue sitka trees that marked his boundary, through the imposing iron gate and up the dull pink composition drive that led to his equally imposing-looking house.

Bower Place, as he had named his house, was both a source of pleasure and irritation to him. Pleasure, because he had designed it himself. Its situation was one of the best in the town and its value had risen phenomenally in the last five years. He had paid old Brettt five hundred pounds for the two acres in 1949, and it had cost him four thousand to build the house. Now he wouldn't take a penny less than twenty thousand for the place, not with the money he had spent on it lately, and if only his ground had access to the river that would put another five thousand on it.

This was the irritation, the fact that Arthur Brett, with all that river frontage, wouldn't sell him a yard of it. He was as stubborn as his old man had been. There he was, without a penny to bless himself with – it took all his salary to keep his place going – yet he wouldn't part with one of his six acres. It was sheer spite, that's what it was; Arthur was jealous of him because he had got the post he thought should have been his by rights.

At times he became so angry that he thought he'd sell his place to a speculator and let him run up a twenty-storey block of flats. That would fix Brett. And it could be done. Oh yes, it could be done. At other times he could see the council confiscating some of Brett's six acres, and running up council houses. What did he want with six acres anyway? He never touched his land, it was like an African jungle.

He entered the house and marched through the hall, throwing his hat on to the marble and gilt hallstand, then went into the lounge where his wife and two daughters were seated. They all looked at him, and his wife spoke first. She said briefly, "Well, what have you done about it?"

"I spoke to him."

"Who?"

"Cotton, of course."

She rose to her feet. "It was him then?"

"Well, not by what he makes out. He said it was some other fellows in the shop. But he's in charge. What did happen?" He turned now towards his younger daughter, where she was sitting on the couch, one leg curled under her.

"Nothing as far as I'm concerned."

"Nothing as far as you're concerned!" His thick greying eyebrows were beetling. "Well, well! this is news. The other three were concerned; their parents were concerned. I suppose what shocked their girls didn't shock you."

"I didn't hear anything, Father."

"You were with them, weren't you?"

"Yes, of course."

"And you didn't hear anything?"

"I was thinking. I didn't even know the boys were at the window."

"Boys! Boys! They were men, and they were throwing filth down on you and you tell me you didn't hear them?"

The girl turned her head on to her shoulder and closed her eyes, and her mother said sharply, "Vanessa! Now don't take that attitude, your father is talking to you."

Vanessa Ratcliffe unwound herself from the couch and stood up straight and looked at her father. She was almost as tall as he, and a good three inches taller than her

21

mother. Her hair was a dark chestnut and fell straight on to her shoulders at the front, but tapered to a point in the middle of her back. Her eyes were brown and round, and the skin over her cheekbones spread to her lower lids without making the slightest hollow. Overall, her face was long and thin, but her lips were full, and when she smiled the corners of her mouth looked square. Her body was unformed and flat. In appearance, she took after neither her mother nor father, nor did she hold any resemblance to her elder sister, Susan, because Susan was a replica of their mother; with Ray, her ten-year-old brother, who had been sent out of the room a few minutes earlier, she had one thing in common, the colour of her hair.

Vanessa was sixteen years old and she was at the turbulent, unrestful stage of adolescence. For weeks now she had been irritated by her family, her girl friends, and everyone about her; what was more, she was experiencing a feeling that both frightened and intrigued her. She knew what it was all about but she could do nothing about it. They talked about it at school, but that didn't help, only tended to make it worse.

"I asked you a question."

"I've told you, Father. I don't remember hearing anything, only the boys . . . men shouting. Anyway," she shrugged her shoulders, "they always shout down at the girls, and that's why they go along that path. They needn't, you know."

"Do you mean to tell me that they go along there . . .?"

"Yes, Father, I do. Lucy Fulton goes that way every day just to egg them on."

Jonathan Ratcliffe swallowed deeply, then said, "Well, the Fultons didn't phone me, but Mrs. Herring did, and Kathy Young's mother. Was this the first time they'd been that way?"

"I don't know because I don't usually go home with

22

them. But anyway, why should those two make such a fuss? You should hear how they talk."

"Be quiet!" Jonathan Ratcliffe looked as if he were about to burst. "What are things coming to? Been attending the Convent school since they could walk and you telling me they . . . ." His indignation wouldn't allow him to go on.

"Well they do. And after all," she gave a little laugh, "we're not infants you know, Father; I'm sixteen and a half and Kathy Young is seventeen . . . ."

"Be quiet, girl! I don't care if you're twenty-six and a half, I wouldn't expect you to listen unmoved to the spewing of the fitting-shop louts. The trouble with you, girl, is you've no sense of dignity. The Convent has failed lamentably there. Don't you realize that you're the daughter of one of the leading families of this town." He almost said "THE leading family". "And what are people going to think if you take such talk casually, while other girls are squirming . . . . Where are you going?"

"Upstairs to do my prep."

"Well, get that defiant look off your face; and bang that door after you if you dare."

When the door was not closed at all Jane Ratcliffe hurried down the room and shut it; then returning to the fireplace and looking at her husband, she said in her prim, thin voice, "Now you'll understand when I tell you what I've got to put up with; she's getting more difficult every day. I never had this with Susan." She looked at her elder daughter. "She's getting worse."

"It's a phase; it'll pass." Susan smiled at her mother knowingly. She had no great love for her sister – they had always been at loggerheads – but since her engagement she had felt much more kindly disposed towards her. She knew what was wrong with Vanessa; she was suffering from the same complaint herself, but soon that feeling would be alleviated; only four months and she would be married. She wished it was four weeks . . . four days .

23

four minutes. Yes, four minutes. Oh, she knew what was the matter with Vanessa all right. And if her mother had any sense she'd understand too. But sex was a taboo subject in this household. Her mother would have you believe that babies came by kissing. "Mind, Susan; if a boy should try to kiss you keep your lips closed. Mind, now; keep your lips closed." That was the sex instruction she'd had. When she had children she'd tell them the whole caboodle at ten. Yes, ten. Ten wasn't too young; just look at Ray. He didn't need any sex training that little devil; you could see the knowledge in his eyes. Give him another five or six years and her father would really know what trouble meant, she was sure of that. But she was getting out of it, and oh, Lord! wasn't she thankful. No more church twice on Sundays. Brian's connections might be county and titled, but she felt sure of one thing, they were as godless as they came.

When her mother said to her father, "I told Emily," Susan rose to her feet; she just couldn't sit and listen to another debate on Emily.

"Do you think that was wise?" Jonathan Ratcliffe looked at his wife under gathered brows.

"Yes, I do. You see, she took the call from Mavis Herring, and as usual she had her ears cocked, and when Mavis said point blank that her Rona had stated that Angus Cotton was one of the men, well, I inadvertently repeated the name Angus Cotton. I said, just like that, Angus Cotton? Are you sure? And there was Emily standing at the kitchen door all eyes and ears, so I just had to tell her. But, as I said, I think it was best; she has heard our side of it now, and when she gets home and hears Angus ranting off because he was called over the coals she'll understand why. Oh!" She pursed her lips and her left eye twitched in a nervous fashion. "It's all so annoying. Why do we have to be bothered with such things at a time like this when I've so much on my mind and Brian's people coming

24

at the weekend? By the way, you didn't really go for Angus, did you?"

Jonathan Ratcliffe now bent his head forward and hunched his shoulders up, and the action told her that he was deeply irritated, and this came over clearly in his voice as he snapped, "Yes, I went for him. But not as much as I would have liked to. It maddens me to think that I have to put up with that ignorant upstart's attitude simply because we cannot do without his mother . . . . Look, Jane." He now stabbed his finger towards her. "I'm sure if you put yourself out and went around the agencies you'd come across someone."

"Don't talk nonsense, Jonathan." Jane Ratcliffe drew herself up to the limit of her five feet four inches. "You know for a fact that I need another two in the house and can't get them."

"Well, you should do what Irene is doing." He jerked his head backwards in the direction of the Brett house. "Take an au pair girl."

Jane Ratcliffe turned her head towards the french windows and focused her eyes on a white-painted, wrought-iron chair standing on the terrace, and she surveyed it for almost a minute before she said, "We've had all that out before. I'm not having any more foreigners in the house; I'm not going through that again and I think it very tactless of you, to say the least, to re-open the subject."

Oh, my God! Jonathan Ratcliffe almost said the words aloud but his Chapel training prevented it. He could blaspheme and swear in his mind, but not even his wife's finickiness, nor her narrow outlook with regard to pretty Swedish girls would permit him to take the Lord's name openly in vain. He turned and left her without further words, and as he reached the top of the broad shallow stairs he saw his younger daughter coming out of her bedroom. She turned her head in his direction for a moment, then turned it away again. There was something defiant in the action; there was something defiant in the way she

25

walked to the bathroom; her whole body was expressing defiance. He wasn't startled when the desire came to him that he wished it were possible to take a horse whip to her. Fifty years ago he could have done it. He remembered his mother saying that her father had horse-whipped her because she had committed the deadly sin of entering a theatre. It didn't matter if the play was Uncle Tom's Cabin, she had disobeyed his wishes, and she carried one of the marks of his anger visible on her neck for the rest of her life. He had never felt sorry that his mother should be so treated; he had been in entire agreement with his grandfather's attitude. A man had to stand by his principles, he had to be master in his own house. It might be considered an old-fashioned adage, but he thanked God that it still held true in some families.

As the bathroom door closed and he opened his bedroom door he thought, "Yes, one of these days I will chastise you, madam." But as he took off his coat he remembered her saying she was sixteen and a half years old. Soon she'd be beyond the age of open chastisement. Well, he would see, he would see.

24 RYDER'S ROW

As Rosie's laugh burst forth Emily put her hands up and grabbed handfuls of her son's hair and, shaking his head none too gently, she grinned widely back into his face, saying, "Aye. An' you will an' all." Then giving him a push, she ended, " But in the meantime, you'll bloody well wear these shirts for work else I'll know the reason why."

The three of them were laughing unrestrainedly now, Angus with his hand covering his face, Rosie leaning over the table, her forearms buried in the pile of old clothes, while Emily, her head back, her mouth open, thumped her broad knees with her clenched fists; then, wiping the back of her hand across her nose and mouth, she exclaimed, "Well, this won't do. We don't get paid for laughin'. Get that clobber off the table and let's get somethin' to eat. What you got ready?"

Rosie lifted up the assortment of clothes and threw them into an old armchair, saying, "Soup, and fish and chips. They'll be soggy by now; I got them nearly an hour ago. An' some Ambrosia rice. By the way, what did you pay for that lot?"

"Four and six."

"Go on! There's three dresses and two skirts there."

"I paid four and six, I tell you, I didn't pinch them."

"That's because you didn't get a chance. Who was on the counter?" Angus cast his eyes sideways at his mother, and she said, "Old fat arse Flanagan. Nobody's going to pinch much when she's around; although I saw Alice Brownlow stuff somethin' in her bag. Eeh! she's barefaced, that one. Did you hear that Millie Taylor was caught again yesterday in the supermarket? She'll go along the line as sure as life this time. This must be her tenth nap. Well, it serves her right; you can be too greedy."

"Oh, aye. Well, you remember that, Mrs. Cotton, when your fingers start to itch . . . now remember." As Angus

24 Ryder's Row

Looking down on Ryder's Row from the embankment you could well imagine you were viewing the efforts of a model railway enthusiast who had stuck a short row of houses next to the goods yard at the foot of the embankment to give a natural touch to his lay-out.

The cottages were surrounded on three sides by the accoutrements of the railway company, the embankment, the goods yard, and the cleaning sheds; the end of the row fronted the main road that ran between Fellburn and Newcastle.

Over the years the occupants of the Row had become immune to the clanking and clashing of wagons, to the hissing of steam, and now the thunder of diesel engines. Some of them had been born amid the noise, and Emily Cotton was one of these.

The Cottons had always considered themselves fortunate that they lived in the last house because their back yard was twice the size of any other in the Row, and they had only one wall through which could permeate their neighbours' conversation and their own loud interchange.

Saturday morning was usually the time when their interchange was at its loudest and most penetrating, for on a Saturday morning neither Angus Cotton nor his sister, Rose, nor Emily was at work. But on this particular Saturday morning the intermittent exchange between Angus and Rosie had been comparatively quiet. Although neither of them would admit it openly, they thought the house dead when their mother wasn't in it. Without her, there was no incentive to have a bust-up, or a cracking laugh. They sometimes said, "Coo! itn't it peaceful without her"; then they would look at the clock and wish the hours away until she burst in on them.

"She's late, isn't she?" Angus put his head into the narrow scullery and looked at Rosie where she was emptying two tins of soup at once into a pan.

"I bet she's gone to the jumble on the way back; trust her not to miss that."

"Workin' Saturday mornin'! They'll have her there on Sunday after this. Why the hell doesn't she give it up! There's no need for her to stay on there; she's done enough, she's past it."

"Don't you tell her that." Rosie jerked her black hair out of her eyes. "She'd scalp you."

"Well, let's face it. She can't do it all. Just look at this place. It's like a pig-sty; she's had enough by the time she gets in, and she doesn't need the money now. I'm goin' to have it out with her."

"Don't be so bloomin' daft, our Angus, and use your loaf. You know old Ratcliffe would wangle you out of the shop if mam left there .... You know it."

"I bloody well know nowt of the sort." Angus thrust his square chin aggressively towards her. "That's what I'm wantin' to put to the test. What do you think I feel like, being carried on her shoulders . . . at least that's what they think. But let me tell you, I got into that shop through my ability. Mark you that, through my ability."

"All right; don't bawl your head off, I can hear you."

The clank, clank, clank of shunting wagons filled the silence between them, until Rosie said, "Here she is."

As the back gate opened there came the sound of a train whistle and it seemed to pipe Emily Cotton into the house. She came in backwards, thrusting her thick, firm buttocks against the door, and from her arms she dropped on to

the table an assortment of garments, exclaiming "Th What do you think of that lot?"

"Oh, Mam! Look at the bread." Rosie retrieved loaf from underneath the clothes, then swiftly began p ing up one article after another. Holding a jumper up front of her, she said, "Oh, this is all right. What did y give for it?"

"Threepence."

"Here, I got you a couple of shirts; they'll do for wor for you." Emily threw two garments towards her son an he caught them, and without looking at them he threw them on to a chair, saying, "I've told you, Mam. I don't like wearin' other blokes' gear."

"You were bloody glad to wear other blokes' gear, let me tell you, once on a time."

"Well, I'm not any more, Mam; so don't get them for me."

"God!" Emily Cotton lowered herself into a straight-backed chair and lifting one foot slowly up on to her knee she stroked her swollen ankle vigorously, and it was to it she addressed her remarks as she said, "Talk about out of the frying-pan into the fire, I've spent most of my bloody life with upstarts. That lot along there; their noses in the bloody air so much they have to have their necks massaged. And now I come to me own house and me son tells me that he's got too damned big to wear another bloke's shirts. Let me tell you," she lifted her head to him, "you'll never be able to buy shirts of that quality in your lifetime. Let me tell you that."

Angus stared at his mother for a moment. Then, the corner of his mouth moving upwards, he went towards her and, leaning forward, put his big hands on her shoulders and brought his face down within an inch of hers and said, "Emily Cotton, that's where you're wrong. One of these days I'm goin' out and I'm goin' to buy six of the best bloodiest silk shirts in all this bloody town, and I'm goin' to wear them for work just to let them see."

turned to go out of the kitchen Emily threw an old woollen tea cosy at his head, saying, "Snotty young bugger!"

A few minutes later, when they sat down to their meal at the small square table in the middle of the kitchen, Rosie remarked, on a laugh, "You know, Mam, I've often wondered how you manage not to come out with something up there."

"Oh, you have, have you? Well, I'll tell you, Rosie." Emily's voice took on a pseudo-refined note. "It's because I know how to pass meself. I always suit me language to the company I'm in – when in Rome they say – an' I'm tellin' you there's nobody can act more refined than meself when I like."

As Angus drew his hand slowly down his face her voice suddenly changed and she bellowed at him, "You take the bloody micky, me lad, and I'll skite you out of that door."

"Who's taking the micky?" His brown eyes were dancing as he looked at her. "Of course you can pass yourself. You wouldn't have survived so long up there if you hadn't been able to. But, you know, there's somethin' I've often wondered an' all, Mam; I've wondered what effect a real good mouthful of yours would have on them."

Once more they were laughing, spluttering over their soup. When the laughter subsided Angus asked, "Did you hear anything more about yesterday's business?"

"Not much," said Emily. "Only she informed me that the master was very vexed at the whole affair." She inclined her head deeply towards Angus, and he inclined his back and said, "Oh, aye."

"She was at her most buttery this mornin'. She impressed on me that the master didn't hold you responsible; it was them awful common fellows that you work with."

"What did you say to that?"

"Nothin', I kept me silence. I find it pays with her. Say nowt and speed the work up and she gets into a tizzy. Oh, don't you worry, I can manage her all right. You

33

don't live with somebody five days a week for eighteen years and not know them inside out. I've been along of her more than I've been with either of you." She nodded from one to the other. "That's strange to say, isn't it?"

"And you don't like her?"

Emily looked at her son and said slowly, "I don't dislike her. I sort of understand her. She's a damned upstart, but she's got it from him, because he's a sanctimonious, hymn-singing, big-headed nowt. An' that's only half of it, because he's deep and calculating into the bargain. An' that Susan takes after him. An' I'm another one that'll be delighted when the wedding comes off, for then she'll be away from under me feet."

"Have you seen much of her fellow?" asked Rosie.

"Oh, he's been in twice this week. He's not a bad sort . . . . I'll tell you somethin'. He's not got one quarter of the side they have. Although he has one uncle a lord and one an admiral, he acts just like any other fellow. 'Hello, Emily', he says. 'How goes it?' "

"He doesn't; you're kiddin'." Rosie flapped her hand at her mother.

"I'm not kiddin'. An' don't you start mickying either. That's what he said. He came into the kitchen when I was gettin' lunch, and that's what he said. 'Hello, Emily. How goes it? What you hashin' up?' "

"He did?"

"Aye, he did. An' I'll tell you something else. He said I was a fine cook. An' that's more than me family's ever said to me."

"But your family never tastes your cookin', so how are we to judge? I ask you. How are we to judge?" Angus spread his hand out, palm upwards, giving emphasis to the question, and he expected her to laugh or come out with a mouthful at him. But when she dropped her fork, which was halfway to her mouth, back on to her plate and, looking at it, said dully, "I'm sorry I've neglected you," his face showed utter dismay.

"In the name of God, woman!" He scraped his chair back. "Don't be so bloody soft. You know I was only pulling your leg. If you don't cook at the week-end it's our fault because we won't let you. Isn't it, Rosie?"

"Aye, Mam. Look." Rosie put her hand gently on her mother's thick arm. "You're tired, that's what it is. He was only pullin' your leg. You neglect us! As Angus says, don't talk so dippy; where do you think we'd have been if it hadn't been for you goin' out to work. We've never wanted for anything in our lives, an' it's thanks to you."

Emily bowed her head and closed her eyelids tightly, and as the tears welled up they came one to each side of her. Their concern making them tender, they put their hands about her shoulders.

"Look," said Angus; "You're in need of a holiday, a break . . . a long one."

"I'm in need of no holiday." Emily's voice was quiet.

"Wel, you want a change, Mam." Rosie stroked the blatantly dyed black hair. "What about going to the club the night; you haven't been for weeks. That's an idea, isn't it?" She looked up at Angus. "I'll get Stan to come along. We were going to the pictures, but he doesn't mind where he goes as long as he can have his slap and tickle." She pressed her lips together and giggled, then said, "What about it, eh Angus, the club?"

"I'm game. It should be a good night. We'll have a knees-up, eh?" He brought his face down to his mother's, and she blinked rapidly and sniffed, then smiled and said, "Aye, that'll do me good, a knees-up, even if I can't get me feet off the floor." She looked at her swollen legs. "Anyway, I think I'll go and put them up for an hour now." She rose stiffly to her feet, and Rosie went with her along the narrow passage and watched her mount the stairs before returning to the kitchen. There she looked at Angus and said, "Funny. I've not seen her like that afore."

"She's tired." Angus's voice was low. "I'm tellin' you, she's tired, she's worn out."

"But she's not old," said Rosie sadly; "she's just fifty odd."

"Well she's had enough in the last twenty years to make her feel eighty. I wonder she hasn't cracked up afore now."

"But I've always thought she was as strong as a horse."

"Horses get old. Don't you know that? Even horses get old and tired . . . Go on up and see how she is."

When Rosie entered her mother's room Emily was lying on the bed, her stockinged feet showing the prominent hump of bunions. Her stomach was pressing up a hillock under her skirt band and her square, heavy face looked pallid in contrast to the colour of her hair.

"You all right, Mam?"

"Oh aye, lass; just a bit tired."

Rosie sat on the edge of the bed. "Anything worryin' you?"

"Aye." Emily stared at her daughter for a full minute before saying, "Yes, there's somethin' worryin' me."

"What then?"

"Angus."

"Angus? Why you worrying about him? He's all right. He's fine and fixed."

"Aye, he's fine, but he's not really fixed, not securely fixed. Do you know something?" Emily pulled herself up on the pillows and, supporting herself on her elbow, she leant towards her daughter and whispered, "If I was to leave up there the morrow he would have Angus out of that shop afore you could blink."

"Mr. Ratcliffe! He couldn't do that, Mam. He'd have to have a reason. If he sacked him for nothing he'd have the whole shop out, the whole place out. You remember last year when they came out because of John Petrick. They were out three weeks but they got him reinstated in the end. They couldn't do anything to Angus."

"There's ways and means, lass. An' I bet you what you like he'd have put the whole blame for yesterday's business on him if they weren't frightened of losin' me."

"Well, I can understand them not wanting to lose you, Mam, because they won't get anybody like you in a hurry." Rosie patted her mother's hand, and Emily said firmly, but without bumptiousness, "I know that, an' they know that, and the missus knows if it wasn't for Angus I'd have left there two or three years back." Her voice suddenly droppped and she said, "I'm tired, Rosie." Then she put in quickly, "I'm not bad, I'm just tired. Tired, lass, tired of working for other folks. I want to stay in me own house and get it shipshape an' have the meals ready for you both when you come in . . . Aw, I know you won't be here much longer, you'll be gettin' married. And Angus an' all, he'll find somebody to his likin' afore long, if he doesnt take May, and then likely I'll be wishin' I had a job. But I can always get a job. Aw, that doesn't worry me, but in the meantime I want a space, not just a week off, or even a fortnight – she's promised me a fortnight – I want a month, two, three, a year."

"Oh, Mam!" Rosie dropped sideways and laid her head against her mother's shoulder and her voice had a broken sound as she said again, "Aw, Mam."

"There, there, don't upset yourself. And mind," she pushed her daughter's head away from her, "now don't you bloody well go downstairs and tell him. Now mind you."

"I'm not daft, Mam. But I can tell you this. He could get a job anywhere. There's dozens of places he could start the morrow, on Monday at any rate." She gave a little laugh now.

"Yes, I know that, but not with the prospects there are at Affleck's. Mr. Brett recommended him to chargehand and he can recommend him further. I want to see him be something, lass, not just a workman like his dad and my dad and their dads afore them. I want to see our Angus rise, and he can, given half a chance. You know it was only because of the set-up in this house that he left school when he did to help look after your dad, an' him being

37

bad so long. You see," she swung her legs over the edge of the bed until she was sitting side by side with Rosie, and she started to pull the knuckle of each finger in turn as she went on, "you need education to rise, not so much brains. Ratcliffe hasn't any more brains than a louse to my mind but he had education. An' look where it got him. A grammar school education and a few kicks in the backside and he's at the top of the tree now. Aye, you need education and our Angus hasn't it, not the kind he needs to push him on, so he's got to get there in some other way."

"But where do you expect him to get, Mam? He's in charge of his shop; he'll not get much higher than that in Affleck's."

Emily turned her face towards her daughter and the words came under her breath, but they were weighty as she said, "He could get himself into the drawin' office where the draughtsmen are. That's why he's been goin' to evening classes on the quiet. He doesn't know that I know he's been goin'. Did you know owt about it?"

"No, Mam. Evening classes! Our Angus?"

"Aye, our Angus."

"He's twenty-four!"

"Twenty-four or not, he's goin'. But mind you —" she poked her finger into Rosie's chest — "don't you let on for God's sake, else he'll stop. You know what his temper's like. If he wants us to know he'll tell us in his own good time. Now go on downstairs afore he comes up an' tell him I'm all right."

When Rosie entered the kitchen again Angus asked, "How is she?" and Rosie replied, "She's all right. She's goin' to have a nap."

"All right. All right. She's not all right. An' I know why she won't leave up there, she thinks it'll affect me. I know, and she's a bloody old fool. He can do nothing to me and he knows it. You know something?" He turned round and looked at Rosie across the table. "That man Ratcliffe has hated my guts since I was a nipper?"

"But why?"

"I think I know; in a sort of way I know." He went and looked out of the window and down the narrow back yard. Then he said musingly, "It was him that stopped me playing with Van. I remember the day. It was just after Dad died. Me Aunt Mary had you, an' me mam told me to go up there after school and she'd slip me a bite to eat. She was workin' late because they were havin' a dinner or somethin — they gave dinners when they couldn't meet their grocery bills. Anyway, this day I was keeping out of the way round the back when Van comes on me. She was about five at the time. Well, there happened to be a garden barrer on the back path, you know one of those wooden ones, an' I put her in it and started to wheel her up and down. An' she laughed so much I thought she would burst. It must have been her laughin' that brought his lordship round, and he bellowed so loudly that he startled me and I nearly upset the barrer and her an' all. After he had ordered her in he stood looking at me with a look on his face that he sometimes has now, as if he considers me so much slime that should be washed down the drain. Yet even on that day he didn't go for Mam and tear her off a strip. But I never got the chance to play with Van again. Anyway, I've worked out this theory about Ratcliffe's attitude to me. It's just this. He can show his dislike for me and nothin' comes of it, but if he did it to Mam she would leave, and knowing this he not only hates me guts but her's an' all."

"Go on. You're just imagining things. They think the world of her."

"Think the world of her! Why? They think the world of her because she's necessary to them. They won't get a woman like Mam the day. Who they goin' to get to work from eight till five for five quid a week, turning her hand to anything from cooking to waiting on the 'At Home'

do's and their blasted dinners? Think the world of her!
If she died the morrow they wouldn't come to her
funeral."

"Oh, you're too bitter against them, our Angus."

"Not me, I've just got them taped, him most of all.
He'd like to kick her backside out of the door. You see
she doesn't kowtow to him, she answers him straight —
without the bloodies of course."

They both laughed softly now, and Rosie said, "Eeh!
I wonder what they'd think if they heard her going on
sometimes?"

"Do them good. God! wouldn't I like to hear her let
rip at them." He boxed the air and Rosie said, "Well,
that reminds me. When you're gettin' it out of your
system why aren't you at the match the day? Is your
back still hurting?"

"I've left." He was still punching the air, dancing round
the table now, boxer-fashion, on his toes.

"You've left?" Her exclamation was high.

"Aye."

"Are you barmy altogether? You broke your neck to
get in, and it was an honour."

He stopped abruptly and repeated, "An honour? From
who?"

"Well." Rosie tossed her head. "With Callow, the
solicitor, playin', and that young Brownlow in the accountant's office."

"To hell! Who's Callow, the solicitor, and Brownlow?
Don't forget Ted Robson's the star player, and he's a
bricklayer. And Andy Thompson, what does he do? He
carts ballast. If they had to depend on the white collar
bods they wouldn't have a team at all. Honour!"

"Well it was," Rosie persisted. "It isn't everybody who
is asked to join the Rugby team in this town. You must
be barmy leaving it."

"Well, I have left."

"Does me mam know?"

"No, she doesn't."

"When did this happen?"

"Two weeks ago, if you want to know."

"When you hurt your back?"

"Yes, when I hurt me back; when somebody hurt me back, jumping on it with both feet. For the last year I've been asking meself what's it all about. Why get half-killed every week? I've had me ribs nearly kicked in, me shins torn. There was one time last year I nearly had me neck broke. And so I asked meself why I was doing it? And then when you're playin' away, the drink. Swimming in it. I don't mind a drink, you know I like a drink, but oh, God! the stupid things they get up to, the way they carry on. I used to an' all, I did me share, but I happened to be solid and sober one night when I went along to the Bull late. They had been at it a couple of hours, and aw, it turned me stomach over. They had put a nappie on Bill Webster. That's all he had on, a nappie, an' there he was sittin' in the middle of the floor sucking his thumb and slobberin', and Alec Turner was playin' the mother. I tell you, Rosie, I nearly spewed."

"Well, it's only a bit of fun."

"Well, it's not my kind of fun." He nodded his head at her.

"You know what, our Angus?" She pursed her lips and grinned. "I think you're goin' through a bad time. It can't be adolescence, so it must be an early change. I should warn May."

The old tea cosy flew through the air again and she ran into the scullery laughing, and he was laughing as he went into the front room, which was his room.

The front room was twelve feet by nine. In it was a single divan bed, a new acquisition, an old chest of drawers, a hanging wardrobe, a small table in the corner near the window, and a gas fire in front of an open grate. The floor was covered with blue-and-white check linoleum and there were blue cotton curtains at the windows. The

41

room was tidy and, if not bright, it was clean. No matter what condition the rest of the house got into Emily saw to this room.

Early change. He grinned to himself and jerked his head, then pulled a straight-backed chair up to the table on which were a number of books and some drawing paper, but he didn't start to work. He rested his elbow on the table and supported his chin on his hand, and he gazed through the narrow aperture of the curtains, across the street to the high, faceless wall of the railway sheds. An early change. Well, he might not be going through an early change but there was something wrong with him. He didn't know what, except, as he put it, he was at sixes and sevens with himself. He knew this much though. If it wasn't for his mam he would pack up the morrow and clear out, he would that. Ratcliffe, Afflecks, the lot would go to hell . . . . What about May? Oh, May an' all for that matter.

THE LARCHES

The Larches

As they went out of the door it began to rain and Rosie said, "Oh lor! me hair'll be flat. Why the devil can't we have a car, our Angus? Nearly everybody else in the street's got one 'cept us."

"Aye; and look at them." He thumbed a derelict looking specimen they were passing. "I'll get a car when I can afford a decent one, not one from the scrap."

"You'll get no car at all," said Emily, "if you want to stay alive. Remember Sammy Cullen afore Christmas. I bet where he is the night he wishes he had never seen a car."

"His was an old wreck, Mam," said Rosie. "You can get a nearly new one for a couple of hundred from Hallows."

"Listen her!" exclaimed Angus. "A couple of hundred! Why don't you get Stan to fork out and buy you a car?"

"He will an' all. That's what he's goin' to do if he wins the talent spot next week, goin' to put it down on one."

Angus gave a ha-ha of a laugh; then nudging his mother, he said, "Why don't we go in for the talent spot, Mam, eh? You could do your bit poetry, you know.

"Between the dark and the daylight,
When the night is beginning to lower,
Comes a pause in the day's occupations
That is known as the children's hour.
I hear in the chamber above me
The patter of little feet . . . ."

45

He was pushed into the gutter. "You'll hear the crack of me hand across your lug, me lad, if you don't stop takin' the micky. I'll tell you one thing, they learnt you poetry in my day. Aye, at a council school at that."

"Eeh! The Children's Hour." Rosie shook her head. "It used to petrify me, that, Mam, when you used to say it to me.

'I have you fast in my fortress
And will not let you depart
But put you down in the dungeon
In the round tower of my heart.'

You used to say it to me to send me to sleep but it always sent me into nightmares; I was always cryin' to get out of dungeons."

They were laughing hilariously as they boarded the bus. They were still laughing and talking, and all at once, when they alighted in the main street, and they were a few yards from the club entrance and passing a tobacconist's, when Angus said, "You go on in, I'm goin' to get some baccy."

"Baccy? You?" Rosie had hold of his arm.

"Aye, baccy, me. I've decided to smoke a pipe. Better for your lungs, they tell you."

Their laughter vied with the noise of the traffic, and as they parted he tried to control his face before entering the shop.

Carsons was a big shop, the best in the town. A number of people were inside, and he did not notice the young girl until she moved a step to allow a man to pass her, and then he said, "Why, hello, Van." He had almost said Miss Van. It was just a habit, the Miss. Sometimes he added it to her name and sometimes he didn't.

"Oh, hello, Angus." Her face, which had been solemn in repose, brightened.

He bent his head down to her. "You takin' to smokin'?"

"No." She smiled widely at him. "It's father's birthday on Monday."

46

He looked her up and down, then whispered, "I didn't recognise you without your school rig; you know, it's the first time I've seen you out of a school uniform in years." He jerked his head. "You look different."

She stretched her face slightly up to his and whispered back, "And you know something, Angus? I feel different."

They both chuckled, then moved a step forward as another customer left the counter. They were silent for a moment, he staring ahead towards the cigarette-laden shelves; then turning to her again, he whispered under his breath, "Don't often see you down this way," and she answered as softly, "I don't often get down this way; I've been let out." And they exchanged an understanding smile.

When her turn came to be served she asked for a box of cigars and paid over thirty shillings for them. As she turned from the counter he said, 'Be seeing you, Van." And she nodded at him and answered, "Yes. Be seeing you, Angus."

A minute or so later, when he left the shop, she was standing in the shelter of the doorway and she turned to him and said, "What a night! I'm going to wait here until the bus comes across the road and then make a dive for it."

He peered at her in the dim light, saying, "This is one time when I wish I had a car. We were just talking about a car when we left the house, me mother and Rosie. They said I should have a car."

"Are they here?" She nodded towards the street.

"They're in the club; we're goin' to make a night of it." The corner of his mouth moved characteristically upwards.

She looked into his face, hers unsmiling now, and she said, "You do enjoy yourselves, don't you? I mean Emily and Rosie and you, you do enjoy yourselves."

"Oh, I don't know, not more than anybody else. Life's very dull at times." In his mind he was talking to a very young girl, a girl who had everything, yet whom he was sorry for in a way, whom he had always been sorry for in

47

a way. He said now, "It's about time you splashed out at dances, isn't it? County balls an' that?"

"The school dance is as far as I've got so far, Angus; but I'll likely start in the autumn."

"Well, that's something to look forward to." He paused and stretched his thick neck upwards out of his collar before saying, "By the way, Van, there's something I'd like you to get clear." He now rubbed the side of his forefinger across his chin. "It's about yesterday's business. You know I wouldn't have let that happen if I could have helped it, but the lads—"

Her gloved fingers lightly flicked his sleeve. "Look, Angus, forget it. All that fuss. They ask for what they get, I know that."

"Yes, but nevertheless, the fellows should mind their tongues . . . I didn't know you came along that way?"

"I don't as a rule, but I was going to my friend's house and apparently she uses it as a short cut," her lips pressed together for a moment, "because she likes to egg them on."

He stood looking down at her. She was wise in a way was Van. He'd always felt that. Different from the rest, inside as well as in appearance. She was turning into a lovely looking lass, and she would get lovelier. With startling suddenness there came into his chest, just below the ribs, a strange feeling, and for a moment he felt he had been cut off from life; he felt empty, sort of lost. The feeling so enveloped him that he didn't notice a car drawing up to the kerb. When a man got out and came into the shop doorway, Vanessa said, "Oh, hello, Brett," and the man answered on a surprised note, "Why! Vanessa." Then he looked at Angus and added, "Hello there, Angus." He didn't show any surprise that Angus Cotton, one of the floor men, should be standing in a doorway talking to the manager's daughter. But, on the other hand, Angus showed a great deal of embarrassment.

"Hello, Mr. Brett," he said; then added quickly, "Van

48

. . . Miss Van here got caught in the rain. She's waitin'
for a bus."

"Waiting for a bus? Well, it's a good job I came along.
I won't be a minute, Vanessa. Go on in the car; Irene's
there."

"Oh thanks. That's fine. Good-bye, Angus." She smiled
at him.

"Good-bye, Van." They were alone again for a moment.
"Be seeing you."

"Yes; Be seeing you, Angus."

As she got into the back of the car she said, "Hello
Irene," and Irene Brett turned round in her seat and
said, "Hello, Vanessa. A beastly night, isn't it?" Then
after a slight pause she added, "Wasn't that Emily's son
you were talking to?"

"Yes, Irene. I just met him in the shop a minute ago."

Vanessa always thought of the woman she had known
from a small child as Irene Brett, not Auntie Irene. Susan
called her Auntie, but she herself had stubbornly refused
to call their neighbour Auntie, or her husband Uncle.
She had even amazed her parents by going so far as to
address Arthur Brett by his surname. When she was
asked why, she said she didn't like the name Arthur, she
liked Brett, and so he had been Brett to her ever since.

This familiarity had always incensed Irene Brett. She
now sat looking at the rain-smeared windscreen, and she
was again feeling annoyed that she could find nothing to
say to this girl. She had always considered Vanessa a deep,
withdrawn type of girl, and she felt now that she was
indeed right about her being deep. She didn't believe for
a moment that she had met Angus Cotton by accident.
This wasn't the first time she had seen them together; a
fortnight ago she had seen them both standing talking
outside the Technical School. Now what would she want
outside the Technical School? It was miles away from the
Convent, and from Brampton Hill. She had felt for a long
time that Jonathan and Jane were going to have trouble

with this one. They weren't going to be able to plan her life as they had done Susan's. Anyway, perhaps they'd be satisfied in wangling one daughter into the fringes of the titled set. They'd never let up, those two, get there or die.

Her thoughts, touching on the second main grievance of her life, gathered momentum and she became lost in her hate, and she started as the door opened and her husband took his seat, saying over his shoulder, "Don't often see you in the town, Vanessa."

"No, I don't often come down. But it's Father's birthday. I was getting him a present."

"It's his birthday is it?"

"Yes, he'll be fifty on Monday."

"Fifty! Well, well. Yes . . . yes, he will be fifty." He was talking as if to himself. When he got the car going he added, "Time doesn't stand still; no, time doesn't stand still."

There wasn't another word spoken until they turned from Brampton Hill into the side road; then Vanessa said, "Just drop me at your gate, Brett, that'll be all right."

"No, I'll take you along."

"No, please. It's eased off."

"All right, just as you say."

When she got out of the car she said, "Thanks for the lift, Brett. Good-night, Irene."

They both said together, "God-night, Vanessa."

A few minutes later they went up the steps, through the glass-covered lobby and into the dark, panelled hall, and there, as Irene Brett took off her hat and coat, she remarked casually, "Well, what do you think of that?"

"What?"

"Her standing talking to that Angus Cotton."

He hadn't looked at her before, but now he turned round and faced her. Then after staring at her for a moment, he said, "Angus Cotton and Vanessa? Well, why shouldn't she talk to him? They've known each other all their lives. I remember them playing together."

She threw up her head, closed her eyes and turned from him, and as she went into the high-ceilinged, old-fashioned looking drawing-room, she said, "Your simplicity makes me want to scream. It must be all of ten years or more since Jonathan put a stop to that. But of course you wouldn't remember anything so mundane."

She turned round now and watched him coming slowly into the room, and when he came near her she said, "I saw them together outside the Technical School only a few days ago. And that's not the only time."

Arthur Brett surveyed his wife. There were times when he had to screw his eyes up to get her into focus, when he had to remind himself that he had lived with this woman for twenty-five years, that she wasn't a stranger whom he didn't know. He said quietly to her, "What are you trying to make of it?"

"What am I trying to make of it?" She stressed the I. "I'm only making a statement. What do you think would be Jonathan's reaction if he knew that she was talking to that fellow in the main street?"

"I don't know, Irene; and I don't care very much what Jonathan would think. But I would think it strange if those two met in the street and passed each other. And whether Jonathan stopped them playing together years ago or not, I can recall when Angus was a big lump of a lad and Vanessa was seven or eight or more seeing them together in the garden."

"Well, you've seen something that nobody else saw, because if either Jonathan or Jane had known there'd have been an abrupt stop put to it. And I think a stop should be put to this if they don't want consequences . . . . That fellow! He's like a great big Irish navvy. I think at least Jane should know about it."

"And I think," there was a hardness in Arthur Brett's usually soft, lazy-sounding voice now, "I think you should mind your own business and not take it out of Jane through Vanessa."

51

"Take it out of . . .! What are you talking about? What are you insinuating?"

"Just that you're not too pleased, are you, that Jane is getting Susan married into the Braintrees. But you can't do much about that so you intend to make her uneasy through Vanessa. That's it, isn't it?"

'How dare you! How dare you suggest such a thing. You're making me out to be a vile, mischief-making . . . ."

"I'm not making you out to be anything but what you are, Irene." As he turned from her she hissed at him under her breath, "Don't leave me like that, Arthur. Listen. Listen to me. Do you hear?"

Not until he was at the room door did he turn, and then he said quietly, "I'm not going to listen to you, Irene; I don't happen to be a member of one of your committees, nor a fellow councillor whom you are rating, nor yet a delinquent up before you on the bench. There are a number of things you can't make me do, Irene, and that's one of them; listen to you."

When he closed the door behind him and she was alone she stood with her two hands pressed tightly over her thin lips. She could understand why women committed murder. He hadn't the gumption he was born with, yet he was inflexible about what he considered his ideals, his principles. Oh, God, how had she of all people got stuck with someone like him! She knew the answer to this, but she had long refused to think about it.

She now walked to the couch, and with her hands still in the same position she sat herself down. She did not lean back against the couch for support, her thin body remained erect. She had a good figure and she looked after it, as she did her complexion and her hair. She was looked upon as a smart woman, but no one had ever said she was good-looking or pretty . . . or charming, but she was often referred to as clever and business-like. She was a committee woman and could get things done, at least outside her own house and family.

After a moment she lowered her hands to her lap and her eyes moved slowly around the room. She almost hated this room, this whole house, as much as she did its owner. The place had never been redecorated inside or out for years, yet he had only to sell two or three acres of land and the whole place could be renovated. Even if he could have been persuaded to sell some of the furniture, some of these ugly monstrosities, this would have gone a long way towards lightening and refurnishing the house.

There was a Queen Anne secretaire on the landing for which he had been offered three hundred pounds, and in a corner, over there, in the recess that hardly saw the light of day, was a William and Mary side-table. There was a very old mahogany commode in Colin's bedroom that would be worth a small fortune at Sotheby's. There were French chairs dotted all over the house, the tapestry so threadbare the wadding was sticking through, and there was no hope of having them re-covered; he wouldn't even allow her to put loose covers on them. There wasn't one of the twelve rooms in the house that didn't hold a piece of furniture that would bring in hundreds, but because his grandfather had furnished this house for his bride in 1892 he thought that was sufficient reason why it should remain as it was for his life. She knew that he had even made a will to the effect that all the furniture couldn't be sold on his death; certain pieces he had willed to the three boys with a request that they would think twice before parting with them. He had dared to tell her that he was going to do this. Spite. Spite, that's what it was, and all because she wouldn't supply him with his needs. His needs indeed! If he came into her room again she would tear his face off. Only last week he had dared to try to get into bed with her. Why? Why? When he cared as little for her as she did for him. She had warded him off for years with the excuse that she didn't want any more children, and nothing was safe . . . . And nothing was safe. Michael, her youngest son, was only six years old. Fancy, on the verge of forty having become pregnant again! The shame of it almost killed her. She had hardly been able to face the boys . . . . Boys? Colin had been almost a man then: eighteen, and Paul thirteen.

And last night he had dared to try it on again, even knowing how she felt about him. Again she had to ask herself, Why?

Upstairs in his room, Arthur Brett was asking himself the same question. Why? Why, when their love was dead, so dead you forgot when it had died, did you re-visit the corpse? Why did you want to put your arms around it, put your mouth on its mouth, press your body into it, work over it, struggle with it, even knowing it wouldn't move? It never had moved during all the years of their married life. The act had been an act of sufferance on her side and had brought him humiliation; yet he suffered humiliation a thousandfold in going to her and begging for his body's easement. Why? Why didn't he go down to Bog's End? He could find ease in Bog's End. He could reel off the names of at least eight men he knew on his floor who visited Bog's End regularly. He had just to say one word to Will Hobson and he'd be fixed up. The times he had made up his mind to say that word to Will. He would be determined when he had left the house in the morning that the first thing he'd do would be to see Will and put an end to this torment. He always got as far as seeing Will but he never mentioned Bog's End. Again why?

Perhaps it was because at these moments he would remember that but for his grandfather's taste for high living, and his father's easy going-ness and lack of business sense, he might to-day be Will Hodson's employer, because the firm of Affleck and Tate had once belonged to the Bretts. His grandmother's name was Affleck. She had brought the business – much smaller than it was now admittedly, but nevertheless a thriving concern – she had brought it to one Arthur Brett, a handsome, loving, carefree individual, who had a taste for good furniture, good wine, entertaining, and horses, which tastes he indulged right up to the middle of the thirties. He died at the table drinking wine; he actually died in toasting his white-haired and still beautiful wife. It was all very romantic.

He could remember the night his grandfather died as if it was yesterday. It was a beautiful summer evening, and he was home from boarding-school. He was sitting at his grandmother's right hand and he was looking at her profile as she gazed down the table towards her big, corpulent, but still handsome husband. When he fell forward over the table she gave a thin high scream and then became quite still. Three days later she herself died. His father said that was as it should be; they both had enjoyed life and one couldn't exist without the other.

His own father had almost repeated the pattern in his approach to life and way of living. It wasn't until Arthur himself was seventeen that he realized that Affleck and Tate was no longer their firm, that the shares had been sold gradually until their holdings were now non-existent, and that all that remained of the once-affluent Afflecks was the house and land; and, of course, the furniture, the furniture which his father wouldn't part with even to keep up some kind of appearance in the town.

He was nineteen when he met Irene Bailey, and she was a year older than him, and he hadn't thought he was deceiving her by not explaining the financial position in which his parents stood. After all, thinking socially, she was of little consequence in the town. Her father was a schoolteacher, elementary. She was attractive and vivacious, and he had fallen deeply in love with her, besides which he was full of admiration for her. She hadn't got to the high school, but she had supplemented her elementary education by going to night school. She could

55

talk intelligently; she only had to have a smattering of any subject and she could give the impression of knowledge.

He knew she was flattered by his attention; also that she was impressed by the big house, and the fact that he was the only son of the Bretts, and that they were Affleck and Tate.

He had told her casually before they were married that they were no longer Affleck and Tate, and he imagined at the time that it had meant nothing to her, but he knew now that she married him because she thought she could do something with him, restore him to the lost eminence of his grandfather, if not in the works, then along other lines.

But he was not cut out for other lines; except perhaps he could have been manager of Affleck and Tate. Oh yes, yes, he could have been manager, and he should have been manager because, after all, Affleck and Tate was in his blood so to speak. Yet all this had been forgotten when a certain Jonathan Ratcliffe, whom incidentally he had befriended when he first came into the drawing-office, inveigled himself into the good books of the board, by what method he had never been able to find out, and he had been too proud to enquire. Of course there had been the usual tittle-tattle about sucking up; but any move upwards brought this reaction. Anyway, Jonathan had gone from the drawing-office to the building across the yard, and there had become assistant to the under-manager, Rowland. Yet he must be fair. That was likely as far as he would have got if both Bowden, who was manager at the time, and Rowland, who took his place, hadn't died within the next five years.

Life was odd. He went to the window and looked out through the leafless trees. There, in the distance, he could see Jonathan's house. It was lit up. They were entertaining again, likely Susan's fiancé's people. He liked entertaining did Jonathan; it was a mark of his power. They were rarely asked next door, because he embarrassed Jonathan. He also knew he angered him. He had still things Jonathan wanted, the river frontage, for instance, and the land, all of it. The land. Oh, yes, all of the land.

He turned from the window and went out of the room and was crossing the landing when his eldest son, Colin, came up the stairs. They blinked at each other over the distance and Colin's look said, "You two been at it again?"

Arthur knew that his eldest son saw him through the eyes of his mother. This didn't boost one's morale. Still he had the consolation of Paul. Paul was different. Paul was the replica of himself, quiet, easy going; clever in a way. But what was the use of being clever in a way, you had to be clever in all ways. He doubted somehow if Paul would be any different from himself in this way either. He had no push. He wanted to meander through life like they both used to meander at night through the wood, then sit in the old summerhouse looking at the river and talk, or be silent, and sometimes laugh. Paul was the only real companion he'd had in his life. Irene had made certain of Colin and was making certain of Michael, but she could do nothing with Paul. Paul had stuck to him as if he was his own sweat.

Irene had made no fuss about Paul going to college. He knew that she had welcomed the fact that the other part of her husband would be out of the house. She was at her worst during the holidays, but the holidays were the only thing he lived for. And this year they would be short, at least for him, because Paul was going abroad on a walking tour. He had wanted him to go along, and if there had only been the two of them he would have jumped at the chance, but he couldn't see himself being one of a party of four exuberant youths.

After his bath he went straight to bed. This wouldn't interfere with the routine of the house; he rarely had anything to eat after teatime. Later on, when they had all retired, he might go down to the kitchen and make him-

57

self a hot drink and sit by the stove. He liked sitting by the stove. He had sat a lot in the kitchen when he was a boy; it had been a different stove then. The old one had exploded one day and the cook had fainted. She had been a big old Irish woman, and when she came round the first thing she said was, "Oh God, have I been blown into heaven?" And they had all laughed and laughed. They had laughed a lot in this house at one time. Everybody in it had been compatible; there had been no in-law trouble when he was young. His mother and father had lived all their married life with his grandfather and grandmother, and he himself had brought his bride to live with his mother and father. It was from then that the laughter had eased off.

It was around ten o'clock when he heard Irene come upstairs and go to her room. She did not look in on him. That, too, had ceased a long time ago. He lay for a time, his book lying on top of the quilt, his two hands flat on the open pages, and he staring down at them as he asked himself questions to which there were no answers. When eleven o'clock struck he switched the light off and got up and opened the curtains. He was surprised to see the moon shining brightly. The rain had stopped and the tangled garden below him and the long stretch of wood beyond looked like an enchanted forest. He pulled his dressing-gown about him and sat on the broad window-sill, with his knees up under his chin. He could still do that for he wasn't pot-bellied. There was no movement outside, no wind; March was in but she was with-holding her signs. It could have been a June evening except that it would be cold out. He had always wanted to write poetry; there seemed such a lot of poetry locked up inside if him. He could think poetry but he couldn't get it from his head to his hands. He envied people who could write. There must be great easement in writing, pouring out your feelings and being able to read them back to yourself. Not only must it be alleviative, but also satisfactory.

That's why he missed Paul so much. Paul, in a way, had been his form of release, his outlet.

As he stared at the treetops his eyes were caught by a movement down below to the left of him. There was a shadow crossing the open space, which was the north side of the Ratcliffes' garden. There were no open spaces in his garden. It took gardeners to create open spaces, and he himself was no gardener for the simple reason he hated to cut anything down, even weeds. Killing in any way was abhorrent to him, but he didn't give this reason for the neglect of his garden. He just said that he was no gardener, also that he was innately lazy.

The shadow disappeared, then re-appeared again in a patch of moonlight. It was making for the gate in his boundary fence, the gate which allowed the Ratcliffes' access to the river bank, his river bank. He had had the gate made when Jonathan first built the house. A second before the figure disappeared again into the shadows he recognised Vanessa. Now what would Vanessa be doing out at this time of night? He turned and glanced at the clock. Ten minutes to twelve. He now turned his gaze towards the Ratcliffes' house. The lights were all out.

Once more he focused his gaze in the direction of the gate. It was impossible to see if she had come into the wood. But she had been making for the gate. When, five minutes later, he had not seen her return up the garden, the reason for her midnight stroll came to him as he remembered what Irene had said earlier in the evening, and he muttered aloud, "Oh no! No!"

It was one thing Angus Cotton speaking to her in the street, but it was entirely another thing meeting her secretly, and at this time of night. The wire fencing at the bottom of the wood was broken in several places where it bordered the side road. The children were always coming in for cob nuts or bluebells. Angus could easily come in that way and walk along by the river bank to the summerhouse.

59

God! No! He liked Angus. He was a good, honest fellow, and he had brains of a sort, but to start anything with Vanessa! He began swiftly to pull his trousers on. One thing was certain. If there was anything in this, Jonathan would blame him for giving the fellow ideas above his station. He had already used that very term.

He got into his coat, took his shoes in his hand, then opened the door softly, and, crossing the landing, he went down the back stairs that led directly into the kitchen, then let himself out at the side door.

The night air made him shiver. As he took the side path around what had once been the rose garden he asked himself what he would say to them. Well, he could just be taking a stroll. That was it. He couldn't sleep and had come out for some air. Then he would get Angus on one side and let him have it. Oh yes, he'd let him have it. This kind of thing couldn't go on. It wasn't only because Jonatnan would blame him, it was because a girl like Vanessa mustn't get herself mixed up with a fellow like Angus. No matter how decent he was, it just wouldn't work out. He liked reading mythology and tales of princesses and plough boys, but these were only to entertain that section of the mind that remained for ever in youth. The fate of the princess and the plough boy in real life could only spell disaster. In a sort of way his own romance had been like the prince and the beggar maid. Not that Irene would thank him for placing her in that category.

The path was well worn, and last year's leaves had been trodden into mush by his own feet. He entered the wood, and although he was in deep shadow he found his way unerringly between the great oak tree which dominated the top of the wood and the forked group of three birch trunks that stood to the right of it; then through a thicket of spidery hazel trees, and on to a pathway again. He was careful to keep to the path so as not to tread on to the carpet of wood anemones and the sprouting daffodils and narcissus. In another week or so the wood would be a picture of white and gold with a sprinkling of blue, and when the blue took over he would think again the sky had fallen. He now turned sharp right and to the gate that gave access to the wood. It was open, pushed back on its rusty hinge. He left it like that, then walked quickly in the direction of the river and the summerhouse.

He paused by the landing stage and looked along the bank and up the rise to where the summerhouse stood. The moon was lighting up the scene as if it was daylight. He strained his ears but could hear no sound of voices. God, but this was going to be awkward. Yet she might not be there at all, she might have gone back. No, she would have closed the gate after her if she had gone back. They always closed the gate so that Michael's puppy wouldn't again get through into Jonathan's garden and play havoc among the formal beds. No, somehow he had no doubt but that she was still here, and in the summerhouse. Well – he squared his shoulders – he couldn't stay out all night, he'd better get it over with. His feet made no sound on the grass bank as he approached the wooden structure that had a disintegrating veranda and a thatched roof in a similar state. Three steps along the veranda took him to the door. To his surprise it was open and, further to his surprise, there was Vanessa, her hand held tightly against her cheek, sitting on the slatted form staring at him.

"Vanessa!"

"Oh, Brett. Oh!" She put her other hand up to her face and closed her eyes. "Oh, you did give me a start." She swallowed deeply now as she gazed up at him, "I . . . I nearly had a fit."

He was blacking out the moonlight, and in the shadow of himself he could only see the dark gleam of her eyes, their brown now appearing like pieces of jet. "What on earth are you doing here, on your own?"

"Oh, well." She rose to her feet, then dropped her head and said again, "Oh, you did give me a fright, Brett.'

"You're shaking." He had hold of her arm. "Sit down. I . . . I didn't mean to frighten you. But why are you out here at this time of night?"

"Oh, I often come down. I hope you don't mind, Brett."

"Mind? Of course not. But why?"

"Well, I suppose it's because I'm restless, I can't sleep. This is only the second time I've been here this year; it's a bit cold yet." She shrugged her shoulders upwards around her chin. "I started to come down last summer. I could have sat in our garden but it wasn't the same, I wanted to look at the river. You really don't mind?"

"Don't be silly." He turned his head away from her. Then looking at her quickly again, he asked, "You're . . . you're not in trouble of any sort?"

"No. No, of course not, Brett. Trouble? What trouble could I be in?" This was followed by an embarrassed silence. She was sixteen and a half, as she had informed her father, and she knew what trouble she could be in, but she didn't think Brett was referring to that kind of trouble. Cecilia Tomache had had to leave school last year because of a similar trouble, but she was well over seventeen. She said airily now, "Well, it's now my turn to ask why you are out at this hour?"

"That's easy to answer. I saw you coming down, and I may as well tell you I wondered what you were up to."

"Oh, Brett, you didn't!"

"I did, young woman, I did."

They were laughing softly together. "Who did you expect to find me with?"

"Well now." It would never do to tell her the truth, so he stroked his chin and pretended to think deeply before he said, "Seeing that Susan might well one day be Lady Braintree I thought you would at least be hobnobbing with a count." He nodded at her. "Yes, a count, Italian. But on second thought, no. Italian counts are two-a-penny, and it would have to be someone exclusive for you, a prince. Yes . . . . Now who are the eligible princes? There's not many left. Now let's see . . . ."

"Oh, Brett, you are funny." She pushed him. "I'll settle for something less than a prince."

"Well, don't go too low. Now mind, I'm telling you." He wagged his finger at her. "Aim high. Aim high, young woman."

The moonlight was falling across their faces, just below their eyes, but he could see the expression in hers as she said, "Who are you thinking about, Brett, when you say I should aim high? Me, or mother and father?"

It was a sobering question, and the bantering went out of his voice as he answered, "I wasn't thinking of them, I was merely being funny. When the time comes, high or low, you'll know."

He had said to her, high or low, yet a few minutes ago he had been worried stiff in case she had given her young freshness to someone like Angus Cotton. People never said what they meant. He was no exception.

She was looking out of the door now down the slope on to the moonlight water and she said, "I want to get married some time, Brett, but I . . . I don't want it manoeuvred, like Susan's. Brian's young, but if he had been as old as father I think she would have been manoeuvred into it, and she herself would have wanted to be manoeuvred into it, she's got a thing about titles. She's as bad as mother." She turned her head sharply towards him. "People make me sick, Brett."

"People make me sick too, Vanessa." He laughed tolerantly.

"Yes, I should imagine they do, Brett, because you've had what is known as a dirty deal, haven't you?"

His eyes widened as he stared at her. Then he said, "How did you come by that impression?"

"Oh!" She shook her head quickly. "Father, Mother, the things they say. Father's guilt complex. He feels awfully guilty about you. I know he does; that's why he blusters."

"Nonsense, nonsense, Vanessa. Good gracious, child, you do have queer ideas about some things."

"I haven't, Brett. You know I haven't. And I'm not a child, I'm going on seventeen and I'm very, very worldly." She bowed her head in a deep obeisance towards him, and he threw back his head and laughed aloud, only to check it quickly as he whispered, "I could be heard from the road, and if the night patrol was passing, he'd be in here like a shot. And what would he think, finding us here at this time of the night, eh?"

"He'd think the worst, Brett."

"Vanessa!" There was astonishment in his voice, yet he was still laughing.

"I told you I'm very worldly."

He looked at her with his head on one side. "You're very sweet, Van. I used to call you that when you were young but your father didn't like it. Vanessa is her name, Vanessa she must be called . . . . Come on, I think we'd both better be making for indoors." He rose to his feet and put out his hand and pulled her upwards, and as they went out on to the veranda she said, "Paul will soon be home; you'll be happy then, Brett, won't you?"

He stopped dead and stared at her. "What makes you think I'm unhappy without Paul, Vanessa?"

"Oh, I don't know, just the way you look, sad like, lost. Yet you never look like that when you're with Paul. You know when you were together at Christmas, you remember at the party, I thought to myself you were like twins."

"Oh, my dear, that's the best compliment I've had in my life. Thank you, Vanessa, thank you." He bowed deeply from the waist.

"I mean it." She turned from him and went down the steps on to the grassy slope, saying over her shoulder, "I like Paul, I like Paul better than anybody I know, except

64

you." She was laughing widely as she turned her glance back towards him.

He laughed back at her, then said, "I am deeply honoured, ma'am, deeply honoured." And he added, "Seriously, I am."

"I am looking forward to Paul coming. He's good fun."

"You like Paul, really like him?"

"Yes, yes, I do. Would you like me to marry Paul, Brett?"

"Vanessa, what's got into you to-night? It must be the moon."

"Yes, I think it is the moon because I'm being very forward, aren't I? I'm not usually like this, am I? They say I don't talk enough. They think I'm reserved. Sulky, Father calls it. But I've always talked with you, and I can feel forward with you and know you'll not tick me off."

Again they were laughing, smothered laughter.

"But would you, would you like me to marry Paul, Brett?"

"Since you ask, Vanessa, I would. It would make me very happy if you married Paul. But that's up to you and Paul."

"Yes, that's up to me and Paul, and Paul doesn't even know I exist."

"Nonsense, Paul's very fond of you. I know that."

"Yes, as the kid next door."

"Well, you know," he said thoughtfully, "up till last summer, even up till Christmas, even up to yesterday, you did appear like the kid next door, but not any longer." He held up his hand warningly against her attack, and they were laughing softly again as they entered the shadows of the trees. He whispered to her now, "Keep your voice down," and they said nothing further until they reached the gate, and there, looking up at him, she murmured below her breath, "I feel better, better than I've done for weeks. There was a dinner to-night, and, oh, it was boring."

"You were down for dinner?"

"Yes, of course. Don't you know that I'm a young lady and must be initiated into society?" The bantering tone left her voice and she said, "You know, sometimes, Brett, I think I'm in one of Jane Austen's novels; the pattern in our house is just like that. Mother talks about 'getting one ready'. In this day and age, 'getting one ready'! I ask you. When they are already talking of school children getting married and going back to school. It's true, it was on the telly. She's still living in her youth, even in her own mother's youth. There's no fun, Brett. You know, down on the main street where I was to-night, you know when I was talking to Angus, there's a club. They were going, his sister and Emily, and they would be laughing and singing and enjoying themselves up till midnight. It made me feel sad, forgotten somehow. Not that I want to go to clubs, but some of the girls from school, younger than me, they go out on a Saturday night to dances. The Golf Club have a wonderful dance once a month. But what happens to me? I'm allowed down to dinner to be 'got ready'. Got ready for what, Brett? Not to get married, not really, you don't really need to be got ready to get married, do you? I should imagine that comes naturally, doesn't it?"

"Well." He was stumped, he was stumped by the whole train of her conversation.

"I know what I'm being got ready for, Brett. I'm being got ready to hook someone in the Braintree set. Oh, I know all about it, and it makes me furious inside."

"Take it slowly, dear," he said gently. "I know how you feel, I really do, and when Paul comes home you'll go off to a dance together. It'll be arranged in some way."

She sighed deeply. "It won't be arranged, it can't, Father will see to that, and in any case I wouldn't want to go to a dance with Paul because it would be on sufferance."

"Don't talk nonsense, he'd be delighted to take you, because, you know, you're a very, very attractive young

66

lady. In fact, I could say truthfully you're a very beautiful young lady when you're not scowling, and if I'm not mistaken you're going to cause some havoc in the male world before you're much older."

"Do you think so, Brett?" Her voice was eager. "Really? You're not just being soothing?"

"No, I'm not just being soothing. It's a prophesy, and all my prophesies come true." He raised his hand, and again they were laughing gently. Now he pushed her through the gateway, saying, "How do you get in?"

"Up the fire escape, on to the second landing, and once I'm there and anyone should open their door I'm just coming from the bathroom."

"You're a minx."

"How did you get out?"

"Down the back stairway." Again he pushed her. "Go on, sleep well. See you to-morrow."

She moved a step from him, then turned swiftly towards him and, reaching up, she kissed him on the chin, saying, "You are the nicest man I know, the very nicest."

He stood perfectly still until he imagined she had reached the side of the house where the fire escape was, then he moved slowly up through the wood, his head bent on his chest, and when he re-entered his room again he switched on the light and looked at himself closely in the mirror. Then he held his hand a few inches from his face as if he was cupping the face that had kissed his.

As he went to sleep he thought, "And I went out to tear a strip off Angus Cotton!"

PART ONE

I

Vanessa just managed to board the train with the assistance of a lift and an, "In you go!" from a porter. She stumbled over the feet of the second-class passengers and excused herself; then she went out into the corridor and down the train towards the few first-class compartments. She was passing the last compartment in the corridor when the sight of the sole occupant of it brought her to a halt and she said, "Why! hello, Angus."

"Oh, hello." Angus got hastily to his feet, dropping the paper to the floor as he did so. He retrieved it and threw it on to the seat before saying, "Fancy meeting you here."

"Yes." She nodded and smiled at him.

"Lookin' for a seat?" He looked down at her.

She hesitated just a moment, and his chin jerked up as he said, "Oh, you're going down to the first. I'm sorry."

"Don't be silly." She moved into the compartment and sat down; immediately he sat opposite to her, saying, "You're not at school the day? That's a daft question, but I mean . . . ."

"I've been to the dentist."

"In Newcastle?" His thick, sandy, well-defined eyebrows moved upwards. I thought we had an overflow of them in Fellburn."

"I had to see a specialist. I'm getting an extra ration." She pressed the corner of her mouth back and upwards to reveal a small tooth jutting out between the roots of two others.

"Good lord! Cutting your milk teeth again? Aw," his smile widened, "in your case it would be a wisdom tooth."

She laughed. "Wisdom, huh! Wisdom. By the way, while we're explaining why we aren't at our particular jobs, why aren't you at work?"

"Oh." He leant back. "I've been to a funeral."

"A funeral?"

"Yes; me uncle's. We haven't seen him for years, ten or more, but me mother thought somebody should go. It wasn't decent like," he mimicked Emily's words "to let him be put away and not one of the family near him."

"But why didn't she . . . ?" Her voice trailed off and she ended lamely, "Oh yes. Oh yes, the company."

He nodded at her slowly and repeated, "Yes, the company."

"But if she had asked mother, I'm sure it could have been arranged."

He stared at her. He didn't say she did ask mother, but that mother said it would be very inconvenient and wouldn't it be simpler for Rosie to attend the funeral? No, Rosie was just a lass and, what was more, she couldn't abide funerals. Then it must be arranged that Angus should have the day off; she would see the master. And she had seen the master, and here he was.

His silence and his intent look implied the facts of the case to Vanessa and she thought, "Oh, Mother!" Then merely for something to say she said naively, "But how are they managing in your shop without you?"

His bellow of a laugh could have been heard above the noise of the train and he wiped his eyes and said, "You know, it's funny but I've never been able to make out how the firm managed to carry on afore I got into the shop. An' you know something else?" He now leant forward and rested his elbows on his knees and brought his face level with hers. "I bet there's twice as much work done in that shop that day, because, you see, I've got a friend, oh a very dear friend." He stretched his upper lip

72

well over his teeth and pulled a face before he continued, "One, Jim Taggart. He likes me so much that he'll get his blokes to work twice as hard when I'm out of the way and he'll say to me the morrow, 'What do you think of that, Angus? We didn't slack, eh?' but what he's really sayin' is, 'I can get twice as much work out of the . . . out of them than you, boy.'"

"He sounds a horrible individual."

"He's not really, he's just ambitious; it's funny what ambition can do to you. It made me hate his guts; it's also made me take up evening classes just to show him that I'm goin' places."

"You're going to evening classes, Angus?"

"Yes, the Tech. You know; I met you outside."

"Oh, I thought you were just passing, I didn't realize."

The eyes looking into his were full of interest; her smile was sweet. She was slim and long and beautiful. He gazed at her. Who would have thought she would have grown into this? And there was more to come. She would be a stunner in a few years' time. She could get anybody . . . anybody. Bye, she looked lovely. And she was lovely, because besides everything else she had a nice nature. As his mother always said, she'd been nice right from a bairn. And to think that he once used to put his arms around her and hump her up on to his bike or lift her into the barrow. She would have forgotten all that but he never would. If he had been brought up differently perhaps he would have had a girl like her, beautiful and untouched. Aye, she looked untouched, not like the paw-patterned misses that got in the club and thereabouts. Not like May . . . funny about May. He had thought he loved her until the night she had told him she had been with two other blokes. She felt she had to tell him, she said, because she loved him. He had been with her himself more times than he could remember, but he had intended to marry her, so it was different. But from then he just couldn't. He had scudded away like a frightened rabbit; or a better

73

description in his case, with his bulk, would be like a shy-
ing buffalo. He knew his attitude was unreasonable, oh
aye, he knew that, but it was different for a man. A fellow
had to have it; it was as necessary as a morning cuppa, or
the evening pint; but with a lass . . . well, it was different.
Oh yes, he had worked that out an' all. If they all pre-
served their virginity it would be pretty hard on the males
in general. But there would always be lasses who wanted
it and no responsibility, no marriage ties, they wanted it
for the cash they could get out of it . . . Yet May hadn't
wanted cash. Give May her due, the only thing May had
wanted was him. He felt bad about May, but there it was.
He had this kink in him, and he couldn't do anything
about it. If and when he married he'd like to make sure
he was the first buyer at that particular stall, but as things
went the day she'd have to be pretty young or so bloody
ugly that nobody would have wanted to try their luck. He
laughed inwardly, and it brought a quirk to his lips, and
Vanessa asked, "What's tickling you, Angus?"

"Oh!" he straightened up. "I was just thinking about
something." He leant back against the seat. "What are
you going to do when you leave school?"

She, too, leant her head back against the seat then she
turned it towards the window and looked out on to a
stretch of green countryside that lay between the towns
as she said musingly, "I don't know. Sometimes I think
one thing, and then another, I just don't know."

"What do your people want you to be?"

"Oh." She was looking at him again, her face stretched,
her brown eyes wide, the thick lashes on her lower lids
forming dark circles on her high cheekbones. "A duchess.
A countess. Queen of the Outer Isles."

They were laughing together and he brought his head
forward as he said, "You've got them weighed up,
Vanessa."

Her face suddenly became straight. Yes, she had her
people weighed up, but she knew it wasn't right to discuss

74

them with Angus Cotton, nor have him laugh at them. With Brett, yes, but not Angus for, after all, his mother was their daily.

Oh lord! lord, stop it! It was as if she was being reprimanded by an elder self. You're talking like Susan. He's right, I've got them weighed up; he's got them weighed up; and Emily's got them weighed up. They know as much about us as we do ourselves, more, in fact, being lookers-on. She was fond of Emily, very fond of her, and not in the way her mother was either. Her mother kept saying, "What would I do without Emily?" but she wasn't thinking of Emily, she was thinking of herself and the difficulty in getting staff. Emily was a common woman; she talked common and she acted common, yet there was something lovable about her. She was the only one who had cuddled her. She used to do it on the quiet in the kitchen. She could never remember her mother cuddling her. Angus was like his mother. He, too, was what you would call common; but he was nice for all that. There was something about Angus that she liked. It was odd when she came to think about it but there were only two men with whom she could really talk without stopping to think of every word she said. Angus was one, and Brett the other. They seemed alike in some way. Yet they were as far apart as the poles; Brett with his soft, cultured way of speaking, against Angus with his hard, thick, North-country intonation and his appalling lack of grammar.

She said seriously now, "Emily's feet are badly swollen."

"Aye, yes; I've noticed that." His tone matched his cynical look.

"She should rest more. I mean when she gets home."

He stared at her for a full minute before saying quickly, "She's got a house to look after besides yours, you know. She's got me coming in at night, tearing hungry, and Rosie. She needs to eat an 'all."

"Oh, I'm sorry, I really am, Angus. I didn't think."

75

"It's all right, oh, it's all right. But I know you're right, she should rest. I might as well tell you, I've been at her to leave your place for a long time now."

Her hand went instinctively to her lips and her face showed dismay. "No, Angus! Oh, the house wouldn't be the same without her. As for mother, well, she'd go round the bend. The people we've had over the last three years, part-time dailies, au-pairs, gentlewomen," she poked her face towards him on the last title, "the lot. But whoever came or went, Emily was there. I think Mother would really go potty if Emily left. And she knows it's hard on her, Angus; and she does try to get help for her. She's even offered them factory wages, but they just won't do housework."

"Can you blame them?" The question was soft.

"What? Oh! Well, I suppose not."

"Have you ever done housework?"

"I do my own room at times."

He stared at her again without speaking, then laughed gently as he said, "And why should you do housework or do your own room when you're going to be a duchess, or a countess, or Queen of the Outer Isles?"

"Oh, Angus, you're making fun of me."

"No, I'm not. No, honest, 'cos I could see you carryin' any of those positions off right to the T."

"I couldn't, Angus. Susan could, but not me. And I would get bored."

"Bored? Not you. Wait till you get going and you'll enjoy yourself, you'll be belle of the ball, top of the pops, the lot."

Her face was bright with laughter again. "You're very comforting, Angus. You know, you always were. I'm so glad I ran into you. I was feeling down in the dumps, and this," she pointed to the offending tooth, "this has been giving me gyp for days. Look, we're running in. Hasn't the time flown?"

He stood up. "Yes, that's the quickest half-hour I've

76

known for a long while. I wish the time went like that at work."

They went into the corridor and walked to the end of the coach, and when the train stopped he got out and gallantly helped her down the high step on to the platform. As they went through the barrier together a young man standing among a group waiting to get on to the platform said, "Hello there, Vanessa."

She turned her head and answered on a high note, "Oh, hello there, Colin. You going into town?"

"Yes."

"I've just been."

He nodded at her, then looked to the side where stood Angus Cotton; then he nodded again. "Good-bye," he said.

"Good-bye, Colin. Be seeing you."

"That was Colin Brett." She looked at Angus as they went out into the station yard and he said, "Aye, I know."

"Oh!" Her voice was hesitant now. "I thought perhaps you mightn't know him; he doesn't work in the yard, he's an accountant in Forrester's."

Oh, aye, an accountant in Forrester's, was he? By the look he had given him you'd think he was God Almighty in paradise. He knew Colin Brett all right; they were both of the same age. He had played with him once or twice when he had gone up to the house, but Colin Brett wasn't the kind who would remember that. Oh no, he was an accountant in Forrester's. He'd likely be a member of the Conservative Club and the Golf Club. Had he been a member of the Rugby Club he would have spoken to him in the dresing-room, he would have drunk with him in the pub afterwards, but he would hardly have recognized him in the street, particularly if he was with any of his women folk. Oh, aye, they were living in an age of social equality. Social equality, his backside!

"I'm gettin' the bus here," he said abruptly. "Been nice seein' you."

"It was nice seeing you, Angus. I'll tell Emily I came down with you."

"Do." He nodded at her, then turned on his heel and crossed the road to the bus station; and she walked some distance behind him wondering at his sudden change of manner. She had to get the bus, too, not the same one as he was getting but the one next to it; he could have walked across the road with her, he had walked out of the station with her. But all of a sudden he had looked grim and bad-tempered, like Emily did when something upset her. Had she upset him? Had she said anything? Oh, bust and botheration. That was people. Everybody seemed at sixes and sevens lately.

When she boarded her bus she saw him standing on the pavement opposite his; he was talking to a girl. She was of medium height and a blonde. Her skirt was well above her knees; she was wearing a short, hairy coat like imitation fur. She looked common.

As she took her seat in the bus she did not retract her use of the word this time for the girl did look common, cheap. Well, she supposed that was the kind of girl Angus would go for. Men usually went for blondes, they said, some time or other.

As the bus turned out of the square it came to her with a kind of shock that Angus was a man. He was no longer a youth or a young fellow, he was a man. A big, virile, rough, coarse man, yet she had chatted to him in the train as if there was no difference between them with regard to age. Somehow she didn't think she'd ever chat to him again like that.

The house was quiet when she entered, it seemed empty. She looked into the lounge but no one was there. In the dining-room the table was set for dinner. There were eight places. This was the second time the Braintrees had been here within the last three weeks. The table looked nice, all gold and silver, the gold being the daffodil heads her mother had arranged in a flowing line down the centre of the table. She used to cringe when, as a child, she saw her mother wiring the heads for a flower display. Her mother was very clever at arranging flowers.

When she went into the kitchen Emily was at the stove. "Oh, hello there. You back? Did it hurt?" she said.

"No, not at all. Well, he didn't do much. I've got to go again next week. By the way, guess who I came home with on the train?"

"The Lord Mayor." Emily closed the oven door and added, "Would you like a cup of tea?"

"Oh, yes, Emily, if there's any going . . . Where's Mother?" Her voice had dropped on the question and Emily answered as quietly, "Upstairs, having a nap afore the fray. She's jiggered."

As Emily took down two cups and saucers from the cupboard Vanessa looked at the back of her legs. There was no shape in them; her ankles were the same width as her broad calves.

"What are you looking at? Oh, me feet? Oh, they're giving me gyp the day; I feel they're going to bust any minute." She put the cups and saucers on the table. "I'm gonna put them in some epsom salts as soon as I get home."

"After you've made the dinner for Angus and Rosie?"

"What's that you say?" Emily held her head to one side and screwed up her eyes.

"I came back in the train with Angus."

"Aw, you did, did you?" Emily now took the kettle from the Aga plate and mashed the tea. "And he told you that I'm a poor soul who has to go home and cook for the family, eh?"

"No, no, he didn't, not like that, but he said he'd been trying to get you to leave us."

"Oh, that! You don't want to listen to him. And look, Miss Van." She turned quickly. "Don't you go scaring your ma. Well, what I mean is the missus has got enough on her plate without worrying about being left high and dry. By the way." She leant against the rail of the stove and a smile spread over her broad, flat face. "That one that came for interview this mornin', she took one look at the place and skited out of the gate as if we had turned a hose on her."

"She wouldn't even give it a try."

"Give it a try? You should have heard what she said. An' what she wanted. Double time for waiting on dinner at night. I said to the missus she should have asked her if she thought this was a factory. I tell you, they don't want work, Miss Van; they won't work the day."

As Emily again turned to the stove and lifted the tea-pot Vanessa once more let her gaze drop to the feet encased in a pair of old leather slippers that had once belonged to her father. Her father had big feet, he took size ten, yet the slippers, stretched as they were, were still too small for Emily's feet.

"You should put your feet up in the afternoon, Emily. You know, Mother told you to."

"Well, I've had them up. I've just got off me . . . I just got out of the chair a minute or so afore you got in. I haven't done a hand's turn since half-past two."

"What's happening to-night?"

Emily handed Vanessa a cup of tea, then said, "Oh, I'm slipping home for an hour, then coming back."

"It wouldn't surprise me if Angus doesn't let you."

Emily now turned fully about and surveyed the only member of this household for whom she had any liking, and she said tersely, "Since when did Angus Cotton tell me what and what not to do? It's all arranged. Miss Susan's dropping me off in the car at half-past five and picking me up an hour later, and let Angus have anything to say on the matter and he'll get a mouth . . . I'll tell him some-thin' that he won't forget in a hurry. Because he can boss the men under him at the works it doesn't say he can do the same at home. An' I've told him." She jerked her head. The statement carried pride that her son was in the position to boss men, and this fact was not lost on Vanessa.

"Have a piece of cake?" Emily asked the question with a conspiratorial air. "Walnut cream sponge."

"Oh, yes, Emily, please."

Emily went to the pantry and returned with a large shive of cake and, placing it before Vanessa, said, "Get it down you in case we should have visitors."

It was a rule that "the children" weren't to eat in the kitchen, and Emily had always seen that Susan complied with it and also Master Ray. Oh yes, she kept firmly to the order where that young demon was concerned. She spoke of Ray now, saying, "Oh, by the way, we had some high jinks here just afore lunch. His nibs climbed the spout and got stuck on the roof near the garret. How, in the name of God, he got up there nobody knows. He got up but he couldn't come down." Her body began to shake with laughter now.

"What happened?" Vanessa, too, was laughing quietly.

"Thay had to phone the works for extra ladders."

"No! Never."

"I's the truth I'm tellin' you. They brought a lorry and two blokes, and one of them went up and got him. Oh, you should have heard the master."

"Where's Ray now?"

"In his room . . . It'll be nice when the holidays are over, peaceful like. Thank God for schools, I say."

Vanessa was laughing openly with her hand over her mouth to still the sound; then rising and taking the plate to the sink, she said, "Thanks, Emily; that was lovely."

"'Leave those, I'll see to them."

"No, no, I'll rinse them."

"Leave them and go on your way. Go on."

Vanessa rinsed the plate and cup and saucer under the hot tap; then turning and bowing her head stiffly towards Emily, she said, "There." It was as if she had assisted her with some major household task, and the look on Emily's face seemed to bear this out as she said, "You always were stubborn, Miss Van. But get along with you; you don't want your mother to come down and find you here. Go on now."

As Vanessa ran lightly up the stairs she thought again of Emily's feet, and the thought took her into the bathroom that she shared with Susan, and there, from her own particular cupboard, she took a plastic bag and filled it almost to the top with a proprietary brand of bath salts that promised to relieve all the aches and pains the body harboured.

Downstairs again, she went hurriedly into the kitchen where Emily was sitting down now and, putting the bag in her lap, said under her breath, "These are very special salts. Bathe your feet with them, they're bound to do them good."

"Aw, lass, aw, that's real thoughtful of you, Miss Van. Ah, that is. Thanks."

Vanessa stood for a moment looking down into the smiling face; then she ran out of the kitchen and up the stairs again with a strange feeling of happiness inside her. There was something in what you learned at church, she supposed. Kindness had its own reward. She felt very good.

The dinner was over. Emily, her feet encased in black shoes, had brought the coffee into the drawing-room and now Susan and Brian were going to run her home. They had just gone out of the room together. They looked happy and self-satisfied. Vanessa thought perhaps Susan, too, was feeling the rewards of charity. The conversation over the last fifteen minutes had been between her mother, Mrs. Braintree and Susan, and it concerned Emily. Their mother said, as always, she didn't know how she would exist without Emily. She spoke of Emily as if she was a very old family retainer. She said as much without actually using the term. Mrs. Braintree said how lucky she was to have such a faithful servant, yet such service could only have been maintained through kindness. Susan put in with deceptive casualness that she was in the habit of running Emily to and from her home. Her mother said it was all a matter of consideration.

The Braintrees had brought their younger son with them. He was eighteen years old and and pimply. His name was Alan and he talked big about cars. He was standing now, talking to her father. She watched her mother rise from her chair and come towards her. She was smiling. She still smiled as she bent over her and said under her breath, "What is the matter with you, Vanessa? Have you gone dumb all of a sudden? Why can't you talk to Alan?"

"Because he wants to talk, you can't get a word in." Vanessa's face looked sulky.

"Don't be difficult, child. Your father's noticed it. You're being difficult. You don't want to make him angry, do you? Now you get up and go and talk to Alan."

As she looked back into her mother's face Vanessa almost said, "He's no good wasting time on, he'll never come into the title, not unless Brian dies," but what she said was, "I'd like to go upstairs."

"You'll do nothing of the kind. You'll stay here until they go."

As she turned away she was smiling again.

After a while Vanessa rose to her feet and gradually made her way towards Alan Braintree, but he took no notice of her; he continued to talk cars to her father. Cars were his only interest, the only thing he could talk about. What was more he did not want to be left alone with Vanessa Ratcliffe. She made him uneasy. She was one of those clever sticks of girls, and he had no time for clever sticks.

Half an hour later, when Susan and Brian returned, they all sat down to a game of bridge. It was a comparatively short game and the guests left at half-past eleven.

At twelve o'clock all the lights in the house were out, and at five past twelve Vanessa went down the fire escape and into the garden. It was moonlight again, but to-night the clouds were scudding across the sky and the wind was high.

It was nearly four weeks since Brett had found her in the summerhouse, and she had been down there at least half-a-dozen times since. Twice when it was black dark. She had been a bit scared those times, yet excited. The first time she had gone into the woods after that particular night she had half expected Brett to appear again, and on each occasion since she had hoped she might see him. He was nice, was Brett. But to-night she didn't expect to see him. It was too late; the whole world was asleep.

She could have fallen asleep at any time during the dinner or after, particularly during the bridge, but now she felt wide awake. She had never felt so wide awake and so filled with unrest. She felt unhappy. Was it because Susan was so happy? Was she jealous of Susan? Yes, she supposed she was. She wasn't jealous of her having Brian, or marrying into the Braintress, but she was jealous of her getting married. She was nodding at herself as she went through the gate and into the deep shadow. One had to be honest with oneself.

Perhaps if she had a boy she would feel different. But boys didn't make for her. Look at Alan to-night. Not that she'd wanted anyone like him, the spotty oaf. But still, he hadn't been attracted to her at all. Boys didn't seem to be atracted to her; what was wrong with her? Rona and Kathy, they'd had boys since they were fourteen. Of course, their mothers hadn't known, but Rona's mother knew now, and Kathy took Harold Blackett home. And neither Rona nor Kathy were good-looking. She considered she was better looking than either of them; she wasn't being conceited. No, because she knew she wasn't as good-looking as Lucy Fulton, because Lucy was beautiful. But she wasn't bad-looking; she had nice hair and

84

eyes. So, what was wrong with her? It was the same when she went to a party. Look at the parties last Christmas. All the necking that went on, but the boy that was with her just sat and played with her fingers. There must be something wrong with her somewhere. It must be something inside that boys sensed.

Further on, the wind lashed a branch against her face and she covered her cheek and bent her head against the pain of it. When she looked up again she saw the figure crossing a dappled moonlit space. First of all her heart seemed to stop still in fright because it didn't look like Brett, not as tall; then she realized he was walking with his head down. Before he was aware of her she called softly, "Brett! Is that you, Brett?" She watched him stand motionless, looking in her direction, and when she reached him she said, "You gave me a start again, I didn't think it was you. What would have happened if it hadn't been you?"

He didn't speak, he just stared into her face, which was illuminated in moving patterns of moonlight.

"What's the matter, Brett? Are you sick?"

"No, no. I had the beast of a headache, I had to come out. But . . . but why are you out at this time? It's well past midnight."

"I couldn't sleep." She turned away from him, walking in the direction of the river. "I felt all het up inside. Oh, I don't know." She turned again, expecting to find him by her side, but when she looked back he was still standing in the same place, and she retraced a few steps and said anxiously, "There's something wrong, Brett. What is it? What's the matter? You . . . There's nothing happened to Paul?"

"Oh, no, no; he's all right."

"You've heard from him?"

"Yes, we had a letter yesterday."

"Is he having a good time?"

"By all accounts, the time of his life."

85

"You're missing him, aren't you? Going off like that the second day of his holiday. You . . . You didn't expect it."

"Oh, yes. Yes, I did."

"No, not until the summer, and remember," she gave a little laugh, "he was going to take me to dances. You promised." She took hold of his arm and shook it. She was endeavouring in her own way to lighten whatever depression had fallen on him, because even in this light she could see that his face was almost the colour of chalk. He never had much colour but she had never seen him looking so pale.

"Come on," she coaxed. "Come on down to the summer-house and let's talk."

"No, not at this hour. You'd best get back indoors. What if they should miss you?" His voice was stiff.

"They won't miss me."

"I'm going up, Vanessa; it's late."

"All right then." She made her voice sound a little huffy. "You go on up and I'll go and sit in the summer-house and muse."

She had gone half-a-dozen steps towards the river again when he joined her. He had his head bent once more, and he muttered something that she couldn't hear above the wind, but she didn't question what he had said. She suddenly felt gay and excited. It must be the wind and the moonlight and the fact that she—and Brett—must be the only people in Fellburn to be walking in a wood at this time of night.

When she slipped her hand into his arm she brought him to a stop again and he turned his face to hers, pleading with her now. "Van, be a good girl, come on back."

"Look, we're there." She pointed across the clearing to the summerhouse, then tugged him forward.

They sat on the step and she pulled the rush mat from the middle of the floor to make the seat more comfortable, and then, joining her hands round her knees, she said,

86

"There." She had the same feeling now as when she had taken Emily the bath salts, she felt good. What she was doing she felt was good for Brett. He was lonely. She knew that he didn't get on with Irene. She had gauged that much from snatches of conversation she had overheard between her mother and father, and latterly between her mother and Susan.

"What is it, Brett?" she said now. "You're worried. You can tell me. Is it about the yard?"

He was about to say no, but he said, "Yes." He'd have to tell her something. "Your father gave me the chance to go to Holland, Germany and round and about. You know Mr. Cribber is in hospital and likely to be there for the next two or three months. He's the representative. Your father wanted me to take his place. Temporary, that is . . ."

"And you're going to?"

"No. No, I turned it down."

"But why? Why, Brett? It would be a kind of holiday for you."

"Oh, for a number of reasons. But the main one, I think, was I'd have to be away from here for weeks on end. You know I've never been away from this place for longer than three weeks in my life, and even after a week I long to be back."

"You are funny, Brett."

"Yes, I suppose so."

Their faces were turned to each other, and she nodded slowly at him as she said, "But I can understand. I can understand how you feel. It's the trees and the river and the house, and it's yours. Yes, I can understand. I often wish we had a bit of woodland. Oh. Oh," she put her hand on his arm again, "I don't mean that you should sell it to father. I would say don't sell it to father, hang on to it. I would if it were mine. But I would like a garden with trees in it. Ours is so formal, you feel you're in the park. I wouldn't be surprised any day to see some women

87

coming through the gate pushing prams.' She laughed, but he didn't laugh with her.

She said now, "Are you worried because you refused? I mean, did it upset Father? He hates doing anything without getting loud applause."

"Oh, Vanessa!" Now he was laughing a little.

"Oh, I know I shouldn't talk like that, but you see I know him. I've said that before to you, haven't I, that I know him?" She joined her hands once more round her knees and began to sway a little back and forwards as she asked, "Why isn't love a sort of natural thing like growing hair or cutting your second teeth, I mean loving your parents. You're theirs and they've brought you up, and you should just love them out of gratitude if for nothing else. It worries me." She stopped swaying and turned her face towards him again and repeated, "It worries me. Can you understand that, Brett? I don't love them and it worries me."

He nodded, then said thickly, "You can't love to order, even your parents."

"I think about it a lot, Brett, I mean loving people. I . . . I can't even like them. There are so few people I really like. I thought I used to like Rona and Kathy and Lucy, but I don't any more. I used to have a thing about Kathy when I was fourteen and now I think she's silly and I was stupid for having a pash on her. And, I . . . I don't like Susan, Brett. Fancy me saying that about my own sister, but I don't like her. And Ray. At times I loathe Ray. You know the only person I like in our house is Emily. She's fat and at times doesn't look over-clean, and she's common. I mean . . . Well, Mother says she's common, they all say she's common. They need her services but behind her back they say she's common. And she is, but I like her. Why should I like her better than Susan or Mother or Father?"

"I can't answer you that one, Vanessa; perhaps because she's more natural, hasn't got so many skins."

"Do you dislike people, Brett?"

"No, not really. I find it hard to dislike people."

"Even Father?"

"Yes. Yes, even Jonathan."

"As you get older will it become easier to love people?"

"In your case perhaps." He smiled tenderly at her. "You'll find somebody that stirs you, makes you feel warm, somebody that you can't bear to live without seeing every minute of the day and night; you'll love like that one day, then everything will be ironed out. You're going through a difficult period; it happens to us all."

She said now, "You know I was thinking to-day there were only two men I could talk to, Angus and . . . and you. I could love you, Brett."

She didn't know why she had said it, perhaps because he needed comfort. When she leant her head on his shoulder and put her hand through his arm, the result of her action surprised and frightened her for a moment; she felt his whole body quivering, and then to her dismay she saw his head droop deep over his knees, and she watched him cover his face and his hands.

"Brett! Brett! What is it? Oh, Brett, don't. Don't. What have I done? What have I said?" She put her arms round his shoulders, and when her hand covered his it became wet with his tears. "Oh, Brett, Brett. Dear Brett." She pulled him round to her. His head drooped on to her shoulder; his wet face was buried in her neck. When she heard him murmur, "Oh God! Oh God" as if he was in pain, she held him more tightly to her, stroking his hair, patting him, soothing him. When, a few minutes later, she held his tear-stained face between her hands and looked into his eyes she became consumed with pity and love, a first love, a love that expected no future, a love that consumed itself in its very creation, a love that was made up of curiosity and desire.

When, locked together, they dropped sideways on to the wooden floor, he hoisted her farther into the summerhouse, and when his hands moved over her she could not have stopped him if she had wanted to for the gentle Brett had vanished and a strange man was tearing her apart, choking her with his tongue and rending her in two with his body.

Her curiosity was being satisfied.

2

"It's the beer talking," said Emily.

"Now, Mam, it isn't the beer. I haven't passed me quota; I've had me six and that's all."

"You can't kid me."

"No, I can't kid you, Mam." Angus bent over the back of the chair where Emily was sitting with her feet up on a cracket, and he nipped one of her sagging chins as he repeated dramatically, "No, I can't kid you. I'll have to confess, I've had a drop of hard."

"I knew it, else you wouldn't be talkin' so damn soft. You know you can't carry it. As for this hair-brained scheme of joining up with Fred Singleton, you can forget it. You're not leaving the yard. Head of a shop at your age and wantin' to give it up. And for what? To start a one-man . . . all right, a two-men, haulage business, when the neighbourhood is infested with haulage businesses."

"I know that, Mam, the big bods. But . . . but the big bods can't carry all the work they've got in. That's what I've been tellin' you. They sub-contract, you know, let it out."

"I know all about it." Emily now brought her feet from the cracket. "And I'm tellin' you this, you're not puttin' your bit of money into any bloody racket Fred Singleton can think up."

"Fred's a good lad."

"Then why hasn't he made his fortune afore now?"

"For the simple reason he didn't have enough to start

with; he's just got one lorry and he's on his own. Now if he had two or three . . ."

"Bought with your money like."

"Aye, bought with my money like, then we would be in clover."

"Do you know where the most clover grows, Angus Cotton? In the Bankruptcy Court. You big gowk, I'll talk to you in the mornin' when you're sober."

Angus was standing with his hand to his brow and his eyes closed when the door opened and Rosie came in, accompanied by Stan, and before they had time to close the door Emily cried at them, "You want to hear what this 'n is on about now; he's talkin' of puttin' his bit in with Fred Singleton and startin' a haulage business. Haulage, I ask you. Bloody silly bugger."

Rosie looked from Angus where he was sitting at the end of the table now, his head resting on one hand, an oily smile covering his face and his lips moving back and forward over each other, and she laughed outright. Their Angus always looked funny when he was carrying a drop; he was never bad-tempered, like some. Wanting to rouse her mother still further and wanting a laugh, she said, "Well I don't think it's a bad idea, not really. I mean if you put five thousand down and pay the rest in instalments."

Angus let out a roar of a laugh and cried, "Aw, Rosie! Aw, Rosie! That's good. Trust you."

"I don't see anythin' to laugh at." Emily was glaring at Rosie now. "He's serious, it isn't a joke. He started this afore he went out an' he was solid and sober then." She turned to Stan now and demanded, "What do you think, Stan? You're on the factory side of cement, you should have your ear to the ground about this kind of thing, haulage."

"Well." Stan walked to the table and took a seat opposite Angus. Then looking at Emily, he said, "If you had a

92

few hundred about you, and the strength of a bull an' plenty of nerve you could get through."

"There you are. There you are." Angus's arm was extended high above his head. "Nerve, he said. And the strenth of a bull; and a few hundred. Is anybody more qualified than me?" He got to his feet and banged his chest with his clenched fists. "Oo! Oo! . . . Oo! Oo!"

The Tarzan call was too much for Emily. She joined in the laughter and she laughed till the tears ran down her face . . .

But Emily didn't laugh the following morning when Angus informed her he was going to have a run out with Fred Singleton. But she did not go for him either, she pleaded with him.

"Look, lad," she said. "It's only three hundred and seventy-five but it's taken a bit of gettin'. Don't be a bloody fool, lad."

"Listen, Mam." He was speaking as quietly as she was. "I'm not bein' any kind of a bloody fool, I'm not committing meself, I'm just goin' out to see this lorry."

"If Fred Singleton thinks he's on a good thing why can't he buy another lorry?"

Angus sighed. "Aw, Mum, he's got a wife and six kids and his widowed mother living with him. It takes every penny. But he tells me at times he can turn forty a week, not all the time, but pretty often. But with a couple of lorries running and the prospect of more there's no reason why it shouldn't be forty every week."

"As long as it lasts, lad; these buildings won't be goin' up for ever."

"You heard Stan last night, Mam. They've got plans out for along the river that'll take another ten years."

"Listen. Listen to me. I don't want you to leave the yard. There's a sort of, well, call it status, or prestige or whatever you like, but you're chargehand of your shop an' you've got it."

"God, Mam." His tone was scathing. "Chargehands an'

foremen, they're two a penny. As for prestige, that went down the sink years ago. You're living in the past, Mam. Men don't look up to them a step above them these days, they spit in their eye. You should hear Jim Taggart at me."

"What's Jim Taggart? Scum. Scum, that's all he is."

"Well, there's a lot of scum about and you find that out once you've been put over them. Anyway, Mam, I've got a fancy for being me own boss."

"Well, what about all this evening-class business you've been goin' at?"

'Oh that'll come in handy, nothin's ever lost."

"And what if you want to get married and your money goes down the drain?"

"If I want to get married, Mam! Who's talking of gettin' married?"

She turned from him and went into the scullery, and from there she shouted, "May was round here last night. She had been to the club lookin' for you."

"Oh, aye."

"You're not playin' fair by May, Angus."

"That's my business, Mam."

"It can be your business but I still say you're not playing fair by her. Three years you've known her; you should be married now, with a bairn."

"Oh, for God's sake! Look, Mam, you can stick your finger in any pie that I'm eatin', but with regard to May, or any other piece, that's my business. Now, I'm tellin' you." He walked towards the scullery door and addressed her back. "I'll marry when I think fit, May or anybody else I want to, but it'll be when I want to. Now understand that."

He went out without saying good-bye, but the frame of his mind was conveyed to her as he banged the door, and she hurried into the front-room and watched him go down the street. He was a fine figure of a man, and he was as well put on as any gentleman in the town. He knew how to dress did her Angus. The cut of his overcoat suited his broad shoulders. He was wearing one of those new velour sporty hats. She shook her head. It was a motion of pride, but as she turned from the window she exclaimed aloud, "The stubborn bugger."

Angus went with Fred Singleton in his old car to Morpeth. He saw the lorry that was for sale, but thought they were asking about twice what it was worth, and so they returned the way they had gone, nothing settled.

On the return journey they stopped just before closing time and had a drink and discussed the situation for the twentieth time. "I'm not going to jump into anything, Fred; I've got a good job as you know, an' what's more I've got me mam to consider. As I say there's plenty of time."

"There's not, you know, Angus; there's not. There's other fellows borrowing money to start up."

"Well, why don't you borrow to get another lorry?"

"Well, as I've told you, I'd have to take on another bloke. What I want is a partner, somebody who'll carry his weight, like you. Tough, with a level head on him. And, I don't mind admitting this to you Angus, somebody who'll be able to do the correspondence like, the writin' and bargainin'. I'm not much good at it. If I did things in writin' I would get farther, but everythin' is by word of mouth, you know."

Angus nodded, then said, "I'm sorry, Fred, but I'm gonna leave it for the time being. Not too long; no, not too long, but just for a week or so. I've got to consider, you see."

It started to rain as they left the pub and when they were about two miles outside of Fellburn and taking a side road that was bordered by the open fell, Angus suddenly said, "Hold your hand a minute, Fred, stop her!"

"What!"

"Stop the car. Stop her a minute."

When the car had stopped Angus swung round in his seat and looked out of the rear window. Then, leaning across Fred, he said, "Pull the window down a minute, I want to see over there."

Over there was a young girl walking by herself. She had a raincoat on with the collar turned up and a scarf round her head. She was walking with her hands in her pockets and her shoulders hunched.

"Who is it? Somebody you know?"

"Aye." Angus nodded his head. "I wonder what she's doin' out up here on her own, in the rain. Hang on a minute, will you?"

Fred grinned and said, "Oh aye; I've all the time in the world."

Angus got out of the car and went up the bank on to the fell. The girl had her back to him now, but there was no mistaking Vanessa. He would have picked out her walk and her style from a hundred; but he didn't call her name until he came abreast of her, about six yards distant, and then she turned and looked at him and he said, "I thought it was you. What you doin' up here in the wet? You lost?"

She stared at him, her mouth slightly open; then she said, "Oh, hello, Angus."

"You lost? I mean it's pourin'. Do you like being out in the wet?"

"I don't mind. I wanted to have a long walk."

"Do you want a lift back?" He nodded over towards the car. "There's another two miles to go, three to your place."

She followed his gaze, then said, "No. No, thanks."

He was now standing in front of her and he peered at her through the driving rain for a moment before saying, "You all right?"

"Yes, yes."

"You look peaked."

"Oh, I'm all right."

96

"Look." He came close to her. "You're not tellin' the truth, are you? You're not all right. What's up?"

"Nothing nothing."

"Mam said you'd been off colour and had a cold, tummy upset; you'd been off school for a week or two."

"Yes, I have. I've had a cold but it's better now."

"Well, you don't look better. And you won't stay better long in this. Come on, get into the car." He put out his hand towards her but she shrank back, saying, "No, no; I want to walk."

He continued to look at her for some minutes before he said, "All right," then turned abruptly away and went towards the car. And there, bending down to Fred, who was sitting smoking, he said, "Do you mind finishin' on your own? I feel I'd better see her home."

"Oh, aye. But you're not goin' to enjoy yourself very much, it beltin' like this."

"Oh, it's nothing like that, man." Angus put his fist against Fred's shoulder. "She's the daughter, you know, where Mam works. She's been ill and I think she still is. She looks odd to me; I think I'd better see to her."

"Please yourself. But . . . but you'll think about the other, won't you?"

"Aye. Yes, I promise, Fred, I'll think about it. And I'll let you know one way or the other in a week or two. All right?"

"All right." Fred's face looked crestfallen as he moved off, and Angus, turning, went on to the fell again. Vanessa was some distance further away now and he had to hurry to catch up with her. When he came to her side he said, "Well now, which is the shortest way home?"

She stopped and again she looked at him with her mouth open. Then lowering her head and moving it from side to side, she said, "Look, Angus, I'm all right, really I am."

"Well, if you're all right, it's a poor look-out for the bad 'uns. It strikes me you should be in bed. You look as

97

white as lint and you're shiverin'." He put his hand on her arm. "Come on. An' I'm standing no nonsense; if we're going to walk we're going to do it briskly. And you want to get home and get into bed. You shouldn't pick days like this to take a tramp; although," he remarked as if to himself, "it wasn't so bad earlier on. But this is our summer, flaming June. Look, we'll cross over the top," he pointed into the distance, "an' go down by the river and over the stepping stones. That'll cut almost a mile off and bring us to the end of Mr. Brett's wood."

When her body jerked he thought she had stumbled, and he put out his other hand to steady her.

They walked some distance in silence, until it became embarrassing to him and he said, "Mam tells me you're leaving school at the end of this term."

"Yes."

"I thought you were staying on until you were seventeen next year?"

"I'm seventeen in August." For the first time she turned and looked at him. "In exactly six weeks and two days I'll be seventeen."

He was slightly nonplussed by both her voice and her manner but he said airily, "Well, it's plain to be seen you've got it worked out to the hour."

"Yes, to the hour."

What was wrong with her? There was something amiss. He hadn't seen her for some time, not since that day they had travelled up from Newcastle and he had got himself narked by the way young Brett had looked at him, and he had left her abruptly. Surely, she in her turn hadn't been narked about his manner . . . . Could be, could be. What did she expect him to do? Bow and scrape. He said, "Haven't seen you for some time, not since that day when we came up on the train together. I . . . I had to leave you rather sharp, there was somebody I wanted to see."

She was looking at him again. She didn't for the moment know what he was talking about; and then she remembered him walking away and talking to the cheap-looking girl.

CHEAP LOOKING. CHEAP LOOKING. CHEAP LOOKING.

The words were re-echoing in her mind, as words were doing a lot lately. Significant words such as cheap, consequences, retribution, sin, scandal, death, suicide, water. Yes, water. But she would never drown, she was too good a swimmer; and they hadn't gas in the house, only electricity and the Aga. This only left the aspirins, there were all kinds of aspirins in the bathroom cupboard. If only Brett would come back. If he knew he would do something about it. He would take her away. She hadn't a doubt but that he would take her away.

For days after it happened she hadn't been able to think of him without wanting to be sick. For days and days after, she could feel his body on hers; she could see his part naked flesh as he rolled off her exhausted, finished. When she had finally come to herself she had for the first time experienced loathing, loathing of herself and him. But it was too late, the thing was done, the beastly horrible slimy thing was accomplished.

Some parts of the episode had faded from her mind and there was only a feeling left about them, but she still remembered the sound and sight of his crying. He had started to cry again, he had cried as he had kissed her all over; he had cried until she had kicked herself free from him and run through the wood in panic. And the panic was still with her, and only his presence could ease it.

If she could only hide her panic until he came back then it would be all right, they would go away. He would get a divorce and they would marry. That's how things were done.

"What? I'm sorry I wasn't paying attention."

"I said, had you decided on anything, a job or anything?"

"No. That is Mother and Father want me to go to

France to stay with a family; my French is weak." She tried to put a smile to her words but it wouldn't come.

He helped her across the stepping stones; then they went up the bank and along the towpath that ran by the side of the river, and fifteen minutes later they came out into the lane where the wire fence that bordered the Brett ground ran down into the river. She had her head down as she walked up the narrow lane towards the road. They were about half-way along the lane, and silent once more, when her name being called brought them both to a startled halt. There were two voices calling "Hi, Vanessa! Hi, Vanessa!" and the voices appeared to be coming out of the air.

She looked up into the trees, and Angus's gaze followed hers and he said, "There's somebody up there in the trees."

She was walking on again. "It's Ray," she said, "and Michael Brett. They've built a platform in the oak."

"Good for them. But it gave me a bit of a gliff hearin' your name being called out of the sky." He was looking at her profile, waiting for her to say something, but she didn't, and when they came to the end of the lane he stopped and said, "Well, here's the parting of the ways. Now you take my advice and go to bed; you look as if you're sickenin' for something. Have you had the doctor?"

"No; I'm all right really and . . . . Thanks." Her voice trailed off, and he added with a smile, "For forcing meself on you? But me mam would never have forgiven me if I'd left you up there in the rain all by yourself. You looked lost." He leant his head slightly to the side. "If you go on this way you'll be losin' your looks, you know, an' you don't want that to happen, do you? What's the duke or the count goin' to say?"

When she swung away from him without a word of good-bye he stood gazing after her until she disappeared into her own gateway; then he turned towards home . . . .

Emily was having her Sunday afternoon rest when he

arrived, and he went straight upstairs and into her room. She was sitting up in bed with a cup of tea in her hand and she said "Oh, so you're back. Well, what's happened?"

"Enough of that after." He sat down heavily on the foot of the bed and began: "Look, Mam, when we were comin' down the fell lane about two miles out, Fred and me in the car, I saw Van meandering across the fells in the rain and I got out and asked if she would like a lift, but she wouldn't come, and she was in such a state that I let Fred go on and I brought her back."

"Here?" Emily straightened herself up.

"No, no. Don't get yourself agitated. I mean home; we came the river way. She was in a state, Mam. She looks bad."

Emily lay back and closed her eyes for a moment before saying "Oh, she's been like that for a week or two. The missus hasn't known what to do with her, nor me for that matter. We used to have a crack at one time but I've not been able to get a word out of her, not for days. It's exam. nerves, that's what the missus says."

"Exam nerves? Good God, is that what it is?"

"Yes, they all get it when they're sitting for 'O' levels; sick, tummy upsets, the lot."

"Christ!" He banged his forehead with his double fist. "Me thinking she was going into the old-fashioned decline or somethin'. Well, I'll be jiggered. You know, she hardly opened her mouth all the way, and when she did she was so bloomin' dramatic you'd think she was rehearsing for a play. Once or twice I could have laughed, but then she looked so bad."

"Oh, they take it seriously." Emily nodded. "I remember Miss Susan and her 'O' levels. She was sick, an' in the night an' all, and the lazy little beggar wouldn't get up. I remember that bed I had to tackle the next mornin'. Well now, tell me what happened about Singleton."

"Oh, they were asking too much, far too much. I told

them when the came down to practically half I'd think about it."

"What did Fred say?"

"I told him that I'd give him me answer one way or the other in a few weeks' time."

"Well, it'll be the other if I've got anything to do with it."

He stood up, then poked his head down to her and said, "Yes, Mam. Yes, Mam."

"Go on with you."

"Where's Rosie?"

"She's in her room. There should be some tea in the pot."

"I'm not havin' your leavings, I'm goin' to make fresh."

"You don't need to make fresh, it's just been made."

As he went out of the room he said to her over his shoulder, "Don't be so stingy; you'd think you bought it. I like making fresh pots of God Almighty Ratcliffe's tea. Anyway, I brought his daughter home out of the wet." He pushed his head back round the door towards her. "That's a good 'un. It's the title of a story: Out of the Wet."

"You're not just wet, lad, you're drippin'." Emily lay back and gurgled at her own joke; then she emptied her cup, saying to herself, "Thank God. But he's got sense, our Angus. I needn't have worried."

3

"You're mad. You must be mad."

"Yes, we're all slightly mad, Mrs. Ratcliffe."

"But you are." She checked herself from adding, "or drunk." It was a well-known fact that he was a tippler; hadn't Mrs. Carey objected to his breath when he visited her? She would change; she had been thinking about it for a long time.

The doctor seemed to read her thoughts, and he buttoned up his coat briskly as he said, "Mad, drunk, or daft, Mrs. Ratcliffe, your daughter is pregnant."

There was the word again; it hadn't really registered the first time. Pregnant. PREGNANT. Oh. no, no! This couldn't happen to them. Not only was he mad, she was going mad. The wedding in six weeks' time. Their position. Oh, Jonathan! He would go insane. This would drive him insane. Jonathan couldn't stand things like this. When they happened to other people's daughters he condemned them out of hand; but to his daughter! Where? How? What had they done to deserve this? WHAT? The question was spiralling in her head. She heard the doctor say, "Come.along now, sit down. It isn't the end of the world; these things are happening every day."

Every day. Every day. Every day. The words carried her into a dead faint.

Doctor Carr went to the drawing-room door and in no small voice yelled, "Emily! Emily!"

"Aye, doctor. What is it?" Emily came scurrying across

the hall. It was one of the quirks of the social set-up that Doctor Carr should also be her doctor.

"Your mistress has fainted."

"God God! What caused it?" She was hurrying past him to the couch.

"She's had a bit of a shock."

"About . . . about Miss Van?" She was loosening the front of Jane Ratcliffe's dress as she spoke, and she turned her shrewd glance up at the doctor.

"Yes, about Miss Van."

"Has she caught something? Infectious or something? She'll go mad," she nodded down towards the prostrate figure, "if anything happens to put a spoke in the weddin'."

"This will put the spoke in a number of things, Emily, if I'm not mistaken. Look, go and make a cup of tea. And be quick about it."

Emily straightened up and was in the act of hurrying away when she turned and looked at him and said, "God Almighty! You don't mean . . .?"

"Yes, I do mean." He nodded at her. "And go on and get that tea made."

Oh no! No! What's the world comin' to? NO! Not Miss Van. God in Heaven! She went into the kitchen and stood gripping the edge of the table. That's what had been wrong with her all these weeks. But who would have suspected Miss Van! Examination nerves, everybody said. Aw, no! No! She just wouldn't believe it. She rammed the kettle on to the top of the hot plate. But the doctor . . . the doctor had just examined her. The missus had insisted on him coming because Van wouldn't get up out of bed to go to school. She kept saying she wasn't feeling well, and begod, she wouldn't be feeling well . . . . But who? . . . Who did the child know? Child? She was a child no longer, she was nearly seventeen. She herself had been married a week after her seventeenth birthday. But in this class, this house, it was different; they were still

104

children at that age. Aw, she answered herself, there were no children these days. But, in any case, God strike them down dead the one who had brought it about. It would be Van this would happen to, the nicest of the bunch; it always happened to the nice ones. "Hurry up you!" She scraped the kettle backwards and forwards on the hot plate.

The master? Oh, God Almighty! There'd be high jinks the night. When he got wind of this they'd have to tie him down, because he was a sanctimonious prig, was Jonathan Ratcliffe. He went to the most fashionable church in the town and subscribed handsomely to the fashionable charities, but let a fellow come to the door and ask for a bite, as they used to years ago – not now; they didn't need to now – and he showed them what charity was. Oh, there'd be hell to pay the night in this house.

When she took the tray of tea into the room Jane Ratcliffe was sitting up, her head supported in the wing of the couch, and as Emily held the cup to her lips Doctor Carr said, "I think your husband should be here. May I use your phone?"

For answer Jane Ratcliffe just raised her eyes.

It took some minutes to convince Jonathan Ratcliffe's secretary that the doctor had no intention of leaving a message and that he intended to speak to Mr. Ratcliffe.

"Yes?" Jonathan's voice was abrupt, and Doctor Carr's matched it as he said, "This is Carr speaking. I think it would be wise if you came home for a while."

"Home? What on earth for? What's the matter? Something happened?"

"Yes, something's happened, Mr. Ratcliffe."

Doctor Carr's words were clipped. "Your wife has collapsed."

"My wife! But . . . but I thought you were calling to see Vanessa."

"I have seen Vanessa."

"What's the matter with her?"

"I don't think we can go into this on the phone; you'd better come home. I can't stay; I have another call to make, I'm late already." On this he banged down the phone, returned to the drawing-room and said quietly, "He'll be here shortly. Now just take it calmly. I'm leaving you some tablets. If you need me give me a ring."

Jane Ratcliffe didn't speak, she didn't even move her head; she was in a state of shock.

At the door Doctor Carr motioned Emily towards him, and as he picked his bag up from the hall table he said under his breath, "The one upstairs could do with a drink too, Emily."

"Aye, Doctor, aye. I'll see to it."

But Emily didn't get the chance to take a tray upstairs until fifteen minutes later, because her missus kept hanging on to her hand, staring up into her face while not uttering a word. That was, until the master walked into the room, and then she released Emily and whimpered, "Oh, Jonathan."

Emily hurried out of the room with the tea tray in her hand and, standing in the hall for a minute, she wondered whether she could get a cup upstairs in time to fortify the lass before he started on her.

A few seconds later she knocked gently on Vanessa's door, then went in.

Vanessa was sitting on the side of the bed in her dressing gown. To Emily she looked all eyes, teeth and hair. She said softly, "You could do with a cup, lass?"

"Emily."

Emily looked at the quivering face, and she said, "Aye. What is it, hinny?" She was no longer talking to Miss Vanessa, only to a lass, who, like many another, and better, before her, had been laid down.

"Oh, Emily!"

"Now, now, now, don't take on. Drink this up. You'll be havin' visitors in a minute; your father's downstairs."

The cup rattled on the saucer and Emily had to steady it. "Come on now, drink it up."

Before Vanessa had drunk half the cup of tea there came the sound of quick muted footsteps across the landing; then the door was thrust open.

Jonathan Ratcliffe stood aside to allow Emily to leave the room, and he allowed his wife to pass in; then he closed the door quietly, which spoke of the control he had put himself under. But when he looked at his daughter sitting with bowed head on the side of the bed his control vanished, and he almost sprang towards her.

"Look at me!"

Her head remained bowed until his hand shot out and jerked her chin up. He did not say, "Is this true?" but "You dirty, dirty little slut! You filthy little slut!" There were dobbles of saliva spurting from between his clenched teeth. "Who was it?"

Petrified, she stared up into his face. This it what she had been afraid of, this moment, in case her fear of him would cause her to betray Brett. She knew she must do nothing until Brett came and he would do the telling. He would stand up to her father. This once he would stand up to her father.

"Answer me, girl."

When the only answer he got was the wide stare from her eyes it was too much. He struck her once, twice, three times before she fell backwards over the bed.

Jane Ratcliffe was clinging to him now crying, "Jonathan! Jonathan, no! Not that." She forced him back. Afraid herself now of the wild stare in his eyes which he kept fixed on his daughter. Using all her strength, she led him out of the room.

On the landing, he stood, his eyes unblinking as he fought the desire to return to the room and tear every stitch off her and flay her until she cried out for mercy. He should have done it. He glared at his wife for a full minute; then, taking a handkerchief, he rubbed the sweat and saliva from around his mouth.

"What's to be done? What's to be done?" Jane was whimpering now.

He moved down the landing, still wiping his mouth; then ground out through his handkerchief, "She'll have it taken away."

Taken away? But Jonathan, that's illegal."

"Don't be stupid, woman!" He turned on her "Nothing's illegal if you can pay well enough for it. But one thing is certain; there's going to be no baby born on the side in this house. And think, just think what this will mean if the Braintrees get wind of it; it could ruin everything. Their outlook might be modern but they're narrow underneath. Remember the other night? Remember when he was on about cleaning up certain quarters of the town?" He put his hand to his head, then turned and looked towards Vanessa's room again and asked, "Who? Who? That's what I want to know." When he brought his infuriated gaze round to her he demanded, "Have you no idea?"

She shook her head in bewilderment. "I can't think. I don't know . . . anyone."

"Well, you should know, woman. It's your duty to know. There's a man somewhere, boy or man; she can't be having a baby through auto-suggestion."

As they went down the stairs Ray came from the narrow passage that led to the second bathroom and he watched his parents' heads disappear before turning and looking towards Vanessa's door. Vanessa was going to have a baby. He knew how people had babies; Clive at school, had told him. He had shown him how it was done in the lavatories . . . . He bit on his lip. Vanessa was going to have a baby. He was grinning as he went out down the back staircase to Michael's tree house. He would whistle to Michael, he should be back from school now. He would tell him Vanessa was going to have a baby.

Emily stood at the table and looked at Angus where he was standing with his coat in his hand. He had taken it off but he hadn't hung it up. She said, "I wanted to tell you afore Rosie got in. I promised him faithfully I wouldn't utter a word. He got me in the study and made me swear I wouldn't let on. They're goin' to have it taken away as far as I can gather . . . . Don't look like that, lad, but I know how you feel. I've never got such a gliff in me life. Honest to God, I was floored."

"Can't be true." Angus's voice was rumbling in his throat "Van? No, not her. She's only a kid and –"

"Look, lad, you know as well as me, they're hardly out of the cradle afore they're fallin' with bairns these days. You haven't to go any further than three doors down. Fourteen years old."

"Oh, I know, I know." His voice was suddenly high and harsh. "But you don't judge the world on Betty Halliday, do you? We're talking about Vanessa Ratcliffe . . . . How did it happen? Was she raped?"

"Oh, lad!" Emily put her hand to her head, swinging it from side to side. "You're askin' me, and they're askin' her, and they can't get one word out of her. And they don't know any fellow she's been with. She doesn't go round with fellows; she hasn't even got a boy friend. There were three lasses, Lucy Fulton, Kathy Young, and that Rona girl. They come to the house for tea. Those are all she ever sees. At least, that's what everybody thought . . . . And then they nearly had another casualty on their hands. I thought Susan was going to go clean up the pole. She went up the stairs and I heard her screaming from down in the kitchen. The missus had to go up an' stop her. You know, it could put a spoke in that one's wheel, a scandal like this." Emily sighed now and ended, "Well, there's nowt we can do about it, so go and have a wash, and by that time your tea'll be ready."

He went towards the scullery, saying, "I've got no appetite the night, I'll just have a cup of tea for now."

"You'll eat your tea. I've cooked it." She was barking at him.

In the scullery he stripped off his shirt and went to the sink and began to wash himself, pausing every now and again to stare at the wall. He felt sick, actually sick, like he did sometimes on a Sunday morning when he had gone over his quota on a Saturday night, and he knew this was only the beginning. Later on to-night, when he was in bed and could think quietly, it would be worse.

As he dried himself he stood looking out of the window on to the back yard, and he did not think, "Poor kid. What luck!" but aggressively, "Why had she to do it? Her! She had been a kind of symbol to him, the queen who smiled at the shoemaker, the princess who touched the hand of the swine herd." He had likened her to the characters in the books that had once been Susan's and hers and had been passed on to Rosie. She had been in his mind something so aloof that even when he thought of her he had to look upwards. She was, he realized at this moment with a mixture of astonishment and scorn at himself for being such a fool, the reason why he had cooled off May when she let on about having the other fellows. He had indeed been a bloody fool. He didn't like feeling a bloody fool. He turned to the kitchen door and said, "She could have been attacked or somethin'."

"I don't think so, lad," said Emily flatly. "If that had happened she would have come home in a state at the time. Lasses don't keep things like that to themselves. No, it was no rape to my way of thinkin'. But whoever it is, she's keepin' mum about him. But, oh, the look on her face as she sat on the side of that bed when I took a cup of tea up to her. That is afore he saw her. She looked like all the lost souls in the Bible; all eyes she was and them full of fear. Oh, I can't explain how she looked. And them gettin' the doctor for exam. nerves. That's the only funny part about it."

He turned back into the scullery. Funny part . . . exam.

nerves. By aye. She had exam. nerves all right. That is why she had been wandering around the fells in the rain and he had taken her home as if she was a little bairn who had lost her way. Oh, she must have been laughing up her sleeve at him. God, but wasn't he the bloodiest of bloody fools. He recalled how he felt as he walked by her side, proud, sort of humble and grateful, all mixed up together. He had always felt grateful to her because she spoke to him. But all the while they had walked over the fells she was pregnant. She had been with a fellow. She knew all about it.

He wondered how many times she had done it, and who with. Likely some pimply groping grammar-school twirp, some sixth former; a boy at school, but a man when he got out of the gates and stuffed his school cap in his pocket.

"Come an' get your tea."

He went into the kitchen and, looking down at the two chops bordered by fried potatoes and tomatoes, he said, "I couldn't stomach it."

Emily glared at him for a moment; then, wagging her head, she said flatly, "All right, we'll say nothin' more about it. I'll warm it up after for you. Go and get yourself changed and have a pint; you'll feel better."

Yes, he'd get himself changed and have a pint. But he wouldn't feel better; he'd only feel more of a so and so fool because the beer would unlock the secret places in himself, that only it and dreams had the power to do; places in which he would wander as he had done on the fells the other day and hold conversations with her. He didn't just talk at these times, he conversed, speaking correctly. He always spoke correctly in the secret places; there was nothing about himself to be ashamed of in the secret places. He had no need to be aggressive in the secret places for there he had an ease of mind and a demeanour that could only elicit admiration – and from the one person he wanted, had always wanted, admiration . . . .

He returned at eleven o'clock. He had been on the hard, and Emily had to put him to bed and she was dismayed. She had always known he was fond of Miss Vanessa, right from she was a bairn, but not all that fond. You see, you thought you knew everything, but there were things you didn't know, even about your own.

In the kitchen Rosie asked, "What's brought this on in the middle of the week?" and Emily replied, "Miss Van; he's cut up."

"Huh!" said Rosie. "What the hell for! That's rich, that is. He wants to tell that to May."

"Now, now," said Emily. "You can be sorry for her."

"Sorry for her, me backside. She had everything, an' she wanted that an' all; she couldn't wait. She's asked for it, an' boy, she's got it. Sorry for her! You're askin' something, aren't you? She always got on my wick."

What Rosie was saying was that she had sense enough to be jealous of the advantages that had fallen to the lot of Vanessa Ratcliffe and she was now feeling a little compensation for the gaucheness that she experienced whenever she was in Vanessa's company. That Vanessa was nearly three years younger than herself made no difference, it was her manner that created the disadvantage.

4

Irene Brett hadn't been so happy for years. She couldn't wait to go next door to offer her condolences.

She had made her son repeat again and again what Ray had said to him, and she linked this with having seen Doctor Carr driving in next door when she was coming home not more than two hours ago. She wished her patience would allow her to wait until the day after tomorrow when Arthur would be home. Not that he would feel as she did because in a way he had been fond of Vanessa, always taking her part; but he would be bound to feel some satisfaction over this calamity falling on Jonathan. As great as the difference was between her and Arthur, she could, she told herself, joy with him in this. How are the mighty fallen. Ah, yes, that saying was applicable to their neighbour. It was another Jonathan in the Bible it was said of. She would have to look it up so that she could quote it pat to Arthur when she told him; and she would also point out to him that she had been justified in her suspicions. She could almost say she had been expecting this outcome; she had always know that, beneath that reserve, Vanessa was a cheap little piece. Her choice of a partner had proved that; she couldn't have picked much lower. Really, really, when you came to think about it.

She looked at the clock; it was turned seven. She would go next door now . . . .

Susan opened the door to her and her manner indicated

the state of her mind for she stammered and said, "Oh, hel-lo, Auntie;" then added, "Mother's resting."

"Yes, I expect she is, Susan, but I just want to see her for a minute." She slipped into the hall and turned and faced Susan, who was slowly closing the door. Then bending towards her, she whispered, "I . . . I don't know whether to believe it or not, children carry such tales, but if it isn't true, your mother should do something with Ray."

"Ray!" Susan moved her head in small jerks. "What's . . . what's Ray done?"

"It's not what Ray's done, it's what he's said. Look, Susan; is your mother in the lounge?" She turned and walked across the hall, and Susan, after a moment's hesitation, followed her almost at a run and pushed open the door, saying, "It's Aunt Irene, Mother."

Jane Ratcliffe turned sharply round. Her face was pale and her eyes red, and on the sight of Irene Brett she turned as sharply away again, saying, "Oh, Irene, I've got a headache."

"Yes, dear, I expect you have. I . . . I was just saying to Susan. I thought I had better come over. It's about Vanessa."

Jane Ratcliffe looked as if she had been frozen into stillnes. Her body slightly twisted, she stood gaping at Irene Brett, then she almost whimpered "Vanessa?"

"Yes." Irene's voice was low and sympathetic. "Ray has told Michael something utterly fantastic and I think you should speak to him." She looked now from Jane to Susan, and unmercifully she went on, "He said that . . . . Well, I really don't know how to put it, but he said that . . . well, the fact is he said that she is going to have a baby." Her voice faded away as if in shock, and for the second time that day Jane Ratcliffe almost fainted. She groped backwards at a chair and sat down; then looked up at her daughter, and Susan turned away and walked towards the fireplace.

"Oh, I am sorry, Jane. Oh, I am. It's appalling. What can I say? What a terrible thing to happen. I . . . I didn't believe it, but, well, if it's true he should be horse-whipped, or put in jail. If I had him up before me, oh I would give him enough time to cool him down I can assure you. It's a pity the birch has gone. I say that again and again."

Both Susan and her mother were staring at Irene now.

"You know who . . . who it is?" It was Susan asking the question, and Irene looked at her and her eyebrows moved slowly upwards as she asked on a high, surprised note that sounded genuine, "Don't you?"

Susan turned her gaze on her mother, and Jane Ratcliffe, calling to her aid all the dignity of which she was capable, straightened her back and said, "Who do you imagine has done this thing to Vanessa, Irene?" She asked the question as if she herself already knew the name of the perpetrator.

"Well," Irene shook her head as if in perplexity. "I mean . . . . Well, I thought. Well, it's no use beating about the bush. I've told Arthur about the number of times I've seen them together, and Michael saw them last Sunday from up in the tree house. He saw them coming across the river. He was with Ray; they shouted to them."

"They shouted to them! Who? Who was with her?"

"Why Angus, Emily's Angus. Didn't you know?"

Jane's hand went slowly to her throat. She told herself that she mustn't faint, not again. She had thought that nothing worse could happen, but it had, and the consequences were terrifying. Angus Cotton . . . Emily's Angus. NO. She could never have degraded herself with Angus Cotton; he must have taken advantage of her. That was the only thing; he had taken advantage of her. Yes! Yes! That was it, and she was frightened to say anything, knowing how they all valued Emily's services . . . . Emily's services? Oh, no! Oh, no! This would mean she would lose Emily. It was too awful. What would Jonathan say?

What was more to the point, what would he do? In anger Jonathan could be terrible. Oh, why had this come upon them? Why? And Irene Brett standing there gloating. She got to her feet, saying, "If you'll excuse me, Irene. I'm sure you understand . . . ."

"Yes, yes, of course, Jane; I understand. And if there's anything I can do, anything at all, I'll only be too –"

"Thank you. Show Irene out, Susan." She didn't say Aunt Irene, and the tone she used and the words themselves were in the form of an insult, as she meant them to be; and of this Irene Brett was aware, but she continued to smile her sympathetic smile, and she touched Susan's hand at the door as she said, "Good-bye, Susan dear. And I wouldn't let it upset any of your plans."

"Cat! Mean, narrow-faced cat!" Susan was speaking aloud as she re-entered the lounge, and going straight to her mother she stood before her and cried, "Angus Cotton. No wonder she wouldn't say anything. Angus Cotton. Dear Lord! Can you believe it, Mother? Angus Cotton!"

Jane Ratcliffe could believe it; yes, she could believe it. Vanessa had always been fond of Emily's Angus. But she knew she must never voice this. She looked up at Susan and said, "He must have forced her."

Susan was scornful. "She's not a child."

"She'd be a child in his hands; he's a great big bulky individual."

Susan turned away, her face screwed up in distaste, saying, "Bulky. Horible. That big oaf!" Then swinging round again, she demanded, "What am I going to do? It's out now; it'll be all over the town to-morrow. I could murder that boy." She clenched her fists, then ended, "Why did you have to talk in front of him?"

"Don't be silly," said Jane Ratcliffe wearily. "As if we would have said anything if we had known he was about. He must have been outside the door or somewhere when we were upstairs." She put her hands to her head as she added, "And when your father comes in I just daren't think what will happen. I just daren't think."

"I can see something even worse than that. Just think what will happen when you confront Emily with this tomorrow morning. Have you thought of that?"

Yes, in a way she had thought of it. Not what Emily's reactions would be, but that Emily would now leave her. The thing she feared had come upon her.

Emily stood for a full minute without speaking; then she startled her mistress by yelling, "You're a bloody liar! And she is an' all if she says it's him."

"Emily! You're forgetting yourself." Jane Ratcliffe's pale, pained countenance flushed.

"Forgettin' meself? You stand there and accuse my Angus of puttin' her in the family way. Miss Van who he thinks about as a child still, an' you tell me I'm forgettin' meself."

"Well, there's no need for language."

"No need you say, no need? Begod! you'll hear somethin' more than this afore you're finished. Wait till he gets wind of it. Just wait till Angus gets wind of this. Anyway, who said this? Did she say it was him?"

"No, but . . . but deducing from what we know it can only be him. She's been seen a number of times with him lately."

"Where, might I ask?"

"Well, they were seen coming across the river last Sunday. And they've been seen in the town together . . . . She doesn't know anyone else, Emily – she hasn't any boyfriends – he can be the only one . . . ."

"Listen to her." Emily banged her head with her fist. "You're talkin' through the fat of your neck, woman." Gone was the cultivated servile manner of years. Her mistress was now just a woman who was accusing her son of taking down a girl. She could have been May's mother, or that of any lass in Ryder's Row. "There must be thirty thousand blokes in this town altogether," she flung one arm wide, "and you're pickin' on him because they were seen talkin' together. He's always talked to her. Or I could say, she's talked to him. She's never passed him in the street like the rest of you." She turned her glare on Susan, who was standing gripping the back of a chair. "Let me tell you, I know my Angus, and he would as soon have broken into the Convent and raped one of the nuns as he would have done that lass up there." She thumbed the ceiling. "Well now. Well now." She was tearing off her apron. "This is the end. I've stood you, the lot of you, for years, but this has put paid to it. But afore I go I'm havin' a word with your daughter."

"You're not to go upstairs."

"I'm goin' to see her and you're not goin' to stop me." Emily glared into Jane Ratcliffe's face.

"She'll only say to you what she said to us, that it wasn't him. She's maintaining that because she doesn't want to cause further trouble."

"Further trouble!" Emily brought her chin into her neck. "You don't know anythin' about it yet. Wait till my Angus hears of it, then you'll know what trouble means."

As she marched out of the room and across the hall Jonathan Ratcliffe came down the stairs, and he stood in an advantageous position on the bottom step and looked down at her with open loathing on his face; and she glared back at him as she said, "I want to see your daughter."

His teeth moved tightly across each other and he ground through them, "After I have seen your son. And if you know what's good for both of you, you won't go yelling your head off about this."

"Huh!" She gave a mirthless laugh. "I've just told her." She nodded back towards the drawing-room door where Jane Ratcliffe was standing. "I've just told her you don't know what you're in for when he gets wind of it . . . Yelling me head off. Huh!"

"I know what I'm in for." His voice was deadly calm

now. "But as yet your son doesn't. He's the one you should worry about. Now I presume you're going; well do, and as quickly as possible."

She was nonplussed for a moment by his manner. She looked up into his thin, bony face, then she turned her gaze on the woman for whom she had worked for years, and her lip curled upwards from her teeth and, squaring her shoulders, she walked from them with exaggerated dignity.

In the kitchen she grabbed her hat and coat from behind the scullery door, screwed her feet into her outdoor shoes, tore her aprons out of a drawer, then went to a cupboard to find a piece of paper with which to wrap them, and as she pulled it out she saw a tarnished silver milk jug and sugar basin. They were among other oddments that her mistress had pushed away in this cupboard from time to time to save cleaning. With a swift movement she grabbed them up and put them in the middle of her aprons. She had worked for these, and much more, they were only Elkington A1 silver, not solid, but they would fetch something. Aye, by God she had worked for them; she wasn't going out empty-handed. And if she had only thought of it at the time she would have asked for a week's money in lieu of notice, but she had been paid last night.

Without a backward glance she walked out of the kitchen, banging the door behind her, but when she left the drive and entered the road she had to stop and lean against the railings for a moment because her whole body was shaking. What should she do now? His lordship there would go to the office within the next half-hour and send for Angus, and if he threw it at him the same way as the missus had throw it at herself then only the Lord knew what would happen. She had better go to the works and warn him. But how she was going to put it she didn't know . . . .

It was a bus ride and twenty minutes later when she

came to the gates of Affleck and Tate and told the gate man she wanted to see her son.

"Oh!" he said. "Angus Cotton? Oh well, look. Just follow the road straight on, take the first turning right across the open space, and anybody there will tell you where his shop is."

Another seven minutes and she saw him coming towards her and her throat swelled and her body began to shake again.

"What is it?" He was holding her arm. "Something happened to Rosie?"

She shook her head. "Is there any place I can sit down for a minute?"

He looked about him. There was a wooden cask lying on its side, and with a heave he righted it and pushed it against the wall, then led her to it. "What is it?" he said again anxiously.

She looked up into his big, rugged face, tender at the moment with his concern for her. She wetted her lips, but she couldn't speak because she was realizing that he would now lose his job. In some way or another Ratcliffe would get rid of him; if not altogether, because of the Union he'd knock him to the bottom again.

"Look. Look, what's happened? Why aren't you at work?"

She grabbed hold of his hands. "Listen to what I'm gona tell you, an' don't go mad, don't shout." She looked about her at the different men moving about the yard. "I . . . I went in this mornin' like . . . like ordinary, you know, an' . . . an' she sent for me. Susan come and said – I'd just got me hat and coat off and me shoes changed – and she said her mother wanted to speak to me. I went in never thinkin', and then –" She tightened the pressure on his hands, swallowed again and shook her head before muttering, "Now, Angus, please, please, for God's sake don't go mad, but," she had to close her eyes as she whispered it, "they're blamin' you for Vanessa."

When there was no movement of his hands within hers, when there was no yell or volley of oaths, she opened her eyes and looked up into his face, and then she realized he hadn't taken it in; or, if he had he thought it was funny. He was actually smiling. And then he took his hands from hers and, going to the wall, put his forearm on it and dropped his head against his wrist, and his shoulders began to shake. But he made no sound. Then turning, he looked at her and said, "They're blaming me for dropping Van?"

She nodded at him.

"You mean," his voice was louder now, "you mean they're blaming me?" He dug his fingers hard into his chest, making a metallic sound. "Christ! You're joking, aren't you?"

"No, son, I'm not jokin'. I came straightaway 'cos when he gets in," she jerked her head upwards, "he'll likely be sendin' for you."

"Huh!" His sandy brows knit together and again he said, "Huh!" It was the beginning of a deep laugh that never materialised. He looked up at the high façade of the shops; then looking down at her again he said, "Well, they must be bloody well hard up to pin it on somebody when they've picked on me. But why me?"

"Because you're the only one who she's been seen with. That's what they said."

"What did she say?"

"I didn't see her; they wouldn't let me. But the missus said they had faced her with it but she kept denying it because she—she didn't want to cause trouble."

"Cause trouble did you say?" He was bending over her, his look full of mock enquiry. Then straightening himself, he said, "God Almighty! Mam, it's bloody well fantastic, isn't it? Me an' her!"

"You've said it, lad, fantastic. What'll you say when he sends for you?" She was breathing more evenly; she was relieved beyond measure that he had so far taken it sort of calm like.

"What'll I say?" he said. "Now, you leave it to me. Oh, just leave it to me. But you're wrong, Mam, about one thing. He won't send for me here, not about that he won't. He won't want the whole place to know about that, not if I know Mr. Ratcliffe. He'll want it hushed and he'll hush me up an' all one way or another. You'll see, I'll either be pushed out, or," he bent his head towards her again, "I'll be pushed up."

"Pushed up?"

"Aye, Mam, pushed up, to keep me quiet." He jerked his head slightly.

She now stood up, and they looked at each other. Then she said grimly, "Knowin' you, an' your kind of reaction, it'll be the out not the up you'll get."

"True, true, Mam, but just you wait. He'll try it on, you'll see. That's if the lady concerned doesn't name the right man and straighten things out, and herself into the bargain." His voice now ended on a bitter note. He put out his hand and said grimly, "Come on; I'll take you to the bus, an' you get home and put your feet up. There's one thing." His voice lightened just the slightest. "You'll be able to have your house clean again and the meal on the table when we come in. It's odd how things happen . . . I've had to become a dad-dy," he drew the word out, "before I could get you to leave your job, Mrs. Cotton."

He put her on the bus outside the work gates, and he left her with a smile. But it disappeared immediately he re-entered the gates. His reaction now were becoming normal to him. His temper was beginning to boil. His thoughts, bitter and cynical, made his face hard and ugly, yet there was among them a feeling he couldn't pin down. It would be later in the day when he would realize that he was flattered that the Ratcliffes should even think he had given their daughter a baby . . .

It was an uneasy morning in the shop, uneasy for all the

workers; even old Danny Fuller enquired what had got into him. "Don't bark me head off, lad," he said. "If you want me to do anythin' just ask me, but don't bark me head off."

It was round half-past eleven when the call came.

"You're wanted up top," said the messenger boy. "Boss's office."

But when he got up top, his body stiff with tension, he was confronted by Mr. Wilton.

Mr. Ratcliffe, Mr. Wilton said, was indisposed. He wanted these papers immediately and he wanted him, Angus Cotton, to deliver them. Why this should be, Mr. Wilton didn't know. But, it wasn't altogether unexpected. Brett had been trying for a long time to give Cotton another push up. But he was no favourite of the boss, nor of himself. He didn't like the fellow, or the idea of him getting any status.

He handed Angus the envelope, and Angus looked at it and all he said was "Thanks"; then turned on his heel and walked out.

Jane Ratcliffe herself opened the door to him as Susan had refused to do this office. After barely glancing at him she inclined her head to indicate that he should enter the house, then she led the way to her husband's study where she opened the door and again indicated by a movement of her head that Angus should enter the room.

Jonathan Ratcliffe was in a place of authority behind his desk, which was set in a corner of the room with a window to the side of it so that the light fell fully on anyone who was sitting on the chair in front of him.

But Jonathan Ratcliffe did not ask Angus to be seated. He himself sat, his hands gripping the arms of the revolving chair, and stared at the figure confronting him. He had disliked many people in his life, he had hated a few, but the combined hate he had ever experienced was nothing compared to the feeling he had for the man opposite to him. He had sat here for the last half-an-hour thinking about this man, his thoughts taking him right back, back to the day he had first seen him, when he had disliked him on sight. Even as a boy there had been something about Emily Cotton's son that caused him to grit his teeth, and as the years mounted so did his dislike. He saw Angus Cotton as a brash, utterly common individual; added to this he was powerfully built, making his own thin frame appear like a reed, which did not improve matters.

He glared up at him now. This was the man who had dared to handle his daughter. Her loud screams and protests had only convinced him more firmly that it was nobody else but this obnoxious individual who had brought her low.

He was preparing himself to speak, to say one word, "WELL?" but before he could utter it Angus threw the envelope on to the blotting pad, remarking caustically, "You wanted that. Or did you?"

It was with something akin to a feeling of triumph that he saw Ratcliffe's jaws tighten until the cheekbones shone white through his skin. He could get this man on the raw; he had always known it. He, too, had his memories from a boy. Perhaps his determination not to knuckle under to him right from the start was the reaction to hearing his mother saying, "Yes, ma'am," and "Yes, sir." His mother wasn't made for knuckling under either, but she'd had to do it. They'd had to eat.

Ratcliffe picked up the envelope and slapped it on the table as if it were a cane, saying as he did so, "You know the real reason why I sent for you."

"Aye!" The words sounded casual. "I understand I'm giving your daughter a baby."

"You dirty . . . !"

"Hold it. Hold it." The careless attitude was gone. Angus was leaning over the desk, his hands flat on it. "I'm warning you. Don't use any of those terms on me."

Jonathan Ratcliffe had to swing his chair round before he could rise. Then when he was on his feet he said, "You've taken advantage of a young girl of good family; you've taken advantage of the fact that your mother . . ."

"I'll take advantage of the fact that we're alone here without witnesses and bust your mouth open for you, MR. RATCLIFFE, and then I'll bloody well take you to Court. How would you like that? Justice is impartial. That's what they say. Well, I would see that it was impartial in this case."

For a second Jonathan Ratcliffe knew a moment's fear. It was two-pronged. It was a fear of being physically handled, also the fear that he had made a mistake. But this reasoning was quick to reassure him on the latter point. Last night they had gone over everybody she knew; there was not one boy they could name that she had seen more than once in the last six months. They had gone over her movements for weeks past. She had been in the house most evenings doing her homework. When she went to the pictures it was with Kathy, or Rona, and, he, himself, had picked them up in the car, having insisted on this because the High Street was usually full of hooligans at night. The only person she had been seen with was this man here. He had made it his business this morning to go next door and have a word with Irene Brett. She said she had seen them together at least four times during the past few weeks. She told him of the night she had seen them standing in the shop doorway together, and Arthur had insisted on bringing her home. She also remembered to tell him of the time Colin had seen them coming off the train together.

Added to this was the tale his son had gone over for him yet again, of how he had seen his sister being helped over the stepping stones in the river by Angus. They had come from over the fells and they had come up the road and stood talking near the railings. He had shouted to them and then Angus had gone away.

He said grimly, "Threatening won't help you any, Cotton. We may be in Court together yet, but I'll give you a guess as to who will be on trial, and what is more I haven't to guess why you have done this." He leaned forward again. "You wanted to inveigle yourself in, didn't you? You were determined to get up into the drawing-office by whatever means in your power. You couldn't get there owing to your lack of education and limited brains so you used . . ."

Angus's arm flashed upwards, his fist doubled and looking like a huge hammer head, but whether it was the width of the table between them and the fact that Jonathan Ratcliffe stumbled back against the wall, or that in the nick of time he realized what he was about to do, his fist dropped with a crash on to the oak desk, the force lifting up a cut-glass inkwell from its brass stand, and as is shuddered back into place again he bent his head deeply over his chest and drew the air into his lungs. After a moment he lifted his eyes to where Jonathan Ratcliffe was still standing against the wall, his face looking like a piece of new lint, and he muttered thickly, "You and your bloody job! You can stick it. Right from this minute, you can stick it. Do you hear? I'm finished. As for brains. I've got more in me little finger than you've got in your whole body. The whole works, the whole town knows how you got into the top office, by leap-frogging poor Mr. Brett . . . Sucking up. Do you know what your nickname is in the yard, and around? Do you know it?" He was yelling now. "It's Tit Ratcliffe. That doesn't need much working out, does it? Tit Ratcliffe, the biggest sucker-up in the game an' the biggest upstart into the bargain, because your father was no better than any of ours. A little huckster grocer's shop, that's what he had. But he scraped and saved and sent you to college, and what did you learn there? To suck up, Mr. Ratcliffe!" He gave an imitation of spitting. Then straightening himself, he ended. "There's one thing I want afore I go, an' you'll not get me out of this house unless you do it. You'll bring her in here, and she'll face me, and she'll tell you if it was me or not." There was a long pause before he said, "Well, get going an' ring your bell."

And Jonathan Ratcliffe did just that. He rang the bell. He was shivering with rage and humiliation; the only thing he wanted now was to get this man out of his sight. There was part of him wishing that the position was reversed, at least physically, that he was broad and tough and had fists like hammers because with them he would batter Angus Cotton to a pulp. Tit Ratcliffe! How dare he! . . . How dare THEY!

When the door opened he did not look at his wife but muttered in a voice that she did not recognize, "Bring her down."

During the time they waited Ratcliffe sat down before his desk again and Angus stood facing the door, and when she came in he hardly recognised her. Not only were her eyes swollen but her whole face was swollen, and there was a dark patch on her cheekbone as if she'd had a blow. She looked even younger than when he had last seen her walking on the fells in the rain, and . . . she looked frightened.

After a moment's hesitation she came straight to him and, standing in front of him, she looked up into his face and said, 'I . . . I'm sorry, Angus. I told them. I've told them but they still won't believe me. I'm sorry. Oh, I am sorry."

Her words, instead of convincing her father and mother, only proved to them still further that this was the man, and that because of her fear she was frightened to name him; fear of what might happen to him at the works, and through that how Emily would be affected, because they knew she had always been very fond of Emily too.

Angus, now looking down at her, asked quietly but stiffly, "Have I ever touched you?"

For answer she lowered her head and shook it slowly.

127

"Have I ever made any improper suggestion to you, or said anything out of place?"

Again there was a shake of her head.

"They say you're goin' to have a baby and I'm the father."

Her head went further down and still kept shaking.

"If they're right then I should marry you, shouldn't I?"

He had never intended to say any such thing and his words came as a shock to her and brought her head up with a jerk. "But . . . but you won't. I mean, you're not . . ." the look on her face made him sick; the prospect had terrified her.

She turned frantically now and looked from her mother to her father, and she said again, "He's not! He's not!" She cupped her face with her hands and began to rock herself and Jonathan Ratcliffe cried sternly, "That's enough!" then nodded to his wife, and she came forward and took hold of Vanessa's arm and led her from the room.

But before she passed through the door Vanessa turned and looked over her shoulder at Angus and whimpered again, "I'm sorry, Angus. I'm sorry."

Now Angus moved towards the door, but he, too, turned before he reached it and he asked tersely but rather flatly now, "Well, does that convince you?"

Jonathan Ratcliffe wanted to bawl a loud "No!" but what he wanted above all things at the moment was to be rid of this man, and so he remained silent.

A few minutes after the front door banged Jane Ratcliffe came into the study and, moving slowly towards her husband, she said, "He wouldn't admit it?"

"No; but it's him all right. I'm more convinced than ever now. Did you see how she went on? 'I'm sorry Angus. I'm sorry Angus. I'm sorry.' She'll be sorrier before she finishes." He gulped in his throat. Then nervously moving papers about on his desk, he said, "I'm going into Newcastle to see Muxlington again. I'm sure he could do it, but he won't. But he'll arrange about London. You can say she's going to visit relatives, anything. When she comes back and there's no sign of it, it'll give the lie to Irene's tongue."

"People will still think . . ."

"Yes, they'll still think," he said bitterly. "And they'll always think. And they'll know, but she won't have any baby." He turned on her. "Understand Jane. She's not going to have any baby."

"Doctor Carr?"

"I'll settle with Doctor Carr. He can't do anything. She'll have a miscarriage. Anybody can have a miscarriage. And if he knows what's good for him he'll keep his tongue quiet, else he'll find himself and his bottle out of practice. He's not fit to be on the books anyway. Now go up and tell her what's arranged. And stand no nonsense. Tell her from me, if she knows what's good for her she'll comply . . . and quietly."

But Vanessa didn't comply, and quietly. She wasn't going to London, she said; she wasn't going to have the baby taken away.

Then what, asked her mother, did she intend to do?

Vanessa could give no answer to this question until to-morrow. Brett would be here to-morrow, and when he knew what had happened everything would be smoothed out. There would be trouble. Oh yes, there would be more trouble. But they would be away from it all. To-morrow night she would go down to the summerhouse as soon as it was dark, and he would be there because Irene would certainly put him in the picture the minute he got indoors. She would have her cases packed ready and then they would go off. They would go through the wood, out into the main road that way. She could see it all plainly.

"You're not to think of seeing him again. Do you hear me, Vanessa?"

"What . . . . You mean, Angus?"

Jane Ratcliffe bit on her lip. Her daughter wasn't stupid, far from it, she was much brighter than Susan, yet her responses were those of some dim child. "Who do you think I mean, girl? And don't take that attitude with me. There's only one person responsible for your condition . . . at least I hope so." The implication startled even herself, together with the fact that she had voiced it. "Now I've told you. Your father is arranging for you to go to London. You'll go into a nursing home, and when it's all over you'll go to Great-Aunt Jean's and stay there until your father considers it fit for you to come home again."

"Oh no, I won't. I won't go to Great-Aunt Jean's." Vanessa was startled into protest. "You're not going to shut me away with Great-Aunt Jean, out in the wilds in Scotland, so don't think you are."

She was about to protest further when she reminded herself there was no need. Great-Aunt Jean who lived in a cottage on a hill six miles from a town, surrounded by her hens, dogs and goats, with her Bible-reading and hymn-singing – the only form of entertainment she allowed – Great-Aunt Jean wouldn't see her, whatever happened, she would die first. But there would be no need for that. She must be quiet and just let them think she was going to go along with them. She turned from her mother and sat down and looked out of the window, and Jane Ratcliffe, taking her change of attitude for acceptance of the situation, said firmly, "There now, let's hear no more protests. The time is past for that attitude. It's all settled." Then she went downstairs to tell her husband.

Vanessa spent the following day cleaning her room, and Susan's. Since, her mother said, she had been the means of depriving them of Emily's services she would have to learn to do things for herself in future. She also delegated to her the cleaning of the two bathrooms, and she ordered her to have her meals in the kitchen because her father couldn't bear to sit at table with her . . . .

By six o'clock she knew that Brett was home. Ray brought the information into the house. She heard him call, "Did you know Uncle Brett was home, Mammy? He's brought Michael a cowboy outfit with a gun. Not a real one but pretty like it. It shoots pellets. It's in a holster."

That evening was the longest she had spent in her life. She sat looking out of the window in the direction of the larches. She could see part of the side of the house through the trees, but she wouldn't be able to see him until he came right to the fence that divided the grounds. And he didn't come. He wouldn't come out until it was dark and they were all in bed.

She herself was in bed pretending to be asleep when her mother looked in before going to her room. She felt her standing staring towards the bed, then the door clicked shut. She waited a full half hour before she went down the fire escape. She didn't take her cases with her; he mightn't be able to get away immediately, he would have to go to the bank for money to-morrow. She had thought about all this. But she'd take them and hide them in the wood when the arrangements were made.

There was a moon due but it wasn't up yet, but she had a torch with her. She was trembling from head to foot as she neared the river. She wondered what he would look like. Remembering him over the past weeks he had seemed to get younger and younger until she imagined he was almost her own age.

She knew he was in the summerhouse before she reached it. She stood below the steps and played the light through the open doorway, and there he stood. His face was brown, for he had been in the sun for the last three weeks, yet it was an odd kind of brown, and he didn't look young, not even youngish; he looked old, very old . . . and different.

She whispered softly, "Brett!" but he didn't answer her, he just stared into the light.

She couldn't bear the look on his face; it looked all twisted and misshapen. She switched off the light and said, "Say something. Say something to me, Brett.'

For answer he reached out and pulled her to him and

pressed his lips to her forehead, and she clung to him for a moment before bursting into tears. He still held her as he led her the few steps to the wooden seat and they sat down together. He did not say, "There, there, don't cry"; he uttered no word of comfort, and after a while his silence told on her and she pulled herself from his arms and peered at him in the darkness. "It's been awful, Brett," she said. She heard him gulping in his throat before he spoke. Then his words sounded ordinary and not suited to the occasion. "Yes," he said, "it must have been."

"I haven't told them, or anyone. No one knows, Brett."

"Thank you, my dear." He could have been giving thanks for someone offering him bread and butter, and his peculiar attitude eventually got through to her and she exclaimed on a high note, "Brett, I'm going to have a baby!"

She thought he said, "Oh, Christ!" Then he was holding her hand and talking. "I'm sorry. I'm sorry Vanessa. You'll never live long enough to know how sorry I am. I didn't stay away because of this. You understand? I stayed away because I couldn't bear to see you. I didn't know this had happened. I thought it might, but again I dismissed the idea. Most . . . most women don't at their . . . ." She felt the movement of his body as he swung his head widely on his shoulders. "It was just that I wanted to pull myself together. When . . . when I finished the firm's business I got in touch with your father and asked him if I could stay on for my holiday. I wanted time, time, and . . . ." he almost added, "enough satisfaction for my body's needs to keep me away from you." And he had certainly done his best in that direction during the past three weeks. No man could have done more.

She put in breathlessly now. "What are we going to do, Brett?" She felt she must give him a lead because she wanted to be reassured quickly that he was going to take her away, but when after a moment he asked flatly, "What can we do, child?" she was stunned into silence. And now he was asking her, "What did they say? What do they intend to do?"

"They . . . they want to send me to London to have it taken away."

"Well . . . well, that's the best thing, dear."

"But Brett! Brett!" Her voice sounded full of terror. "I can't. I won't. I won't have one of those operations. It showed about them on television. People die."

"Hush, dear. Hush. It won't be that kind of an operation. They'll send you to a clinic, to a good man. Those girls who die, they go to old women in back streets, ignorant people. You'll be all right. And when you come back . . . ."

She withdrew her hands slowly from his. She was no longer peering at him. Her eyes were wide, staring out of her head into the blackness, and her voice sounded like that of a child's who had been told that they weren't going on holiday after all. "But . . . but I thought you would take me away, Brett. I thought we would go away. You don't love Irene. You said you didn't. You said that night you had never loved her for years; she was cold and hard. You said she was. You said if only you could take me away –" "Fly away with you, my princess," were the words he had used – "you could get a divorce and . . . and we could be married. I . . . I want to have the baby, I really do, Brett, I do. I feel I would like a baby, but . . . but not unless I'm married. I want to be married, Brett." Her voice, filled with pleading and fear, was like a thin whistle coming up from her bowels.

When he groped over her knees for her hands she felt herself shrinking inwardly, yet she allowed him to bring them to his chest and press them there as he said, "Oh, my darling, Vanessa, if only we could. If only we could. But it's impossible, child. There's so many things against it. You see, it would be difficult, almost impossible, for me to get started again at my time of life. And I haven't any money by me, and we'd have to live some place. What is more, Irene would never divorce me, never. I know that. And there's . . . ." He stopped abruptly. It was impossible to say to her, "And there's this house and the wood. I couldn't live long away from either." What was more he couldn't bear the thought of starting a family again. He had no real love for children, which was likely why his own sons, with the exception of Paul, had never responded to him. You only got back what you gave out. He was well aware of that. When he heard her catch her breath on a sob he wondered if he would have been kinder to lie and tell her they were going away, say to-morrow or the day after – but in the long run that would only make things harder for her.

From five minutes after he had entered the house this afternoon he knew exactly what he was going to do. As he listened to Irene pouring out her spleen, openly gloating over what had befallen Vanessa, he knew then what he must do, and now, holding the child's hands, his decision was firmer than ever. If only he had the courage to take her away. But he hadn't. He hadn't the courage to start all over again, to face up to the responsibilities that would attend such an action. Yet at the same time he hadn't the courage to live without her. He was a weak man and he knew it. Life had been pretty bleak before the night he had come down into the wood to send Angus Cotton packing; but since then it had been sheer hell.

When she withdrew her hands from his he said, "It's going to be all right, Vanessa. Everything is going to be all right. It wouldn't work with you and me. In a year's time, even in a few weeks' time, you would regret having tied yourself to me. You're young; you haven't started to live yet. I've done you a great injustice, a great harm, but . . . but do what they advise and it will be all right. You can start again, and to-morrow morning," he coughed here, "you can tell your mother and father just how it happened and they'll understand."

"You mean . . . you mean I'm to tell them, not you?"

"Yes, my dear. They must have kept at you to know."

"Yes, yes, they have." Her voice sounded far away. "But they think it's Angus, Angus Cotton."

"What!" He was on his feet. He seemed to have come alive for the first time since their meeting. "You mean . . .? Have they tackled him with it?"

"Yes. Father . . . Father brought him to the house yesterday. Emily . . . Emily's left. She was in a state."

"And you let them think this."

"No, no! I told them flatly that it wasn't him but they wouldn't believe me. You see, Irene came over and told Mother that she had seen us together a number of times . . . and then Ray and Michael had seen us too."

"Irene came and . . . ." His voice trailed away.

"Yes, and from what I understand she seemed very pleased about it all." There was a sound of bitterness in Vanessa's voice now. "She's never liked me and she's jealous of Susan marrying well. I think she hopes that this will, in some way, put a stop to it. Mother and Father are afraid of the same thing. I've to be got out of the way, hushed up. They're going to send me to Great-Aunt Jean's, up in the wilds of Scotland, after I come back from London." She was talking dully now as if she was accepting what had been arranged for her.

He asked quietly, "Have you seen Angus?"

"Only yesterday morning in the study. He was very angry."

Brett made no comment on this but, putting his hand out blindly until he found her arm, he drew her to her feet, saying, "Come along, dear. Come along. And believe me, it's going to be all right. To-morrow you can explain everything. It'll be all right."

"What . . . what about you? What will happen to you?"

"Don't worry about me, dear, everything will work out to-morrow. You'll see." He led her up the bank and through the wood, and at the gate they stopped and he drew her into his arms and, putting his lips against her brow, he held them there tightly for a moment, then said thickly, "I just want you to remember one thing. No matter what happens remember this. I love you. I've loved you for a long time, but I've only been aware of it in the past few months. Thank you, dear." When he pressed her away from him she muttered, "Will I see you to-morrow?" She was crying bitterly now.

"Yes, you'll see me to-morrow."

He stood on the same spot for almost ten minutes after she was gone, then he walked slowly up through the trees. He let himself in by the side door and went upstairs; but he didn't go to his own room, he went to his wife's.

After he had switched on the light he stood with his back to the door. Irene, blinking, pulled herself up in the bed and said, "Yes, yes. What is it? ... Oh!" She focussed him through narrowed lids, then asked, "Is it Michael? Is he sick?"

"No, it's not Michael." He moved slowly towards the bed, and by the time he had reached the foot she had pulled the coverlet up under her chin. The action was a defensive one that a timid woman might take, but there was no timidity about her voice when she said, "We've had all this out. No. Do you hear, no."

He stood staring at her, not speaking. He watched her thin mouth form into a button that aged her.

She was hissing at him now. "You're not back five minutes and this starts again. I thought you would have learned more sense."

"Do you know something?" His voice was quiet, even gentle. "I wouldn't want to take you, Irene, if you were stark naked doing a fandango. I saw a naked woman doing that dance when I was abroad. She was fat and ugly and her skin was greasy. Moreover, she smelt. But you know something? Given the choice, I'd take her any day in the week rather than touch you with my little finger . . . . Does that surprise you, Irene?"

Her mouth had slackened. It was slightly agape. "You've

136

been drinking," she said under her breath. "You could never carry your drink."

"No, I haven't been drinking, and you know it. I'm solid and sober and I'm going to talk to you. We've never talked for years, and this will be the last time I'll talk to you, and for that I'm grateful." He paused, and they stared unblinking at each other, until he said, "Do you know what you are, Irene? Fundamentally, you're a mean, narrow-minded bitch. You're a woman who has fought her way into positions in this town on my name, on my father's name, and his father's name. You're uneducated, unintelligent and without the slightest scrap of breeding. You've had a shot at imitating these various qualities, and you've hoodwinked a few into believing they are your own, but they're only a few. Besides which, Irene, you're cruel. It's a hobby with you, cruelty."

Her lips trembled before she put in, "Are . . . are you quite finished?"

"No, not by a long chalk. I'm coming to our neighbours now. Jonathan did me a dirty turn some years ago, but what happened was my own fault. Jonathan got the post over my head because he was ambitious. I'm not. And you've never forgiven him or his, not, let me stress, because of me but because of how it affected you. You saw yourself as the wife of the manager of Affleck and Tate's. You would have carried it off with a high hand, but not half as successfully as Jane has done. She's a snob of the first water, she's a social climber, but, unlike you, she came from a decent family."

"Get out!"

"I'm not going out until I'm ready, Irene. As I said, we're going to talk. I'm going to talk. Now you, in a way, are on a par with Jonathan. You both came originally from the gutters of Fellburn. Your father was an elementary schoolteacher; his father had been a little grocer and his grandfather . . . . You didn't know I knew this, but his grandfather, together with your great-grandfather were well known taggereen men in Bog's End. They both had donkeys and flat carts and they gathered scrap. A couple of Steptoes, but not quite so famous I should say."

Her hair was pulled tight back in curlers held in place by an invisible net, and the skin at her temples now showed the veins standing up like pieces of thick blue string.

As he paused again they held each other's glance, hers wide, bitter, full of hatred, his scornful, sad, and bitter too. He moved from one foot to the other before going on. "Your chagrin gave you sleepless nights when Susan burst into the titled set, didn't it? So you looked around for something to spoil, something to smash, and you found it, didn't you? You found it when you saw Vanessa talking to Angus Cotton. Your mean little mind put two and two together and made a dozen. They couldn't be talking unless they were up to something, and so what did you do? You flew next door and named the man, the father of Vanessa's child, didn't you? . . . DIDN'T YOU?" His voice had suddenly exploded in a shout and she leant towards him, gritting out between her teeth, "Stop it! Stop it! Do you want to raise the house?"

"Yes. Yes, I would like to raise the house. I have something very interesting to say." There was a considerable silence now and his voice had dropped when he spoke again. "First, I want to ask you. Do you really, in your heart of hearts, think Vanessa was having an affair with Angus Cotton?"

"There was no need to think," her voice was thin, low and bitter, "there's enough proof. And I've seen them together again and again. And the children –"

"Yes, I know all about that. The children saw them together. But . . . but he's not the father of her child."

"How do you know? What do you know about it? You've been away for weeks, and you took your time in coming –"

"Yes, I took my time in coming back, because I was afraid to face up to my responsibilities. I still am."

"What are you talking about?"

"If you weren't so dull, woman, you'd realize without me having to put it into words . . . . I'm the father of Vanessa's child."

Slowly she leant back against the bed head. She thought for a moment she was going to have a seizure of some sort. She had to wait seconds, minutes, before her heart stopped racing. Then she muttered, "You're mad. You're sex mad. It's because you wanted her. I don't doubt but that you wanted her. You've thought of nothing but sex for years. But you, you, wouldn't have dared . . . . You . . . ."

"Well, I did dare. I had one short amazingly glorious moment of living down in the summerhouse."

Her eyes were like pieces of flint piercing him. "I – I don't believe you; you're just making it up. Wishful thinking, that's what it is, wishful thinking. I deal with people like you every week in the courts, people who say they've done things because they want to do them but are afraid to. I don't doubt but you wanted one glorious moment, but you would never have dared, never."

"Well, I tell you I did dare, Irene. And Vanessa has been waiting for me coming back before she spoke. She's been very, very brave. She wanted me to take her away. And oh, I would have dearly loved to have done just that. And I would if I'd been younger, and with more nerve and some money behind me. Yet if I could have done this she wouldn't have been happy. She's made for someone young, and she'll get someone young. A girl like her must be made happy, because you know why? She's kind, and kind people, even if they're the biggest rogues or scamps in the world, they're happy, they're made happy in some way. I've seen it again and again . . . . Of course there are exceptions. I was kind to you, Irene. And my people were kind to you. But my mother's last years were made miserable through you, and all my married years have been made miserable through you . . . . Well, it's finished. Or nearly so. By the way, I'd better tell you I made another will some time ago. Funny, but I must have known this was coming. I've made a stipulation in it that the land and house, when it is sold, mustn't be divided, it must be sold as one and the money that it brings is to go into trust until Michael is twenty-one. Then it is to be divided between the three boys. I've also left special pieces of furniture to Paul alone. You, my dear, will have the interest on the money until Michael comes of age. After that you are at the mercy of your three sons."

She was unable to speak. Her whole body was shaking as if with an ague. When he said, "Good-bye, Irene," and turned slowly from her she knew what he was going to do. The only thing she didn't know was how he was going to do it. But she didn't get out of bed or say one word to stop him.

5

Vanessa had sat by her bedroom window until almost two o'clock in the morning, and when she eventually did go to bed she didn't sleep, at least for a long time. When she heard her mother's voice saying stiffly, "Vanessa! Vanessa! It's almost eight o'clock. Come along," she imagined she had been asleep only a few minutes.

At half-past eight she went downstairs and into the morning room. She had stopped being sick these last two or three mornings and had felt hungry, yet at the same time she thought it wasn't right somehow that she should eat at all.

She had the morning room to herself; her father had already had his breakfast and would now be in his study where he would stay until after nine. There was some bacon under cover on an electrically heated plate, and as she served herself she thought, "I can't eat, I can't"; yet she ate the bacon and had two cups of coffee and some toast and marmalade.

The sun was shining full into the room and she looked about it, seeming to see it for the first time. It was a beautiful room. Pale grey walls, thick pink satin curtains, two large mushroom-coloured rugs on the polished parquet floor. The sideboard with its gleaming silver, most of which was now going to be put away, and the period dining chairs with their seats and backs upholstered in rose. This had always been her favourite room, and perhaps after to-day, or to-morrow, or the next day she wouldn't see it any more. After she had told them about Brett – and how she was going to deliver this bombshell she didn't really know – she was going to tell them something else. She was going to tell them she meant to get a job of some kind, any kind, and, what was more, she was going to have the baby because the prospect of having the baby in six months' time was less frightening to her than having it taken away now. She knew that when she told them what she intended to do her father would bring his authority to bear, and if he couldn't force her to go to London he would send her somewhere. It wouldn't matter much to him where she went during the next few weeks as long as she was out of his sight, and not an embarrassment to them all until the wedding was over.

But she was fully aware that she couldn't stand up to her father on her own regarding the baby, particularly when he knew it was Brett's. He would be madder than ever at this disclosure. He would see it as a personal affront, and she daren't think of his reaction. She would need a higher authority to fall back on and she knew she would find that authority in Doctor Carr. She would go to Doctor Carr and say, "I want to have this baby, I don't want it to be taken away." And she could hear him now exclaiming loudly, "If you want to have it, you have it; you're strong and healthy. Don't let me hear any talk of you having it taken away." After that, let her father try and send her to London. Abortions were illegal and people could go to prison for doing them, or aiding them.

One minute her chin was jerking upwards in support of her thoughts, the next she had her face buried in her hands biting on the pad of her thumb to stop herself crying. She wished she had someone she could talk to. She felt dreadful inside, lonely, lost, all mixed up and confused.

She sat now, telling herself that she didn't know her own mind from one day to the next, because this time yesterday she was just longing to see Brett, knowing that he would take her away, and last night when she knew that he was going to do no such thing she had been sick. Even when she saw him as a timid, vacillating old man, she had still been sick with disappointment, and fear of what was going to happen to her. Yet this morning, when her mother had wakened her, she was filled with relief that they hadn't gone away together, that she wasn't going to marry him.

It was as she sat wishing that the day was over and shuddering inwardly at the repercussion her news would have on the two households that she heard the screaming. It was quite near, it seemed to be in the garden.

When she hastily pulled open the french windows and stood on the paved terrace the screaming filled the air. She saw her mother come to the drawing-room window, then her father come round by the side of the house. He looked along towards her, then her mother came through the morning room and on to the terrace beside her and she asked, "What is it? Who is it?"

"Next door." Jonathan Ratcliffe moved down the garden, saying over his shoulder. "It sounds like Michael."

The screaming now seemed to come from the top of the trees, and when her mother followed her father she followed them both, and then they were all standing by the gate looking into the wood, looking at Irene and Colin Brett. Irene was standing with one clenched fist pressed against her cheek, she was looking upwards into the tree house. Colin, too, was looking upwards. He was calling, "Michael! Michael! Do you hear. Come down. I'll only have to come and fetch you. Come down."

"What is it? What's the matter?" They all went through the gate and into the wood, Vanessa still walking a few yards behind her parents. As another series of screams came from the tree, Colin mounted the rickety ladder.

"What is it, Irene? What is it? What's upset him?"

Irene Brett turned and looked at Jonathan Ratcliffe, then she looked at Jane, and she gulped and moved her head twice before she said in a strangely controlled voice, "He . . . he found his father in the cellar. Arthur . . . Arthur's hanged himself."

No one moved for a moment. Then Jonathan said, "Oh no! No!" And Jane put her two hands up and covered her cheeks, a characteristic gesture when she was without words. Then they both went to Irene's side, and they murmured over her. But she did not look at them, she looked straight between them and to their daughter, and she said again, "Arthur hanged himself in the cellar. Do you hear?"

Both Jonathan and Jane Ratcliffe imagined she was repeating herself in this way because she was distraught, but Vanessa was aware that she was telling her she knew why her husband had hanged himself. It was in the hate in her eyes, and she was sending it like an arrow into her. Turning, she flew back through the wood and up the garden, and her parents made no comment on her actions because they knew their daughter had been very fond of Arthur Brett.

Back in her room, Arthur's death was having a strange effect on Vanessa; she was experiencing both anger and resentment against him. Her reasoning told her that resentment towards Brett should have taken effect weeks ago when she knew he had given her a baby. Yet her condition had evoked no such feeling. But his deliberate death had.

She saw him in this moment as Irene had seen him, and she hated him. She told herself that she should have known when he cried that he had no guts, gumption, nothing. He had used his tears to gain her sympathy, to get her to touch him, to hold him. She was glad he was dead, she was, she was. She stood in front of the long mirror and nodded at herself, nodded at her long white face, at her long, thin, leggy body, nodded at her stomach which was showing a slight fullness beneath her dress.

144

When she lay on top of the bed and buried her face in the pillow she asked herself what she was going to do now. Would she tell them, or would she leave it to Irene? He had told Irene. The thought brought her upwards. He must have told Irene last night after he had left her. She knew what would happen now. When her parents took Irene back to the house she would tell them why her husband had committed suicide, it was all because of their daughter. Oh dear Lord, dear Lord. Like her mother, she was holding her face in her hands.

It was nearly an hour later when her parents returned to the house. She was glad she was alone to meet them. Susan was staying with Brian's people for a week. She didn't think she could have borne to see Susan's face when she knew who it was who had given her the child. Her scorn and distaste would have been too much, even worse than when she had thought it was Angus, for after all Angus was young.

She was standing waiting for them when they came into the lounge. She watched her father go and sit down in the big chair to the side of the fireplace. She watched her mother sit down on the couch. And she looked at them and waited, but neither of them looked at her. Then her mother said to her father, "What on earth could have made him do it? The trip was successful wasn't it? Nothing went wrong there?"

"No, nothing went wrong there. Nothing could go wrong there, the stuff sells itself. He got the orders. He was only going to be out there six weeks, which was more than ample, but when I knew Cribber wouldn't be able to start again for at least another six months I phoned and asked him if he would like to go on to Germany and Italy. He seemed quite pleased about it. Then just before he was due to come back he phoned me and said he was going to take his holiday out there, was it all right?"

"Do you think something could have happened on his holiday?"

"How should I know?" He got to his feet. "She says she doesn't know anything, yet I feel she knows something, that look on her face. She's a bitter pill, is Irene. They've never hit it off for years. I could have understood him doing it if he had been at home for weeks and they'd been having one of their periodical rows, but he just came back yesterday . . . . Ah well, I'll have to get to the office. You'd better keep looking in," he nodded at his wife, "she's going to need all the help she can get. As for that boy, this'll leave a mark on him for life."

He went out into the hall, and after a moment Jane Ratcliffe followed him, at least as far as the lounge door, and there she seemed to become aware for the first time that Vanessa was in the room and she turned to her and said, "You can dust the drawing-room and dining-room. I've got a woman coming for interview at half-past eleven, put her in the morning-room, and should I happen to be next door ring me."

She wasn't going to tell. Irene Brett wasn't going to tell. She stood gaping towards the closed door. What should she do? If she didn't tell the truth they would still blame Angus, but if she told the truth now they would blame her for Brett committing suicide. She couldn't stand that on top of everything else. And it looked as if Irene didn't want it known. Yes, it looked like that because she'd had plenty of time to tell them. What must she do? She'd have to think.

Five days later Arthur Brett was buried. At the inquest they had brought in a verdict of death while the balance of his mind was disturbed. On the day of the funeral, at which all the professional people in the town were at least represented, the local evening newspaper gave the event full-page coverage. It said that Arthur Brett was a descendant of one of the oldest families in the county. There had been Bretts in Fellburn for the last two hundred and fifty years and that the early Bretts had once occupied the

146

Moat House and owned considerable stretches of land on the outskirts of the town. It went on to say that the late Mr. Brett's grandfather had married one Alice Affleck whose family had started the engineering firm of Affleck and Tate.

After reading the report Jonathan Ratcliffe handed it to his wife, and after she had read it she laid the paper down before saying, "It sounds all very fine, but she is left practically penniless. Fancy him making a will like that; he must have hated her."

"Well, you haven't had to wait all this time to realize that, have you?" he said tartly. "But, you know he wasn't only hitting at her when he made that will." His lips were in a tight, thin line now and his voice was bitter. "He was hitting at me. By what I gather from Colin the land is tied up tighter than ever. It cannot be sold without the house."

"Would you buy it if it was put up?"

"Of course I'd buy it. That's a silly question to ask. But I don't want the house. I'd pull the place down, it's dropping to bits anyway."

"Did Colin say there was anything against their selling?"

"No; but he'll have Paul to deal with there because he's as daft about the place as Arthur was."

"Are you going to give her a pension?"

"Yes, she'll get the usual, what he had paid in for."

"Nothing more?"

"I have little say in that. Any suggestion like that would have to go before the board. And anyway," he turned his face fully towards her, "the more she has the longer she's likely to stay there. She likes prestige, does Irene, as you know. But," he rose to his feet, "we'll talk about that later. There's plenty of time to deal with that. At present we've enough difficulties of our own. Have you told her?"

"Yes."

"And she's ready?"

"She didn't say anything."

"You've got her packed?"

"Yes . . . . Jonathan."

"Yes, what is it?"

"I'm worried about this. At least I'm worried about what Doctor Carr might do. You know she said . . . ."

"It doesn't for one single moment matter what she said. And I don't believe she went to Carr. Why didn't he get in touch with me, eh?"

"Well, he hasn't had much time, it was only yesterday."

"If she had been to him at all he'd have been on that phone before now. And I was ready for him. I know a thing or two about Carr that will check his tongue . . . . By the way, have you written to your Aunt Jean?"

"Yes . . . I've asked her to answer by return."

"Well, that'll be settled. She'll go there straight from the clinic."

"She says she won't."

"Oh, does she?" His mouth formed a straight line again. "Well, it's your business to see that she does. You'll be up there, and you'll take her yourself. And you can tell her that if she knows what's good for her she'll do what she's told." He paused; then looking upwards, he added, "It might make a deeper impression if I tell her myself. Go and fetch her down."

As his wife moved towards the door he said, "By the way, you didn't leave her in alone? This afternoon, I mean."

She turned towards him. "No, of course not," she said; "Susan was here."

He nodded; then said under his breath, "I wouldn't put it past her to try and sneak out to meet that oaf. If she got what she deserves I'd make him marry her. That would be an object lesson all right . . . . Go on, bring her."

He had taken up his stand with his back to the fire, his

arms crossed, and he looked towards the door as his wife re-entered the room again. She had one hand cupping her face, in the other she held a letter. She held it out to him without a word, and he met her halfway across the room and snatched it from her and read:

"Dear Mother and Father,
    I am not going to London, I am going to have the baby. Doctor Carr said I should. I told you last night but you didn't believe me. What I didn't tell you was he said if you force me to go to a clinic he'll take the matter up. I'm going to get work as I told you. I have taken my bank book. I don't want you to worry about me so I'll write you every week. I'll be all right, I've arranged to stay with a friend. I am sorry I've caused you all this trouble. Tell Susan I am sorry and I hope the wedding goes off all right and she's very happy. Please believe I am very, very sorry that I have upset you.
                    Vanessa."

It was too much, he actually took the Lord's name in vain. "God!" He held his head. "Where? How long? Ask Susan!" He was yelling now.

"How can I, she's out with Brian?"

"God!" he repeated again as he walked up and down; then smoothing out the letter that he had crumpled in his fist he said aloud, "I am staying with a friend"; rounding on his wife now he cried, "A friend! Which friend has she that'll take her? Which friend knows about her condition? One friend, Cotton."

"No, no, Jonathan, she would never go to Emily . . . I mean to him."

"Then tell me which friend she has gone to?" He nearly knocked her on to her back as he turned and

149

marched out of the room, and she ran after him, crying, "Where are you going, Jonathan?"

He was at the door which led into the garage from the kitchen when he barked, "Where do you think? I'll break her neck . . . and his . . . We'll be the laughing-stock of the town one daughter marrying into the county, the other into Bog's End, and her pregnant!"

"Jonathan!" Her voice was loud now and stern. "Don't publicise us, not in that quarter. Keep your temper."

He got into the car and from there he looked at her. Drawing in a deep breath, he bowed his head. "Yes," his voice was low now, "yes, you're right. Keep my temper. But wait till I get her back here, just wait. I'll flay her. God! See if I don't."

Three times he had blasphemed aloud, which proved to his wife the extent of the depth to which he was moved.

Ryder's Row wasn't new to Jonathan Ratcliffe. He had once or twice, in the early days, brought Emily home after a late session of washing-up from a dinner party, but now, when he drove up the narrow street and he had to edge the Bentley into the space between the railway wall and a dilapidated Rover the rage within him increased. People owning cars in this street!

He knocked twice on the door, the second time banging with his fist. He heard someone shouting, "Turn that down will you! There's somebody at the front door." The music of either the wireless or television was lowered as the door opened and in the light of the dim passage bulb he saw the towering bulk of Angus Cotton in his shirt sleeves, neck open showing a dark growth of hair on his chest, and his rage was inflamed still further. This was the man who had dared to touch something that belonged to him, something that was part of him. Again the wish came that he could change places with him psysically, just for one minute.

150

"I've come for my daughter." He had to thrust the words out of his mouth.

"You've what? What the hell are you on about now! Look, what d'you want here?"

"Don't ask the road; you know. Where is she?"

"God Almighty! You must be bonkers, man."

"Who is it? Who is it, Angus?" Emily came into the dim light. Then seeing the visitor she exclaimed, "Why sir!" only to have her words cut off by Angus crying, "Sir, be damned! Do you know what he's here for? He's here to take his daughter home."

"Van?"

"Aye, Van. He thinks she's here. I ask you! They won't be told, will they?" Angus turned from his mother and, glaring at Ratcliffe, shouted, "You won't be told. You won't believe the truth."

"Keep your voice down." Emily's own voice was low and harsh. "You don't want the street to know."

"It doesn't matter a bloody damn to me who knows. I'm not afraid of anythin', or ashamed either. Has she run away then?"

When no answer came from Ratcliffe, Angus cried, "Good for her. Good for her."

For a moment Jonathan Ratcliffe stood bewildered. He hadn't had the smallest doubt in his mind but that he would find her here. He didn't believe that Cotton had nothing to do with Vanessa's condition, but he did believe him when he said she wasn't here. So when Emily said, "Come in and see for yourself, if that will satisfy you," he turned on his heel and walked to his car. And Angus moved on to the step and watched him, his whole body quivering the while. He stood there until the lights of the car disappeared from the street. Then returning to the kitchen, where Emily stood waiting for him, he asked her grimly, "Well, what do you say to that?"

Emily sighed and shook her head. Sitting down heavily, she said, "All I can say, lad, is they're dead sure it's you."

"You know somethin', Mam?" He leant towards her. "If I knew as much a few months ago as I do now, it would have been."

"Don't say that, Angus."

"I'm sayin' it, Mam, and you can believe me. God! I stuck that girl on a pedestal from when she was that high." He pointed down to the level of his knee. "You know I did. As hard bitten as I am I was still under the impression – because I wanted to be under the impression. Oh aye, because I wanted to be under the impression – that there were some virgins left, and she was top of the list . . . top of the pops. Aye, top of the pops. An' all the time she was messing about with some pimply schoolboy."

"How do you know that it was a schoolboy?"

"I don't know, but ask yourself. She was at the Convent school, wasn't she? If she had been goin' out with a fellow regular, I mean like one of the Braintree set, they would have named him surely, but she was seen with nobody but me. She's likely met the bloke on her way from school; there's plenty of lanes between the Convent and Brampton Hill. There's also the golf course and Poulter's Wood."

"Oh, Angus, don't say that."

'Well, it wasn't another bloody immaculate conception, was it?"

"Oh!" Emily rested her face on her hands and muttered, "I don't want to laugh, it's no laughin' matter."

"No begod, it's no laughin' matter." He, too, sat down, and after a moment he spoke as if to himself, saying, "I wonder where she's gone."

"They'll find her. They'll put the polis on her."

"I wonder."

"Of course they will." Emily's voice was high. "She's only sixteen, well seventeen in a day or so. But she's nothin' but a bairn."

Nothing but a bairn. Huh! Angus got to his feet now and walked out of the kichen and into his room and sat down in the wooden chair opposite the little table. His

152

forearms resting on the table, taking the weight of his slumped shoulders, he stared down at the drawing paper and pencils, and his aggressiveness seeped from him. After a while his eyes lifted to the hanging shelf attached to the wall. His hand went up and he pulled one of the books down and looked at the title. It read "The King's English, by H. W. Fowler and S. G. Fowler." It was her who had made him buy that book, her and the fact of being put in charge of the fitting shop. Not that he needed grammar in the fitting shop, he had all the language necessary for the fitting shop, but he knew he wasn't going to stay in the fitting shop. Yet that wasn't the real reason why he bought the book; it was because of how she talked. It had happened he had met her on her way to school one afternoon last year. She was carrying a great armful of flowers, white and pink, and he had admired them and asked their name, and she had said they were called Esther Reads. They were quite a common flower really, she said, at least the white ones were, and she had pointed through the park railings and said, "Look! There they are, those are they." It had been that last bit, "those are they." It sounded all wrong. Surely it should have been "those are them". He knew his grammar was bad, but he felt he was right about that bit, for whoever said those are they. It was like saying "was you?" and his grammar wasn't so bad that he said "was you?" So, he had gone and bought this book. But far from helping him it had only confused him further; he hadn't been able to find out from it if "those are they" was right or not. One thing the book did bring home to him was the fact that he'd never be able to understand grammar. He had never heard of gerunds. What were gerunds anyway? And compound possessives? One thing only came out of buying the book, and that was a begrudging admiration for those who did speak correctly. He thought that they must have had their work cut out to learn, and understand, all these two fellows said was necessary to speak English properly.

153

He recalled feeling a bit down and browned off for a few days after buying the book but it had soon passed. He had a home-spun philosophy of his own: If you couldn't do one thing then try something else.

He could draw, he was a good drawer. But now the chance to draw had been whipped away from him. The drawing office, any drawing office, was now as far from his reach as the moon, that was unless he did the thing properly and went every evening to a technical school, and it was too late for that. Anyway, he had burnt his boats. He was committed now for good or ill to cartage; he had gone in with Fred Singleton. To-morrow he was to collect his lorry and start. And all this had come about through Van Ratcliffe.

Where was she? Where had she gone? Certainly not to any of the family friends else he wouldn't have come tearing around here. The bloody nerve of the man. He was sure, wasn't he? He was so sure. He picked up the book and rammed it back on to the hanging shelf. Je-hov-ah he would like to get even with that bloke. Wouldn't he just. He'd give half his life, or sell his soul, to get even with him. But what chance had he of that, apart from going and shooting him? And he could understand now why blokes got shot. Yes, he could that!

The door opened and Rosie put her head into the room. "I hear you've had a visitor," she said.

He got to his feet and smiled wryly, saying, "Aye. You missed it; you shouldn't have gone to the pictures."

"Mam's brewed up. Come on, have a cupper." She moved towards him, smiling now and adding, "Because, you know, this is the last night of Angus Cotton, Fitter; from the-morrow mornin', boy, you'll be Angus Cotton of Cotton and Singleton, Haulage Contractors. Just think of that, lad." She pushed him hard in the chest, and he, punching her back playfully on the jaw, said, "Aye, just think of that."

"Come on." She pulled him towards the door. "I bet

you what you like you'll remember this night. Won't he, Ma?" she called to Emily who was sitting with her feet on a modern oxidised kerb fronting the old-fashioned grate. "When he's got his big house and his Rolls won't he look back to the night and say, 'Remember?' you know, like they do on the telly where the poor lad makes good and buys out the lord of the manor, together with his mama and his papa." She was giggling. "That sounded funny, Mama and Papa."

"Funny or not," Emily's voice was flat and there was no smile on her face as she said, "there's many a true word spoken in joke, and I know this much, he'll see his day yet with that bugger."

On this prophecy Angus jerked his head, whether hopefully or hopelessly it was hard to tell.

A few minutes later, when Rosie had poured out the tea and they were sitting at the table amid an unusual silence, she remarked, "I wonder where she's got to? She's going to find it chilly out there in the big, big world is Miss Vanessa. It'll be like being thrown in from the deep end."

Aye, thought Angus, just like that, being thrown in from the deep end.

6

Susan's wedding was over. It had been a big affair; half the county had been there. Vanessa's absence had not been remarked upon. One thing education did, it enabled one to be tactful, at least before the parties concerned.

Jane Ratcliffe explained her daughter's absence by saying that she was on the Continent touring with friends. It was rather an inopportune time for her to be away from home, but one of the party had dropped out and Vanessa had been so anxious to go. She was very adventurous was Vanessa. And she wrote every week, such interesting letters.

The recipients of this information smiled and nodded and said how nice for Vanessa, it was what every young girl should do, travel and have experience.

Jane Ratcliffe wondered if there was a double meaning behind these smiling replies. She also wondered where her daughter was. Two postmarks had said London, another Brighton, another Eastbourne, one as far away as Torquay. She had been forced to show Vanessa's note and her first letter to Doctor Carr because he had become difficult. He had acted as if they had done away with her. She had become very frightened about his attitude, but Jonathan had taken care of him and they had changed their doctor.

Jonathan said he had washed his hands of Vanessa once and for all, he never wanted to see her again. She herself wasn't so adamant; after all, she was her daughter and she was so young. She still felt the matter should be placed in the hands of the police, but Jonathan went almost mad if she brought up the subject. Perhaps it was because Rowland, the Chief Constable, was a member of his club, and Jonathan thought a lot about his status in his club, yet it would reflect badly on them if Vanessa had the baby in some charity home and the fact was discovered. But she couldn't make Jonathan see this. She was at the other end of the country, he said, and let her stay there. Far better that than under their noses and consorting with that lout; at least she'd had the sense to break away from him.

The house seemed very empty now without Susan, and when Ray started boarding-school – another decision of Jonathan's – she wouldn't know what to do with herself. She would have to take up some charity work to fill in her time. The house was no great concern now, for she had been fortunate enough to get a woman equally as good as Emily, if not better. She had thought for years that the world would come to an end if ever she lost Emily, but, you see, everybody could be done without. This had proved it.

PART TWO

I

It was Rosie who first found out where Vanessa was. It happened while she and Stan were in Newcastle. They had arrived at three o'clock with the intention of looking round before going to the cinema, but they were back in Fellburn by five o'clock.

Angus was in the house but he hadn't yet changed. He had finished work at twelve and spent the hours since going over his lorry in the shed that Singleton rented as a garage. He had bought it cheap and it was acting cheap. In the last three months he had learned a great deal about the mechanics of an engine. He'd had to or go bust, for during the first week the lorry had broken down four times. He knew he had been done over his purchase, and he put it down to experience; it would all add up to knowledge when next he went lorry hunting, but by the look of things at present, he was telling himself, that would be some time ahead. Forty quid a week they could make each, Fred had said. The highest he had touched was thirty. Last week he was down to twenty-four. They both worked all the hours that God sent, but their lorries were not big enough or good enough. The business that had passed them by in the last four weeks made him literally sick, yet he knew that even with new lorries two men on their own weren't going to get very far. He wanted half-a-dozen lorries at least, and the same number of men to go with them. He also told himself he wanted the moon. At the rate he was saving now it would take him a year to buy one lorry and that second-hand. He could have got one on the never-never but he didn't want to start that. He was against hire purchase because he had seen too many of the swabs coming claiming the stuff back around the doors; no, he wanted to pay on the nail. It might be frustrating waiting, but that was what he'd have to put up with. There was another thing. Once he started the never-never business Fred would keep him at it. He was finding he had to be firm with Fred; he was too slap-dash, too easy going.

He was looking dolefully down at the exercise book in which he did his accounts when the door opened and Rosie came in, still in her out-door things. "What do you think," she said, excitedly. "I've seen her."

"You've seen who?" She could have been meaning any-one at the moment.

"Miss Van, of course."

His face was straight as he asked, "Where?"

"In Newcastle. Come on, come into the kitchen, I'm not going to tell it twice." She turned about and left him, and he followed, but slowly.

"Well, go on," said Emily. "Where . . . where did you see her? Stop muckin' about an' tell us."

"You'll never guess, not in a thousand years. Not her. Would they, Stan?" She looked from Stan to Angus, but Angus didn't speak, he just waited. And then she looked at her mother again and said almost gleefully, "Servin' in a greengrocer's. A potty, dirty little greengrocer's. Wasn't she, Stan?"

"Not Miss Van, no!"

"Aye, Mam, MISS VAN. It was her, Stan, wasn't it? She looked at Stan for confirmation, and Stan nodded. "You said it was."

"It was." She looked from one to the other. "We had just got out of the bus station and gone round by the pig market. Stan wanted to have a look at the river and I wanted to go and have a look at the flats, you know where

162

Kyle Street used to be. We were wandering about there, and then we came to some of the streets that hadn't been pulled down yet, old mucky places you know, worse than anything round here."

"Go on, get on with it," said Emily impatiently.

"I am, Mam, I am. I'm just tellin' you, I'm givin' you the settin'. Well, we saw this little greengrocer's, you know, that sells everything; candles, firewood, the lot, a real huckster shop. There was some pomegranates in a box outside and Stan here says he wants one and I said I'd like one an' all. It would be like being a kid again eatin' pomegranates in the street. Well, Stan went to the door where there was an old woman servin', and there was a lass inside serving somebody else, an' it was as I stood by the window that I recognized her. It was Miss Van."

"Couldn't be. She could get a job anywhere. She wouldn't want to go into a huckster shop; she would go into one of the big stores . . . ."

"Mam," said Rosie slowly and patiently, "she couldn't go into one of the big stores an' she wouldn't get a job any place, not lookin' like she does . . . she's big."

"God in heaven! Did you speak to her?"

"No, course not, I kept out of the way, she didn't know Stan. You know I've never cottoned to her but I felt sorry for her for a minute servin' in that bruised apple dump."

She looked at Angus as he said, "You could have made a mistake."

"I'm not daft, our Angus; I know her as well as you do."

"Where did you say the shop was?"

"I told you, where they haven't started pullin' down yet. I don't know what the name of the street was. Do you, Stan?"

Stan shook his head, then said, "No; but I remember that it was near Murphy Street and it was the end one. There was a big open space filled with rubble behind it." He added, "I've heard a lot about her but I'd never seen her afore. She's a good-lookin' piece, even if she's —"

163

"Watch it! Watch it!" Rosie dug him hard in the ribs and they both laughed; but Emily and Angus didn't join in.

"You goin' to the club, our Angus?" Rosie now asked. and he answered, "Aye, I might as well. But I'm goin' down to the baths first."

"You were there last night." Rosie's voice was high.

"Aye, well. And I'm goin' the night again." His tone said, "What you trying to make of it?" He stared at her for a minute before he turned away and went into his room, and Emily, now bending towards Rosie, whispered thickly, "You shouldn't have let on."

"Let on?" She screwed up her face at her mother. "What do you mean?"

Her voice lower still, Emily said, "Don't be a stupid bugger; about Miss Van."

"Why not for?" Rosie was whispering back.

"Because it's ten to one if she's in a plight he'll do somethin'."

"Don't be so daft, Mam." Rosie pulled her chin to her neck, "And him being accused of droppin' her. He's not barmy altogether."

"You don't know him like I do, and he is barmy about some things. If he wasn't barmy he would have married May years ago."

Rosie now turned her head slowly and looked towards the front-room door and she asked under her breath, "You mean . . . you mean he's been struck with her?" Her tone was incredulous, and her mother whispered sharply, "I mean no such thing, he knows his place, but, as I said, if she was in a fix he could be sorry for her an' want to do somethin'. He's not barmy you say, an' I say he's bloody well barmy in some ways."

During the next week Angus came home every night about the usual time. He would have a wash in the sink or take his soap and towel and go down to the public baths three streets away. It all depended on what he had been loading during the day. Monday night he stayed indoors; Tuesday night he went to the club – Stan gave Rosie this information the following day – Wednesday night he stayed at home again; Thursday night he went to the pictures, and on Friday night he was going to the dogs. But on Friday afternoon he took his lorry into Newcastle.

He found Murphy Street and parked the lorry near a mound of rubble. Dusting down his coat and adjusting his cap he went up the first street and found the huckster shop. There were pomegranates in a box outside, and onions and soft tomatoes. He looked through the window but could see only an oldish woman. He bit tight on his lip before he entered the shop and the oldish woman said, "What can I get you?"

"I'll have a pound of apples, please."

As she went to weigh the apples he looked towards the little back shop but could see or hear no one. "You've got a young lady helping you?" he asked.

Her eyes narrowed and she peered up at him without speaking, and he said, "Haven't you?"

"What business is it of yours?"

"It happens that I know her. Can I have a word with her?" He looked towards the back shop again, and she said, "She's not here, she's off bad."

"Bad?"

"Aye, that's what I said, bad."

"You . . . you mean the baby, it's . . . ."

"No, I don't mean the baby, it's not due yet. You know about that, but I don't suppose . . . ." She looked him up and down and didn't finish, but he finished for her. "That it could be me. That's what you mean, isn't it?"

"I didn't say nowt of the sort."

"You didn't need to. Where's she livin'?"

"Why should I tell you that?"

He stared at her and decided to tell her the truth, for

her sort could keep mum and he'd have had his journey for nothing, and another night of thinking ahead of him. "Well you see the truth is me mother used to work for her family and she's been worried since she ran away."

"And so you want to go back and tell her where she's living so she can carry it to the lass's folks?"

"Nothin' of the sort. Me mother doesn't work for them any more and she's no intention of letting on about her. I just want to see her and have a word with her."

The woman stared at him again, then said, "It's funny you findin' her; her people haven't done much searchin'. I don't know what kind of folks they are to let her be on her own, an' her in her state. She's nowt more than a bairn herself and no more fit to be left on her own than a new bride in a barracks."

He hadn't heard that one before. He must remember that one – A new bride in a barracks.

"It's a good job she stumbled on Nell Crawford's house when looking for a room; if she had got in some places I could speak of, even in her condition, she'd have been eaten alive. But Nell's is all right, an' clean."

"Where's this Nell Crawford's?" he said.

The woman moved her head impatiently. He had only to go out into the street, she said, and ask to be directed to Nell Crawford's and anybody in this district would show him the way. It's 132 Batterby Bay Road," she said.

Batterby Bay Road! God! Of all the places she could have landed in she had to land in Batterby Bay Road. Nell Crawford, whoever she was, might run a clean house but, if she was in Batterby Bay Road, he'd like to bet his life it was the only one there. He said "Thanks" and turned on his heel, and when she sad, "You havn't paid for the apples," he said, "Oh, I'm sorry. How much?"

"One and fourpence."

He gave her the money and went out of the shop and he sat in the cab of his lorry for a few minutes biting on his lip. Batterby Bay Road! Good God! They made them

166

in Batterby Bay Road; it was a training school for them. He'd first walked down Batterby Bay Road when he was fifteen. It was on a Saturday night, and he and three mates had come into Newcastle and had dared each other to go down the road.

They had gone down it, but they had come out the other end quicker than they had entered it. They had thought they were great guys to go down Batterby Bay Road and had bragged about it for weeks afterwards, but each one of them had been scared stiff by the tarts. Tarts of all types, tall and short, young, middle-aged and old 'uns. Not one of them had started yet. Talked about it never-ending, but never got down to it, and, all the opportunity in the world offered them, they didn't that night either.

He took the lorry right to the door of number 132. It was a tall, double-fronted terraced house. It had undoubtedly at one time been the home of a middle-class family. Now its ten rooms had ten separate occupants. Their names were on dirty pieces of paper pinned on a board inside the dim hallway; even the paper bearing the name V. Ratcliffe was thumb-marked. There was a glass door leading out of the lobby, but he found it locked. Looking to the side he saw a bell. He did not hear it ring, but after a few minutes there came the sound of footsteps on the other side of the door, and as it was opened a voice said, "Haven't you got your key?"

The woman stared up at Angus and added, "Oh, what do you want? I'm full up."

"I've come to see a Miss Ratcliffe."

She was now looking at him in the same way as the woman in the greengrocer's shop. Then she said, "Ee'. You have, have ya. And what would you be wantin' with her?"

"That's my business." He stepped towards the door with the intention of entering, but her thin arms checked him with a force that was surprising.

"Don't rush it, lad. Don't rush it. And let me tell you somethin'. If you're after anythin' you've come to the wrong shop."

He closed his eyes for a second and turned his head to the side, then said, "Look Missus, what I want is to have a word with Miss Ratcliffe. I happen to know her. Will you tell her that Angus Cotton is here?"

She wagged her head in small movements and her lids blinked over her round black eyes; then she said, "I'm not deaf. Stay where you are."

As she mounted the stairs he watched her, and when she was half up them she turned and looked down at him, scrutinising him from head to foot as if she couldn't make him out. Then she continued on her way.

It was a full five minutes before she returned and her manner was unchanged. She said briefly, "It's the top floor, number eight. And you'd better mind your head on the ceiling on the top flight."

He was glad she had warned him about the ceiling. The third flight of stairs was dark and he had almost to grope his way up them. The top landing was lit by a fanlight in the roof and the door to the left of him was marked number eight.

He was again nipping his lip as he knocked on the door. After a moment it was opened and she was standing looking at him. She was wearing a loose kind of dressing-gown and he reckoned she must have just got out of bed. Her face, as his mother had once described it, looked all eyes and teeth. He had always thought he had never seen hair the colour of hers, a real chestnut with a gleam of dark red in it. There was no gleam in it to-day, it was dull and lank. When her lips began to tremble he said, "Hello, Van."

"He-llo, Angus." She gulped on his name. Then standing aside, she said, "Wo . . . n't you come in?"

He walked into the attic room and tried not to notice how it looked, but his immediate impression made him compare it with the home she had left, and he thought, it's unbelieveable! His own home left a lot to be desired, but it was Buckingham Palace compared to this. There was a narrow iron bed under the sloping roof, there was one chair and a small square deal table; there was a hanging wardrobe attached to the ceiling at its highest point near the little four-paned window, and beside a much-battered chest of drawers there stood on the floor a tin tray, on which was a gas-ring and a kettle. When he turned and looked at her she dropped her head and said below her breath, "Don't say it, Angus. Don't say it." Then her head still bowed, she said, "Won't you sit down?" She motioned towards the chair; at the same time she sat down on the foot of the bed.

When he was seated he dropped his hands between his kness and tried to think of something to say, but found it impossible. Of the two, she seemed more in control of the situation. "How is Emily?" she asked.

Even now he couldn't answer her right away; then after a moment he said, "Oh, she's fine."

"Has . . . has she got a new job?"

"No, no. I don't want her to go out any more; she's done enough."

"Yes, of course."

There was silence between them again, and in the silence the smell of the place filled his nostrils. The air was dank, dirty, thick. He imagined that the walls were impregnated with muck. He longed to turn round and throw the window open, but the room was chilly. His eyes moved about, looking for a means of heating, and then he saw a tiny gas-fire by the wall at the head of the bed.

When they both broke the silence together he smiled and nodded at her, giving her place, and she said, "I was going to ask where you are working now."

"Oh." He straightened his back against the chair, "I'm on me own, I'm me own boss. I'm in partnership with a fellow called Singleton. Haulage, you know, contracting. It's working out fine." He wanted to assure her about that at least.

"Oh, I'm glad, Angus." Her head drooped for a moment before she raised her eyes to his again and said, "I'm . . . I'm sorry, Angus, about the trouble I brought on you and the others."

"Oh, you've got no need to worry about that. If that's all you're worried about you can put your mind at rest. It did us both a good turn. I mean me mam and me. It set me up on me own, and mam's a new woman now she's had a rest."

"I'm glad," she said again.

Now his face became straight and he stared at her blankly for a moment before asking, "And what about you?"

When she made no reply he leant slightly forward and said under his breath, "This is no place for you, Van. Why don't you go home?"

"No! I'll never do that, Angus."

"But why? They're your people."

She looked at him for a time before saying, "Yes, they're my people. And if I'd gone on the streets they couldn't have treated me worse. They were terrified, really terrified, about me having the baby. Not because of what it might do to me, but because of the effect it would have on their prestige. You see . . . father was determined that I got rid of it, and, and I didn't want to." There was a firmness in her voice now that hadn't been there before.

"Well, you know I think he was right. I do. I don't hold with a damn thing he's ever done or said, in fact I might as well tell you I hate his guts, but on that score I think he was right. You could have started again." She was looking downwards, and he stumbled on, "You know what I mean. You're young, you would have forgotten all about this, and they would have stood by you and seen you all right."

She was gazing into his face now and there was a deep bitterness in her voice as she said, "They would have stood be me, but how? They intended that after I came out of the clinic in London I should stay indefinitely with a great-aunt in Scotland. She lives miles and miles off the beaten track. She has an old couple who look after her. They are over seventy. There's nobody young within miles. The minister visits them on Sunday and they have prayers. He's made a special journey out to her for years hoping that when she dies he'll be taken care of. They haven't a car. There's one taxi down in the village, and that's miles away. I was there last year for a week . . . . Mother, too, wants to be remembered in her will." Her tone was cynical now. "So I was packed off there as a sort of insurance premium to be raked off later. After two days I thought I would go mad."

As Angus listened to her talking in a way that surprised him he realized that, although she still looked very young, the girl he had known was gone. But then that was to be expected; the girl would have ceased to be when she started the bairn. It was as his mother said, he was barmy in some ways. Into the silence that had fallen on them he said, "You've been bad, I mean ill?" and she answered, "I caught a chill. The shop is rather draughty where I work."

"Yes, I know." He nodded at her.

"How . . . how did you find out?" she asked.

"I didn't, it was Rosie. They passed the place last Saturday and saw you."

"Will . . . will she talk? What I mean is, Angus, I . . . I don't want anyone to know I'm here. You see, I write home every week and my letters go from as far away as London, Devon, and places like that. I give them to Mr. Noakes. He's . . . he's in number nine." She nodded towards the door. "He's a long-distance lorry driver. He, he posts them in London for me, and gets one of his work mates to post them some other place."

A long-distance lorry driver, Mr. Noakes. And what did Mr. Noakes expect for his kind service? Long-distance lorry drivers who picked up any slimy piece that thumbed them from the gutter. She didn't know what she was askin' for. Doubtless Mr. Noakes would one day inform her. After the bairn was born likely, if not afore; it all depended on how desperate was his need.

She seemed to sense his reaction to what she had just told him and she said, "He's a very nice man, kind, oldish." When she shuddered he said, "You're cold, I'm keepin' you out of bed. Can't . . . can't you light the fire?"

"Oh, yes. I have it on most of the time but it got a little too hot and I put it out."

He didn't believe her, but he didn't go and light it. Instead, he said, "Where do you eat?"

"I usually have my lunch in a café in the town and bring something in for an evening meal. I manage all right."

"Van." He got to his feet. "I've got to be going now, I've got a load waiting for me," he nodded towards the window, "but I'd like to come and see you again. Can I?"

She shook her head slowly, then said, "No, Angus. I don't think it would be right. If they ever found out you know what they'd say; they would put –"

"Aye, I know what they'd say, and what they would put together. Well, they would be bloody well wrong, wouldn't they?" He lowered his head and said, "I'm sorry." When he looked at her she was smiling slightly, the first time the muscles of her face had moved upwards since he saw her, and she said quietly, "Don't apologise; I've enlarged my vocabulary quite a bit in the last few months. It, it isn't that I don't want to see you, Angus, it's been wonderful seeing you but, but I don't want to cause any more trouble, and you know it would only lead to –"

"Well,' he said briskly, "let me deal with the trouble and whatever it leads to. Now look. You get back into bed and I'll call later on and bring something back for you to eat. And in the meantime you tell that one down-stairs that my intentions are honourable." He felt he had said the wrong thing, and he blustered, "Well, I've got to go. There'll be so much ballast waitin' at yon end they'll have me scalped. I'll be seein' you. Now get back into bed. I can't say what time, after six though. Aye, it'll be well after six."

She was standing at the foot of the bed holding the iron rail with both hands, and she said softly, "Good-bye, Angus."

He forgot about the ceiling as he went down the stairs and cursed as he hit his head; then he took the other flights two at a time.

He had already lost two loads but he finished early, parked the lorry in the garage, then went straight to the baths, where he hired a towel and soap. He reached home at five-thirty, and sat down immediately to his tea.

"Aren't you going to have a wash?" said Emily.

"Don't I look clean?" He turned his head towards her. "I had a bath afore I came in."

Ten minutes later when the room door closed on him, Rosie said, "Him and his baths, he'll wash himself away! In the end it would be cheaper to put one in the wash-house. He said that years ago, didn't he?"

"Where's he off to in this rush?" asked Emily under her breath. "The dogs don't start afore eight."

"Why don't you ask him?"

Ten minutes later, when he came out of the room, Emily did ask him. Casually she said, "Where you off to, lad?" and he answered without blinking, "I'm goin' along to see a fellow about a lorry. This one's drivin' me up the wall; it only goes when it's pushed."

"A lorry?" Emily's brows gathered suspiciously. "You never mentioned it afore."

"I couldn't, I only heard of it this afternoon. A fellow on the site told me I might pick up one cheap."

"The other one was cheap, and look what it's brought you."

"Well, I've got me eyes open this time. Be seein' you." As he went out of the front door he knew that they would both be looking at each other and wondering. Well, he would let them wonder for a little while until he knew what he was going to do. He'd have to do something, but what he wasn't sure. Well, not really.

2

This was his sixth visit to number 132 Batterby Bay Road, and he brought with him, on this occasion, two bags of fish and chips, two half-pint bottles of pale ale, a sliced loaf, a half-pound of Danish butter, and half a pound of cheese. It was Monday and she had started work to-day.

He knocked on the door and entered when she said, "Come in." He hadn't seen her since Friday night and he had worked late on Saturday to make up for lost time, and then to allay his mother's suspicions he had gone to the club as usual; and yesterday he had made himself lie in, after which he had followed the usual Sunday routine. He had gone along to the pub for a couple of pints with Stan, and they had come back, had their dinner and, when his mother had gone upstairs to put her feet up, he had left the kitchen to Rosie and Stan and gone and lain down on his bed; and in the evening they had all gone to the club again, for as his mother had said it was often better on a Sunday night than it was on a Saturday. But here he was, here he was where his thoughts had been every minute during this last week and all the week-end.

He stared at her. She was looking different. She was no longer wearing the slack dressing-gown thing but had on a brown woollen dress that hadn't been cut for maternity.

It was evident that she hadn't expected him so soon, because when he entered the room she was going towards the wardrobe, and he watched her take the dressing-gown from it. When she was about to put it on he said quietly,

175

"Leave that off." She turned a surprised look towards him, and as he dropped his purchases upon the table he added, "You don't have to hide yourself."

When he turned towards her she was standing in much the same attitude as her mother was wont to do, she was cupping her cheeks with her hands, "Oh, Angus!" she said, and to this he replied brusquely, "Never mind 'oh, Angus'! Get those plates out and let's have this while it's hot. I got skate. I don't know whether you like skate or not, I like it."

She had never tasted skate; she couldn't remember having it at home, but she said, "Yes, I like skate." So deep was her gratitude to him that if he had brought in fried dog she would have eaten it. She brought a dinner-plate and a tea-plate to the table; the smaller one she set before herself, and he said, "You'll have to sport another meal-size plate, eh?"

"Yes, I must get another plate. She doesn't provide for visitors."

"She doesn't provide for boarders, if you ask me." He looked disdainfully round the room.

"It's better than some, Angus.'

He paused with a chip to his mouth, saying, "You're kiddin'."

"No, I'm not. There was a place farther down the street. It was terrible, dreadful. And at least the people in this house work."

"Well, didn't the people in that house?" He was quizzing her.

"Yes." She had her eyes cast downwards. "Yes, I suppose so, work of a kind."

"Aye, of a kind," he repeated. Then turning the conversation abruptly, he added, "We're goin' out."

"What!"

"You heard what I said." He poked his big face towards her. "We're goin' out."

"No, Angus, no. What if we were seen together?"

"You frightened?" He placed his knife and fork down on the table, and she was quick to assure him, "Oh, not that way, Angus. Not what you mean, no, but I'm frightened that someone might see us and tell Father, and if he saw us together then nothing on earth would convince him but that –"

"Look, Van. Get it into your head he's convinced already. God Almighty steppin' out of heaven wouldn't convince him otherwise. I told you he came to the house when you ran off, and although he believed you weren't there at that minute he believed that I knew where you were. I'm sure of it."

"Well, I don't want to prove him right, Angus."

"Now let's get this straight, Van. You can't stay in this place for ever, you can't come from that stinkin' little shop and bury yourself under this roof seven nights a week until the bairn's born. And that's another point. We've got to talk about this . . . . It's no use sticking your head in the sand." He looked at her downcast face. "What's going to happen when it's born? You goin' to have it adopted?" He waited, and after a while she said, "I . . . I suppose I should, yet I don't know. I keep thinking first one way then another. It seems stupid having gone through all this then letting it be adopted. If that's what I'm going to do I think it would have been simpler to have done what they wanted in the first place . . . .'

"Aye, it would," he put in. "As I said, that's one thing him and me agree on, it would. It would have saved you a lot of trouble and worry, because as it is, you know yourself, you can't keep it. Now where could you keep a bairn here? You could hump him along to the shop and put him in a basket out at the back. That's easy fixed, it's been done afore. I spent me early years in a clothes basket in people's wash-houses when me mother went out doin' a day's washin'; under the table in different kitchens when she went out cleanin'; and once, she tells me, I spent three weeks in a hen cree. The old dear she worked for couldn't

177

stand bairns, and there was an empty hen cree at the bottom of the garden, and there me mother used to dump me." He was smiling now. "So you see you could manage that part, that would be easy. But this here house is the problem. You'd have to hump up water from the next landing, and take it down again and empty it. And, you must remember, a bairn needs a lot of water." He almost added, "And makes a lot an' all," but refrained. "You've got some thinkin' to do about this, Van."

She kept her head lowered as she said, "I do nothing else but think."

"Is there nobody you could go to? I mean, none of your relations or friends?"

"Not one of them who wouldn't be embarrassed to see me and who wouldn't immediately get in touch with Father." Now she raised her eyes to his and said quietly, "But I'll manage. I've got this far and I'll manage."

"Manage be damned!" He jerked his head – he had ceased to apologise to her for swearing. "You're only at the beginning of it, an' what's more you know nothin' about bairns. By the way, have you made arrangements about having it?"

"Yes, yes, I've done that."

"Do you go to a clinic, or one of them places?"

"No, I went once, but there were so many people there I . . . I was afraid someone might see me."

"But you can't hide away for ever."

"I . . . I'm not going to. It's just till it's born, and then the thing will be done and he can't do anything about it."

"Only press you to get it adopted. That's the tack he'll take then."

"No, I don't think he would do that. I don't think he ever wants to see me again. I think he'd show me the door if I did go home."

"How did your mother react to it?"

"She is guided by Father, she always has been."

He rose from the chair and walked down the middle of

the attic. He had to keep in the middle to prevent bumping his head. And he walked the length of the room twice before he spoke again, and then he had his back to her as he asked, "The fellow. Couldn't he marry you?"

He waited for her answer, and when none was forthcoming he turned and looked at her. She was sitting staring down at her hands resting on the mound of her stomach, and he went to her now and, dropping on his hunkers before her, he put his hand under her chin and pushed it upwards and asked again, "Couldn't he?"

"No." She shook her head.

"Why?"

"It's . . . it's impossible."

"Nothing's impossible."

"That is."

They stared at each other for a moment. Then he rose to his feet and, drawing in a deep breath, said flatly, "Well, you can't go on like this, you just can't.'

"Other girls do. They survive."

"Aye, but other girls aren't like you."

"You'd be surprised. I've seen girls at the clinic. The look in their eyes. You can tell us. Oh, you'd be surprised."

"Nothin' surprises me, Van. And anyway, I'm not concerned what happens to other girls, I'm just concerned at the moment at what's gonna happen to you."

She was staring up at him, and slowly her face crumpled; then her body bent forward and she was sobbing into her hands.

When his arms went about her and his hands felt her shoulder blades under her dress his own body stiffened against the touch of her. But only for a moment; then he was clasping her tightly and saying, "There now, there now. It's all right." But the more he soothed her the more she cried. "Look." He brought her damp hair from her brow and face. "Don't carry on like that, it'll only upset you. An' the bairn as well. Come on, come on, stop it. Give over. Look, give over."

But she couldn't stop, she couldn't give over. She had cried before, she had cried night after night when she had first came to this room, but it wasn't this kind of crying. This was a deluge of weeping; the force of it was a hurricane shaking her body. He became worried, not only for her, but that at any moment one of them across the landing would come to the door. That bloke Noakes, whom he had met once and whose age and manner had allayed any suspicions he had had of him, but who in his turn might be thinking her visitor was up to something. He implored her now, "Van! Van! Don't. Aw, don't."

He led her to the edge of the bed and, pressing her backwards, he said, "There, there, lie down."

She was lying on her side now, her face covered with her hands, and he knelt by the bed and held her wrists, and he wished his mother was here – his mother would have known what to do. If she went on like this she'd really be ill. She wasn't only crying, it was more like hysteria. The cure for hysteria, he had read, was a good slap along the lug; well, he couldn't administer that kind of shock treatment, but he could give her a shock. Aye, it was one way to do it.

He had wondered all the week-end how he would put it over and what her reaction would be. Well, now was the opportune time to try it out. He pulled her hands roughly from her face and putting his own down close to hers he said firmly, "Listen, Van. Listen to what I'm going to say to you. Now listen . . . Will you marry me?"

It worked. After a few minutes her sobs turned to intermittent shudders, and then she was staring at him. Her breath still coming in gasps, her eyes puckered, she was staring into his face. Then stammering, she asked, "W . . . what did you s . . . say?"

"You heard what I said all right, but I'll say it again. Will you marry me? Under ordinary circumstances this could never have happened, you know it, and I know it, but you're not livin' under ordinary circumstances, are you? That's not sayin' what I've got to offer you is a piece of cake, God knows it's far from it, but . . . but it would get you out of this. And I'll have you off me mind sort of, not worryin' every hour of the day what's happening to you in this warren of pimps and whores. Our house is not a palace, you might think it's a slum, but God, it's better than this, and you'll have me mum to see to you. What about it?"

"Oh, Angus, Angus." Her face crumpled again, and he shook her hands roughly, saying harshly under his breath, "Now don't start that again, you'll make yourself bad."

She was biting tight down on her lip as he said, "Think about it. I don't want yes or no now, just think about it. But as I see it, when you're drowning in the deep sea you don't turn your nose up at a floating plank."

She tugged her hands from his and again her face was covered, and again she was crying, but quietly, and he stood up now and walked to the table, and from there, with his back to her, he said, "I know it'll be a big comedown for you. I might be looked on as a bit of a catch round our quarter, but from the place where you're standin' I'm less than the dust beneath thy chariot wheels, sort of, an' if you did decide to come to our place," he didn't say "to marry me," now, "you'd have to stand the racket. And it would hit you from a good many sides. You'd be livin' atween the devil and the deep sea. Your own folks wouldn't own you ever again, so you've got to think on that, and my kind would be suspicious. So I'm warnin' you, do a bit of thinkin' about it. I'll be back the morrow night. But mind, don't think I'm blackmailing you or anything like that, for if you do say no you haven't seen the last of me."

When he turned to her she was sitting up, leaning wearily against the iron rails of the bed. He came and looked down at her and he put out his hand and lightly took the hair from behind one ear, and as he touched her the tears welled in her eyes again, and he said brusquely. "Now, now, stop it. I'm off. Well, you have it. Chew on it. I'll see you the morrow night." As he reached the door he turned to her and said, "Think hard; it's usually for life."

When he reached the bottom of the stairs he stood in the darkness and wiped the sweat from his face. God! Where in hell's name had he got the nerve from. And if she said no, what then? Aye, what then? He knew what then. His self-esteem would never rise to the surface again. He would shout louder, bluster more and belly laugh at every opportunity, but under his skin he'd be grovelling in the deep, deep chasm that held his self-disdain.

He didn't go straight home but called in a pub and had a double whisky. When he reached the house there was only his mother in and he was glad of this.

She greeted him rather tersely as he threw off his hat and coat, and when he took his seat opposite to her at the side of the fireplace she looked at him and waited. In a way she knew what was coming, but still wouldn't believe it.

"I've been to see Van, Mam," he said.

"Tell me somethin' I don't know," she answered; then went on looking at a magazine she had been reading.

"Now, look!" He pointed his index finger at her as if it was a gun. "Don't you start."

"You're a bloody fool." She was on her feet, and he cried back at her, "Aye, I know I'm a bloody fool. But I'm not the first, an' I won't be the last. Are you going to listen to me or not?"

She walked over to the dresser and snatched up a cup and saucer from the rack; then coming to the fire and lifting up a brown teapot that had been standing on the hob for the past hour she returned to the table and poured herself out a cup of tea that looked like tar.

"I'm askin' you." He, too, was standing now, leaning on the table looking down at her, "Are you goin' to listen me out?"

"I haven't much choice, have I? I have to listen you out apparently whether I like it or not."

He bowed his head and fought to control his temper. Then, his voice deep in his throat, he said, "She's in a frightful state, Mam. Rosie saw where she's workin'. That's bad enough. But if you saw the house where she's livin', you wouldn't believe it; you just wouldn't, Mam."

"Whose fault is that?"

"We're not talkin' about faults or blame or anythin' else. By the way, I thought you liked her; I thought you liked her the best of the bunch."

"Aye, I liked her, but I don't like the idea of you gettin' yourself mixed up with her. You got blamed for somethin' you didn't do, and now you're walkin' right into their hands. Do you think anybody would believe that you're not the father now?"

"Do you know somethin'?" His voice was deceptively low. "I don't care a monkey's cuss what anybody believes. They'll believe what they like in any case, no matter what you say, or I say, or God Almighty says, but I would have thought that you might have had a different attitude, especially under the circumstanmes."

"What did you expect? The old family retainer with the heart of gold? . . . Well," she leant towards him and thumbed her chest, "that isn't a picture of me. Charity begins at home. What charity I have is needed here. As for her, she should be in her own home, an' gettin' charity there."

"Well, she thinks different, Mam. And so do I."

"You do, do you?"

"Aye, I do."

"And what can you do about it, do you think, except make a bloody fool of yourself?"

"It isn't what I can do about it, Mam, it's what I'm goin' to do. Bloody fool or not."

She stared fixedly at him before she asked, "You're goin' to live with her then?"

"Live with her!" He sounded slightly shocked. "No I'm not going to live with her, I'm going to marry her." He didn't add now, "If she'll have me."

"Christ Almighty!" Slowly she subsided back into her chair. After all, she hadn't expected this. She had expected him to say he was going to look after her or some such damn silly thing. She had even expected him to ask if she could come here to be looked after. Aye, that's what she had expected. But, marry her! Her son, Angus Cotton, marry the daughter of Affleck and Tate's manager! Jonathan Ratcliffe's daughter. He was stark, staring, bloody mad, and she said that to him. "You're stark, staring, bloody mad. You don't know what you're talkin' about. You! You goin' to marry Miss Vanessa Ratcliffe? Aw, lad!" she shook her head slowly at him while she smiled mirthlessly.

"Not so much of the aw lad. What's wrong with me, anyway? Oh, I know I haven't had an education to match hers, but who's fault is that? It isn't mine. But it's not too late. An' what the hell does education matter after all? It's money that counts, money that sets you up. When you have money you get things, an' they change you. I've seen it."

"Shut up." Her voice was quiet.

"Look!" He almost pounced on her. "Don't tell me to shut up, Mam. An' listen to me. I'm goin' to make money, I'm goin' to change—"

"So can a leopard." She was scornful.

"My God!" He was standing straight now, taut. "That's what you think of me, worse than them, and you me own, with the scorn drippin' from your lips."

She looked at him pityingly now. "Aye, that's what I think of you, lad, when you're aimin' at her. I wanted you to rise, I wanted you to rise in Affleck's. I stayed on up there for years just so that it would give you the chance. But I knew how far you could go. You see, I'm of two worlds meself. I've lived up there the best part of eighteen year. You could say it hasn't brushed off on me, an' you'd be right, yet inside I know what's what; I know that oil an' water don't mix. And you and she are oil an' water. And I'm goin' to tell you frankly to your face, lad, that if she's marryin' you she must be pretty desperate."

He swallowed the truth hard. He gulped on it. His lips worked one over the other until there was no saliva left on them. And then he said quietly, "That's it, Mam; she's pretty desperate. You've said it. You've said a mouthful, haven't you? But look you here." His voice was almost gentle now and his movements, when he bent towards her, had no aggressiveness about them, he was just making a plain statement. "I'll surprise you one day. I'll let you see. I'll let you see as well as the rest. From you up to Ratcliffe, I'll let you see. That's a promise, and whatever else I do, or don't do, you know once given I keep me word."

She reached out and picked up the cup of black tea again and as she stirred it she said, her voice as quiet as his now, "There'll be nobody more pleased than me, lad, if you bring it off."

"If I bring it off! But I haven't got a chance in hell. That's what you're thinkin', isn't it?"

She looked at him and her voice still quiet, she asked, "Where do you intend to live?"

"Here. Where else? Here."

"Aw no! No!" Her voice was a roar. You couldn't. Where do you think she's goin' to live in here?"

"There's my room; it's big enough for two."

"But, lad . . . Aw," she was pleading with him now, "what do you think my life is goin' to be like? If you and her are oil and water don't forget I'm on the same side as you. You'll leave her in the mornin' and I'll have her all day. No, no." She shook her head slowly, slowly and widely as she gazed at him standing silent now. And she waited for him to speak; and when he did he said, "And where else could I take her? I can't run two houses, and

185

I'm not leavin' you. As bloody bitchy as you've been, I'm not leavin' you, Mam. You know I wouldn't."

"Look." She waved her hand at him. "You can leave me any day you like, lad. I can fend for meself; I've still got a pair of hands."

"Aye, and a pair of feet that won't carry you much longer." He looked down at her still swollen legs. "Anyway, I'm not taking her anywhere else, I'm bringin' her here." His voice was gritty again. "An' she's stayin' here until I can make other arrangements, arrangements that's goin' to suit both you and her, and me." He thumbed his chest on the "me". "Then we'll talk about it." As he turned from her she said helplessly, "Have you thought about our Rosie? She'll go mad. She never cared for her."

He stood in the kitchen doorway and, looking back at her, said, "That's a pity for Rosie. Anway, she's got Stan. It's about time she was married."

As he turned to go into his room she flung one last missile at him. "What about May?" she cried. "What about May?"

He turned again to her and said deeply and bitterly, "To hell with May. To hell with her and everybody else."

When his door banged she cried at it, "You've played her dirty. She served your purpose for years and you've played her dirty. You'll pay for it, lad, you'll pay for it; you can't get away with those things." Then turning to the fire, she raised her hands and gripped the high mantelpiece and stood staring down on to the flickering coals. Her world had been shattered into smithereens. She wished she was dead.

3

It was three days later that Angus went to see Doctor
Carr. He was the only person he knew who was in sympathy with Vanessa and who might be able to advise him
on how to go about getting married legally without her
parents' consent.

He had been to the reference library and looked up
books on Common Law, but had found nothing to en-
lighten him about a matter of this kind, and he didn't
want to go to a minister until he knew where he stood.
He would, he told himself, feel embarrassed as it was,
going to a parson, as he'd never put his foot inside a
church since he was christened.

Doctor Carr's eyes were whisky hazed as he looked across
his desk at Angus, but nevertheless he listened intently
to him. His interest had been caught from the moment
the young fellow had mentioned the Ratcliffe girl, and
he was both astonished and absolutely tickled pink when
he heard what he intended to do. Lord, but wouldn't this
hit Jonathan Ratcliffe where it hurt most. The situation
gave him a feeling of glee never engendered by the whisky,
without which he was finding, more and more, he was
unable to get through a day's work. But before he advised
the young fellow what to do he would ask him a question.
He asked it bluntly. "You the father of her child?" he
said.

"No, I'm not." The answer was equally blunt.

"Oh, well, you know you'll get the blame for it when you marry her?"

"That doesn't matter to me."

Doctor Carr surveyed Emily Cotton's son. He was a good-looking fellow in a way, well made, tough looking, but working class written all over him. It was a pity he wasn't her type. He said, "I think it's like this. You'd have to have their consent to a register office marriage, but if your banns are called three times at your parish church and nobody raises any objection the marriage can go ahead, and it's legal. I think that's one set-up. It's a bit tricky but it's been done. Anyway there's always the court. You present him with that alternative and if I know Ratcliffe he'll soon sign because in her condition the verdict would be a foregone conclusion. Which parish are you in?" He asked the question of himself. "Oh, you must be in St. Edward's. You frequent any church?"

"No."

"Have you ever?"

"No."

"Where were you christened?"

"I think it was St. Edward's. I don't know but my mother will."

"Well now, if I know anything about St. Edward's, it's dying on its feet, and but for a few old dears that go there the place is almost empty. I don't think the name Ratcliffe will have any significance for them. It's worth trying. I advise you to go and see the minister. He's like his church, very old, and he mumbles, which is another good thing in your favour. Take her along with you. You'll both look like an ordinary couple doing the usual thing." He got to his feet and came round the desk, and when he was confronting Angus, he said, "And good luck to you." He didn't add "You'll need it"; that went without saying.

The following evening Angus brought Vanessa in the lorry to the vicarage, and in a musty, dim lit room he asked that the banns for their marriage should be put up.

The old man repeated her name twice. "Ratcliffe. Ratcliffe," then he peered at her and said, "Hm! Hm! You will want your birth certificate and your parents' consent." They couldn't be sure if he recognised her or not. Angus had the idea that he might not be as old and doddery as he looked.

When they came out Vanessa had her head buried deep in her coat collar. She seemed afraid to look up; or, he wondered, was she ashamed to. He hoisted her up into the cab and then he drove her home to Ryder's Row.

Again there was only Emily in the house. Rosie had refused point-bank to meet her future sister-in-law; there was nobody going to look down her nose at her, not if she could help it. Although Emily had said far better stay and get it over, she had replied, "Not me. You might have to, but not me." And now Emily stood self-consciously in her own kitchen looking at the girl she had practically brought up, and she saw her as a stranger. Physically she was changed. Her body naturally had filled out, not only her stomach but her face, and also naturally she looked older. Emily also saw that the girl had entirely gone. Here was a lass, a lass in a jam, and the jam had made her calculating. That was how she saw Vanessa now, and in consequence the feeling she gave out was one of resentment.

"Well, Mam; here we are." Angus looked at Emily, then turned to Vanessa and said, "Sit down, sit yourself down." But Vanessa did not sit down, she stared back at Emily and said softly, "Hello, Emily."

"Hello." There was no Miss Van now, not even Van.

Angus sensed that the situation was going to be more awkward than he had bargained for, and the best thing he could do was to leave them alone for a while, so loudly he exclaimed, "Look. I'm as hungry as a hunter; I'll slip along and get some fish. All right?" He cast his glance down at Vanessa, and she nodded at him and tried to smile, for he was, she knew, doing his best to help matters along.

They sat silent for a time after the door had banged, before Vanessa said softly, "I'm sorry, Emily."

"Aye. An' you've reason to be; you've brought a lot of trouble on a lot of people." She moved about the kitchen before she went on, "And if he isn't the father why are you marryin' him?"

"Be . . . because I like Angus and because he wanted me to marry him."

"You like him!" Emily stopped and, turning, faced Vanessa. "Lots of people like him. Likin' him isn't enough, it'll be for life. You know likin' isn't enough if he's goin' to look after your bairn and give you some of his own. You don't get by just on likin'. Not one of his own sort wouldn't have got by just on likin' But you've got a thousand and one obstacles in your way; I suppose you know that?"

"Yes, Emily; I know that."

"Look round you. Look round you, lass." She was bending towards her. "This is where we live. This is where he lives. Come here." She pulled Vanessa towards the front room and, thrusting open the door and switching on the light, she said, "This is his room. That will be your room. Look at it."

Vanessa looked. Compared to the one she had just left it could be termed a palace.

"We're cramped for space as it is, but just imagine, with you and the bairn here . . . And there's another thing I'll tell you." She turned her about and, pulling her almost roughly into the middle of the kitchen again and pointing to another door, said, "That's the scullery in there. Talk about swinging a cat. Two of us can only just get in together. And beyond that is the door leading into the yard, and at the bottom is the lav. Not the loo here, the lav. Sick or well, wet or fine, you go down the yard to the lav, or do it in your room and have it under the bed. This is the way some folks still have to live."

Vanessa closed her eyes and Emily, letting go of her

arm, thrust herself around and said, "I'm puttin' it plainly to you; I'm lettin' you see what you're in for. You were brought up with carpets in the lavatories, carpets in the bathrooms, powders and scents and creams, bath sprays, the lot. You're goin' to find this very different."

Vanessa could say nothing in her own defence; there was nothing really to say; she only knew that she wanted to placate Emily. "I've been living without all these things for some months now, Emily," she said. "I'll . . . I'll be quite pleased to live here if . . . if you'll have me."

"If I'll have you?" Emily's voice was flat now and her face held a dead expression as she turned and looked at Vanessa again, "I haven't much choice, lass, have I? I know it's my house; my name appears on the rent book, but Angus has always been the head of it since his dad died, even before, because my man was sick for years. And although I keep sayin' I can look after meself I've been on me feet too long." She slapped her legs. "They're lettin' me down an' they're not going to get any better. I know that. It's water. They'll get worse. All the doctor's medicine won't cure what I've got. I stood in your mother's kitchen for years just for one thing, so that your father would push my lad on. And now see where it's got me. Do you know something?" Again she bent towards Vanessa. "I just can't believe this is happenin'; I think I'm in a sort of a dream, or at the pictures. Daughter of influential man marries fitter . . . Daughter of influential man marries cook's son . . . Daughter of influential man lives in slum. An' that's what the papers 'll say when they get hold of it. At least the local one will, unless your father plonks down on them, 'cos he's got shares in that company, hasn't he?"

Vanessa said nothing. She was trying her hardest not to cry, because she knew that if she cried Angus would blame Emily. She sat down abruptly on a wooden chair near the table and, supporting her face with her hands, she muttered brokenly, "Emily, I said I'm sorry and I am, but . . .

191

but I'm very tired, I'm sort of lost. When . . . when Angus came that day to my room the first time, I was . . . I was thinking about finishing it all. I'd lain in that awful place for three days and the only person I'd seen was my landlady, and then only once. I wanted to die. If I'd had enough aspirins or tablets, I would have taken them. Angus was the first person who had spoken a kind word to me in weeks, except the woman whom I worked for in the greengrocer's shop; and then she was a very brusque kind of person." She lifted her eyes and looked at Emily. She could have added, "Just like you."

There was silence between them again, and Emily turned to the fire and stared into it. Then after a moment she gave a deep sigh and said flatly, "Well, what's done's done, I suppose. But it's no use sayin', lass, that I'm goin' to welcome you with open arms because I can't. And then there's our Rosie. You're goin' to put Rosie at a disadvantage."

"Oh, no. No, I won't, Emily; I – I've always got on with Rosie."

"You've spoken to her kindly, but she's always been tongue-tied in your presence. Think back. Has Rosie ever chatted with you like Angus has? No. There's as big a difference between Rosie and you as between him and you. Only he's got sex on his side. Oh! Oh!" She raised her hand. "He's a man. That breaks down barriers of a sort, but not atween women, not atween lasses. You've got every advantage over my Rosie; and Rosie's no fool, she knows it." She came now to the table and, bending down quite close to Vanessa, she asked quietly, "It isn't his, is it?"

"No, Emily, no."

"Well, why didn't you say who it was and get him to marry you?"

They were staring at each other, and then Vanessa said, "I couldn't do that, Emily."

"Does he know who it is?"

192

"No."

"Do you think that's fair to him?"

Vanessa turned her gaze away, then said, "Fair or not, I can't ever tell him."

Emily straightened up, then walked away, saying, "Well, you're not out of the wood yet. You know what'll happen if your father gets wind of this? He'll come storming along here again . . . ."

"I don't think so, Emily. He'll close his eyes to it. I'm quite dead to them, at least him. I'm sure of that. I've just realised lately that he's always disliked me."

At this point the door was thrust open and Angus came in carrying three paper bags, and the kitchen reeked with the smell of fish and chips.

"Haven't you got the plates warmed?" He looked at his mother. "What you been up to?" His voice was loud, covering the embarrassment that pervaded the three of them.

"Put them in the oven a minute," said Emily; "the plates won't take a tick."

A few minutes later they were sitting at the table eating the fish and chips. At least Emily made an attempt to, but all of a sudden she got to her feet and, taking her plate and thrusting it back in the oven, she said, "It's not ten minutes ago I had me tea, I'll have them after. I'll make a drink." And on this she went into the scullery.

Angus looked up at Vanessa under his eyelids. She had stopped eating. He put his hand out and pressed hers; then silently he mouthed the words, "It'll be all right."

Fifteen minutes later they left the house, and on the journey back to Newcastle they hardly exchanged a word, and not until they were standing in her room did he ask, "How did she take it?"

"Not very well, Angus."

"She'll get over it; she'll come round; I know me mam."

"It isn't fair to her. I . . . we could get a room somewhere . . ."

"We're getting no rooms anywhere, Vanessa. If you're marrying me, as I said you're comin' home; I'm not leaving her to God and good neighbours. There's too many does that the day. Round our place it's littered with old folks livin' alone. Well, she's had it hard enough. And I'm not being easy on her now; I know that, but I'm not making it worse by walking out on her. I explained it all to you . . . ."

"Oh, I know, Angus, I know. I'm sorry, but I've been thinking. Is it wise to . . .?" She stared into his eyes, and after a moment he said, "You're going to marry me. It's settled, so just take things as they come, one at a time. The next hurdle you've got to get over is our Rosie. She won't be as easy as me mam, so prepare yourself . . . . Well now, I'd better be gettin' back; I've got to get up early in the mornin'. I'll see you the morrow night, same time."

He made no move towards her; all he said was, "Ta-rah!" and he smiled at her and went out. And she went and sat on the side of the bed, and slowly her head drooped in her hands and as the tears fell through her fingers she muttered, "Oh, God! Oh, God! What am I doing? It isn't fair to him, it isn't. Oh Brett . . . . You! You!" Her thoughts ground to a standstill on her clenched teeth, and she rocked herself back and forward, much the same as Emily would have done.

4

Jonathan Ratcliffe heard of the banns being called in St. Edward's through Mr. Wilton. Mr. Wilton was standing at the other side of the desk, his face showing deep concern as he explained how he had come by the knowledge. One of the men in the fitting shop had a mother who attended St. Edward's. She had heard the names being called and had put two and two together. Mr. Wilton thought Mr. Ratcliffe should know.

Jonathan Ratcliffe looked at his subordinate and was unable to speak; then after a moment he thanked him and nodded his dismissal. As Mr. Wilton went out of the door he was about to call him back and tell him to keep this knowledge to himself when he realized that Wilton would be the last but one in the whole works who had remained in ignorance of the situation between his daughter and Cotton.

He picked up a steel ruler and endeavoured to break it between his clenched fists. The slut! The low, low slut! The scheming little hussy. It was only three or four days ago that she had written to her mother thanking her for sending her birth certificate, the birth certificate that was supposed to be required by an employer. It had never dawned on them for a moment why she wanted her birth certificate. My God! And she was in the town. But that last letter had been postmarked Islington . . . . Islington. She could never have been in Islington; you had to reside at least three weeks in the parish where you were to be married. The scheming . . . ! The treacherous . . . ! Words failed him. He rang his secretary and told her to get his wife on the phone.

All Jane Ratcliffe could say to her husband's information was, "Oh, no! Oh, no! But how?" and again "Oh, no! Oh, no!" Then she asked, "What are you going to do?"

"I'll tell you when I get in," he answered and rammed the phone down . . . .

And he told her immediately he entered the house, even before he had taken his coat off. After asking, "Is anyone in?" and getting her answer "No," he said, "Can you believe it?"

She shook her head. "No, I can't make it out," she said. "How did she send the letters from those various places?"

"He likely manoeuvred that for her." And he hit on part of the truth by saying, "Lorry driver. Long-distance lorry drivers. That could be it. Taking her letters down there . . . . And to think you sent that birth certificate and it was picked up and returned to this very town."

"How was I to know? What are we going to do?"

"I'm going to put a stop to it. Anyway he can't do it without our consent, but by God he's likely forged that. I know what he's up to. Once he's married her he thinks I'll come round, and there'll be a place for him well up the ladder in Affleck's. He was never more mistaken in his life."

"Do you really think that's his intention?" Her question was tentative and conveyed her doubts and brought him barking, "Of course, woman! I know him and all his type. He thinks I won't be able to bear them being in this town together, not her living in that quarter and us up here. And he's right. But his plans are going a little awry." He now beat his fist into the palm of his hand as he cried, "That girl! she must have a defective streak in her. That's it." He nodded at his wife as if he had discovered the root of the trouble, then went on, "I'll straighten that out when I get her home. I'll have her put in care. I will. I will."

"You're going to fetch her home?"

"Just that. And then we're taking her to your Aunt Jean's, and we're taking her ourselves, every step of the road. And then you're staying with her for as long as is necessary."

"Oh, Jonathan! I . . . I can't do that. How are you going to . . .?"

"Look, woman. Put first things first. I'll manage and see to Ray."

It was as if by speaking his son's name he had conjured the boy up, for he turned his eyes slightly to the side towards the passage leading to the kitchen, and there he saw his son standing. This was a thing that annoyed him about the boy; he was always standing in dark corners listening. He yelled at him, "Come out of that!"

When Ray walked slowly into the hall he said angrily, "You've been listening again."

"Not really. Not really, Father; I was just coming out of the kitchen."

"I've told you about it, haven't I?"

"Yes, Father."

"What did you hear?"

The boy glanced at his mother, then back to his father again and said, "About Vanessa going to marry Angus Cotton."

As Jonathan Ratcliffe ground his teeth his wife said, "It can't do any harm now, no matter what he hears."

As her husband stalked into the drawing-room she took hold of the boy and drew him into the kitchen, and there she said to him, "Now mind, Ray, I'm warning you, don't discuss this with Michael. Remember, Michael is only a little boy; you shouldn't talk to him about things that happen in the house. I've told you, haven't I?"

"Yes, Mother." He stared fixedly at her. He wasn't afraid of his mother; he wasn't really afraid of his father;

197

well, just a little bit. He knew something he would like to tell his father just to see him go red in the face and nearly choke, like he did when he was in a temper. He had forgotten about it for a long time now, but hearing his father talking about Vanessa going to marry Angus had brought it back to his mind. He liked to be able to surprise people. He knew he would have spoken about it before if Uncle Arthur hadn't killed himself, yet he knew that his knowledge was somehow connected with Uncle Arthur killing himself.

The next best thing to surprising his father was to surprise his mother. He said to her now under his breath, "I didn't think Vanessa would marry Angus, I thought she would marry Uncle Arthur."

"What did you say?"

"I said I thought Vanessa would marry Uncle Arthur, that he'd give up Aunt Irene and marry her, Vanessa, like they do after a divorce. There were three boys in our form whose parents were divorced."

Jane Ratcliffe was sitting down now. She had hold of her son's shoulders and was staring into his face. Her lips were moving, but no words issued from them for some time. And then she whispered, "Ray, what are you saying? Come along, tell me what you know. What makes you think Vanessa should have married Uncle Arthur?"

"Well," he shrugged his thin shoulders and moved his dark, satanic eyebrows upwards, "they used to kiss and slop."

She was doing now what she had never done before, she was shaking her son as if he was a rat, and for the first time in his short life he himself was really frightened. When her hands were still again but still gripping his shoulders, she muttered thickly, "Tell me, boy, tell me everything. Everything mind."

His head seemed to be still wobbling and he jerked it once before he said, "Well, I saw them kissing."

"You saw them . . .?" She swallowed deeply. "Yes, go on."

"I used to go out at night down the drainpipe, and one night I saw her go down the wood and when she came back Uncle Arthur was with her, and they stood by the gate talking, and he kissed her. I was up in the tree house."

"Go on."

"And another time I followed her and she and Uncle Brett were in the summerhouse."

His mother was gripping his shoulders so hard that he hunched them up against his head, and when she relaxed her hold and again said, "Go on," he continued, "Well I saw them sitting on the steps. Uncle Arthur was talking and then they were kissing and things."

He was surprised the way his mother started calling on God. He had never heard anybody say things like that, except Emily.

There was a long silence now before she said, "Why didn't you tell me this before?"

"Well – well, I didn't want to give Vanessa away; I – I knew she would get wrong. And then Uncle went away and I forgot about it until he came back."

"What happened when he came back?"

He bowed his head, then said, "She went into the wood, but – but I didn't follow her; I was waiting for Michael. He had promised to sneak out and I thought he would be frightened if I wasn't there and go indoors again. We were going to sleep there all night."

"Yes, yes, go on."

"Well I saw Uncle and Vanessa at the gate, the wood gate, and she was crying and he kissed her."

He was now looking down right on to the crown of his mother's head. He looked at it for a long time before she brought herself up and said to him in a funny voice, "Come on."

When they entered the dining-room she checked what

her husband was about to say in a voice that caught his attention. "Ray's got something to tell you," she said.

He looked at her face for a moment longer, then turned to his son and said, "Yes, what is it?"

"I think you'd better sit down."

He stared at her hard again, but sat down, and she pushed Ray towards him, saying, "Tell your father what you've just told me . . . all of it."

Jonathan Ratcliffe said not one word as his son talked haltingly, but when the boy was finished speaking he rose from the chair, pushed his son to one side and walked out of the room, across the hall and into his study. A moment later Jane Ratcliffe joined him, and at the first sight of him she was afraid of what might happen. He looked as if he was on the point of a seizure. His complexion was both red and grey, and the greyness around his mouth had paled to a sickly white. She dared not speak in case she said the wrong thing and incited him more.

When he spoke he surprised her because he didn't speak immediately of his daughter but of Arthur Brett, and not about what Arthur had done to Vanessa but what Arthur had done to him. "You see," he said; "you see why he did it? To spite me. He planned it; he planned it every step of the road; he did it to get his own back. I always knew he'd do something one day. He took it too quietly years ago, too smoothly. He must have been boiling against me all this time; behind that quiet smile of his he was hatching this. He wanted some way to bring me low, and he knew exactly how to do it. And he timed it, he timed it that the balloon would go up before the wedding. Don't you see? DON'T YOU SEE?"

No, she didn't see, not quite the way he was seeing it. For once she saw a situation in its true light, an older man, an unhappy man, playing on the sensitive nerves of a young girl at her most impressionable age. She dared to say now, "No, don't look at it like that, Jonathan; I'm sure he – "

"You're sure of nothing, woman. I know, I know. Everything fits. He had refused my offer to send him abroad in the first place. Then he got cold feet and thought he'd better get out of the way. The swine. The dirty swine. He expected the balloon to burst while he was away, when she found out she was pregnant . . . and he hoped she would be. You mark my words." He was stabbing his finger towards her. "That's what he was aiming at, her pregnancy. Then he would come back and gloat."

"But," she felt she had to reason with him, "but he took his life, Jonathan. He didn't gloat, he took his life."

"Yes, to spite me, so that people who didn't know the real facts would say he had done it out of frustration. He had done it because I had walked over his head; that's what they would say. He had been brooding over the injustices for years; that's what they did say."

She knew it wasn't any good trying to combat at the moment his irrational way of thinking, nor in fact in the future; Jonathan was a law unto himself; he would think what he wanted to think; but she voiced now what had been in her mind from the moment Ray had spoken. "And we accused Angus," she said.

He stared at her, trying to collect his whirling thoughts, Angus, Angus Cotton. And he was going to marry her. Well, this only confirmed what he had known all along – that slob was determined to rise. Ten minutes ago he was determined to put his spoke in his wheel, but now, no, no, he'd let him get on with it, because one thing was utterly vital: not a breath of this latest development must come to light.

It was evident that she hadn't told Cotton who the father was and he was taking her on trust, on trust that he thought was going to pay off a good dividend later on. Oh yes, Cotton's type did nothing for nothing; he was ambitious, he was a climber. Being one himself, he thought he recognized the same traits when he met them in another man.

She said now, "What are you going to do about them? I mean about them marrying?"

He hadn't enough cool nerve to go on looking at her as he said, "Let them get on with it."

"You mean, you're not going to do anything?" she was addressing his back.

"Just that," He turned to her again. "I'd even give them consent, for this thing mustn't leak out. Do you hear? Fetch that boy in. He's got to understand that he must never mention this to a soul. If she's kept quiet we can keep quiet. We've got to. I – we'd be the laughing stock of the town if it leaked out. The past scandal would be nothing compared to what it would be if it was known that Brett," he ground his teeth, "the dirty, dirty swine had given her the child."

"You don't think they know, they guessed? I mean next door? Irene and Colin and Paul?"

"Don't be stupid, woman." His voice was filled with scorn. "Do you think that Irene would have kept that to herself? And did we guess?"

"No. But knowing Irene. Yes, I think she would have kept it to herself if she had known."

"Nonsense! Nonsense! That kind of a woman couldn't keep anything to herself. Go on and bring the boy in. And one more thing. Don't breathe a word to Susan about this, mind. Do you hear me?"

"I hear you; you've got no need to stress the point," she said.

She did not go immediately into the lounge but stood in the hall trying to collect herself. For weeks now her feelings had been softening towards her errant daughter. She imagined her travelling from one job to another, from one place to another, and the baby's birth getting nearer and nearer, but now her duplicity had wiped away any lingering tenderness. Granted she had been taken advantage of by an older man, but that was no reason why she should now resort to marrying a person like Angus Cotton, someone who was the antithesis of all she had been brought up to expect in a man and a gentleman. She could see herself now accepting the child knowing it was Arthur's, because after all Arthur had been a gentleman; but Emily's Angus! Well, he was nothing more than an uncouth, gauche, ignorant individual, and in marrying him her daughter was indeed sinking to the depths. And there, as Jonathan had implied, she must be allowed to wallow.

It was, after all, a comfort to her that she saw eye to eye with her husband over this unhappy affair.

5

They were married at ten o'clock on a Saturday morning. Emily wasn't present, nor was Rosie, but Stan acted as Angus's best man and the verger made the other witness. When the short service was over Vanessa couldn't believe that she was now married, and to Angus Cotton.

As she stood in the vestry she had an overpowering desire to turn and fly out of the church, fly out of the town, to put as much space between herself and him as possible. But she liked Angus, for he was the only one who had been kind to her, the only one who had stood by her; the only one who had accepted her condition and hadn't asked questions, at least after the night he asked her to marry him. And now she was married to him and the enormity of the step she had taken loomed over her like a dark canopy.

Yet she felt she could live with Angus and know a modicum of happiness if it was possible for them to be alone. But she was going back to that tiny little house which was filled with Emily . . . and Rosie, and she was frightened, frightened of them both.

She had lodged with Stan's mother for the past three weeks, so fulfilling the requirements of living in the parish during the calling of the banns. Stan's mother was a quiet woman who asked no questions and talked mostly about the weather, and her Stan. She wished they were going back there, or that, things being as they were, they were returning straight home – she thought of it now as home –

so that she would get the meeting with her new mother-in-law and sister-in-law over. But Angus had arranged that they would spend the day in Newcastle. She didn't wonder why this was; she knew it had to do with Emily and Rosie.

And it had, it definitely had. Angus thanked Stan and said rather sheepishly they would have a drink later – which term gave no indication of time. Then he bade him good-bye, and Stan, after awkwardly shaking hands with Vanessa, wished her, ironically, the best of luck, following which he took his departure with unconcealed haste.

At this moment, more than at any time in his life, Angus wanted company, lots of company. If someone had told him years ago that one day he could have Aladdin's lamp and three wishes, he would have used all three to wish that he could some day marry a lass like Vanessa Ratcliffe; and now Aladdin's lamp had been rubbed and he had married, not an imitation of Vanessa Ratcliffe, but Vanessa Ratcliffe herself, and the fact had stilled his tongue, made him self-conscious, yet elated, and at the same time sad, sad because his mother had refused to come to the church.

Last night there had been hell to pay. "You still goin' through with it?" she had said. "God Almighty, Mam!" he had bawled back at her. "Haven't you got it into your head yet? I'm marryin' her the morrow. Come hell-fire or high water, I'm marrying her the morrow." And to this she had said quietly, which made it all the worse, "Aye, well, I hope you don't live to regret it."

Then May had come in. One or other of them had used May as a last straw. Neither of them had liked May; May was common. Aye, there were grades below 24 Ryder's Row.

May was standing at the kitchen table when he came out of the room ready to go and meet Vanessa, and she had said, "Hello there, Angus." And he grinned sheepishly and replied, "Oh hello, there, May. How you keepin'?" To which she had replied, "How do you think?" She would never have made this answer, not within those four walls, if she hadn't had his mother and Rosie behind her.

Rosie and his mam had gone upstairs and left them alone and May said to him, "Is it right that you're gettin' married the morrow?" and he had answered quietly, "Yes, May. I'm sorry an' all that, but it's right." And to this, and with her voice as quiet as his, she had said, "You know what you are, Angus Cotton; you're a lousy, rotten twister, you're nothin' but a stinking bugger. I've been good enough for you on an' off for years; I've served your purpose, haven't I? Every time I made a break from you an' got a decent fellow, up you'd pop again and wag your little finger and expect me to come runnin'. And being the bloody fool that I am, I came runnin'. And now this. But don't think you'll get off with it; you'll get paid out one way or the other."

At this point he had asked her had she quite finished, and she had replied, "Not by a long chalk. You'd have been married already, and to me, wouldn't you, if I hadn't been such a bloody fool as to tell you the truth?" Her voice was weighed now with bitterness. "You can do it every night in the week and with as many as you like, can't you? But because I was honest and told you of the other two you cooled off. Like a parson at a strip-tease, you melted away."

When he hadn't answered her she moved towards the door and from there she said, "Well, I wish you joy of her, and from what I hear you'll need it. She'll make you feel like a worm, that's after she gets rid of the bairn. Once she's had the bairn she won't be scared out of her wits any more. She won't want a life-belt then. It makes a difference having a bairn. I should know, shouldn't I? And when she wakes up and sees the big galoot that she's married she'll ask herself if she was clean barmy, because she will wake up. Oh aye, she will, an' then you can look out, Mr. Bloody Big-Head."

What had upset him more than anything she had said was when she looked around the room and put her head back and laughed mirthlessly, saying, "And you're bringing her back to this? God Almighty! Even I wouldn't have stood for that. I'm goin' to wish you luck, big boy, because you're goin' to need it. And how! . . . Who put the overalls in Mrs. Murphy's chowder." She ended on a saying that she usually fitted to situations that puzzled or were beyond her. It had always made him want to belly laugh. May had had the knack of making him belly laugh. Vanessa would never have that kind of knack.

They were sitting in the bus now and he turned to her and asked, "All right?" She smiled faintly at him as she answered, "Yes, Angus." After a moment he said, "We're going to have a spot of lunch, then have a look round." He paused. "Is there anything you would like?"

"Like? What do you mean?"

"Something for yourself." He was smiling into her eyes now. "Wedding present, sort of."

"No, Angus, thank you very much."

"Nothing?" The smile had gone from his face.

"Well," she lowered her head and shook it slightly, "I haven't thought; perhaps later."

"Yes, aye." He looked ahead again.

They had lunch, then they went to the cinema. They sat side by side and he didn't take her hand. He hadn't touched her in any way except to put the ring on her finger. He hadn't even kissed her at the service, and the minister had made no comment on it. What he would do later on the night, he didn't know. The separate beds would help.

That had been another hell-raising moment when the other single bed had been delivered at the house. On this occasion his mother had bawled at him, "Well you are marryin' her, aren't you? Look . . . if you want my advice you'll start the way you mean to go on. There's a sayin': You've made your bed and you must lie on it, but there's

207

another sayin': If you don't make your bed the first night, whether it's through being sozzled or not havin' it in you, then there's little chance you'll do any better the second, or the third."

She was a coarse old bitch when all was said and done, and he had told her so. But she had replied that he was already trying to jump the fence to Van's side where nothing was looked at squarely because it wasn't the thing to do, but he wasn't cut out for politeness, and he would soon find that it was choking him. Her words stirred a tiny fear that she might be right.

It was around seven when they came out of the pictures, and there was a cold drizzle falling, and as they stood under a lamp he said, "What about a bite to eat, eh?"

She pulled her coat collar up under her chin, and she looked up at him for a moment before she answered, "I'd rather go home, Angus."

He smiled broadly. "Good idea. Good idea."

He had wanted to put the going home off to the very last minute when he hoped both Emily and Rosie would be in bed. To-morrow morning everything would look different; everybody would take a different slant at each other; but now she had said she would rather go home, and in a way he knew she was right. Far better get it over with. Anyway, they would likely be out at the club. One thing was certain, Rosie wouldn't be in; Stan would see to that. Stan was a good fellow at bottom.

It took much longer to get from Newcastle to Fellburn by train than it did by lorry, and then they caught a bus from the station to the end of the street. It was pouring with rain when they alighted and he took her by the arm and ran her across the road, and he kept her in the shelter of the railway wall until they were almost opposite the door. But as he made to cross over to the pavement he stopped. He had heard the singing farther up the street but he hadn't thought it was coming from their house. The Conways usually had their wireless blazing away at all hours, but this wasn't the wireless or telly, it was singing. voices singing. There was a difference.

When he pushed open the front door the sound hit them like the backwash of a huge wave. The voices were all raised on the last line of a dated song: "Now is the Hour." His hold tightened on Vanessa's arm as he stared along the dimly lit passage. God! She had gone and got company in, which told him one thing even before he saw her, she was bottled. She wasn't the one for having neighbours in. Only twice before in his life had he known her do this, and on both occasions she had been burnt up inside with anger.

He stood in the kitchen doorway almost in front of Vanessa looking at the company. He was surprised to see Stan there, but the look that Stan gave him said, "I couldn't do anything with them," and he could see that for himself, because Rosie had had a skinful too.

There was Alf Piggott and his missus from down the street, and Bill Wilson and his missus from next door. Bill had his old concertina on his knee; they weren't relying on the television or the wireless the night. His mother always said she hated the sound of Bill's concertina, but she was singing to it now. As the song ended on different notes, the visitors all turned and greeted him, saying in different ways, "Congratulations, lad." They didn't say anything to the bride; they just looked at her, and not at her face but at her distended shape, and grinned.

What Emily said was, "Well, it's a weddin', isn't it?" She stared across the room at her son, but even her glance did not take in Vanessa. "Come on." She got to her feet. "Some of the old 'uns, Bill. Cock-o-doodle. Play Cock-o-doodle. If you don't I'll bloody well do me poetry piece again:

"I hear in the chamber above me the patter of little feet. Da-da, de-da, de-da.

Do you think, O blue-eyed banditti,
Because you have scaled the wall,
Such an old moustache as I am
Is not a match for you all?"

"Cock-o-doodle, for God's sake!" cried Rosie, and after a moment's hesitation Bill was playing "Cock-o-doodle" and Emily and the others were singing. But Emily's voice was louder than the rest.

"Cock-o-doodle, cock-o-doodle,
I'm the cock of the North.
Cock-o-doodle, cock-o-doodle,
I'm the cock of the North.
Me faather went out on a Saturda' night
After giving me ma a bairn;
He filled up with rum
And came doddering back
And tried to give her mairn."

With the quickness of a freak wave, anger rose in him. Grabbing hold of Vanessa, he pushed her past Alf Taggart's chair, then in front of Stan, and to his room door, and, thrusting it open, he went inside with her, saying grimly under his breath, "It'll be all right. Stay there." When he returned to the kitchen his mother was singing,

"He killed five thousand Irishmen
In the battle of the boiling water."

Over and over again he had told her that it wasn't the boiling water, it was the Boyne Water, but now he was boiling. He yelled at her, "Stop it! Do you hear me? Stop it!"

"What! It's a weddin', isn't it? It's a weddin'. Everybody's merry at a weddin'. What do you say, Bill? What do you say, Rosie? We know it's a weddin', don't we?" She punched her daughter on the shoulder, and Rosie punched her back, crying,

"You wouldn't take your mother's device,
You wouldn't take your faather's device,
But you took Barney Rooney's device,
And now you've got your belly full of Barney
    Rooney."

As the company, with the exception of Stan, howled their appreciation of this quip, Angus's hand drew back above his sister's head. It was only Stan catching at his arm and crying, "Steady on! Steady on, Angus," that checked the blow.

"Get out! Do you hear me?" Angus now swept the Piggotts and Wilsons with a look that brought them swiftly to their feet, and when he added, "Quick, the bloody lot of you!" the male in Mr. Piggott rose and he turned on Angus, and shouted, "Now look here, lad, don't try any of your big – "

"OUT!"

"Whose house do you think this is, eh?" Emily grabbed at the back of Angus's coat, and he swung swiftly round, almost sending her to the floor as he said, "Shut your mouth, you!" Then he turned his attention to his sister who was standing by the table blinking at him. "Get up the stairs. "Go on now."

"By damn, you won't tell me what to – "

Stan, now pulling Rosie to the door, said, "Give over. Give over. Look, go on up. Do as he says. I'll see you the morrow."

"You're as bad as him. Why, you bugger, you're as bad as him!"

"Go on." Stan pushed her into the passage and towards the stairs. "Go on now."

There was only Angus and Emily left in the kitchen, but the walls seemed to be pressing outwards with the bitterness between them. Emily was sitting by the table, her forearms on it; she was staring at her hands and her head was moving in small, pathetic jerks. He stared down at her, love, compassion and understanding all fighting for a place in his thoughts, fighting against the words of recrimination he wanted to pour on her, fighting against his hate of her. Bending his big head down to hers, he gritted out below his breath. "That was a bloody dirty trick to play."

Slowly she lifted her eyes to his and her fuddled gaze swept over his face before she brought out thickly, "I take after me son, playin' bloody dirty tricks." He straightened up and her eyes were still holding his when he said, "I'll talk to you in the mornin' when you're sober."

She rose unsteadily to her feet; her eyes had never moved from his face and she took two unsteady steps away from him as she muttered, "I might be sober in the mornin', lad, an' in me right senses, but not you; things'll happen to you from now on like as if you'd taken to drugs. Mark my words. You think she's taken your name but she hasn't, lad; you've taken hers, and you're going to break your bloody neck tryin' to keep up with her. Well, you can go on breakin' it, I'll leave you to it."

She shambled past him and he said nothing, but he turned and watched her go out of the passage and up the stairs. He watched her until he saw her grotesquely swollen feet and ankles disappear from view through the stair railings; then turning to the fire he stood staring down into it, until, with a swift movement, he brought his clenched fist hard against his forehead. The action caused him to screw up his eyes tightly and he held his fist motionless for some minutes before he dropped his hand.

The house was quiet now and he looked towards his room door. Then the habit of years taking over, he followed the nightly pattern and went down to the bottom of the yard.

When he returned to the kitchen he stood confounded for a moment as to how he was going to tell her to do the same. How different it would have been with May; there would have been no feeling of delicacy in mentioning a lavatory to May; rather it would have evoked laughter. He went into the room.

Vanessa had not even taken her outdoor things off. She was sitting on his chair near the little table; her bag was on her knee and her cases were standing near the wall, where he had left them last night. He went to her and said softly, "It's all right; she'd had a drop." He refrained from saying that it was rarely she did anything like this, it would only have worsened matters. He made his lips move into a smile as he added, "She'll be herself in the mornin'."

"She won't, Angus."

"What do you mean?"

"You know what I mean . . . We couldn't . . . ?"

"No, we couldn't, Van." He bent his head down until his face was on a level with hers. "We've had this out. I've got to look after her; not only with money, you understand. Oh, I dare say she would get along with supplementary and one thing and another, but she needs me here; she's always needed me. I explained it all to you about me father. I've been the man in her life, if you can put it like that. She's had nobody else, and she's just lived for me. Whatever happens now I'm stuck with her, whether I like it or not. Sometimes I like it fine, other times, like the night, I don't like it one bit."

Vanessa sat looking at him. She was sick and weary, weary in her mind and body. She wondered vaguely why this should be happening to her, why she had ever let herself be talked into marrying him. She was finding things out about him all the time, things that repulsed her secretly; the depths of his crudity, the depths of his ignorance; yet there were other depths, such as his depths of loyalty, the feeling of responsibility he had towards Emily, which feeling she imagined outweighed all others in his life, even his love for her.

Intuitively, because he had never put it into words, she knew that he was in love with her, that he had always been in love with her, and that although he had found her when she was at rock bottom, he was nevertheless flattered that she should consent to marry him. But he covered this up with his off-hand and casual attitude towards her. She also knew that she was afraid of him, afraid of his body and what it might do to her.

"Come on." He held out his hand, pulling her up. "You're tired. It's been a day. Get ready for bed."

Perhaps it was the small jerk of her fingers within his grasp that made him say brusquely, "Oh, it's all right, don't worry. There," he pointed to the opposite corner from where his bed stood, "that's yours. At least for the time being." He did not add "until the bairn comes". Although why he was considering the bairn he didn't know; they said it thrived on a little action, and women liked it at this time; brought them a sort of comfort. Well maybe. And that was all right if they had been at it from the beginning, but to take her now, no, he couldn't. He looked at her blankly for a moment. She looked neither Vanessa Ratcliffe, Miss Van, nor Vanessa Cotton. She was a girl with a protruding stomach and a weary face, and eyes with a sadness in them that seemed to be drawn from the very pit of her.

When he turned from her and said, "By the way, if you want it, it's down at the bottom of the yard," her head drooped and she went towards the door, pulling off her head scarf as she did so. It was this act that brought a deep embarrassment to them both, for as she flicked the scarf downwards it caught at one of the little ornaments on the mantelpiece and she was only just in time to save it. The ornament was of blue Venetian glass; it was six inches high and stood on a base of silver, so tarnished now as hardly to be recognizable as such. From its narrow base the vase mounted outwards to a fluted top, and as her fingers gripped the scalloped edge she remembered that her mother had always considered it a nice little vase for roses; they didn't topple out. The vase's disappearance had been noted after one of the dailies had left. Over the years the household had come to look on dailies as members of a pilfering gang, for always, after their departure, something was missing, and, as Emily had said to her mother, "It's not a bit of use going after them, they've likely sold it, and you'd have to pin it on them anyway."

She placed the vase slowly back on the mantelpiece among the bric-a-brac. When she lifted her head Angus was looking at her.

"God blast her!" He had forgotten about all her perks, because she hadn't brought home anything of value for some time as there hadn't been anybody to pin the blame on; not that she would have let them stand the racket if there had been any possibility of them being caught. She was thoughtful that way. But the house was dotted with bits and pieces from up there. Why the hell hadn't he thought about it! If she had thought she had purposely done nothing about it. She hadn't thoroughly cleaned this room for weeks now; all she had done was to lick a duster over it. But he himself should have remembered and got rid of the things. There was that silver teapot and jug in the chiffonier in the kitchen. He'd put that in the dustbin first thing in the morning. God! What more could happen?

He went to the door and watched Vanessa walking across the kitchen, and when she went out into the yard he followed into the scullery and put the kettle on. A cup of coffee might help. After making it he put the cups on a tray and took it back into the room; then he waited. It was after he had been waiting ten minutes that it suddenly came to him that she had been a long time. The back door! She could have gone out the back door. He almost leaped across the kitchen, and when he opened the scullery door and saw her standing there about to enter he leaned against the stanchion for a moment and closed his eyes. It took him a few seconds to pull himself together, and then he said, "Are you all right?"

"Yes. Yes, I'm all right." She smiled faintly at him.

"I've made a drink." He led the way into the room and closed the door.

As they drank their coffee he made several light remarks in order to cover up the awkwardness that lay between them. It was an awkwardness that had nothing to do with sex; it was the awkwardness of two diverse personalties thrown into close proximity. After a while he rose and hung his coat up on the back of the door, saying, "It won't look so bad when you titivate it up a bit, new curtains and things. She didn't do anything to it because she thought you'd like to have it your own way."

She, too, rose to her feet. She felt better, quieter inside. She thought the hot coffee must have done her good. She stared at him as he turned towards her. He looked bigger without his coat. The muscles of his arms bulged through his shirt sleeves; his arms looked long and powerful, as did his hands and shoulders; an Irish navvy, one of them had called him. Well, she supposed he did look like an Irish navvy, but he was being kind and thoughtful and she was grateful for any kindness. When he stood in front of her, saying, "Don't worry; it'll be different in the morning. I mean," and jerked his head towards the ceiling, she didn't answer, but on an impulse similar to that which had brought her lips to Brett's cheek with the result that she was now married to Angus Cotton, she leaned forward and placed her lips lightly against the corner of his mouth.

It was the first time their faces had come into contact, and the effect was electrifying. The next minute he had her pressed tightly to him. Her body slightly askew, he held her in a vice as his mouth covered hers. But within a minute they were standing apart again and she was gasping for breath while he wiped the sweat from his face with the back of his hand.

"You shouldn't have done that," he said. "It was all right until you did that. Asking for trouble, aren't you? what do you think I am, eh? Well," he strained his neck

216

up out of his collar, "when I want you I'll take you, in me own time. Get that. In me own time."

She was unable to speak; all she could do was stare at him. She had only meant it to be a sort of thank you for all he had done. She had never really thanked him; he made it so hard. She watched him go to the switch and put the light out. Then his voice came out of the darkness, saying, "Get to bed." And she got to bed. Like a child who had been whipped and was afraid of the lesson being repeated, she scrambled out of her clothes, and because she hadn't unpacked anything she got into her petticoat again, and, groping at the bedclothes, she slid down between the sheets and lay stiff and taut, listening to her heart as its beat thumped in her ears. It was so loud that it shut out the sound of Angus's breathing.

But six feet away Angus listened to her breathing as he lay on his back staring upwards. His mother had been right; he had been a blasted fool, he should have got a double bed. He needn't have touched her; she could have just lain by his side and he could have held her hand. Aw, God, he was kiddin' himself, wasn't he? Lying by her side and holding her hand, when that peck she gave him set him off like a starter gun! But, nevertheless, his mother had something.

Into the silence now there permeated a sound that didn't come from the bed to the left of him but from the ceiling at which his eyes were directed. It was a sound that he hadn't heard for many years, not since the night his dad had died; it was the sound of his mother crying. With a heave he turned on his side and pulled the clothes over his head. Had there ever been a wedding night like this, ever? No! He bet his damned life there never had.

6

Why no one liked the month of November had always, up to now, puzzled Vanessa. She had said once to Susan that it was just a different kind of weather, and all weather was nice. She liked walking in the rain, she liked wind, she liked to lie in bed and hear it whine and moan through the tall chimneys. She particularly liked November, December and January because she associated them with roaring open fires both in the drawing-room and dining-room. She had always had more time to read in the winter. After she had done her homework she would curl up before the fire, preferably in a room which she had to herself, and munch crisps and chew caramels – she didn't care for chocolates.

Now, again, it was November, and she was seeing it as most people saw it; a month of rain, fog, cold, sleet, snow flurries and a half light that bore you down.

At ten o'clock on this particular Wednesday morning she stood in the middle of the kitchen and thought, not for the first time by any means, "I'll go mad, I'll go insane and they'll put me away." She had been married just over three weeks and, mentally, she had gone through more torment during this period than during all the weeks since the night in the summerhouse with Brett. She was learning that there were different kinds of torment. There was the torment of this tiny house, where every word you said above your breath could be heard upstairs, and vice versa, where five steps one way and four the other were all you could do in the privacy of your room.

She knew every square inch of the ground floor of this house, but she didn't know anything about upstairs. Even when she was alone in the house, and that was pretty often, she didn't venture upstairs; upstairs was Emily's and Rosie's rooms, and she didn't want to get any nearer to them than she must. Their resentment of her filled the air when they were indoors, and it stayed with her long after they left the house in the morning, because now Emily was again going to work.

For the first week after Angus had brought her here she was, most of the time, alone with Emily, and Emily would speak to her only when it was necessary. "Well, aren't you goin' to get him his tea ready?" she had said to her on the first Monday.

"I – I don't know what he likes; I'll leave it to you, Emily."

"Oh no, begod, you won't, lass. You're his wife; you've got to cook for him."

She had felt an anger rising in her against Emily, but she had tried to control it. Yet in spite of her effort her voice took on a slight hauteur as she said, "You know for a fact I can't cook, Emily."

"You should have thought of that afore. And don't use that tone to me; I'm not up at the house now."

"I'm not using any tone to you, Emily." Vanessa was beseeching now. "I just want you to help me, show me how to cook."

"I'm sorry; I'll have no time for that, I'm going after a job the morrow," said Emily flatly.

Vanessa had groaned inwardly. That's what Angus feared she would do, go after another job.

But this was only the beginning. There were the evenings when Angus came in and she put before him what she had cooked, and he rarely ate it; but he soon went through the things she hadn't cooked, such as fish and chips, or peas and pies. She said to him, "I'll go to cookery classes once it's over," and he had nodded and smiled at her but hadn't said, "You'll have other things to do besides cookery classes once it's over."

As much in an effort to make conversation as to find out his tastes, she had said to him, "What is your favourite dish?" and when he replied, "Steak and kidney pudding," she had said, "Oh!" There was as much chance of her making a steak and kidney pudding as there was of her making crepe suzette, in fact she might have had more success with the latter as she had tried her hand at pancakes.

On Monday of this week she had bought a cookery book only to find that there wasn't an ingredient in the house that was stated in any of the recipes. So yesterday she had ventured into the centre of the town to buy what was necessary, for she didn't like going into the little shops near the house, because the looks she received said plainly, "So this is who all the trouble's about."

It was while she was waiting for a bus in the main street that she became aware of two women in a car, held up in a line of traffic, almost at the same time as they became aware of her. They were Mrs. Herring and Mrs. Young, the mothers of Kathie and Rona. She had been entertained in their homes countless times, and they had always been charming to her, but now they were surveying her with hard, blank stares. Their eyes, in a way, looked sightless, as if they weren't really seeing her.

She looked away, and it was all she could do not to run away from the bus queue. She had never felt a "bad girl" before, but she did now. She wanted to sink down through the earth.

It was unfortunate that this incident should have followed so closely on a row between Angus and Emily the night before.

"Where you goin'?" Angus had asked his mother.

"Out," Emily had replied.

"You've taken to goin' out a lot of late, haven't you?"

"It's my life, lad. You do what you like with yours, I do what I like with mine. Is there any reason why I shouldn't go out?"

"Aye," he had yelled at her; "every bloody reason under the sun, you awkward old bitch you."

"Don't you call me an awkward old bitch else I'll brain you. As sure as God's me judge, I'll brain you."

"Try it on then. Try it on."

Vanessa had stood in their room, her face held between her two hands, and like a child she had prayed: Dear Lord, make them stop. She was dazed by the yelling and shouting that went on in the house. What should be ordinary conversation was conducted in a tone that would have been used only for deep anger in her own home, and she had rarely heard it until she herself had evoked it. At one point when the swearing was filling the house she thrust her fingers into her ears, and when she extracted them it was to hear Angus yelling, "You've no bloody need to go out workin'. You know you haven't. And Emily's reply, "You're goin' to break stones with a bloody great stick, aren't you? Sixteen pounds! You'd get more sweepin' roads. Your own boss, me backside."

"It was a bad week. I told you . . . in between contracts. Anyway, what the hell has it got to do with you what I make and what I don't make? I pay the rent and every other bloody commitment in the house, so what you talking about?"

As the door banged before he had finished speaking, Rosie's voice took over from her mother's. "You should be bloody well ashamed of yourself, our Angus, speakin' to her like that."

"Now you, YOU keep your trap shut. I'm standin' none of it from you, because you've turned out to be nothin' more than a damned little upstart. That's what you are. And you've got nothing to be uppish about.'

"There you're wrong; I have got something to be uppish

about. And I'm going to remain uppish. I'm not like some people I know gettin' me belly filled at the first opportun – "

When the sound of the blow came to her, Vanessa threw herself on the bed and buried her face in the pillow. A few minutes later when she raised her head she expected to hear Rosie crying, but Rosie's voice, as strident as ever, was yelling, "You great, big, soft nowt. Don't think you'll frighten me. And you lift your hand again and, begod, I'll do what me mam threatened, I'll brain you. Now mind, I'm warnin' you."

She had sat on the edge of the bed gripping her hands on the dome of her stomach. She felt dazed by it all. She knew she'd never, never get used to it, at the same time she was amazed by the fact that this was how people lived, had gone on living for years and years. Emily and Rosie and Angus hadn't just started shouting at each other since she had come into the house. Everybody in this neighbourhood seemed to shout. They shouted greetings across the narrow streets as if they were miles away; even the tenants in the new block of flats round the corner in the main street, they shouted from their upper windows down to the children in the play yards. Life here was one big shout, when it should have been a whisper, because there was hardly space to breathe. Perhaps it was because they lived in such close proximity to each other that made them want to shout, to break out.

It had been nearly fifteen minutes later when Angus came into the room, and after looking at her face he said, "Don't look so worried; there's nobody been murdered."

"You surprise me."

He had turned swiftly on her. This was a tone, she knew, she must never use to him. It was the tone she had used to Emily, the tone of her class, slightly haughty, supercilious, condescending, and he reacted to it as such. "Look, this is our way." He was yelling at her now. "It means nothing, well, not all that. It'll work out. I keep telling you it'll work out. I know her." His voice dropped.

"And Rosie?"

"Aw, Rosie. She's jealous of you, that's what's the matter with Rosie. I always had a soft spot for her. She's jealous of you."

Following this he had gone to the little table in the corner and sat down with his exercise books, working out figures, and she had taken up her knitting. She was knitting a baby coat; she could knit and sew quite well. They had taught her something in the Convent. It would have been better if they had taught her Domestic Science, but they only taught that to those who wanted to go in for it. There had been no need for her to study Domestic Science. Somewhere inside she was laughing derisively. She had taken languages, German and French, instead of a meat pudding. She would have given all her knowledge, however limited, to be able to make a meat pudding.

They had been sitting in silence for some time when he turned to her abruptly and said, "What I want is another couple of lorries, besides two new ones to replace the crates we've got. I missed a job the day because we weren't big enough; a fellow said it would take six lorries but he'd stretch a point if I had four.

She had no interest in his business or the lorries that he had or hadn't got, but she said, "Can't you go to the bank and get the money?"

"Oh my God, Van." He smiled pityingly. "I'm down to one hundred and twenty-five quid. I don't have a bank account; our dealings are strictly cash. It helps with the tax man an' all. But go to the bank you say. You're talkin' daft."

She suddenly put down her knitting and straightened her back, and her tone changed again, not to the one that would anger him, but to one filled with protest as she said, "I'm not a fool altogether, Angus."

"Look honey, I didn't say you were." He was leaning

over the back of the chair towards her. "But it's just that you've got a different slant on things."

"I haven't got a different slant on things, not with reference to the bank. What I meant was, couldn't you go to the bank and raise a loan? I know you've got no money in the bank."

He pulled a chair round until he was facing her, his knees almost touching hers, and he said, "Oh, I see. But I ask you; what have I got as security? We don't own this place, not that that would mean very much if we did. I've got nothing as security except a broken-down lorry, the other one is Fred's."

"Has he no security?"

"Insecurity; a wife and six bairns."

She said, "You mentioned an insurance some time ago."

"Oh, that. It isn't due for another eight years. And then what is it? Three hundred pounds."

"How long was it for?"

"Fifteen years. I've paid seven."

"Wouldn't they take that as part security?"

"And me not paid half yet? I don't know about that. But," he jerked his head, "I could see. It's an idea. You've given me an idea." His smile widened and he leant nearer to her and asked now softly, in the voice that he kept for her alone, "How you feelin'?" These were the only words that his tenderness seemed to supply him with: "How you feelin'?"

"All right," she said.

"You always say you're all right. If you were peggin' out you would say you were all right, wouldn't you, because it's the thing to say?"

"But I am feeling all right."

"No, you're not; you're feeling bloody miserable. There I go." He wagged his head. "I told you I was goin' to stop swearing in front of you."

"It doesn't matter."

"But it does. If I said I was going to stop swearin' I should stop swearin'; at least in front of you."

She wanted to say, "The more you try the more it will emphasise the difference. Don't change yourself; it'll be better that way."

He looked down at his hands, the nails all broken, the finger tips as hard as pieces of dried leather, and he said, "You're having it pretty rough, but believe me once it's over everything will be all right, you'll see. And we'll go out; we'll start going places; I'll take you round; we'll enjoy ourselves . . . Oh," he wagged his hand at her, "she'll look after the bairn; she'll be in her seventh heaven havin' a bairn to see to. You'll see. I'm tellin' you. And by that time business will have bucked up, and I'll bet what you like we'll have a car. Not a new one, oh no, not yet, because every spare penny I make I want to push into the business. It's going to be big, I'm tellin' you." He turned his head almost on to his shoulder and nodded it as if she was contradicting him, and he said again, "I'm telling you. It's a prophecy if ever there was one, it's going to be big. I mean it to be big. I generally get what I want." He brought his head slowly towards her again and his hand went out and touched hers.

She always shivered when he touched her. She wasn't repulsed by him, but nevertheless she couldn't stop her limbs shivering when her flesh made contact with his, and each time he was aware of this. She knew it angered him, but he endeavoured not to show it.

He had left the house at seven o'clock this morning, before either Emily or Rosie had come downstairs, and when they did come down she heard them talking. They intended she should.

She felt sick and ill this morning, not only in her body but in her mind. A dark depression had fallen on her. Her thoughts were going round in circles, she couldn't see ahead, yet when she looked back into the past all was brightness. She had had a wonderful home, wonderful parents; she even saw her father as kindly and good, and her mother as sympathetic. She had been going to wear the most gorgeous dress as bridesmaid to Susan. There would have been marvellous people at the wedding. Never before had she thought of Susan's friends or the Braintrees as marvellous, but now, in retrospect, they were all charming and kindly; and none of them raised their voices when speaking. What had segregated her from this wonderful past? It was Brett. He should have known what would happen. But she mustn't blame Brett, at least not all the way. She had liked Brett; she could say she had loved Brett. He was a gentleman, except when . . . Her mind shut out the picture of the moments during which Brett had ceased to be a gentleman.

Emily's voice penetrated the fog of her depression as she called to Rosie, "Times have changed, lass, times have changed. I was goin' at it scrubbin' for nine hours a day up till twenty-four hours afore you were born, not sittin' on me arse all day. Aye, times have changed."

When finally the door banged for the second time and she had the house to herself she got up and dressed. She knew what she was going to do, and she knew that she should have done it sooner. She should have done it instead of marrying Angus. She had brought trouble on him and parted him from his family. As Rosie had made it plain a number of times, they had been a happy family once.

She got dressed and went to the little shop around the corner. They hadn't any large packets of aspirins, only strips. She asked for four. At the next shop she bought a box holding twenty-five, and now she was standing in the kitchen and the aspirins were on the table before her.

She knew she must leave some word for Angus, so she went into the room and looked for a piece of drawing paper on which to write, but there was none on the table. There was a piece of paper sticking between two books and she pulled it out, and with it Fowler's "King's English." She had been surprised to find that on the bookshelf. Angus and Fowler's "King's English." She smiled a pitying smile. He tried, did Angus, he tried. Perhaps she could have helped him here. No, he would never have allowed her to help him with his grammar because that would have meant facing the fact that he needed help in that direction. There was a pride in him that mustn't be hurt. She took the piece of paper and a pencil into the kitchen and she wrote on it: "I'm sorry, Angus. It was a great mistake; I should never have let you do it. Emily was right. It would never have worked out. Thank you for all the kindness you have shown me. You have nothing to regret, believe me, because you're the only one who has given me a kind word during all these awful months. Thank you, Angus. Vanessa." She read what she had written and felt that she hadn't expressed herself clearly, hadn't thanked him enough, then she went into the scullery and brought back a glass of water, and, opening the aspirins, she dropped thirty into the water and slowly stirred them. They took a long time to dissolve, and as she waited she thought, I wonder if I'll see Brett. Odd, us both going out the same way; but I could never have hanged myself. When eventually the liquid was a milky mass of whirling particles she raised the glass to her lips. Her hand began to tremble now; then her body; and she knew if she hesitated for one moment longer she wouldn't do it.

When the glass was empty she shuddered and gritted her teeth against the taste; then she put her forearms on the table and sat gazing down at the letter she had written and she wondered how long it would be before the aspirins took effect.

7

They were at break in the canteen. Rosie, Freda Armstrong, her pal and fellow machinist, and two other girls. They were seated at their usual table in the corner and Freda was pouring sympathy over Rosie. The expression of her sympathy was questionable but nevertheless sincere. "You look awful, Rosie girl," she was saying. "Cor! your face is green. I've never seen you as bad as this; it makes you look fifty. You should go home, shouldn't she?"

One of the other girls nodded and said "Aye. I would tell the boss, Rosie. Tell her you can't stick it, she's all right. She has it herself." There was a giggle at this which turned into a laugh when Freda added seriously, "Now you ain't got no proof of that, now have you? Her sex's been in question afore the day."

Rosie did not join her laughter to the others but said, "I wouldn't have come in this mornin' but it meant stayin' at home with that 'un. God, what a life it is now. You've got no idea."

"Does she still put it on?" One of the girls asked, and Rosie replied, "No, by God, she doesn't put it on with me. I'd swipe her mouth for her if she did. She knows better. She keeps out of me way. Our Angus. Of all the bloody fools, our Angus . . . Oh, my God, I do feel sick."

"If you don't do it for free like you should get married, Rosie, that's what you should do. They say it clears up once you start."

"It all goes into the first bairn," said the other girl.

"Aw, shut your traps," said Rosie, straightening herself up. "Married, bairns; I'm livin' with it. I don't want to hear any more about marriage, or bairns, so shut up."

There was silence at the table until the pain in Rosie's stomach brought her bending again, and after a moment she stood up, saying, "I'm goin' to be sick."

Ten minutes later Rosie went to the forewoman and told her that she'd have to go home. And fifteen minutes later, when she entered the house, she was still in pain and still feeling sick, but the moment she opened the kitchen door and saw Vanessa sitting at the table with a glazed look on her face and the table strewn with the covers of numerous aspirins she forgot about how she herself was feeling. "God Almighty!" She put her hand across her mouth; then diving across the room she cried, "What you done?"

Vanessa's lips moved but no sound came from them, and slowly her head sank on to her arm.

"Oh, God! God Almighty!" The words seemed to issue out of the top of Rosie's head. Then pulling Vanessa upwards, she shook her and cried, "You bloody young fool you! You bloody young fool. What you done, Oh, my God!" She let Vanessa's head and shoulders drop to the table again; then she grabbed the letter and scanned the first few lines, before throwing it down and crying, "Mam! Mam!" She was running between the scullery door and the passage like someone demented. Her mother was at her job. Mrs. Wilson next door? No, no, she was a big mouth; there would be trouble. She'd have to get the doctor, and her mother, but if she left her she could die. You made them sick. Yes, that's what you did, you made them sick. What did you make them sick with? Oh, my God! She pulled Vanessa up again and shook her. "Get up, Van," she implored as she unconsciously used her name. "Van! Van! Do you hear me? Come on. Come on." She was in tears now as she pleaded.

Salt water. Aye, salt water. She dashed to the cupboard

and, getting a packet of salt, poured a third of it into a mug and filled it with warm water from the kettle standing on the hob. She was talking and crying and swearing as she worked. "Bloody fool! I knew something like this would happen. Our Angus, you should be battered. That's what you should be, battered. You should never have brought her here. She can't stand it, she's not made for it. God! if she dies. Come on. Come on." She grabbed hold of Vanessa's shoulder, but when her head still lolled forward she gripped her hair and pulled her head up and, leaning her back in the chair, she whispered, "Get this down you. It's going to make you sick. Can you hear me?"

Half the liquid ran over Vanessa's face, but some went down her throat as she gasped and gulped.

Now Rosie tried to get her to her feet but it was impossible, and once more she slumped across the table.

There was nothing for it, Rosie knew, but to get her mother and the doctor. She had her mother's phone number. If she could get a taxi she could be here in ten minutes. She looked once more at the inert figure, then flew out of the house and down to the corner of the street and across the road to where there was a telephone kiosk. When a strange voice answered her ring she asked if she could speak to Mrs. Cotton, it was very important.

When her mother came to the phone, she said quickly, "Mam, you've got to come. Listen. She's tried to do herself in. Get a taxi, do you hear?"

There was no answer from the other end and she yelled, "Do you hear me, Mam?" and she thought she heard her mother say, "Aye, I heard you," before the click of the phone came to her. She was gasping herself now, and on the point of being actually sick as she phoned Doctor Carr. Fortunately, he was still in his surgery and she began by saying, "Doctor Carr?" and when he answered "Yes," she said, "Do – do you remember Vanessa Ratcliffe? She – she married my brother, Angus."

When again he said, "Yes, yes, I remember," she said "Well, she's tried to do herself in, in our house."

"What with?" he asked sharply now.

"With aspirins."

"What have you done?"

"I've given her salt and water; that's all I could think of."

"I'll be with you in a minute."

"Ta, thanks doctor."

She ran out of the box, across the road again, just missing being run down by a bus, down the street and into the house. It was very quiet and she stood for a moment looking down at the relaxed figure lying across the table, and she put her double fists over her mouth and whispered to her, "Don't die. For God's sake, don't die."

She continued to stare at her, not knowing what to do. She couldn't get her to her feet on her own, so perhaps it was better just to leave her there.

Emily was the first to arrive. It couldn't have been five minutes since she got the phone call. She must have walked straight out of the house, for she was without hat or coat and was wearing a blue print dress with a big white bibbed apron over it. She, like Rosie, stood just within the door and gazed for a moment at the inert figure. Her face looked bleached. Then she whispered in much the same way as Rosie had done, "Oh, God Almighty! . . . Did you do anything?" Her lips were quivering as she asked the question.

"I – I gave her salt water to make her sick, but it hasn't."

"Get at the other side of her. Hoist her up. Keep her walking. That's what we must do, keep her walking. Did you get the doctor?"

"Yes, he's comin'. He should be here any minute."

It was as much as they could do between them to support Vanessa. They pulled her arms around their shoulders and Emily thrust her arm around Vanessa's

231

waist, and they managed to walk her up and down the kitchen twice. And then they could go no further. As they sat her in the chair again her body heaved and out of her mouth frothed the salt water and some of the liquid she had swallowed earlier.

"That's it, get it up, lass. Get it up." Emily now started to rub her back with a large circling movement, talking in a coaxing, wheedling voice as she did so. "Come on, come on, have another try. Doesn't matter about the floor." It was as if Vanessa had pointed out that she was being sick all over the floor. "If that's all we've got to worry about then we're all right. Come on, lass, get it up."

"Hoist her again," she said to Rosie, and as they were about to resume the walk the door opened and the doctor came in.

"Has she got it up?" he asked abruptly.

"Just a bit, Doctor," said Emily.

"How many has she taken?"

"There's the papers." She pointed to the table. "Twenty, thirty. I don't know."

He opened his bag quickly and filled a syringe. Then baring Vanessa's arm, he pressed the needle in gently. "Get a bowl or something," he said without turning his head.

It was Rosie who ran to the kitchen for a bowl and placed it at Vanessa's feet.

"Shall we walk her again, Doctor?" asked Emily.

"No, she'll be sick in a minute . . . I hope." He slanted a bleary glance towards Emily, asking now, "What's brought this to a head?"

Emily's eyes were cast down and she muttered something, and he repeated scathingly, "You couldn't say? You couldn't say?"

Emily's head jerked up quickly in the old aggressive manner, only to turn sideways, and, her face averted, she said, "It's been difficult all round, Doctor; the blame isn't all mine."

"No, I dare say not, but you could have helped." He was patting Vanessa's cheeks now, first one and then the other, keeping her head up the while. "By all accounts, you've been giving her hell."

Again Emily's head swung upwards; then after a pause she said, "You've had your ear to the ground, haven't you?"

"I didn't have to put it that far to hear what she's been going through. Angus did a decent thing, if you could use an old phrase, a noble thing, not that it was purely altruistic on his part; nevertheless, he did what many another wouldn't have done, no matter what his feelings. But you've done your best to spoil it, Emily."

"Begod, look here – "

"Don't shout; I should think you've done enough of that."

"What do you know about it?" Emily turned her back on him, and he said, "Quite a bit; we've all got crosses to bear. And if I hadn't had my ear to the ground, I would still have known your reaction to the present set-up. You seem to forget I've known you for the last twenty-five years."

It was in her mind to say, "And me you, you drunken slob," but this wasn't the time for retaliation. Perhaps she had retaliated too much. Aye, what he said was true, but who was he to say it, anyway?

The sound of Vanessa retching brought her swiftly round and as she saw the volume of water spurt from the girl's mouth she said deep within her, "Thank God. Oh, thank God."

"Oh de-ar, oh de-ar, oh de-ar me," Vanessa groaned, and Doctor Carr said, "You're all right." He was now holding her head against his breast, and as she moaned again he stroked the hair back from her head. "There now, it's all over. You'll feel better soon."

She opened her eyes dazedly and muttered, "I'm sick."

"Yes. It's all to the good; it's all to the good." He

nodded towards Emily now and said, "We'll get her to bed."

Emily and Rosie between them undressed her. Rosie supported her as Emily pulled off her clothes. Neither of them spoke until the doctor, standing at the foot of the bed, said, "Where's Angus working?"

"He's on haulage. He's with Fred Singleton; they're running a sideline on their own."

"Can you get him?"

Emily looked at Rosie, and Rosie said, "They're under contract to Farrer's."

"Well, I would phone Farrer's and get him here. I think he should see this."

"Yes, Doctor." Rosie ran out of the room. She had forgotten entirely about the pain in her stomach and her own sickness.

Emily, now standing close to the doctor at the foot of the bed, asked under her breath, "Will it harm the bairn?" and he raised his eyebrows and said, "That's to be seen. It could bring it on . . . . Has she been going to the clinic?"

"No, not that I know."

"Well, you should have seen to it, woman." He poked his face towards her, and his attitude now brought no feeling of retaliation to her because her conscience was working against her. What she said was, "Aye, I suppose I should. I should have done many things, but bein' meself I didn't."

"Being yourself, you're a stubborn, ignorant individual. You know that, don't you?"

"Yes, I know it, Doctor, and I don't need you to rub it in; it takes every man to look to his own house." They stared at each other; then she added more calmly, "How was I to know she was working up to this?"

His voice, too, was calmer now as he said, "You've known her for years. You knew her background, soft, easy, filled with refinements. Your own sense should have told

234

you what this set-up would do to her." He jerked his chin twice as he looked round the room.

"She seemed to be fallin' in. I thought she was settlin', makin' the best of a bad job. She doesn't show things very much. How was I to know?"

"You, with your experience of people, should know that there are greater conflicts fought beneath the skin than in any open battle. She couldn't get rid of her inhibitions by yelling and shouting; it isn't done in her quarter. You know that, Emily. Their battles are fought quietly, secretly, not like round here." Again his chin jerked twice. "You should know that it's a saving grace to be able to bawl your head off. There's very few suicides in this quarter, whereas in the Brampton Hill area there were four last year, one a close neighbour of hers. If any of them from that quarter had one such row as you have on a Saturday night, say, it would break up the entire family for ever. She's from a different world, Emily. You should have realized that . . . . But it's not too late."

Vanessa moaned now and Doctor Carr went to her side, and when he touched her forehead she muttered, "Angus. I'm sorry, Angus."

"Don't worry. Don't talk any more. Go to sleep; you're all right."

She opened her eyes, then shook her head slightly and whispered, "Doctor Carr."

"Go to sleep."

Rosie came back into the room now. She was panting, and she said, "They're goin' to tell him when he comes back for his next load."

The doctor walked into the kitchen and Emily, about to follow him, said to Rosie, "Stay with her a minute, will you?" Then she pulled the door closed before she asked, "What are you goin' to do about it? Will you have to report it?"

"I should, yes."

"But must you?" She was staring hard at him.

And he returned her stare for a full minute before he asked, "Does anybody else know?"

"I'll find out." She went into the bedroom and came out within a minute, saying, "No. Rosie's got her head screwed on right. She phoned for me; she didn't even go next door. They'll think it's a miscarriage coming."

He was nodding at her. "What did she tell them when she got on the phone to Angus?"

Once more Emily went into the room, and when she came back she said, "She told them to tell him that Vanessa had been taken bad, that's all."

Again they were staring hard at each other; then he said, "There's a possibility she might make a second attempt, and the next time when she's found she'll likely to be too far gone to be sick."

"No such thing, no such thing," said Emily. "She won't do it again; I'll see to that. I'm staying here. I'll see to her; I promise you."

"Well, we'll see." He sighed; then went to his bag, closed it, picked up his coat from a chair, put it on, and, going towards the door, said, "I'll be in my surgery around one-thirty. Send Angus along to see me then."

"Yes, Doctor." She came close to him again and muttered softly, "Thanks. I promise you things'll be different. I'll see to her."

"You've nearly been too late, remember that."

She closed her eyes and shook her head, as she said, "Don't worry. It's somethin' I won't forget in a hurry."

Half-an-hour later the lorry stopped at the door, and Angus burst into the house. "What is it?" he demanded. "What's happened her?"

"She's all right," said Emily from the other side of the table. "Don't go in for a minute; Rosie's in there with her. You'd better read this." She handed him Vanessa's letter. It was no use with-holding it from him because Vanessa would ask him if he had got it when she came round.

His mouth was agape when he stopped reading and he put his hand up and ran it slowly through his rough hair. He did it a second time before he muttered, "Aw, no. No."

Emily, her lips compressed to stop them trembling, stared at her son. The dark stubble round his chin was standing out against the dead whiteness of his face. There was a grey dust on his hair and shoulders. He looked all white and grey. She dreaded his onslaught; she dreaded to hear the truth from him that she was to blame for this; and she waited silently. And to her surprise he didn't break the silence, but moved slowly across the room and opened the door.

Rosie was sitting by the head of the bed. She had her hands clasped tightly between her knees; she looked like a very young girl, and she, too, was evidently waiting for the onslaught. She stared at her brother and rose to her feet as he came to the bed. She tried to say something but couldn't. He didn't look at her, and after a moment she went out into the kitchen.

Angus stared down on the long pale face. Her hair was scattered over the pillow. It looked dank and tousy. She looked almost dead. He couldn't take it in that she had tried to die. His mind seemed to have got stuck for he was still repeating to himself "Aw, no. No." Then slowly he began to tell himself things and ask himself questions. He should have realized she was at this pitch. But how could he have told? She had been so quiet; she didn't talk much, and when she did she gave no indication of how she was feeling.

He was a thick-headed numbskull; he had been mad to marry her in the first place; but having done so he should never have brought her back here. Yet what could he have done? AYE, WHAT COULD HE HAVE DONE?; Not married her at all; just been friendly to her until she had got on her feet. He had rushed her, taken advantage of the fix she was in.

He knelt down by the bed and, enclosing her thin hands between his two hard dirt-covered ones, he whispered, "Van! Aw, Van!" He had the desire to lay his head down on her chest and cry.

When she neither moved nor spoke he realized she was asleep, and after a moment he got to his feet and went into the kitchen.

They were waiting for him, standing stiffly within arm's length of each other looking towards the door. He knew they were expecting him to blow them sky high, but he couldn't, he didn't feel that he had a shout or a bawl left in him. He had the sensation of being winded. Moreover, he knew it would achieve nothing to blame his mother now. She couldn't have acted differently if she had tried; she had acted according to her nature, as he himself had, as Rosie had. As he walked towards the table he asked, "Who found her?"

The moderation of his tongue loosened Rosie's tongue, and she said, "Me. I – I had to come home, I had the cramp, and when I got in she was sittin' there." She pointed to the chair. "I – I nearly went mad meself." She shook her head. "I rung me mam –" she nodded towards Emily, who was staring at her son, and then she ended, "And I rang the doctor."

"What did he say?" He was addressing his mother, and Emily moved her tongue over her lips for a moment. She wasn't going to repeat what the doctor said, she wasn't a fool; anyway, he'd likely open his mouth to him when he went along. And that's what she told him. "He says you've got to go and see him about half-past one."

"Does – does he think it'll affect the bairn?"

Emily glanced down for a moment. "It might, he says; we've got to wait and see."

He dropped suddenly on to a chair and he looked downwards as he asked, "Have you got anythin' in, a drop of hard anywhere?"

She shook her head. "No, but Rosie will slip along and get you somethin', won't you, Rosie?"

"Aye; it won't take a minute."

They were both openly eager in their placating of him.

"It doesn't matter," he said. "Coffee will do, black." He put his elbow on the table and rested his head in his hands. After a time he got to his feet as quickly as he had sat down and, going to the fireplace, stared into the fire as he said quietly, "There's got to be a change, Mam."

It was some seconds before she answered, and then briefly. "Aye," she said.

"I've got to get her away from here."

"It would be best," she said.

"I – I can't do it at once, not straightaway; I'll have to look for something."

"I understand that." She was supporting herself against the edge of the table, the nails of one hand digging into the underside of the wood. "But until you do," she said, "I'll see to things. I'll see she's all right."

He turned and looked at her squarely but didn't speak, and she said, "I'm gettin' Rosie to phone Mrs. McVeigh. I never liked working for her anyway; she's a mean scrub. I'll be glad to be back home."

He surprised and broke her down at the same time by saying, "Thanks, Mam."

"Don't" she turned from him, her voice harsh, her manner almost back to normal, "don't heap coals of fire on me head; you know in your heart you're blamin' me for what's happened the day and . . . and, although I don't blame you, I'll remind you that I didn't start this. However," she turned on him quickly before he had any time to reply, "it's done and I'm not very proud of me share in it, but as I've said, as long as she's here I'll see to her."

Rosie came in from the scullery, a cup of coffee in one hand and a sugar basin in the other, and she stood mutely before him while he ladled three spoonfuls of sugar into the cup. She wanted to say, "I'm sorry," but you didn't say you were sorry, not openly; you didn't ask for forgiveness, although you might crave it badly to take the fear away from you, the fear that told you that if Vanessa had died you yourself would have been more than a little to blame, for, to use her own words, she had been a bloody stinker.

Her tone when she said quietly, "I made it strong," was in itself a plea for forgiveness, and when he answered quietly, "Ta. Ta, Rosie," the words were a form of absolution.

They were all sitting quiet now, still somewhat stunned but united, and all three were strangely at peace.

It was as he had been telling Van all the while, things would work out, but when the thought came to him how nearly they hadn't he had to get up quickly and go down the yard.

8

Three weeks later Vanessa lost her baby. Doctor Carr ordered her into hospital on the Friday night and the baby was taken away on the Sunday afternoon. It was eight days later when she returned home. Angus brought her in a taxi, and as soon as she entered the house she noticed a difference, particularly in their room. There were new curtains at the window; the furniture had been polished and there was a cherry-coloured wall-to-wall carpet covering the floor. The room had been papered in a plain grey paper and the old pictures hadn't been re-hung. The single beds were still there, but they both had new candlewick spreads. She paused in the doorway, then looked at Angus and smiled weakly as she said, "It's nice, lovely. Thank you."

He wished she didn't always thank him, not in that polite way anyhow. He said, "Rosie picked the colours; I wasn't any good at it, and me mam not much better." He turned and looked at Rosie where she was standing well back in the kitchen, and Vanessa turned towards her, too, and across the distance she again spoke her thanks, in that quiet, polite, courteous way, which would have be-fitted an elderly woman but sounded strange coming from this young girl.

Rosie nodded and smiled self-consciously. She couldn't see herself ever liking her sister-in-law; you never really liked anybody who always seemed to put you at a dis-advantage; yet she no longer detested the sight of her. She

241

took a step forward, saying, "I thought the cherry and grey would go nice together."

"It does. It looks lovely," Vanessa moved into the room and to a coffee table on which was now set tea for two people. There were two cups and saucers and a milk jug and sugar basin to match, a plate of bread and butter and another of small cakes. She looked down at it; then turned and looked at Emily, and Emily said, "I thought you'd like to eat in here."

"No, Emily, no." There was a firmness about the shake of her head that silenced the three people looking at her, until Angus said, "It's all arranged, don't worry; we'll eat here."

"No, Angus." She looked straight into his face for a moment, then turned to Emily and said again, "No, Emily. We eat as before."

"Oh, then have it your own way." Angus was tossing his head. It was as if he was giving in reluctantly to some outrageous demand, but what the three women knew in their different ways was, he was pleased and relieved at her decision.

The pattern now was different. The atmosphere in the house was light, even gay, but whereas before Angus had felt that his marriage, for good or ill, was an established fact, he no longer had this feeling of security concerning it, for as each day passed and Vanessa returned to full health, he felt that she could walk out on him any minute; there was nothing to hold her. She wasn't dependent on him to look after her and her child; she could go any place and get a job. She had the looks and figure that models were made out of; she was almost eighteen and she hadn't begun to live; she didn't know yet what it was all about.

Each night when he came back from work he felt sick, until he saw she was still there. He felt that there was one solution to it all; he had to put her in a position similar to the one she had just got out of, and everything would be as it was before.

"Go gently with her," Doctor Carr had told him. "She's of a different calibre to you. You've got to realize that. Modern, swingin, or what-have-you, as brash as they are to-day, early environment counts." He hadn't minced his words had Doctor Carr. "You're mother's been an old swine to her," he said. Then he waved his hand and silenced him by adding, "I've got three hundred patients in your quarter and four of them are in your street, one next door. You cannot stop people talking." And then he had ended, "I'm telling you, go gently with her. It'll pay off in the long run."

Well he had gone gently for two months, he was burnt up inside. There was no May to go to now to relieve the pressure, and he wasn't picking anybody up. He thought too much of his skin for that; he didn't want to catch anything.

So, like a man who proposed to seduce the girl of his fancy, he planned in his mind how he would take her. They would go out the morrow night, it being Saturday; he would take her to some posh restaurant and they'd have a good dinner and a bottle of wine, and then later . . . well, that was up to him.

As he had been doing every week for the past two months, he called in at the estate agents' office to ask if they had found anything in the way of a flat for him, and to-day Reg Walker, who incidentally had at one time lived in Ryder's Row, greeted him with, "No, there's nothing in the way of a flat, Angus, but I wonder you don't go in for a house, or a bungalow."

"Oh, that's in the far future for me. What I want before a house or a bungalow is a couple of lorries."

"It's a pity," said Reg Walker; "a bungalow came on my books yesterday and it's a snip. It's on the outskirts. Bit out for most people. An old couple had it and they died within a month of each other and their only son is in Australia, and he's given us the O.K. to sell it. Do you remember Arthur Ridley? You know, they had the little hardware shop at the corner of Wolf Lane."

"Yes," nodded Angus. "Yes, I remember them."

"Well, it's him. I mean his people. He wrote me from Australia and asked me to get rid of the bungalow and furniture; they hadn't any money except a small insurance that paid for the funeral. He's cagey is Arthur Ridley. He once had a huge bill in from a solicitor for something and he's never dealt with them since. That's how I've come to be handling it."

"Aye." Angus jerked his head. "What you askin' for it?"

"Well, it's in need of decoration inside and repair outside, and the garden's overgrown. If it was all done up it would bring anybody's four thousand, and then it would be cheap."

"Oh, aye." Again Angus jerked his head, laughing now.

"I'm on the level, Angus." Reg Walker nodded at him. "I stated a price of two thousand five hundred and Arthur Ridley agreed, so it'll go for that. And I'm telling you, these days it's an absolute snip. And there's nearly three quarters of an acre of land with it, and you know what land is the day."

Again Angus said, "Oh, aye," but now he neither shook his head nor laughed. He hadn't been doing too badly these last few weeks, in fact he and Fred had split seventy pounds for each of the last five weeks. Of course there was tax off that; but then there were the Saturday runs he did and the three Sunday mornings. They had been for cash and had brought in over eighty pounds. Things were looking up, but he could do nothing big until he got more lorries, and he wanted those more than a house, but he said, "Have you put it in the paper?"

"Yes; it'll be out the morrow."

Angus bit on his lip. "When could I see it?"

"Any time you like. Run you out now if you like."

"Well, there's no time like the present."

And so Angus went to see the bungalow, and he immediately agreed with Reg that it was a good buy, an excellent buy. It had six rooms, bathroom and garage, and it overlooked the river and a fine stretch of country. He stood in the road looking back over the tangled garden towards the roof of the bungalow. This was the answer, but it would mean good-bye to the lorries for some time to come because he would still have to help his mother. And taking the bungalow was only the beginning. There would be the repayments, rates, electricity . . . and a phone, not to mention furnishing the whole place. He said to Reg Walker, "Will you give me until five o'clock?"

"Aye," said Reg. "And I won't mention it to anybody in the meantime. But mind, you'll have to make up your mind then. I can't hold it, and I dare say after it comes out the morrow it'll be gone by Monday."

"I'll let you know by five," said Angus

He didn't get into the house until half-past six. Emily had the tea set waiting. "You're late," she said; "I thought you must have run into Van."

"Run into Van?" He looked towards the room door. "She's not in?"

"No, she went out early this afternoon; she was going to do a bit of shoppin' or somethin'."

As he moved slowly towards their room she said, "Now don't go in there on that carpet with your boots on. I've told you," and he stopped and looked down at the floor for a moment, then sat down by the side of the fireplace and took off his heavy boots and put on a pair of slippers that were resting on the fender.

"Get your wash . . . You're not goin' to the baths the night?"

"No . . . She's never been out at this time."

"She could have gone to Newcastle." Emily was bending down to the oven.

245

"What would she want in Newcastle, there's plenty of shops here? What was she after, do you know?"

Emily lifted a pie from the oven. Its top was brown and there was a pattern of pastry leaves around the edges. It could have been cooked for the table at Bower Place. She said now, "Stop your worryin'. Surely she can go out for five minutes . . ."

"It isn't five minutes if she went out this afternoon."

"Well, anyway, you're not very early yourself; you're nearly an hour past your time. Where've you been?"

He got to his feet and went into the scullery and, stripping to the waist, he started to wash himself before he called out to her, "I've been after a bungalow."

She was at the scullery door, looking at him. "A bungalow?" Her voice was high.

"Aye. Reg Walker had a snip on his books; he offered it to me. I had to make up me mind for five o'clock; it was as quick as that."

"How much?"

"Two thousand five hundred."

"Oh, my God!"

"It's worth four thousand, even as it stands. It wants doing up."

"That'll take some payin' for. What'll happen to the lorries you were goin' after?"

"They'll have to wait. First things first."

As he reached for a towel he paused and looked at her and said, "You'll be all right . . . I'll see to you."

"Now look." Her voice was high and held the old aggressive quality. "Don't you bother about me, lad; I can take care of meself. And there's always supplementary. I don't see why I shouldn't get it; every other bugger in the street's on it. You look after yourself . . . and her. Anyway, if Stan and Rosie marry, an' they're bound to, they'll come in with me, so don't let anythin' at this end put you off."

He nodded at her.

246

A few minutes later, back in the kitchen, he said "Hold it for another ten minutes or so until I get changed; she'll likely be in by then."

In the room the fire was burning brightly; it looked comfortable and cheery. Inwardly he was delighted at the change in the room, but it was still small, and to her it must appear like a box.

Where was the? Had she gone? He brought his forefinger to his teeth and bit the end completely off his nail. It would be just like the thing, wouldn't it, him getting the bungalow and her going off all in the same day. What would he do without her? How could he go on without her? How did he go on before he had her? And yet he'd never had her in that sense. He had lived in this room with her for weeks on end and he'd never had her. It was all going to happen to-morrow night. He was barmy, mad. Be nice to her, gentle, Doctor Carr had said. Gentle be damned. He should have taken his rights weeks ago; that would have settled it. She would likely have been well on the way now with another. God it was as his mother had said, he was soft, barmy, a blasted fool. He had worked his guts out these last few weeks to get the money to put down for the lorries and now what had he done with it? Given Reg Walker fifty pounds in advance, and promised him another two hundred and fifty the morrow. That would take every penny of his capital and push him back a year, two years; in fact he might never get on his feet again. Well, it served him right . . . And wouldn't there be some laughter round the doors when they knew she had left him high and dry. They had been waiting for it, betting on it . . . Aw, he knew them.

He went to the narrow mantelpiece and, leaning his forearms along it, he dropped his head on to them and groaned inwardly.

When he heard his mother's voice saying, "Hello, we thought you had got lost," he almost sprang to the little table in the corner of the room, and when she opened the door he was emptying his back trouser pocket of notes and silver.

"Hello, there." He smiled at her. "You look froze. Where've you been?" He continued to smile at her as he walked towards her.

"I went into Newcastle."

"Oh. Mam thought you might." He was nodding at her.

She was taking off her hat and coat. "It's raw," she said, "bitter; it's nice to see a fire." She bent forward and held her hands down to the blaze and, looking over her shoulder, said, "You were late, too?"

"Yes. Yes, I've been doing a bit of business . . . What have you been up to? Shoppin'?"

She turned and hunched her shoulders up over her long neck, then smoothed down her mauve woollen dress over her flat stomach before saying, "I've been after a job."

When he made no comment on this she said, "Don't be vexed."

"Vexed! Me? I'm not vexed. What kind of a job?"

"In one of the stores, Daintrees."

"Oh. It's a classy shop that."

"Yes." She nodded. "Quite nice. You don't mind?"

If he didn't know what he was going to do to-morrow night, or to-night for that matter, he would have said, "Mind? You're bloody well right, I do mind. If you can't fill your time in then I'll have to give you something to fill it in with, won't I?" but what he said was, "I've got a surpise for you an' all."

"You have?" She waited.

"How would you like a bungalow?"

"Bungalow!" She brought her head forward, her smile widening her large mouth.

"Aye, I've bought one."

She moved a step towards him. "You've bought a bungalow? What . . . what kind?" She didn't say, "You bought a bungalow without me seeing it? I mightn't even like it."

"Big one. Six rooms. The lot. There was no time to let

you know. I had to make up me mind by five o'clock. It's a snip. I'll run you out first thing in the mornin' to see it."

"Where is it?" Her face was bright and eager.

"Oh, it's a bit outside. Collier Road way, on a rise. You can see the river from the windows."

The river. Her throat constricted just the slightest; the smile was fading from her face when she brought it back again and said, "Oh, that sounds lovely. Is it going to cost a lot?"

"No. As I said, it's a snip. Two thousand five hundred. It's worth four, even as it stands. Get it put into shape and you can add another two on to that."

She glaced towards the door, then said under her breath, "But, Emily."

"She knows; she's glad."

"Are you goin' to let this get spoilt?" Emily's voice, coming from the other room, made them both grimace, then laugh gently, and he pushed her towards the door, saying, "I'll be there in a tick."

As Vanessa entered the kitchen Rosie came down the stairs, and she asked immediately, under her breath, "Did you get it?" and Vanessa nodded and said, "Yes."

"What they payin' you?"

"Six pounds ten."

Rosie shrugged her shoulders. "That isn't very much; in fact it's nowt. And then you've got your fares to pay."

"That's only to start with, sort of training period. I'll get commission on sales after two months."

"What did he say?" Rosie jerked her head backwards

"Oh, he doesn't mind."

"Coo!" Rosie again jerked her head; "that's a surprise."

"What's a surprise?" Angus came into the room, buttoning his shirt up, and Rosie said, "It's none of your business."

"Have you told her?" He looked from his mother to Vanessa, and when Vanessa shook her head and his mother said "No, I've not had time, she's just come down," he turned to Rosie and said, "I've got a bungalow."

"A bungalow? You come into some money or summat? A bungalow? When did this all happen?"

When they sat down to their meal he explained briefly how it had all happened, and then Rosie voiced what was in the back of his mind all the time. "Well, that's put paid to you're gettin' any more lorries, at least for some time," she said, " 'cos you'll need furniture and things. Good job you started work." She nodded at Vanessa, and Vanessa, after a moment, said, "Yes. Yes, it is." She herself had forgotten about the lorries for the moment, and yet they hadn't been out of her mind for weeks past; the job she had got to-day was in a way connected with the lorries.

It was as they finished the meal that Angus, suddenly determining in his mind to push personal matters forward a little, said, "What about us all goin' to the club to celebrate? Friday night's a good night."

Neither Emily nor Rosie made any rejoinder, but after a moment's pause Vanessa said, "Yes. Yes, that's a good idea."

"Oh, I don't feel like it," said Emily sitting back in the chair. "Me feet's killin' me."

It wouldn't have taxed Emily's feet very much in visiting the club. She would have loved to have gone along to-night and had a bit of a sing-song. It was what she needed, to be in a crowd and yell her head off, but the last time they had gone to the club altogether it hadn't been a success. It was Vanessa's initiation, so to speak, into their kind of entertainment and she had smiled all the while, even laughed at some of the turns, but Emily hadn't seen her almost since she was a bairn not to know that it was a façade covering her real feelings. She knew that even if Vanessa had been challenged she wouldn't have admitted to her opinion of the company, of the drinking, singing, rocketing company, where, although the men were well put on and the women wore dresses

250

that were a good imitation of the Bower Place lot, they acted as they had always done. It would have taken somebody like Miss Susan to say outright, "Common individuals!"

Rosie wanted Vanessa to accompany them to the club no more than her mother, so she said brightly, "Why the club? Look, our Angus, why don't you take Van along to some place like Donovan's? Now, that would be a night out, sort of celebration for her getting her job."

Donovan's." Angus cocked his chin in the air and repeated, "Donovan's. Aye." He looked at Vanessa. "Would you like to go to Donovan's?"

"I've never been, I don't know what it's like." She glanced at Rosie, and Rosie said, "Oh, it's posh is Donovan's. That's where all the Rugby players get on a Saturday night. Angus used to go, didn't you?"

"Oh, well." He moved his head from side to side. "I've been a couple of times, but –" he turned to Vanessa – "I wouldn't take you there on a Saturday night." Then bending towards her he added jocularly, "But this is Friday. We'll go to Donovan's, eh?"

"Is it . . . is it evening dress or . . . ?"

"No anything," he answered.

"Your blue one," Rosie put in, "that he bought you for Christmas. That would do. It's smart and warm and it's your colour. You look smashing in it."

Vanessa smiled at Rosie. When Rosie was kind to her, as now, she ceased to think, "If only you had been like this from the beginning I wouldn't have done it."

The shame of trying to take her own life was still with her. She felt that her action had been the admission of utter failure. She was like Brett. Brett had given her the child, then had taken his life because he couldn't face up to the consequences. They were a pair, weak; nice, but weak. His weakness had created the child and her weakness had killed it. No matter what Doctor Carr said to the contrary, she would always feel that it was through her attempted suicide that the child had died. It had been shocked into death when on the point of coming alive.

"You're for it, aren't you?" Angus's question brought her mind quickly to the present, and she answered eagerly, "Yes, yes, of course. I'd love it. That's if we're not too late. I've got to get ready and it's after seven."

"Oh, places like those don't get going until nine or ten."

"Well, don't sit there," said Emily, energetically now. "An' don't you go on stuffing yourself." She nodded at Angus. "Else what's the good you payin' for a meal?"

As he got to his feet he bent towards her, saying, "I bet you a shilling that no matter what we pay it won't be half as good as this." He was trying to please her in all way these days. She was all right was his mam; he had always known it . . .

Half-an-hour later they were both ready, and Emily, looking at them as they stood side by side in the kitchen, thought that whatever differences there was underneath it didn't show much when they were dressed up. She was proud of the way Angus was turned out; nothing flashy about him; he could have come from Brampton Hill itself. He knew how to dress, did Angus, and how to carry himself. He had been to Donovan's before and mixed with them lot. Oh, she had no fear of how he would carry himself in that swell place.

"Bye-bye," said Vanessa, looking from Emily to Rosie; and they didn't answer as was usual with them, saying, "Ta-rah," but said, "Bye-bye . . . And enjoy yourselves," they both added.

"Don't wait up mind." Angus turned from the door and Emily answered robustly, "Wait up for you? What would I wait up for you for? Go on, get yourself away."

As they stood waiting at the corner of the street for a bus he looked at Vanessa and said, "There's one thing missing."

"What's that?"

252

"A car. People don't go by bus to Donovan's. You can't get near it for cars."

"Well, we can get off at the stop before and pretend we've left ours parked at the end of the road."

He dug her gently in the ribs and jerked his head as he said, "You've got something."

He was happy as he had never been happy before. The happiness banked down on that corner of his mind where were piled his worries.

In the bus she asked, with excitement in her voice, "Is there a place to dance?"

"Aye, a bit of floor, but . . ." He drooped his head to the side to look full into her face. "Do you dance? Funny, I've never asked you; do you dance?"

"I've had lessons." Her brows moved upwards.

"But you've never been on a dance floor?" He felt superior. This he could teach her, anyway, because he was a good dancer. Heavily made as he was, he was light on his feet.

"Once," she said.

"Once!" His look and tone ridiculed her single effort; then he added, "If you stand on me toes I'll yell the place down mind."

When she laughed and looked down at his size ten shoes his happiness moved in all directions through his body; it made him want to grab her to him and hold her tightly, not do anything, just hold her tightly, like his Uncle Dick used to do to his Aunt Ann. They had been married for twenty years but he used to get hold of her and hug her, and she used to laugh up into his face. She was a little woman, round and fat, but there was something between them, a sort of something. He remembered it when he went to his funeral, that day he had met Van in the train. Lord, that seemed ten years ago. Did he ever think then that . . . ? Blimey? He would have asked them to cart him away if he had even dreamed of it.

They got off the bus, and when they reached the hotel

car park where the cars were spilling over on to the drive it looked as if it was a busy night after all.

"We . . . we mightn't get a table." His voice was flat. "I should have had the sense to slip out and phone when I got the idea."

"I don't suppose it would have made much difference; you likely have to book up a day or so ahead. Anyway, we can always try." She smiled consolingly at him, and her eyes lingered on his face. She wasn't ashamed to be out with him; that was something she was grateful for. Another thing she was grateful for was, he didn't raise his voice outside. He could bawl and shout in the house; even in their room he shouted to her in ordinary conversation as if she was at the end of the street, but outside his manner was different. He tried, did Angus. Oh yes, he tried very hard. She wished he would let her help him. She had learned a lot over the past weeks about the man she had married. She knew, for instance, that he was in constant fear that she would leave him now that there was nothing to hold her, only a marriage that could be dissolved quite easily, it never having been consummated. She knew that he didn't want her to go to work in case she would meet someone else. She was getting to understand all his little ways, his moods, but this did not alleviate the fear in which she held him, the fear that would be strengthened or erased completely when he began to make demands of her; and the time for that was very near. She knew it; she felt it; it was very near.

Having left their outer things in the cloakroom they walked side by side past the open cocktail bar, past the main bar, across the deeply carpeted lounge that was studded with small tables and groups of people, and towards the dining-room. When they were almost there he stopped and said, "Would you like a drink first?" He motioned towards one of the tables, and without looking at them she said, "No. No, I would rather not." She felt excited; nervous, and strangely more ill at ease than he was.

"Good evening, sir. Good evening, madam. You have a table reserved?"

"No, I'm sorry," said Angus. "We just came on speck." His voice sounded airy.

"Ah!" The head waiter looked straight into Angus's face, and Angus said, "I'd be obliged if you could find us a table." The words were a promise and the head waiter said, "Well, sir, you're lucky, there's been a cancellation . . . and a very nice table. It's in the alcove. Come this way. This way, madam."

The table was indeed a nice table. It was screened from part of the main room by an ornamental partition, and the head waiter pulled out a chair that backed on to the partition for Vanessa, giving her a view over part of the dining-room towards the space allotted for dancing and to the small platform where four musicians were seated.

When they were alone for a moment Angus drew in a deep breath and adjusted his coat, then said, "Nice?"

"Lovely." She nodded across the table at him.

As the band struck up the wine waiter came to the table and handed Angus the wine list.

"Well now." He looked at it, then across at her and asked, "What do you fancy?"

"I'll have a sherry," she said.

"Dry or sweet, madam?" asked the waiter.

"Dry, please."

Angus, after a pause said, "Make it two."

"And for later, sir; you'd like a little wine with the meal?"

"Yes. Oh, yes." Angus looked at the wine list again. He knew nothing about wines. He could name any make of beer in the country, even the brands that were popular in the South, but of wines he was completely ignorant. He felt the heat of embarrassment creeping up his neck. He saved it getting further by looking over the list and saying to Vanessa, "Have you any particular fancy?"

Intuitively she knew he needed help and she answered, "I would like," she paused as she was about to say, "a white wine." Instead she named it. "A Graves Supèriur or a Liebfraumilch." She looked at Angus, and the waiter looked at Angus, waiting for the final word. And Angus, taking a deep breath, gave him the final word, and he pronounced it almost as Vanessa had done. "Graves Supèriur," he said, nodding once. He couldn't have attempted to pronounce the other tongue-twister.

"Very good, sir. Very good."

When they were alone again, he stared at her, without speaking now. She knew about wines. The space between them was marked again.

She leaned forward and said to him now, under her breath, and as if she had read his thoughts, "I only know about them because father used to discuss them with mother when people were coming for a meal." Her voice trailed away. She knew she had said the wrong thing. As far as she could remember it was the first time she had spoken her father's name to him since they were married. This could spoil everything. She said quickly, "I'm sorry."

"What you sorry for? No need to be sorry because you know the name of a wine." He flapped his hand lightly at her, and ignored the fact that she had mentioned her father.

Then they were ordering dinner. He knew his way about here. This was safer ground; it wasn't the first time he had ordered dinner. That was until he looked at the menu. "What about a shrimp cocktail to start with?" He was bending towards her.

And she answered, "Lovely."

"Two shrimp cocktails."

"And the main course, sir?"

Again Angus looked at her. She was looking at the menu. It was mostly in French.

He too looked at the menu. He looked at it for quite a while; then he raised his eyes to the waiter and said coolly, "A steak for me, medium rare."

"Very good, sir. Very good, and you, madam?"

She did not say Chicken sauté à la Marengo but fried chicken in sauce, please.

When that was over they both relaxed for different reasons.

There were couples dancing on the floor now, and when she began to tap her fingers to the tune he said laughingly, "Now you're not going to get up there and show them until you've had something to eat."

She laughed softly across at him. They both looked across the room when a roar of laughter came from the direction of the cocktail bar, and as the band struck up a number of couples came through from the lounge and began to dance.

Angus, still looking across the room, said, "I didn't think that was allowed; I thought the dancing space was only for the diners." He had the air of a regular patron.

As the noise and the laughter rose above the music, Angus commented, "They're all high. Looks like a Saturday night after all."

"You used to come here on a Saturday night?"

"Once or twice after we finished the game."

"I never knew you played Rugby until to-night."

There was a twisted smile on his face and he looked at her for a full minute before saying, "There's lots of things you don't know about me, Van."

When she lowered her gaze from his he turned it quickly into a joke. "I've got a medal for life-savin'," he said; "I once dived into four feet of water and got a bairn up in the baths." When she gave a little splutter he said, "It's a fact. There was a gang of lads together and some-one shouted that their Willie or some such was drownin' and I ran along and dived in, and it was nearly fifteen minutes later when I came round; I'd hit me head on the bottom."

"Was anyone drowned?"

"I don't know, I've never found out to this day." They were laughing openly now. "And that's not all," he said. "You should have seen what I got for doing a good deed." He lifted the quiff of his sandy hair from his brow. "Have you noticed that?"

She looked at the scar and said, "Yes, I had noticed it, and I wondered how you got it."

"Oh, that was the payment for doing the good deed. I was on top of a bus and a woman was going to go down the stairs. She had a basket of groceries, a huge basket, an' she was hanging on to the top rail. The bus was going round a corner so I said, 'Give it here, missis; I'll take it down for you.' I was a big brawny fellow of fifteen and she said, 'Thanks, lad,' and she went down the stairs and me after her. Only I tripped, and it was the iron rail, you know the rail you hang on to, that stopped me falling into the road and, boy, I've never seen a basket of groceries go so far in me life. Talk about the three loaves and the five fishes."

He had her laughing now, really laughing. Her shoulders were hunched and she had her hand across her mouth, and when she murmured, "Oh, Angus, don't," he warmed to his theme. He was entertaining her; she was happy; it was the first time he had seen her really laugh. He said, "That's nothing. I could fill a book. Every time I've done a good turn in me life I've got it slapped back straight in me face." Somewhere in the back of his mind he knew this was a tactless remark, and at the same time some part of him was praying that this was one time in his life that he wouldn't have his good deed slapped right back into his face, that life would go on from here and that she would never leave him.

"There was Mrs. Halliday's fire,' he said. "You know Mrs. Halliday, five doors down. I was comin' down the street one day and there was smoke comin' out of her window, and she came out yellin' that her gas stove had caught fire, and in dashed brave Angus Cotton. I couldn't get near the stove. 'Have you got any salt?' I yelled. Mam was always douching our fire with salt when the chimney caught ablaze, you know, and Mrs. Halliday yelled back at me, 'What!' and I yelled, 'Salt!' She was a very methodical woman was Mrs. Halliday and she kept a good supply of stuff in the house – everybody used to go and borrow from her. Anyway, when she pointed I picked up the jar of salt, only it wasn't salt it was sugar, and I threw it on the fire. Believe me we were nearly blown over the railway wall."

Her head was down, her hands were joined tightly in her lap, her eyes were wet; she looked up at him from under her thick short lashes and asked, "What was the end to that?"

"The fire brigade. Her whole kitchen was burnt down. Lord, I daren't pass her door for months after that."

Again she said, "Oh, Angus." He was nice. She had always known he was nice. He was trying to make her happy. Oh, if only he could . . .

The steak came medium rare, the chicken and its sauce were delicious. They ate everything on their plates, and then made their choice from a trolley of assorted sweets. Finally there was coffee.

"Will you have it here or in the lounge, sir?"

They decided to have it in the lounge. They walked around the outskirts of the dancing couples, past the head waiter, whom Angus thanked for an excellent meal and supplemented his thanks with a piece of folded paper, and they were again escorted to their seats.

Over the coffee Angus looked at her and asked, "Enjoying it?"

"It's lovely, Angus, wonderful. Do you know," she twisted round to him, "this is the first time I've ever been out to dinner. I've never enjoyed myself like this before, never in my life."

His eyes ranged over her face. All the tenseness had gone from it; she looked soft and warm and beautiful. There was nobody in here who could hold a candle to her; and she had to develop yet. In two or three years' time she'd be a stunner; a little more flesh on her and she'd be something. Did she know that? Was she aware of how she looked to other people? He must keep her. By fair means or foul he must keep her. He knew now that all his life he had wanted her, and he had got her, but when she came awake could he keep her? Because the raw fact was, she wasn't awakened yet, not to anything. She'd had a bairn but it hadn't really touched her.

He got abruptly to his feet now and, buttoning up his coat, said, "We're going into the fray, it's a quick-step. Have you ever done a quick-step?"

She shook her head. "I've done the twist. I can do the twist." She sounded confident.

"Aw, the twist! That went out with the first programme of 'Top of the Pops'. Quick-step's back, à la ballroom dancin; it's all back. I even saw a young lad on the telly the other night in 'Top of the Pops' put his arm round a girl's waist when they were dancing. Do you know somethin'?" He shook his head at her. "It looked quite indecent, it did really."

He had her laughing again when they reached the dance floor. And there he put his arm around her and walked her gently backwards and forwards.

She had a lightness and rhythm all her own, and soon they were moving in motion together and she smiled up at him, pleased that this was so. Two or three times they were bumped into, and occasionally he had to excuse himself for bumping into someone else; the small floor was packed even before the company from the cocktail bar came on to it again.

It was when they were almost knocked off their balance

by a stumbling, laughing couple that Angus said somewhat angrily, "Here, steady on," and, balancing Vanessa, he glared at the back of the man who had bumped into them, and who was evidently far from sober for he had his head on his partner's neck as he shook with laughter. But Angus's tone piercing his mirth, brought him round and he stared from one to the other. Then, his mouth widening, he said, "Ah, Good Lord! Cotton . . . And you!" His eyebrows moved upwards as he contiuued to stare at Vanessa. Then on a hic of a laugh, he said, "Why; would you believe it? Vanessa Ratcliffe!" He poked his head towards her. "You know me. You remember, at Susan's do? Brian Cornell. Fancy seeing you here."

"Yes, fancy," said Angus flatly, putting his arm round Vanessa once more and moving away into the dance.

Within a minute Cornell was at their shoulder again, shouting above the music and the noise, "We'll have to get together, eh?"

Angus made no reply, and a few minutes later he walked Vanessa back to the lounge.

"You know him?"

She screwed up her face as if trying to remember. "Yes, yes, I've seen him before. He came to a party of Susan's. And you . . . you know him, too?"

"He was in the Rugby team. Still is for all I know." He didn't add that Cornell was one of those individuals who would speak to you if he must in the dressing-room, or when he was drunk, as now, but would ignore you flat in the street when he was with his women folk. And they said there was no class distinction these days. God! That was funny. He remembered thinking along the same lines the day he met Colin Brett in the station. "Have another coffee?" he asked her.

"Yes, I think I will."

He leaned towards her. "What about a liqueur? Would you like a liqueur?"

"No." It was a firm no. "And stop throwing your money

about." She was smiling gently at him. "You'll need all you can get from now on."

"Yes," he said, "I know. But this is a night apart."

They were looking at each other; then her head drooped and she moved the spoon around in her cup as she said, "I'm glad I've got a job, Angus; it'll help, won't it?"

He didn't answer her for a moment; and then he said, "I don't want you to go to work, Van. You know that, don't you?"

"But I can't stay at home all day, Angus; there's nothing to do."

"There will be once you get into the bungalow. There'll be more than you can tackle."

Once more their gaze held until he exclaimed, "Aw, don't let's talk about that now. Drink your coffee and then I'll let you stand on me toes again."

She had just put her cup down when there loomed over them the tall, heavy figure of Brian Cornell. "Ha-ha!" He put a hand on each of their shoulders. "I've caught you."

There was the thing about getting to your feet, Angus knew, when another man came to a table when a woman was present, but he remained seated, his head to one side, staring up into the grinning countenance.

"Spare her a minute?" Cornell's voice was thick and fuddled, and his glance merely touched on Angus as he made the request. But it rested heavily on Vanessa as he said briefly, "Dance?"

"She's not dancing any more."

"What!" Cornell straightened himself. "Now, now. Come on, Cotton; don't play the heavy husband. You should have got over that by now. What is it? Four months? six months? Anyway, I knew her before you did." He laughed as he punched Angus not too gently on the back.

"You do remember me, don't you?" He was leaning

262

over Vanessa, his face close to hers. "Susna's party. You know something? I remember thinking than that you'd beat Susan to a frazzle. Come on, give me this dance?" He caught hold of her arm, but she remained seated.

"Leave go of her!" Angus was now on his feet.

"What! Aw, Cotton, be your age." Cornell thrust his arm backwards across Angus's chest. "Don't come the heavy husband, man. You're out of your depths; they don't act like that where she comes from."

His raised voice had attracted the other occupants of the lounge. There was a man sitting to the right of them who had turned completely round and was listening intently to all that was going on.

"I—I don't want to dance, thank you," Vanessa said; then looking from Cornell to Angus she added quickly, "It's about time we were going."

The look she bent on Angus said plainly, "Please, please don't make a scene," and he obeyed it. His jaw stiff, his fists clenched tight, he waited for Cornell to leave them. But Cornell had no intention of leaving them. Sidling down on to the wall seat to the left of Vanessa, he mumbled thickly, "S'prised to see you; didn't think they would let you up out of the ghetto."

The next second Brian Cornell was up on his feet again, brought there by Angus's hands gripping the lapels of his coat.

"Come on outside."

"Go to the devil!" Cornell tugged himself from Angus's hold; then surveyed him with disdain.

"Are you coming outside?"

"You'd better go." The words came from the man who had taken an interest in the proceedings. He was a youngish forty, dapper looking, small.

"Oh, you, Fowler." Cornell turned towards the man. "Well, you keep out of this."

"Are you coming outside or have I to give it to you here?"

"Have it anyway you like, chum, only don't forget you asked for it." Cornell's mouth curled upwards.

As they went through the lounge, Cornell shouted "Arthur! Tony!" but when Arthur and Tony came from the cocktail bar counter they were stayed by the man Cornell had called Fowler. "Hold your hand!" he said. "They'll have it out on their own."

"What the hell is it all about?"

"You can ask Cornell when it's over."

It was quickly over. Out in the open near the car park they squared up to each other.

If Cornell had been sober he would have been a match for Angus, but in his present condition his blows were aimed wildly; not so Angus's. A blow with the right hand to the stomach was immediately followed by a quick left-right to the face. When Cornell stumbled against the wall, his body bent over double, Angus stood back gasping.

There was a small crowd around them now, all men, with the exception of Vanessa, and as she moved to Angus's side he pushed her roughly away muttering, "Go and get your things on."

After a moment's pause she turned to obey him, and it was then she saw one of Cornell's friends, with his fist at shoulder level, making for Angus from behind, but he never reached him, for experiencing a feeling of anger that was quite new to her she sprang forward crying, "Stop it, you drunken beast you." Whether it was the push she gave the man, or the surprise of being attacked by a girl, he stumbled backwards, and those around sniggered. But the sound died swiftly away as Brian Cornell raised himself up and leant against the wall for support. There was blood running from the corner of his mouth and one eye was already swelling.

Another man, going to Cornell's aid, turned and confronted Angus, crying, "You should be damned well ashamed of yourself. If there was a policeman about I'd hand you over. They're never here when they're wanted."

The quiet voice interrupted again, saying, "You're talking to the wrong fellow; he didn't start it."

"I saw what he started; I was in the lounge. He attacked him first."

"Under provocation."

"Come on." Angus pushed Vanessa past the men and into the hotel again, where the manager was waiting in the foyer, his face no longer smiling. His voice stiff, he said, "This is a very unfortunate incident, sir."

"You should be more particular who you let in then, shouldn't you? And you shouldn't keep on serving drink to drunks."

"Angus!" There was deep appeal in Vanessa's voice and he turned to her and, biting on his lip, said harshly, "All right, all right. Get your things."

She wasn't a minute collecing her coat and hat, and when she returned to the hall Angus was talking to the dapper man; at least, the dapper man was talking to Angus. He turned to Vanessa and said, "Now don't let this little incident worry you. I was just telling your husband that should anything come of it he can call on me to say my piece."

"Thank you." She inclined her head towards him, and, looking intently at her, he smiled and said, "You don't know me but I know of you. I happen to be Brian Braintree's half-cousin." Perhaps it was because he felt that both of them stiffened that he added quickly, "But on the poor side. Brian's father and mine are full cousins but they're not on speaking terms; we weren't invited to the wedding." He brought his head forward as he pulled a face. "I recognised you right away. You were at the Taylor's house about three years ago when I was there. You haven't changed much. My name's Fowler, Andrew Fowler."

All she could say was "Oh." Her face was flushed. She knew he was trying to be nice, smooth things over, but she wished he wouldn't. She felt sure that the very mention of him being connected in any way with her family, or the one into which Susan had married, would make Angus angry. But Angus showed no actual resentment towards the man; in fact, he bade him good-night quite civilly, and when he turned towards the door the man turned with them, saying, "I'm off too." And on the steps of the hotel he left them, adding, "Good-bye. And don't let it worry you. Cornell's been asking for that for a long time."

They walked across the drive and round by the car park and to the bus stop almost in silence. It was as they were standing there that Andrew Fowler passed them in the car. Drawing up sharply and backing towards them, he asked, "Can I give you a lift?"

Angus hesitated for a moment, then said, "Thanks," and opened the door and helped Vanessa in.

"Where can I drop you."

"Oh, anywhere near Caxton Bridge," said Angus in an off-hand manner.

They had gone a little way when Fowler dropped his head backwards as he said, "You're in the contracting business, aren't you?"

"Yes. How did you know?"

"Oh, I'm an architect. I remember seeing you down at Ralstons, in the office or somewhere, and somebody happened to remark that you had started up."

Yes, thought Angus to himself; I bet they did. And I bet they added, "That's him that got old Ratcliffe's daughter into trouble." Only the term wouldn't have been as polite as that.

"How's business going?"

"Oh, not too bad. Could be better though."

"How many are you running . . . lorries?"

"Just the two at the moment." He was talking as if the concern was his own.

"Hmm!" There was a silence after this for a while

266

until Andrew Fowler remarked, "You really need more than two, unless you're always going to be dependent on the big firms."

As if he didn't know that.

When they reached the bridge, and the car stopped, Andrew Fowler turned to Angus and, handing him his card, said, "You may want to get in touch with me if they stir anything up about to-night. As I said, I'll vouch for you being provoked. Cornell's a nasty piece of work; I think you'd better know that."

"I already know it; I've met him afore. We were in the Rugby team together."

"Oh!"

"But thanks. Thanks all the same. And thanks for the lift. Good-night."

"Good-night," said Vanessa. "And thank you."

He nodded to them both and said, "Good-night," and drove off.

They walked down the main road and over the traffic lights, past the railway bridge and up the street, and just before they reached the door he pulled her to a stop and, peering at her in the dimness, said, "I'm sorry. It . . . it was such a grand night, but . . . it wasn't really my fault."

"Oh, I know, Angus, I know. He was a horrible beast, and I'm glad that you hit him." There was a vehemence in her voice that he hadn't heard before, and he smiled slightly and said with some surprise, "You are?"

"Yes. I wanted to hit him myself." She, too, was smiling weakly now. "I pushed that other man." She put her hand up to her face as she added, "I've never done that before in my life; but . . . but I wished I'd had a stick or something."

He put his hand out swiftly and grasped her round the shoulders and pressed her to him for a moment; then they went into the house.

Emily was in; so too were Rosie and Stan; and Emily

turned and looked at them in surprise, saying, "Well! you're back early."

"No good?" asked Rosie.

"Very good," said Vanessa. "Very good indeed." She looked from one to the other; then slowly she started to laugh. Leaning against the table she laughed and laughed.

They had never heard her laugh like this; they had never seen her mouth stretch in real laughter. They watched her put her arm around her waist as her laughter grew. It was almost touching on hysteria and they became infected by it. Angus sat heavily down on a chair, and threw his head back. Emily was laughing, as was Rosie and Stan, although they didn't know what they were laughing about.

"What is it? Tell us the joke," Rosie spluttered, and when Vanessa, gasping and holding her chin tightly, said, "He . . . Angus had a fight," Emily's laughter suddenly ceased and she cried, "MY God! You didn't. Not at the Donovan?"

Vanessa was nodding her head when Rosie, who had also stopped laughing, said, "Oh, our Angus. You had a fight in the Donovan? Trust you to show yourself up."

Vanessa was still gasping, and the tears were running down her face, and she tried to check her mirth as she said to Rosie, "But he didn't, he didn't. There was a man and he was bothering me and he wouldn't stop and," she glanced at Angus, and the laughter bubbled in her again, "he – he made him go outside and blacked his eyes." Her long thin body drooped and she collapsed into a chair.

"Oh, my God!" Emily was no longer amused. Staring at Angus now, she asked, "Who was he? Anybody important?"

"Oh, Mam!" He too had stopped laughing. "Important? Who's important? Yes, I suppose you could say he was important. It was Brian Cornell."

"Cornell? You mean the shop Cornell; him who's got the chain stores?"

"Yes, him who's got the chain stores."

"Well mind, you picked on somebody to hit, didn't you?"

"Aye, I picked on somebody to hit, Mam; and I'll hit him again if I meet up with him."

"Good for you," said Stan. "I know a bit about Cornell. Beer and bawd Cornell, they call him, and it isn't spelt b,o,a,r,d. He's no good."

"We agree on that, Stan." said Angus, nodding across the table.

"Aw dear, dear me," said Emily, getting to her feet. "Trust you to get into trouble. I don't know when you have gone out of this house that something hasn't happened to you."

"We had a lovely dinner," said Vanessa now.

"Aye, what did you have?" asked Stan, aiming to change the subject.

And Vanessa told them, and in detail, and she ended, "We had Liebfraumilch with it." They hadn't, but it sounded better than Graves Supèrier.

"Lieb – what? What in the name of goodness is that when you're out?" asked Rosie.

"It's a wine. Angus chose it."

Both Rosie and Emily were looking at Angus as if they had never seen him before. They didn't ask what he knew about this lieb-frau or whatever it was, they just looked at him, and he laughed openly at them. He was suddenly happy again, very happy. She was with him; she had said he had picked that wine. He bent forward now and, pointing his finger at his mother, said, "And there's something more you won't believe. She hit a fellow." He thumbed in the direction of Vanessa; and now they were all looking at Vanessa, and Emily said in a shocked tone, "You didn't, did you?"

"Yes." She nodded her head in small jerks, smiling widely.

"You must be spiffy," said Rosie.

"No, no; I only had a sherry and two glasses of —" she paused — "Leibfraumilch." She brought her head into deep obeisance as she said it again, and Emily said, "Well, I've heard everything. Was it this fellow, this Cornell fellow?"

"No. I don't know who it was, but after Angus had finished with Brian Cornell this man was going to hit him on the back of the head. I could see it coming, and so I pushed him as hard as I could."

After a few seconds of silence the kitchen was suddenly filled with gales and gales of laughter. It mounted and mounted. Rosie leant her head helplessly against her mother's flabby breast and they rocked together. Stan shook, and Angus shook, and Vanessa laid her head or her arms, so helpless had she become with laughing.

Never before in her life had Vanessa experienced this exhilarating feeling of laughter. They had never laughed at home, not really. Smiled; oh yes, all the time. But they had never really laughed. She couldn't remember hearing her father laugh out loud. She had seen him chuckle. Even Susan never laughed outright. It wouldn't be the done thing for Susan. And Ray? Ray made noises of glee but he didn't laugh. Nobody laughed like these people, the people to whom she had linked herself, and in this moment she loved them. And it was in this moment that her love for Angus was born.

It was almost an hour later when they went into their room and there, doubling his fist, he said, "I hadn't realized it before but my knuckles are hurting."

"I bet his face is hurting more."

They were standing looking at each other on the hearth rug in front of the dead fire, and after a moment he put out his hand and touched her cheek and said under his breath, "You've been grand the night, grand."

She looked down; then turned away, saying, "You'd think I'd been in the fight, I feel so tired."

It had been his practice to put the light out when they were about to get undressed. He knew this was a daft idea right from the beginning, but once he had started it, it became a habit. But to-night he didn't put it out. He took off his coat and loosened his tie, then reached for his pyjamas that were underneath the pillow.

Vanessa had her back to him. She had taken off her dress and was standing in her slip. Then he was surprised to see her pull her night-dress over her head and do some wriggling motions under it. When her slip and panties dropped to the floor he thought, "Well! Well!"

He had no tent under which to undress, nor did he need one. As he stripped off his clothes and got into his pyjamas she was getting into bed and she didn't look at him until he came and sat by her side. His weight brought the edge of the divan right down, and she rolled a little towards him. As they stared at each other the sound of Emily's and Rosie's laughter came to them from the rooms above, and, without taking his eyes from hers, he said, "They're happy."

She nodded at him.

"They think you're the tops."

She could say nothing to this. They hadn't always thought her the tops; perhaps it was because they thought she had come down to their level that they had changed their opinion of her.

He said, "It's been a strange night; a lot has happened."

She nodded again; she was unable to speak.

"We could have some good times together, Van." his hand came out and stroked her cheek, then moved down her neck on to the top of her breasts. Her flesh was trembling but she didn't shrink openly from him. Yet she couldn't look at him. He said softly, "Van! Van!" When she didn't answer or look at him, he was about to say, "All right, we'll leave it," but he asked himself was he daft altogether. Lie there half the night awake, his innards churning as if they were filled with boiling oil? The time had passed for words. They were no longer necessary. Get on with it. That's what he had to do, get on with it.

He had made up his mind, hadn't he that it was the night or the morrow night. If this stillness of hers put him off now it would put him off the morrow, and all the morrows.

As he rose quickly from the bed her eyes spring wide and she was staring at him as he crossed the room and put the light out; then he was throwing back her bedclothes and the next minute she was in his arms and his mouth was on hers and his hands were over her; and it was quite different from what it had been with Brett.

9

"You're not taken with it?"

She turned from him and looked about her once more. "Yes, yes; it's very nice." What she wanted to say was "It's wonderful," and it would be wonderful, she thought, decorating it. She was sure she could do it herself, at least inside. And then there was the garden. Angus could dig it and she would plant it with roses and shrubs and perennials . . . . Yes, she could have said "It's wonderful," but instead she said coolly, "It's very nice."

"What's the matter with it? I know it's all brown paint; I don't think it's been painted inside since it was built; but that'll come off. And I'm telling you, if it was done up we wouldn't be getting it for this price."

"That's the point." She turned towards him again. "We can't afford it."

"Now look!" He spread his fingers wide, almost in front of her face. "You leave that to me. I'll manage. Things aren't going to stay as they are; I'm going on and up. You'll see." He jerked his head at her in his characteristic fashion.

She was staring at him in a way she wouldn't have done this time yesterday. There was a confidence about her, an assurance that hadn't been there then. Had it come about because she had defended him last night? Because she had pushed his assailant? Or because she had taken the strain out of her body in loud hilarious laughter? Or had the difference been created because he had made love to her for the first time and she hadn't shrunk from him. Not that she had enjoyed the process. And when afterwards she had lain in his arms and he had fallen asleep, his flesh still pressed against hers, she had asked herself what all the fuss was about, why people craved for this thing, and she remembered her curiosity concerning it that had kept her awake at nights, made her irritable and a willing victim of Brett's.

She also thought that the gigantic consequences of the act was the most illogical, even diabolical, happening nature could have thought up. A second of unison and you filled your body with a child. And then the further illogicality was that the goodness or the badness of the act was decided by a ceremony, during which a man said you are now married and gave you a piece of paper to that effect. She hadn't got to sleep for a long time.

But whatever it was that had changed her, she was undoubtedly different, and Angus naturally put it down to his love-making.

She said to him now, "How much would you have to pay for a good second-hand lorry?"

He screwed up his eyes at her. "Seven hundred; anything less would be like what I've got, held up by paper and string. But . . . but what are you getting at?"

"Take the money that you're going to put down on this and put it on a lorry. You can pay it off by instalments, just as if you were buying this."

He came and stood close to her, his bulging chest almost touching her. "You'd give up this so's I could get a lorry?"

The look in his eyes embarrassed her and she turned her glance away as she said lightly, "Perhaps I'm after something bigger, and the only way to get it is for you to get more business."

He pulled her round squarely to him. "It could mean staying in number twenty-four for God knows how long, you realise that, don't you?"

"Yes."

"And you don't mind?"

The question was silly and he knew it, but when she answered truthfully, "Not as much as I used to," he nodded at her, and after a moment during which his gaze burrowed deep into hers, said, "You'll do." It was a compliment. Then stepping back from her, he ended, "You know, if I give it up I'll lose fifty quid."

Her reaction was immediate. "Oh no! He'll give it back to you."

"I can't see him doing it."

"But I thought you knew him."

"Oh, aye, I know him; but business is business."

"I'll go with you; I'll help to explain."

His head went back and he laughed. Then looking at her again he said, "I think you would an' all."

"Well," she began walking down the narrow hall towards the front door, "you can tell him that when, one day, we go after a bigger place we'll put the business in his hands."

She found herself swung round, and the next minute her breath was taken away with his kisses, which covered her mouth, her eyes, her neck, and she became filled with panic when she thought where his frenzy of loving might lead: daylight would hold no obstacle, they were alone in this house. She managed to press herself from him and to say between gasps, and in an airy fashion, "Come on, come on; there's fifty pounds at stake."

He looked at her, at her flushed skin, which was like tinted cream, and he swallowed deeply; then with a rumbling laugh he pulled her arm tightly against his side, and he held it there as he locked the door. Then they walked down the path, but before they went through the gate he drew her to a stop and, leaning his face close to hers, he said, "I'm so happy I could bust."

The summons came on the Wednesday afternoon. It was served by a policeman.

In the usual way Angus wouldn't have been in the house on a Wednesday afternoon, but he had wanted to show Vanessa the lorry; after all, it was she who had really got things moving.

Reg Walker had given him back his deposit without much demur – a five-pound note had eased the situation here – and on the Saturday afternoon he and Fred Singleton had gone lorry hunting and had found one, but Angus hadn't been able to pick it up until an hour ago, when the owners use for it had come to an end.

Vanessa and Emily had stood on the pavement and admired the new acquisition, which showed up to disadvantage Fred's lorry. They were both on their way to a job, but now they returned to the kitchen and the cups of tea Emily had poured out for them, also to continue the discussion of hiring another man for the old lorry. Angus was eager for this move, but Fred seemed reluctant. Angus was wondering about Fred. There was, he put it to himself, something up with him these days. He hadn't the interest in the business he once had, yet he had started it. It was his missis, Angus thought; she was a nagger. She didn't belong to these parts and had never settled. Doncaster was her home.

Angus was saying, in answer to Fred's statement that it was risky engaging another driver, "You've got to take a risk, man; I've put me lot into that out there," when the knock came on the front door.

Emily returned to the kitchen. She stared at Angus for a full minute before she said, "It's for you. It's the polis."

"The polis?" He looked puzzled, he had forgotten about Friday night. Then under his breath he muttered in horror, "It must have been nicked, the lorry."

Emily shook her head, then stood aside as he thrust himself into the passage. And now she looked at Vanessa, who had come to her side, and whispered, " 'Tisn't the lorry."

Vanessa knew what it was before Angus returned to the

room. He walked past them and to the table, and there he flung down the sheet of paper, then put his fist on it and looked first at Emily then at Vanessa. He looked at her for quite a while before he turned his gaze to Fred, and it was to him he spoke. "That bugger, Cornell, that I told you about; he's summonsing me." He always tried to curtail his swearing in front of Vanessa, but his good intentions went by the board at this moment. "The bastard, summonsing me for assault. I told you, Fred, he started all this. He's a good three inches taller than me and could give me a stone any day, and if one of his blows had contacted, as drunk as he was, I don't suppose I'd have stood much of a chance. He's got fists and feet on him as hard as a bull. I've felt them on the field many a time when we've been in the scrum, and he's summonsing me!"

"Aw, Angus, you don't want nowt like that at this time." Fred pushed his cap on the back of his head. "Summonsing means money, a solicitor. And then there'll be a fine; as likely as not you'll get fined."

"I'll not, you know." Angus rounded on him. "I'll not you know. I'll tell them exactly what happened. And you will an' all, won't you, Van?" He was glaring at her.

"Yes, yes, of course, Angus." Her voice was low but firm.

"There; he'll not get his own way in this. By God, no!"

"What does the charge say?" It was the first time Emily had spoken, and he picked up the paper and after a moment read, "Assault occasioning actual bodily harm."

Emily said nothing for a while, but her colour faded. Then she sat down and muttered, as if to herself, "That's bad . . . You'll have to get help."

"I'll get help all right, don't you worry." He looked at the summons again and said scornfully, "Actual bodily harm!"

"Don't you think you should go and see that Mr. Fowler?"

He stared at Vanessa; then said, "Aye. Fowler . . ." His

voice was high now. "Aye, yes, you've got something there,
Van. Funny, he thought something might come of it. He
said if I should need him he'd speak up for me, but by
damned I never dreamed I would. It just shows you,
doesn't it? It was a little punch up, clean, nothing dirty."
He was speaking to Fred again. "And that was that.
Finished as far as I was concerned. And now this." He
swiped the paper aside; then looking at Vanessa, said,
"I've got to go through the town, I'll drop in and see him
if he's there."

"I'll come with you."

"Oh, there's no need; not yet, anyway."

"I'd like to come."

"Aye, let her go along of you," said Emily, and Angus
shrugged his shoulders. It looked an indefferent, non-
chalant movement, and it covered up the fact that he was
glad she was coming. He turned to Fred. "I shouldn't be
more than fifteen minutes behind you, all right?"

"All right," said Fred. "You be as long as you like."

"Time's money and it looks as if I'm going to need it,
doesn't it?" He nodded from one to the other.

Andrew Fowler's office was a surprise to both of them.
It stood in a new block of buildings. There was a secretary in the outer office, and she asked if they had an
appointment.

"No," said Angus, "but Mr. Fowler told me to look
him up."

The secretary spoke into the phone, and listened, and
she'd hardly replaced the phone and said, "Will you wait
a moment?" when Andrew Fowler appeared at the con-
necting door. He looked pleased to see them. "Hello," he
said; then, "I'm going to give a guess. He didn't waste
much time."

"You're right there." Angus smiled and nodded towards
him, as he handed him the summons.

"Come in." He stood aside and allowed them to walk
into the inner office; and pushing a seat towards Vanessa,

278

he said, "Do sit down." And he motioned to another for Angus to be seated. He did not go round the desk and sit in his chair but perched himself on the corner of the desk, and after reading the summons he looked from one to the other and said, "Well, I'm not at all surprised. He's a vindictive beggar, Cornell, nasty piece of work. But assault occasioning actual bodily harm, that's laying it on. And he'll likely have a good solicitor. You'll have to be well prepared. Have you a solicitor?"

"No, and I don't feel like paying for one. I'll do my own defending. I can only speak the truth, and my wife here will tell exactly what happened. And . . . and then there's you."

"Oh well, you can rely on me. I'll put them in the picture." He laughed now, adding, "And as much as I'd like to hear you defending your own case I think it would be wise to get a solicitor."

"How much would that cost?"

"Oh, it all depends. Fifteen, twenty guineas. If you lose you'll have to pay the costs. And then the fine can be pretty stiff for what's stated here, I think."

"How much?"

"Oh, I'm not sure, fifty I'd say."

They both looked at Vanessa because she had groaned, and she, looking at Fowler, said with a weak smile, "And this morning he bought a new lorry."

"You did?" He looked at Angus with interest, then asked, "You've got another man?"

Angus moved his tongue quickly around his upper lip and after a pause said, "No, not yet; but I've got the promise of a fellow." And he added, "It looks as if I'm going to need half-a-dozen lorries, and the blokes to go with them, afore I'm finished."

"Oh, I don't think it'll be as bad as that. A lot depends on who's on the Bench and how they're feeling."

"And . . . and you don't mind speaking up for me?"

Andrew Fowler looked at the big fellow before him. He

looked rough, he talked rough, but there was something about him that attracted one. It had certainly attracted the daughter of Jonathan Ratcliffe. He would like to know the real ins and outs of how it came about, and he would through time. In the meantime he liked the idea of giving the fellow a hand.

Andrew Fowler was honest enough, as he always was with himself, to see his philanthropic gesture to Cotton as a roundabout way of getting his own back for past slights received from distant relatives. Who knew, but if this rough diamond rose he might come to be an embarrassment to the combined families of Ratcliffe and Braintree. As it was, he must be something of an embarrassment to the Ratcliffes, for had he not stormed the citadel of the mighty and snatched their convent-bred lily white chick from under their noses? Indeed, yes. And from the little he had seen of her the chick was adapting herself to her changed circumstances. She was out to push this rough man of hers. He would like to bet it was she who reminded him about coming here this morning; it was she who certainly had brought up the subject of the lorries again. They said she was only seventeen. She looked older, nineteen at the least. Having a child likely did that; and, of course, being under the tuition of Mr. Angus Cotton.

He chuckled. Andrew Fowler in his puckish way liked people. He liked these two, and no matter how it worked out he would enjoy giving them a lift. And he wouldn't lose anything by it, of that he was sure. Not if young Cotton got some lorries going, he wouldn't. He nodded inwardly and said, "By the way, I'm going to look at a site yon side of Durham some time this week. Plastows have got the contract for excavating. He's not all that big and I know that he's often very glad of an extra lorry or two when any of his fellows are laid off, and this can happen, especially after a long run and they get a bit tired and want a break, a couple of weeks' holiday or something. Will I mention your name?"

"Aye, yes. Thank you very much."

"How are you fixed now?"

"Oh, I'm set for the next month up at the quarry, Peterson's."

"Well, look me up before that . . . Oh, I forgot; we're most certainly sure to meet before then, aren't we?" He slid off the edge of the table, saying, "And don't worry too much about this. If I were you I'd go and have a talk with a solicitor. Millard's a good chap. Millard and Fogerty, you know, in the Market Square."

"Thanks, I'll think about it."

Angus waited until they reached the outer door, and there, turning to Andrew Fowler, he said, "Thanks again for everything."

"A pleasure." Fowler nodded his head. "And don't be afraid to pop in any time."

"I won't. Good-bye."

"Good-bye, Mrs. Cotton." Andrew Fowler inclined his head towards Vanessa, and she answered, "Good-bye, Mr. Fowler." She wanted to thank him, but she refrained; Angus had done that.

In the lorry, Angus turned towards home, and presently he said, "It isn't often you meet blokes like that, is it?"

"No. I think he's very nice; and – and he could be a great help to you."

He glanced quickly towards her; then back to the wheel again before saying, "Do you think so?"

"Yes, yes, I do indeed."

Angus was quiet now. All of a sudden he was wondering why this stranger was going out of his way to help him. Or was he aiming to help himself to something that didn't belong to him? You could never trust blokes and she would catch anybody's eye; and that fellow had a discerning one. Yes, he could say that. He didn't look at her as he asked, "Is he married?"

Vanessa bit on her bottom lip and with a great effort she did not smile or laugh but answered, "I don't know."

"But you had met him before; he said you had."

"Well, if I did I don't remember." Then she added a little comfort. "He's not the kind of man one would remember, is he?" She was learning quickly.

After a while he said, "When we're down this far I'll drop in at the station yard and see if some spares have arrived; those bits I sent for out of the catalogue, you know. You don't mind waiting a minute?"

She smiled and said, "No, of course not."

In the station yard he got out of the cab, saying, "I won't be a tick," and she answered, "Don't hurry. I want a magazine; I'll get it from the stall."

"Well, come on then." He held up his arms and gripped her waist and lifted her down. Whenever he touched her now he wanted to kiss her, and his hands stayed on her longer than was necessary. Her face had been smiling as he lifted her down, very like how she had looked when he used to lift her into the garden barrow. Now, as on the very last time he had done this, he saw her expression change, and for the same reason.

She was looking over his shoulder, and he turned round and saw Jonathan Ratcliffe and his wife passing at a distance of not more than six yards, and in spite of his toughness his heart began to bounce and he was filled with apprehension, as if she'd be snatched away from him.

Vanessa's heart, too, was bouncing; she had an almost irresistible urge to run forward. She knew that her mother would have stopped if her father hadn't been there. It was he who had caught sight of her first, and the look he had sent across the distance told her that he didn't know her, nor did he want to.

She stood watching them until they reached the car, then she turned away and was quite unable to check the flood of tears that rained down her face.

"Get up." His voice was rough and he almost pushed her back into the cab. He revved up the engine as if he were at the start of a race, and he drove out of the yard ahead of Jonathan Ratcliffe's car. "Bloody nowts!" He was muttering under his breath, swearing with every other word; but she remained silent until they reached the house. And when they entered the kitchen Emily asked, "What's happened now?" She moved towards Vanessa, then looking quickly at Angus said, "What is it?"

"I dropped in at the station, and she saw them . . . From up there. And she could have been a mongrel dog for all the notice they took of her."

When Vanessa sat down at the table and dropped her head on to her arms it was Emily who went to her and said comfortingly, "Never mind, lass. Never mind. Time heals everything."

"My – my mother would have stopped. I – I think she would." She raised her head and looked up at Emily. "I'm sure she would."

"Aye, I'm sure she would, lass. But it's him. Men are like that. But one of these days you'll come across your mother on her own and then you can have a crack. You'll see; the opportunity'll present itself, it always does."

Vanessa now looked towards Angus. His face was hard and tight, and she said, "I'm not really dying to see them, or anything like that. It's the truth. I would never go back even if I had the chance; but it was just, just coming on them like that."

"Aye," he said. Then turning abruptly, he added, "I'm off."

She got up hastily and followed him into the passage, and at the door she said quietly, "After all, Angus, they are my people. You," her voice dropped to a whisper, "you – you would defend Emily to the last gasp. You know you would."

"Aye," he said again, "but not if she let me down when I most needed her. That would have finished me. But it's all right." He put out his hand and tapped her cheek. "See you later."

When she returned to the kitchen, Emily said

brusquely, "Take no notice of him. Men look at things differently. Of course you would be upset seein' them; you would have been unnatural if you hadn't. Now go an' wash your face, and I'll make a cup of tea. And then I'm goin' to do a bit of bakin'. I'll show you how; it's about time you learned. You can try your hand at a lemon pie and a fruit loaf; he's fond of both. Go on now."

Vanessa went into the scullery, and as she sluiced her face under the tap she asked herself why had she to run into her parents at this time. She knew that there was always a possibility of meeting up with her mother, or Susan; her father she was less likely to meet as he was in the works all day. She had often pictured meeting her mother, and she always imagined them talking; there would be an interval filled with embarrassment and then they would come together, and talk, because her mother, although narrow, wasn't as hard grained as her father.

But that she should see both her mother and father on this particular day, and when she was with Angus, was most unfortunate. He had enough to think about with the summons. And that was another thing. They had more than likely heard of the fight; such kind of news travelled fast. In their estimation, she would have now sunk even further, if that were possible.

As she swilled the water around the shallow sink there returned to her a momentary longing for the material comforts of her home, the bathroom in particular, and on this thought came regret that she had turned down the bungalow. Oh, she was tired of it all. She had made a mess of her life, if anyone had.

As despondency flooded over her she gazed at herself in the small mirror on the wall to the side of the sink. Her face looked longer; she looked white and miserable. This was how she looked, and felt, before she took the pills. She stepped back from the mirror as if frightened of what she saw. There must be no more of that; she had caused enough trouble to so many people. Her parents might not want to have anything to do with her; nor anyone from her own class; and she was not unaware she was merely living under kindly toleration from the class she was in now, even from Emily and Rosie; but there was one person who did want her, one person all along who had stood by her, and who needed her. And not only sexually. In an odd sort of way she knew that to him she was the equivalent of a gold medal at the Olympic Games, or of a knighthood; in short, she was an honour. Men needed honour, recognition of having done something, acquired something, something that caused other men to look up to them or hate them as Angus did her father.

Angus and her father were opposed in every way. Yet oddly their aims were the same, both were ambitious for recognition.

She thought it strange that she had this knowledge of them while they hadn't it of themselves.

10

The case was due to be heard on Thursday, a day over three weeks since the summons had been issued.

The tension in the house had been mounting over the last few days, and as Rosie had remarked, on a laugh, last night, the case was causing nearly as much interest in the town as a Cup Final. The lasses in the factory were betting on it, as were the people roundabout the doors. Would Cornell, with his money and influence, win by a length? Or would Cotton, who was defending his wife from insults, romp home? It was anybody's guess.

Vanessa herself was very uneasy. Up till two o'clock on the Wednesday afternoon when she returned home – it was half-day closing – she had made her concern centre around the size of the fine that would be imposed on Angus; she wouldn't allow herself to think of an alternative. But once she entered the house the suppressed dread that Angus could be sent to prison burst into the open and she was forced to face it.

She had just got in the door when Emily, turning to her, said, "Aw, there you are, lass. You've just missed him by about five minutes. He came in over the moon. He thought old Cargill and Howard were goin' to be on the Bench the morrow, but old Cargill's laid up, and he hears that Mrs. Brett's takin' his place; so he'll be all right . . . What's the matter? You fellin' funny?"

"Just a bit. I . . . I felt a bit sick in the train."

"It's an empty stomach; that's what's the matter with

you. Get somethin' down you and you'll be all right."
She walked towards the oven. "And you're worryin' about
the morrow. But you can rest your mind easy; everythin'
will go smoothly now. It's ten to one she'll say 'Case Dismissed', like that." She turned and snapped her fingers
towards Vanessa before stooping down and bringing a
dish from the bottom shelf. "Mr. Brett thought a lot of
our Angus. It was a bad day for him and everybody else
when he went . . . . What is it, lass?" She looked towards
Vanessa where she was hurrying into the scullery. Then
going to the door she said, "Well, it's better up, whatever
it is."

A few minutes later Vanessa, returning to the kitchen,
said, "Do you mind if I lie down for a minute, Emily? I
couldn't eat anything yet."

"Go on, lass, go on. Put your feet up. I'll bring you a
cup of tea in. But try an' get over it afore teatime, for he
plans takin' you out somewhere, the pictures, or some
place in Newcastle, because, as he says, if we sit here the
night we'll be jabberin' about nothin' else but the morrow. He should be home early, he says; there was only a
few more loads and they'll be finished up at the quarry.
They're not startin' on a new lot until Monday. Go on
now."

In the room Vanessa stood with her back to the door
and pressed her hand tightly across her mouth, as if to
prevent from escaping the groan that was straining up
through her body. Irene Brett being kind to Angus!

The charge was assault occasioning actual bodily harm.
They had never put it into words in the house but they
all knew that men were sent to prison every day in the
week on that charge.

And Irene Brett was to be Angus's judge! Irene knew
that Brett was the father of her child. She had seen the
knowledge in her eyes the morning Brett died; her look
had been full of bleak hate, and it had found its target.

But Irene had said nothing. Why hadn't she come to the

house and openly accused her of stealing her husband? Of causing his death? She had asked the question of herself at the time, but now she asked herself no longer for she knew the reason why Irene Brett had remained silent. It had been gall to a woman of her calibre that she should lose anything she considered hers, especially to a young, unformed girl, and one of no particular ability; she had kept silent because she couldn't bear the public ignominy of having been passed over.

But at ten o'clock to-morrow morning she would have her revenge. She'd pay her out through Angus, and it would be the maximum sentence she would give. She could almost see his face stretching in surprise that Mrs. Brett should do this to him.

When Emily brought her in the cup of tea she was sitting in the chair by the fire, and Emily said, "Now why don't you take your shoes off and put your feet up?"

"No; it's passing off a little; I'm all right now."

"You don't look it. You never had much colour, but you're as white as a sheet. It's the morrow you're worrying about, I know by meself. Me stomach's been as sick as a dog's, but since he was in and told me about Mrs. Brett I feel better. She does a lot of good work, does Mrs. Brett; she gets things done. Some don't like her. But there it is; if you get things done people don't like you, do they? Now drink that up, and do as I say and put your feet up for a while."

When she was alone again Vanessa joined her hands tightly between her knees and began to rock herself slightly; then, taking off her shoes, she got to her feet and began to walk from one side of the small room to the other . . . She had to do something. She stopped in her pacing. She would go and see her. NO. NO. That would mean going to Brampton Hill and she couldn't bear to go so near her old home. Would she be able to find her in one of the offices in the Town Hall? But wasn't there some rule about getting at the jury? She shook her head. But she wasn't a jury, she was a magistrate. Well, it might still hold good. And what would she say when she did see her? . . . What could she say? "Will you please be lenient with Angus?" No, no; that wasn't the line to take with Irene Brett. She picked up the cup of tea from the low table, and although it was still hot she drank it almost at once; and as she put the cup down again she knew what she was going to do.

A few minutes later, when she again entered the kitchen with her coat on, Emily turned to her in surprise, saying, "Where you off to? What's up?" But all she said was, "You don't have any stamps, do you?" knowing full well that Emily never had any stamps.

"No. What would I do with stamps, lass?"

"I've run out and I want to write a letter. And Angus will be needing some; there's two letters he must get off to-night."

"You don't look fit to go out; I'll go along for you."

"No, no, Emily; the walk will do me good, give me something to do. And when I come back I'll have my dinner."

"Please yourself. Please yourself." There was the old tart note in Emily's voice, but Vanessa was used to it now. As Angus said, it meant nothing.

She hurried down to the bottom of the street, walked along the main road to the pedestrian crossing, crossed over and walked a little further up the far pavement to the telephone kiosk. She knew the number; her mother had at one time frequently phoned next door. She stared down at the phone for a full minute before she picked it up. Then she inserted the coins and dialled Fellburn 538506. She knew it wasn't likely that either Colin or Paul would answer the phone; and if the house was running as it had done for some time past there would be no woman there in the afternoon – Irene had no au pair girl now but a daily who came twice a week in the mornings; so it would be Irene or silence.

When she heard Irene Brett's voice her lips moved but she couldn't speak.

"Hello. This is Fellburn 538506."

"Mrs. Brett?" She did not say Auntie Irene, nor yet Irene.

"Yes." There was a pause. "Who . . . who's speaking?"

"Vanessa . . . Cotton." She had almost said Ratcliffe. There was no sound on the line now, and Vanessa said quickly, "Are you there?"

"What do you want?"

"I just want to tell you something; and . . . and it isn't that Brett was the father of my baby because you already know that, don't you?"

The line seemed to be dead, but Vanessa knew that Irene Brett was still at the other end, and she swallowed and went on, "What I want to tell you is, that if you take out your spite on me through Angus I'll stand up in Court and shout out the reason why you're doing it. If you send Angus to prison he'll come out again, but you'll never be able to come out from where this town will put you. You'll be fin—" There was no longer anyone on the other end of the line, the receiver had been banged down.

She leant against the dust-covered side of the kiosk and closed her eyes for a second. Would she do what she had said she would if Angus received a prison sentence? Would she stand up and cry "She's only doing this for spite because her husband gave me a baby?" She didn't know; she wouldn't know until the moment came. She had already made a name for herself in this town, but if she did that her mother and father, the whole family, and, she imagined, the family that Susan had married into would be bent low with embarrassment. And once sentence was passed, would it help Angus? Perhaps not; the only thing it would do would be to show him that she cared what happened to him. But again, would Angus thank her for publicly naming the father of her child? He had never pressed her to know who it was, but at times she felt his curiosity. How would he respond when he knew it was "Mr. Brett", the man he admired who had done this to her?

Well, whatever she would do to-morrow morning, the main thing was, she felt, she had convinced Irene Brett that she was quite capable of acting on her word.

She came out of the box and walked farther along the road, until she was opposite the little sub post office. And there she waited for an opportunity to cross . . .

As Vanessa had come out of the kiosk Angus had passed her in the lorry. It was impossible in the traffic to attract her attention, but he went round the island and came back up the other side of the road, and as he parked he saw her going into the post office.

He was waiting for her when she came out, and the first thing she said was, "How long have you been here?"

"Oh, only a minute. I . . . I saw you as I was passing." He did not mention seeing her coming out of the phone box, although he wondered who she was phoning; but he said quickly, "Mam all right?"

"Yes, yes, of course. Why shouldn't she be? You were in at dinner time."

"Oh, aye." He stared at her. She looked paler than usual, her eyes larger.

"You all right?" he asked.

"I felt a bit sick when I came in. It was the train; it was packed, being Wednesday; I had to stand all the way. Are you finished for the day?"

"Yes," he answered; "but I've picked up another bit of business that'll keep Fred and me busy until the start of the quarry again. Come on, get in; I can't leave her parked here. And I'll have a cuppa before I put her away."

Seated next to her, he said, "Where to, modam?"

Taking his cue, she replied, "Twent-four Ryder's Row, Cotton."

"Very good, modam."

He had to drive to the next side turning, back into it,

and come down the main road again before he could enter the street, and as he drove he thought, "Why hasn't she said who she was phoning?"

When they entered the house Emily greeted them with, "Oh, there you are. Going out in ones and coming in in twos. I suppose you want a cuppa."

"That's the idea." He nodded at her.

Then she said to him, "I think you should see she goes and lies down; she's out of sorts." She jerked her head towards Vanessa.

"Now, does she ever take notice of anything I say?" He was keeping things light.

Vanessa went into the room and took her coat off, and a few minutes later he joined her. He had a cup of tea in his hand and, sitting down and crossing his legs, he looked at her and asked casually, "Who were you phoning?"

He watched her mouth open and close again and her expression change, her face becoming even paler; and he uncrossed his legs and said, "Well, who were you? I saw you coming out of the box."

She was so taken aback that she hadn't a lie on her lips. He got to his feet and moved slowly towards her, the cup of tea still in his hand, and after surveying her for a moment he asked thickly, "What's the mystery?"

"There's no mystery."

"All right then," he inclined his head towards her patiently, "who were you phoning? It's as simple as that. Give me a straight answer. Who were you phoning?"

When she didn't answer at all but made to turn from him he put the cup down noisily on the table, grabbing her arm at the same time. Then pulling her round to him, he looked deep into her face as he said, "You weren't in the telephone box to rob it, were you? And you weren't in there to do wilful damage, were you? You were in there to phone . . . Who were you phoning?"

"A – a girl in the shop."

"But the shop's closed this afternoon." His voice was very low and ominously quiet.

"I know the shop's closed this afternoon. I—I phoned at her home."

"What's her name?"

This was easy. "Teresa Bumpstead."

"And her number?"

Could she think of a number? Of all the thousands, the millions of numbers in all the directories in the country she couldn't think of one number. All she could remember was that all Newcastle numbers began with 53, and she stammered "Five, three . . ."

"Don't think too hard," he said. Then, his voice rising slightly, he added, "Are you going to tell me the truth?"

If she said "I was phoning Mrs. Brett," he would say, "what the hell did you want to do that for? She's on my side." And he would believe this until to-morrow, when he found she wasn't.

"You were phoning your house, weren't you?"

"Oh, no! No, Angus." Her voice was high with relief. "No, I wouldn't do that." She watched his face relax for a moment, then tighten again as he said, "Well then, it was some bloke . . . Fowler. You were phoning Fowler?"

"Oh, Angus!" She closed her eyes and put her hand to her cheek and smiled faintly. "Why would I want to phone Mr. Fowler?"

"Because he's breaking his neck to help me, and all the while I'm wondering why; and I tell meself I haven't far to look for the reason. Why would he want to help me if it wasn't for you being a sort of distant family connection? . . . And mind," he stabbed his finger at her, "I'm being kind when I think along those lines, 'because he's got an eye wide open, he has."

"Don't be silly." Her voice was harsh now; it was a woman's voice showing impatience with an unreasonable man.

"All right." He turned and walked to the fireplace. "If

it wasn't Fowler, then tell me who it was. Look." He swung round and glared at her fiercely. "It's as easy as that. Just tell me who you were phoning, because I'll not let up on you until I know. I'm made like that. It'll niggle and niggle at me mind, getting bigger and bigger every minute. I've got a mind that makes mountains out of molehills where you're concerned. You know that already, don't you, and you're playing on it?"

"I'm not, Angus. That's unfair; I'm not. I don't play on people's emotions."

Dropping down into the chair, he said, "All right, I'll be reasonable. Let's start from the beginning, eh? You went to the phone; I saw you coming out. You must have gone to phone somebody. I've asked you a simple question and you can't give me a simple answer. Now this is how I look at it. If you've nothing to hide why can't you tell me truthfully who you were phoning?"

She stared down into his face; then said slowly, "All right, Angus; I'll tell you who I was phoning . . . to-morrow dinner-time."

He screwed up his eyes at her. "After the case you mean? Is it to do with the case?"

"Yes and no. There's more to it than that."

"But why did you . . . ? Who did you get in touch with? Look. I'll be all right; you've got no need to worry." He got to his feet and gripped her arms. "If you're worrying about me, stop it. I've got a good solicitor. And there's our Mr. Fowler." He smiled a tight smile and made a deep obeisance with his head. "And above all, I've got somebody on the right side of the Bench, Mrs. Brett."

She lowered her head slightly and she kept her eyes shadowed with her lashes as she said, "I'll tell you to-morrow. Have patience with me, Angus. As I said, there's more in it than that, I mean the case. I—I promise you I'll tell you to-morrow."

After staring at her bent head for a moment his grip on her arms tightened and he shook her once before grinding out below his breath, "You're not going to walk out on me, are you? That's not what you're going to tell me?"

She was looking at him, half-smiling now, as she said quietly, "No, Angus, that's not what I'm going to tell you."

He drew in a deep, shivering breath, and after a moment he said, "Reprieved. For a while at any rate. But one of these days you will, won't you, Van? You'll say to me; I've had enough, I'm going back . . . And you know what I'll do on that day . . . do you? Do you know what I'll do? I'll kill you. I mean it." He nodded his head at her.

She gave a little huh of a laugh and unwittingly her smile held derision as she said, "Well, I won't have to tell you, will I, because now I want to stay alive at least a little longer."

He couldn't stand being laughed at, or taken lightly. He turned away and punched his fist into the palm of one hand, then went to the little table in the corner and sat down, and, picking up the letters that had come that morning, he read them once more. One was a request for his estimate on clearing a building site. It had been sent to him direct, and not to Fred – although Fred always passed any correspondence on to him – and he felt he had Andrew Fowler to thank for it. A lot might depend, he knew, not only on his estimate, but how he got it out and also on the accompanying letter.

He put his hand slowly up to the little bookcase and lifted down Fowler's "King's English," and opened it at a page on which the heading read: "On sustained metaphor". A page of Egyptian hieroglyphics would have posed no greater problem, and he did at this odd moment what he had been wanting to do for weeks, but had been too proud to voice his need. "Will you take me through this?" he said. He lifted up the book to shoulder height but did not turn round, and when she did not answer he moved his head slowly until he had her in the corner of his eye.

Then he said, "It'll be a laugh for you. I've made so many bloomers you could fill a book. 'Those are them' won't be in it. I've got some prize ones."

She was standing by the side of the table now, and she looked into his face, saying softly, "Don't, Angus."

"Don't what?"

She did not add, "You know what I mean," and he pushed it no further.

Taking the book from his hand, she looked at it, saying softly, "I'd love to help you, you know that. There's a lot I don't know, although English was my best subject. We," she glanced down at him, "we could learn together."

He covered her hand on the book, pressing it hard, saying, "You know, this is only another ruse to keep you, you know that, don't you? Everything I do is aimed at keeping you." He was looking at her in a way he some-times did, like a small boy who was asking to be needed, and loved. But he wasn't a small boy, he was a man, a rough, arrogant, bumptious man, who would, as he said, kill her if he thought she was going to leave him.

The issue seemed to have moved away from the tele-phone box to the region of raw emotions, but she could cope with this. And so she turned from him, saying, "Go and put the lorry away. I haven't had any lunch yet; I'll get it, and then we'll go out." She half turned her head. "You were thinking of going out, weren't you?"

"Who told you that? Oh, me mam. She can't keep her mouth shut, that one." He rose swiftly and stalked out of the room, and she heard him crying to Emily, "You and your big mouth, Ma Cotton; you can't even let me spring a little surprise on me own."

He was covering up the things that hurt and embar-rassed him. During the past half hour he had been the questioning jealous husband, the young man pleading for education, two kinds of small boy, one loving, one rough, loud-mouthed, but threading all his attitudes was a man with a deep need.

296

There came, in the region of her heart, a restricted feeling that turned into an ache. The ache spread until her body was filled with it. If he went to prison, what would she do? She'd be lost. Yes, without him she'd be lost. She—she was in love with him. No; not just in love, she loved him. How had it come about that she should love Angus Cotton because he was . . . ? She didn't tell herself all the things he was, but she went over all the things he wasn't. Was, or wasn't, it didn't matter; what did matter was that if he went to prison she wouldn't live until he came out again. She loved him.

They shouted to Angus as he and Vanessa went down the street the following morning: "Good luck, lad." It was as if they had been waiting behind their doors for him. One wit cracked, "See you at the assizes, Angus," and Angus turned a laughing face towards the man and shouted, "And I wouldn't be surprised at that an' all, Jim."

"Ten years' hard, you'll get, Angus, ten years, not a day less. You might as well have been in the train robbery."

"Aye, Mrs. Grant, you're right there; I might as well."

When they were on the bus he turned to her and said, "They were enjoying themselves, weren't they?" There was a kind of pain in the back of his eyes, and she answered softly, "I don't think they meant to be unkind."

"Huh!" He jerked his chin up. "You defending 'me ain folk'? Oh, I know them, I know them all like the back of me hand. They'll all come round and help you when you're in trouble, but that doesn't stop them being happy that you are in trouble, somebody else is getting it, not them . . . Do you follow me?"

Yes, in a way she did follow him, and she was surprised at the depth of his knowledge concerning his . . . ain folk, as he called them.

He kept on talking. "Human nature all over, that is. If you move away from the street you're a nowt, an upstart; if you stay in the street you're a stick-in-the-mud, you've got no gumption. You can never be right. I used to worry about it at one time." He turned his face fully towards her. "Can't imagine me worrying, can you?"

"Yes, Angus, yes, I can imagine you worrying." She had a desire to take his hand; he was worrying now. He had been worrying since he got up. He had never stopped talking, which was proof that he was worrying.

"I used to worry because I couldn't get Mam into a better house. I used to worry because I hadn't got a decent job; then when I got promoted I used to worry in case I got demoted. Still do. And the more I worry the louder I yell." His mouth was wide now and his smile cynical. "I've been yelling since I got up, haven't I"

She wanted to laugh, she wanted to cry. She touched his fingers and found her hand grasped painfully tight.

They got out at the market square and walked across the open space which, to-morrow, would be packed with stalls, and went through the iron gates that guarded the flower-decked space in front of the Town Hall where the Court was being held, and at the bottom of the steps he said, "Are you sure you want to come in?"

"Yes, yes, I want to be there."

"You've a stronger stomach than me mam. Funny isn't it, she just couldn't stand to come and hear it. You'd think I was going to get the long drop. Oh, there they are," he said under his breath, as he saw the solicitor standing in the distance talking to Andrew Fowler. And he added, "I hope they look as happy when it's all over."

The two men were laughing together as Angus and Vanessa came up to them, but they stopped immediately, and when Angus introduced Vanessa to the solicitor, he inclined his head deeply and said, "How do you do, Mrs. Cotton?"

She always felt it strange to be addressed as Mrs. Cotton.

"Our—our opponents are already seated," said Andrew Fowler to Angus, "and our Mr. Cornell's face is still showing signs of the fray." He slanted his glance sideways at

Angus. "It's a good job old Cargill's indisposed and you have Mrs. Brett to deal with."

"Yes, indeed, indeed," said the solicitor. "Although when I saw her upstairs a few minutes ago she looked as if it was a murder charge she had on her hands. Likely suffering from indigestion. But usually she's fair, except for desertion or maintenance, and then, oh dear, does she jump on them. But as you're up for neither," he glanced with a thin smile at Vanessa, "I think we're fairly certain of having her on our side."

His tone changing, he now spoke directly to Angus, saying, "The main issue as I see it is: you were protecting your wife; he was making a nuisance of himself and he did it repeatedly . . . not once, but repeatedly. You had warned him, but he would take no heed. You know the line to take. You were protecting your wife from being annoyed. Mr. Fowler, here, will vouch for all that; we have been all over it. Ah, here we go." He answered the summons of a policeman standing before two double doors at the far end of the hall and he went forward. Angus followed, walking at one side of Vanessa, while Andrew Fowler walked at the other. And so they entered the Court.

Half-an-hour later they re-entered the hall and they stood in a circle, and looked at each other; then Mr. Millard said almost angrily, "It's preposterous, ridiculous. She was utterly bitchy." He looked from Andrew Fowler to Vanessa, and then to Angus again, and repeated, "Utterly, absolutely bitchy. Old Cargill wouldn't have made it anything near as stiff as that even at his worst. It was the maximum."

Angus said nothing. He felt stunned. He was remembering how Mrs. Brett had looked at him as she said, "You're lucky I am not passing a prison sentence on you. I am dealing with you leniently this time, but should you come before this Court again on a similar charge then there'll be no option of a fine, I can assure you of that. This town can do without your sort. Too long we have put up with big heads and bruisers: it has got to stop. Decent people can't have an evening out, or approach an old friend, but they are punched in the face. Their teeth are knocked out . . ."

It was as if she had got the wrong fellow. All she had said to him she should have said to Cornell. And he wasn't the only one who thought so; the whole Court seemed confused. Even Cornell was surprised. Pleased; oh aye, pleased, but nevertheless he was surprised . . . Mrs. Brett! Angus couldn't understand it. He had spoken to her numbers of times since he was a lad; and it was her husband who had pushed him on. He just couldn't understand it. It was as if she had hated his guts. One hundred pounds and costs! It was unbelievable. And besides that, she could have sent him along the line for six months. She had said so. What was the matter with him anyway? Everything was hitting him. It was coming at him from all sides.

He looked along the hall now to where his solicitor and Cornell's were chatting amiably together, quietly and amiably together. Somehow he thought that shouldn't be. Yet they did it on the telly, try to cut each other's throats in the courtroom and pat each other on the back when they came out of it, like "The Defenders".

He wanted to get home out of this; he wanted to think. He felt he had been dealt a dirty deal somehow. He thought again: Mrs. Brett! Mrs. Brett! All right, she could have fined him, but to slam into him in front of everybody like that as if he was one of the local tearaways, why? Why? He said abruptly to Vanessa, "Come on, out of this."

"Just a minute." It was Andrew Fowler touching him on the arm. "I know you're puzzled, " he said soothingly. "So am I. So are they all. But it's over and done with . . . Listen, did you get a letter this morning from Fenwick?"

"Fenwick?" Angus had to think, and Vanessa put in quietly, "Yes, Yes, about estimates."

"Oh aye, I've got a letter."

"Well, it'll be O.K.," said Andrew Fowler; "I'll see to it. Make yourself a good margin. You might have to hire a couple more lorries and more men. Pop in to-morrow and we'll have a word."

"Aye, all right. Thanks." He spoke as if in a daze, and his "Thanks" was desultory, and Vanessa, looking at Andrew Fowler, said firmly, "Thank you, Mr. Fowler."

"It's a pleasure."

He watched them going down the steps. The smile had gone from his face now and he was nipping his lip. There was something fishy here. Why had Mrs. Brett flayed him like that? Evidently he didn't know, he had looked flabbergasted. Cotton had counted on her being on the Bench – her husband had apparently been a kind of benefactor to him when he worked at Affleck and Tate's. Had she taken that attitude because her neighbour's daughter had stepped over the rails? But that was nothing to her, surely. There was something here he would like to get to the bottom of. He liked to get to the bottom of things. Knowledge was power even if you didn't use it. He wondered how he could go about finding out. Well, something would happen that would give him a lead; it usually did.

Three days later not only had he a lead but the whole reason why Irene Brett had come down like a ton of bricks on Angus Cotton.

I I

"It's a bloody shame!" everybody said. They called to him across the main road; "Just heard, Angus. It's a bloody shame." They said it in the street: "A hundred quid and costs! It's a bloody shame, Angus."

Emily said it standing behind the kitchen table. "She didn't!" she said. "Mrs. Brett? No. One hundred pounds and costs? Oh, no! lad."

"She did. But that's not all, Mam. You should have heard her. I mean, if she had gone for Cornell in the same way I could have understood it, everybody could have understood it, couldn't they, Van?" He turned towards Vanessa, but all Vanessa did was nod her head. "She flayed me in front of everybody, talked to me as if I was a tough, running scatty, knocking people on the head in the main street, telling me what she would do if I came afore her again? You know what I feel like doing? . . . Going along there and asking her why, I do, honest to God, Mam."

Vanessa went into the room, took off her coat and stood waiting. In a short while he would get over this shock to some extent, and then he would say, "Ah now, time's up. You're going to tell me who you phoned yesterday." So she wouldn't wait for that, she'd come straight to the point.

When he entered the room she turned stiffly towards him and, looking him straight in the face, said, "I can tell you, Angus, why she did it."

"You?" He moved near to her. "You mean you know why she got at me?"

"Yes . . . You – you wanted to know who I phoned yesterday. Well – well it was her."

"Mrs. Brett?" His eyes were screwed up tightly at the corners.

"Yes; I – I phoned her because I knew that when you came up before her this morning she would get at me through, through you; I was afraid she would give you a prison sentence. I threatened that if she did I would shout it out in the Court."

"Shout what out? What are you talking about, girl? You all right?"

"YES! YES!" She had almost yelled. Then clamping her hand over her mouth, she bowed her head and said, "She hates me because . . . because she knows who was the father of the baby." Her head bent lower and her voice was hardly audible as she ended, "It was Brett, her husband."

From underneath her lowered lids she could see his body up to the waist, and it was perfectly still. Then his silence forced her to raise her head and the expression on his face turned her cold. It had in it the essence of incredulity, but something more, a surprising quality for him to show towards her, disgust. His lips moved well back from his upper teeth before he said, "Mister Brett and you!"

Her head was moving down again and her voice was a whimper. "It just happened. He—he was very sad, lonely, unhappy . . ."

"Christ!" The exclamation was like a crack of a whip. "Aren't all old married men unhappy, lonely, sad? But that doesn't mean you've got to lie with them . . . You and Brett! He was as old as your father . . . Brett!"

As he continued to stare at her he remembered that he had always liked Mr. Brett, that Mr. Brett had been kind to him, but he also remembered, and with a sense of deep shock, that when he wondered who had given her a bairn he had imagined it to be a lad of her own age. He had imagined him carried away on the first real wave of emotion and being borne under with the pressure of it. He had imagined them both fumbling at the act without enjoying it; then the boy skulking away and keeping his tonque quiet while she carried the can. He had even admired her for not revealing who the young fellow was . . . But she had been under the hands of no young fellow, she had been with a man old enough to be her grandfather; aye, he could have been her grandfather.

He had the urge now to take her by the neck and choke her. He had been made a fool of. She had let everybody blame him while she could have put a stop to it, a real stop to it, by naming the fellow next door . . . But there hadn't been any fellow next door had there when the balloon went up? No, he had skedadled, gone touring, supposedly getting orders for the firm; and when he came back and found what happened to her, what did he do? He hanged himself. It was a pity he hadn't done it earlier. How often had he had her?

There was a strange feeling in him now. He didn't want to go near her, or touch her. When she said, "Angus, I'm sorry. Don't look like that. It – it was a sort of accident; it only happened . . ." he put in quickly, "I don't want to hear." He curled his lip at her. "But you know something. I'll tell you something. I thought you had been let down by a young lad, and I could understand that and I could put up with it, but not when it was a bloke like Brett, with a son as old as me, and two others."

He walked towards the door, then turned to her and said in a tone that was frightening because for him it was quiet, "You're no better than the rest. You know something? I wouldn't marry May because I found she'd been with other blokes. Bit illogical you might say, when I've had my whack, but I'm made that way. I stomached what happened to you because, as I said, I thought it was a slip between two young 'uns, not a calculated get-together, as it must have been atween you and him, because a man

304

of Brett's age wouldn't jump in feet first, he'd know he'd have to tread warily until he was sure of his ground. And he was sure, wasn't he?"

She was so stunnned by his attitude that she could make no reply. All her mother and father had said, the treatment she had received from her friends, nothing she had gone through, affected her like Angus's reaction.

When he went out of the room he didn't bang the door behind him. Presently she heard the murmur of his voice coming from the scullery. He would be telling Emily.

He had no need to tell Emily, she already knew. She had picked enough up from standing at the kitchen door to put two and two together, and now she was looking at her son and saying bitterly, "What are you going to do?"

"Nothing." He looked out of the scullery window. "Damn all. What's the good of raking up muck, you only get more smells, and at the present moment me nose is full of them. I couldn't stand any more."

"I thought it must have been a young lad."

"Aye." He turned and looked at her. "Aye, that's what I thought an' all; and I took the rap because of that. But do you think for a moment if I'd guessed it had been Brett I would have? As sorry as I was for her, I would have seen her in hell first."

"Mr. Brett. MR. BRETT. He was a quiet, refined, gentlemanly . . ."

"Oh, Mam, for God's sake come off it. Gentlemanly. They do it an' all; even royalty has to be born. What's maddening me is that I've been made the scapegoat, and that bitch on the bench finished it the day. She's right about one thing though . . ." He jerked his head back towards the room. "It's ten to one if she hadn't got on that phone yesterday and threatened what she might do I might quite easily be along the line at this minute."

Emily shuddered. She knew that what he said was true; he could easily have been along the line. That lot! That lot! Look what they had done to her lad. Turned him

305

into a lorry driver when he should have been in the drawing office. Then fining him a hundred pounds and blamin' him for the bairn, when all the time it was Mr. Brett.

She was working herself up into fury when Angus said, "I'm going."

"Where? Where you off to?"

"To get the lorries ready."

"What time will you be back?"

"I don't know." His voice was flat.

She followed him to the yard door and, her voice a low murmur in case someone was sitting in the lavatory beyond the wall, their ears' cocked, she said, "Don't go and get sozzled; that won't solve matters."

He turned and looked at her once, then moved away down the back lane; and she returned to the scullery, and as she stood gripping her forearms with each hand her anger mounted into a white blaze, strangely not against Vanessa, but against her parents, and the Bretts, the whole family of Bretts, those two grown-up sons who must have been stone blind not to guess what their father was up to.

She was thinking along similar lines to Angus. This thing couldn't have happened like the snap of your fingers. There must have been some outward sign somewhere, to show that Brett – she did not now think of him as Mr. Brett – had his sights on the young lass next door. And next door? Had they been stone blind an' all? God-Almighty Ratcliffe and his missus? And the things they said. Aye. She was recalling practically every word they had said to her regarding Angus, and the manner in which they had said it.

Her anger seemed to lend wings to her feet now and she was upstairs donning her hat and coat and downstairs again within a few minutes. Opening a cupboard, she grabbed up her handbag, looked in it to see if she had enough for the fare, then went out of the house, taking the well-known road towards Brampton Hill again.

12

Irene Brett was pouring tea in the drawing-room. It was seldom she had tea in this room; except when there were visitors, and they were few and far between. But to-day she was serving tea in the drawing-room because Paul was home. It was the first day of the Easter vac and to-morrow he would be off on another of his walking tours. She had little time to impress him, and her future lay very much in his hands; in fact, how long she could remain in this house depended on him.

If everything had gone to Colin, as it should have done, he being the eldest son, she would have known a sense of security, whereas now she felt she was dealing with a younger edition of her husband. She had urged Colin to contest the will, but for some reason or other he wouldn't. This was another thing that irked her; although the brothers were as different in character as chalk from cheese there was an affinity between them that she had no part of.

Her object now was to persuade Paul to sell some of the mouldering antiques in order that she might have the ground floor, at least, redecorated. When she had broached the subject at Christmas he had said neither yes nor no to the matter. He was like his father there, a ditherer . . . His father! When she thought of his father she knew she wouldn't live long enough to erase the hate of him that burned in her. She had always known she was capable of strong emotions, but she had never imagined that a man like Arthur, a weak, vacillating creature such as he could have aroused in her this unrelenting feeling of hate and resentment. And then there was that girl . . . Her thoughts sank into the depths and dragged up adjectives, and it was as much as she could do not to voice them. She had a picture of Vanessa sitting in Court staring at her, daring her to do what she most desired, send Angus Cotton down. She wished now she had defied her threat and done it. Oh, if only she had.

"Been a busy day for you?"

She brought her face round to her son, whom she couldn't look at without seeing his father, and she made herself say lightly, "So-so, rather upsetting; some cases tend to be upsetting."

"You take it all too seriously."

"Perhaps."

"You should have a holiday."

"You know I can't have a holiday, Paul."

He was silent, and the feeling of guilt that he always had now when he was with her mounted. He knew that within a few minutes she would bring up the subject again about selling the furniture. He supposed he would have to give in; although he would like to keep things intact as his father had done. But times were changing. Sooner or later the whole place would have to go, house, land, the lot. It was too big anyway for any one family these days. It had been too big for years. He wished he could feel more sympathy towards her but somehow he couldn't. He had never been able to understand the driving force that animated her thin body. There was too much of his father in him, he supposed. Poor Dad. When his thoughts were touched with pity he always addressed his father in his mind as Dad. He had wanted so little, and that's what he had got, so little. He wished that tomorrow was here and he could get away. The house wasn't the same. Nothing was the same. Perhaps he had grown up suddenly, or perhaps it was the events that had happened in the last year. Whatever it was, life didn't appear bright and starry anymore.

When the ring came on the bell he rose and said, "I'll take it"; and when he opened the front door there stood Emily Cotton. After a moment's pause he said, "Emily! Oh, hello, Emily."

"Your mother in?" No "Master Paul" now.

"Mother? Yes, Yes. You want to see her?"

"Yes, I want to see her."

There was something wrong here; Emily was in fighting mood. He said, "Come in a minute," and when she'd walked past him and stood in the hall he closed the door and went quickly towards the drawing-room door, which he pushed behind him but not closed before he went to his mother and said softly, "It's Emily, Emily Cotton, you know."

He watched the cold blue of her eyes turn to a steely grey and her narrow jaws tighten.

"Will I bring her in?"

"No, I'll see her in the hall . . . Stay here."

When she entered the hall she closed the drawing-room door behind her, then looked across at the cheaply dressed, unshapely woman, and, aiming to take command of the situation, she said, "Yes, Emily. What can I do for you?"

"Don't you come that tone with me, Mrs. Brett; you know what you can do for me. By! you've got a nerve. You know what you are?" Emily advanced two steps. "You're a vindictive bitch, that's what you are."

"How dare you! And stop shouting, woman. You forget yourself."

"I'm tellin' you not to come that line with me. I'm not forgettin' meself; you're the one, Mrs. Magistrate, who forgot yourself when you were up on that bench this mornin'. You forgot why you were put there. You were put there for justice, not to dish out personal spite. An' that's what you did, didn't you? If it hadn't been for

Vanessa phoning you and threatenin' you yesterday that she would broadcast who was the father of her bairn if you sent my Angus along the line, you would have done just that, wouldn't you? You would have sent him up for six months, just to get back at her."

"Be quiet, woman! And get out." Irene was hissing at her now.

But Emily had no intention of being quiet or of leaving until she had had her say, and she said it even louder now.

"Be quiet, you say. When I'm ready an' not afore. I tell you again you're a bloody, vindictive bitch, and that's swearing to it. Your man took a young lass down, a school-girl, and then he took his life because he couldn't face it. An' you knew about it; you knew all this all the time my lad was being blamed for givin' her this bairn, but you let it go on. Councillor Mrs. Irene Brett, Magistrate, Chairman of this an' God knows what else, couldn't stand the racket of being shown up . . ."

"Get out! Do you hear me. GET OUT."

"Aye, I'll get out, but I'm not goin' very far, just to your neighbours . . ."

"You wouldn't dare!"

"I wouldn't what?" Emily was bawling now. "You tell me what I wouldn't dare?"

"I forbid you, woman." They were standing close to each other now, Irene's words spitting between her teeth. "Do you hear. I forbid you. This is between her and me . . . Vanessa."

"Aw, but that's where you've made a mistake. It's not atween you and Vanessa, it's atween you and my lad. His name's been blackened all over this town, and beyont. He had dared to step over the white line and have an affair with one of his betters, that's what was said. A few years ago they would have had him flogged. Old Ratcliffe would have taken a horsewhip to him. Something similar was done to one of the grooms from Brampton Manor, an' that was in the thirties, not so very long ago. But times have

310

changed, except on the bench, where there's upstarts like you . . . An' don't you call me woman . . ." She thrust her lower jaw outwards. "I'm clearin' me lad's name. If it's the last thing I do I'll do that, an' people won't have to guess why he got it hot and hard from you this mornin'."

"It will be you who'll be in Court next if you're not careful." Irene's voice was trembling now, as was her whole body.

"All right, summons me, but you'll have to give me a summons for telling the truth. That's how you'll have to word it. Emily Cotton accused of telling the truth, the suppressed truth."

Emily's eyes were brought for a moment from Irene Brett's bleached face to the open drawing-room door, where stood Paul, so changed that she thought for a moment she was looking at his father.

She turned now and walked towards the front door, and after she had opened it she jerked her head round to give one parting shot, but checked it as she saw Irene Brett and her son staring at each other. She had said enough, she was satisfied, in this quarter anyway. Mrs. Magistrate had her son to deal with, and from the looks of him she was going to have her work cut out.

Her body still quivering with indignation, she marched down the drive along the road, through the open gates and to the house in which, as she herself had said, she had spent a greater length of time over the past eighteen years than she had in her own home. She did not take the tradesman's path to the back door but made for the front door, and as she looked at the car standing on the drive she thought, "Good. Madam Susan's here." Then she pressed the bell with her thumb, holding it tight for some seconds.

The door was opened by a young woman who was wearing a small frilled apron over an ordinary housedress, which in itself told Emily that there was company. "Yes?" said the woman, looking her up and down.

"Your missus in?"

"What do you want?"

"You tell Mrs. Ratcliffe that Emily's here and wants to see her. Just say that." Then she put her hand out quickly, adding, "You needn't close the door; I'm not goin' to pinch anything; I worked here when you were still in nappies. Go and tell her."

The young woman's eyes were wide, but she made no further protest; she had heard of Emily Cotton. Emily followed her slowly and stood in the hall, and as she waited her eyes roamed around, and she noted, with some chagrin, that everything looked as usual. When the lounge door opened the maid came out alone and said to her, "The mistress will see you in a minute." Then she went on into the kitchen, and Emily waited. She waited a full three minutes before her late mistress made her appearance.

Jane Ratcliffe closed the lounge door carefully behind her; then, coming slowly forward, she said unsmilingly, "Good-afternoon, Emily."

Emily did not return the greeting but said, "Do you know why I'm here . . . ?" she had almost said ma'am but checked herself in time.

"No, Emily, I don't know why you're here."

"I've come for an apology."

"For what?"

"You heard, for an apology."

"Come—come into the morning-room, please."

"No, I'm not goin' into any morning-room, missus; what I've got to say I'll say here, where there's ears cocked at the doors, an' they'll be my witnesses . . . Is he in?"

"If you're referring to the master, no, he's not, Emily." Jane Ratcliffe's voice was trembling.

"That's a pity. That is a pity, because it's him I want to see more than you; but you can pass on what Ive got to say. I suppose you know about my lad being up afore the Bench this mornin'. He was up there because he was defending your daughter – for the second time mind –

against a man, a man who was pestering her, and what did he get? He gets fined one hundred pounds an' costs. And, you know, he was lucky to just get fined. If it hadn't been for Van phonin' next door yesterday an' tellin' Madam Councillor, Mrs. Irene Brett, that she would stand up in Court this mornin' and yell the truth at her if she dared send my Angus along the line, he would have been along the line at this minute."

"Emily! Emily, please, come into the morning room."

"I'm not goin' into any mornin'-room; you can save your breath. And I haven't finished yet. You know what Van was goin' to shout at Mrs. Brett, do you?" She bent her body almost double. "She was goin' to shout out the name of the man who gave her the bairn, an' the name was Mr. Brett. Your esteemed neighbour . . . Mr. Brett! That's who gave her the bairn. And his wife knew it, she knew it; an' she knew it was because of that he committed suicide . . . Aye," her voice dropped a tone lower as she looked at Jane Ratcliffe supporting herself by the banister. "I thought you would need some support. But you didn't think me or me lad needed any support, did you? You made him out to be the scum of the earth. He was accused of takin' Van down because he had been seen talkin' to her once or twice, and all the time under your very noses a man old enough to be her grandfather was having his fun with her; an' you knew nowt about it. Of course, of course." Her voice changed. "You could trust people like Mr. Brett; he was a gentleman. The same goes for Mr. Brian Cornell, another gentleman. He can say what he likes and gets off with it, but because my lad had neither money or position he didn't stand a chance."

"Will you please go, Emily!" Jane Ratcliffe's voice had a far-away sound to it. She was standing stiffly upright now staring straight ahead, and Emily said, "Aye, I'll go when I say this. My Angus is a bloody fool, that's what he is, for, knowin' that he was playing into your hands, he goes an' marries her. He marries her out of sympathy 'cos he finds her living in a filthy dump in Newcastle. Do you know Batterby Bay Road? No. I don't suppose you do. But your husband will. Oh, aye, there's not a man in this county who doesn't know of Batterby Bay Road. It's where the prostitutes hang out, an' that's where he found her. And he brought her from there an' married her, and he hadn't," she paused, "he hadn't given her the bairn . . ."

The lounge door was pulled sharply open at this stage and it checked Emily's spate, and she watched Susan Ratcliffe, or Braintree as she now was, going quickly towards her mother, saying, "Come along, dear. Come along."

As Susan put her arms round her mother she turned and looked at Emily and said, "I think you'd better go. You've had your say, now get out."

The young man standing in the doorway didn't speak, but he looked at Emily for a full minute and she at him before she said, "Aye, I'll go. But I haven't finished me say yet; this town's goin' to hear the truth. Your lot's treated my lad as if he was a Geordie lout, an' there's not one of you fit to wipe his boots. Well, now we'll see what the town thinks and how the so-called gentleman from next door'll stand up against Angus Cotton."

There were two reactions to Emily's outburst. The one in Bower Place was that Jonathan Ratcliffe refused to listen to his wife's pleas to move. Angus Cotton wasn't putting him on the run. All right, let the town know, let them talk, but he wasn't going to be frightened out of his home by that young slob.

He was still fighting Angus Cotton, more so now than ever, because Angus Cotton had got the better of him. He was in the right and the town would be laughing. Oh yes, behind their hands they would be laughing. Young Cotton had taken the blame of giving Ratcliffe's daughter a child just so that he could marry her and get his foot in.

Jonathan Ratcliffe was still convinced that Angus

Cotton's motive in marrying Vanessa was to inveigle himself into her family's good books.

The other reaction took place in the kitchen in No. 24 between Emily and Angus. He had been utterly astounded when she told him where she had been. For a moment he could say nothing, then his wrath poured over her. She was a bloody, silly old cow, an interfering, stupid old swine. Why the hell couldn't she mind her own business! Hadn't there been enough talk and tittle-tattle without her going stirring things up? All right, all right, he knew he had been wrongly accused, nobody knew better, but that was his business.

"Thanks!" Emily screamed. "Thanks! That's what I get. You're a bloody, ungrateful sod. Your name's been mud in this place for months now, aye, even round the doors. They said you had a nerve, and it was a dirty trick to take a young lass down like that an' her still at school, and a convent into the bargain. Virgin huntin' in the right place, they said. Taking advantage of his mother being up there, they said. Well then, I was determined they weren't goin' to say that no longer; they were going to know the truth an' this is what I get."

"You haven't got half of it yet. For two pins I'd slap yer mouth for you."

"Begod you would!" She thrust her hand back and grabbed up a large sauce bottle from the dresser; but at this moment Vanessa came out of the room. She stood in the doorway and, her voice louder than it had ever been raised in this house or anywhere before, she cried, "Stop it! Stop it! I'm sick of you, do you hear, the both of you. I'm sick of your shouting and fighting. You're like wild animals, the pair of you. That's all you are, wild animals."

Perhaps it was surprise that silenced them, for they both turned towards her and made no reply; they just looked at her. Her hair was tangled as if she had been running her hands through it; her clothes looked dishevelled as if she had been lying in them; her face was bloated with crying; she looked tired and weary, but above all she looked an angry woman. "All right!" she said. "I'm the cause of all this, but I'm going to end it, I'm leaving." She was looking at Angus directly now. "Do you hear me? I'm leaving?" When he still made no comment she went into the room and banged the door.

There was now exchanged between Emily and Angus a shame-faced look before he went slowly across the kitchen and into the room. With his back to the door he stood for a moment watching her pulling her dresses from the hanging wardrobe in the corner, and when she had put them in the case he approached her and said grimly, "What d'you think you're doing?"

She glanced up at him with a look that was new, because it was defiant. She was looking at him as May might have looked at him when she was on the point of telling him to go to hell.

When he put his hand out and caught hers as she went to close the case, she jerked it away, and he said flatly, "You're not leaving. Make up your mind to that; you're not leaving."

"You can't stop me. If I don't go now I'll go once you leave the house; you can't keep watch over me all the time." She was staring straight into his face, and he held her eyes with an unblinking stare as he said, "You know what I said I'd do to you the other night if ever you left me. Well, you might have thought it was a joke, but it wasn't. If you walk out I'll drop everything till I find you, and I'll bring you back. Every time you go off I'll find you and I'll haul you back again. I mean it."

She stepped back from him as she asked, "Why? Why do you want to keep me here? Yesterday I thought I knew, but not now, because you were disgusted when I told you the truth. You were, you were disgusted. Just because **it** was Brett who was the father you were disgusted. You had already accepted the situation because you thought I had been with a boy. Why, I could have been with a boy

316

twenty times, fifty times and nothing could have happened and you wouldn't have known anything about it, but because this happened with Brett once, just once, your whole attitude towards me changes. It was as if you had suddenly heard that I'd had a baby; or, if you thought it was yours, then found out it was Brett's, you couldn't have reacted worse. I—I can't understand you."

"You can't understand me! That's rich. But then I can't understand meself. I don't know why in hell I bother about you, but I do, so there's a pair of us who can't understand me. But you think it's odd I was disgusted when I heard it was Brett, an' I was disgusted, that's the right word; and it wasn't only because he was an old man, oldish anyway," he flung his head upwards, "but because, well, I liked him. I'd always liked him, and was fool enough to look up to him, thinking he represented something big, something fine, even great." His voice dropped. "I looked up to him the same as I looked up to you . . ."

It was his last words that took all the fight out of her. She turned from him and, going to the little table, sat before it and dropping her head on to her arms began to cry, painful, quiet crying.

He remained where he was, looking at her. The defiant woman was gone, and he saw a young girl again. Once, she said. She had only been with him once. He thought back and tried to remember when Brett had gone abroad. It must have been pretty near when it happened, for it was three months later when he came back, at the time when they were looking for somebody to pin it on. He must have known that there was a chance she might fall and he had scurried away like a frightened rabbit, jumped at the opportunity to get away, because he now recalled that when Mr. Cribber went into hospital, Mr. Bindley was going to get the chance of going out abroad to fill in. He knew this because he often had a word with him at the Tech, where he did spare teaching at nights, but then Brett had gone instead.

She had been left high and dry by them all: Brett, her own family, and now, it must appear to her, that he was another one of them. Quite suddenly it didn't matter any longer who had been the father of her bairn; it was a thing that was over and done with. He went to the case and, lifting the lid, took out her dresses, one by one, and put them over his arm. Then going to her, he said, "Hang these up."

She raised her tear-streaked face and looked at him for a moment before, getting to her feet, and saying, quietly, "No, no, Angus, it's not going to be like that. I don't care what you say, or what you do, I'm . . . I'm going. I'm not living on sufferance any longer."

"Sufferance? What do you mean?"

"Just what I say. You married me because you were sorry for me. I – I thought you loved me; I imagined that you needed me; but now I know that was all girlish imagination. Another reason why you married me was so that you could cock your snoot at my folks. Oh, I know, I know." She flapped her hand in front of her face. "You'll deny it, but it's true. You were letting them see, father in particular, that you could marry anyone you liked, that you were as good as they were. So you married me, but you've never said one endearing word to me in all the months since then. Oh, yes," her voice was scornful now, "you can kiss me and hug me until I can hardly breathe; you can show me how strong you are, what a man you are; but you've never once said you've cared for me. I could have been that May woman you used to know." The impetus went out of her voice and she ended, "You don't really care for me, Angus, so why do you want to keep me? Just to hold me up and say, 'Look what I've got; someone from Brampton Hill'?"

He was shaking his head slowly at her, bewilderment showing in every feature of his face, and, his voice humble now, he said low in his throat, "You've got it all wrong, Van, you've got it all wrong. Admittedly I was shaken

318

when I knew it was Brett, but the feeling's past, it's over. But about the other, how I feel about you, you've got it all wrong. You want fancy words. Well, I'm not up to it. It's almost impossible for me to express how I feel about you in words, but I thought I was showing it in a thousand and one other ways. If it means anything to you, I live in dread every day of you walking out, and that bit about what I would do if ever you left me, about bringing you back, and even polishing you off, it's just talk, wind, the big fellow bellowing . . . Look, if you go out of that door now, Van, I won't try to stop you. I'll know you're going because you can't stand the set-up or me any longer. And don't worry, I won't even ask you to come back, because who in their right senses would want to come back to this?" He flung one arm wide. "Not even an ordinary lass from around the doors would have put up with what you've put up with. I know all this, and I've tried to tell you I know it, but I'm no hand at expressing meself that way. The only thing I can say now, and I've never said it afore, not in so many words is . . . I love you, that I've loved you since you were a nipper, and I'll go on loving you to the end of me days. That's not saying, if you leave me I won't take anybody else. I'm a man, I need some-body, but that isn't love. It's you I love, an' it's you I want. If you go, you go, but if you stay . . . well . . ."

All this time he had been holding her dresses over one arm, and now he went and put them on top of her case again, and when he turned round she was standing near him. But he did not touch her, not even when her hands went up to her face in distress and her fingers pressed so tightly across her mouth that her nose was pushed out of shape did he touch her, not until, her body leaning for-ward, she drooped her head against his shoulder did his arms go around her. And then his face, falling into her hair at the back of her neck, he muttered, "Aw, Van. Van. God, don't you know how I feel about you?"

Her body began to shake again with her sobbing, and,

his own voice thick and broken now, he said, "It's a new start; we'll go on from here, no more looking back. I love you, love you, love you. Do you hear that? Always have and always will. It goes past lovin' what I feel for you. I need words now. I adore you, Van. Aye. I do. I adore you. Teach me words, Van. Teach me words so as I can tell you just how much I adore you . . . But there's one thing I don't need fancy words for, an' it's this." He held her from him and looked deep into her tear-blinded eyes as he ended. "I'm going to make you a promise and I'll carry it through by fair means or foul. I mean to put you back where you belong afore I'm finished. Brampton Hill, or even beyond. Now that's a solemn promise."

When the shaking of her body increased with her sobbing he took it as a sign that she was pleased with the prospect. He was quite mistaken.

PART THREE

I

It was a week before Christmas, almost eighteen months from the day Angus had left Afflecks. Two things of import had happened to him and Vanessa since that day. First, and most important, was that Vanessa was going to have another baby, and it was due any time now. The second thing, and hardly of less importance, was that Angus Cotton was now a haulage contractor with his own name on ten lorries, and a respectable bank balance, together with a less respectable but equally important horde of five-pound notes in a cavity under the floor boards.

Angus's rise in the contracting world had been swift, even taking into account the many men who had made quick piles in this line of business. His success had really started when he thought he was finished altogether. It was on the day Fred Singleton asked him if he would buy his lorry because he was moving – the wife wanted to get back to her people in Doncaster.

Fred had thrown this bombshell on the very day Angus had secured a sub-contract to clear the rubble from a complete street of demolished houses. He had come by the contract through the help of Andrew Fowler, and it was to him he went to say that he couldn't go on with it; one man and one lorry couldn't do the job and he hadn't any cash at the moment to buy Fred Singleton's lorry. It was at this point that Andrew Fowler said "Why don't you strike out on your own? Take a chance, borrow the money. Hire a couple of men and take a chance."

Where, asked Angus, could he borrow the money without any security behind him?

"From me," Andrew Fowler had answered; "at five per cent. I won't be over-charging you or under-charging you. I'm willing to take a chance if you are, and, as you've seen, I can push a lot your way. If you take this chance I think you'll find it very much worth your while – and mine too." He had nodded his head slowly. "We can come to an agreement."

Angus didn't know then whether Andrew Fowler was a bit of a sharp-shooter or not, and even now he didn't know; but what he did know at this present time was that if he kept going ahead during the next two or three years at the rate he had done these past months he would be set fair for the top. And to-night's little transaction would undoubtedly help it along.

"Move over, love," he said. He dropped on to his knees on the hearth rug as he spoke; and as Vanessa rose to her feet he didn't immediately pull the mat back but, putting his arms around her waist, he pressed his face against the bulge of her stomach, and shouted, "Hurry up, you in there. Hurry up. Do you hear me?"

Vanessa gave a contented laugh, saying, "Angus don't. Look, you'll have me over."

" 'Bout time too," he said; " 'bout time." Then poking her stomach again gently he said in a lowered tone, "Get a move on, d'you hear? Somebody else has got claims as well as you, you know."

She turned away, biting on her lip, her head slightly lowered. He was raw, uncouth in many ways, and she doubted if he would ever change. Definitely, the English lessons and selected reading had made no notable impression on him; but it didn't seem to matter, she loved him; she loved him as she hadn't imagined loving anybody. She had never imagined what it would be like to love like she loved him; it was a consuming feeling. Yet she wasn't happy.

She turned now and looked on his bent head as he put a knife down between the two floor boards and prised them upwards, then lifted a metal box on to the mat, from which he began counting out five-pound notes.

When he had counted to eight she said in some surprise, "What are you going to give him?"

"A hundred."

"A hundred pounds, Angus?"

"Aye."

"But – but will he take all that from you?"

"Take me hand off for it an' all." He grinned up at her with slanted glance.

He now replaced the box under the floor boards, and after straightening the mat and putting the chair back on it he counted the money again before putting it in an envelope.

When he looked at Vanessa she shook her head and said, "I can never believe that he takes it."

"You can believe it all right." His head was bouncing up and down. "That's how these blokes get rich, that's how all blokes get rich. You never find a rich honest business man. I mean, not one sticking to the books, everything down in black and white. Such men make a profit but they don't get stinkin' rich. And our kind friend, Mr. Fowler, intends to get . . . stinkin' rich. And he should do with all the pies he's got his fingers in."

"But he helped you at first without taking anything."

"Aye, aye, you're right he did; but he had his eye on the future, and I soon picked things up. I know which side me bread is buttered." He jerked his head at her.

"What if you hadn't given him any money on the side?"

"What do you think? I'd have been dropped. I'd have managed a one-man little business, just keeping afloat but nothing like where I am now, and where Stan is. It would appear we all took a chance and it paid off. Do you know how much Stan picked up last week? Forty-seven quid. Mind you, he had to work for it. And there's our Rosie going on about him coming home late. She doesn't say that when she goes and spends a small fortune on her clothes on a Saturday afternoon. She wants her ears scudded, that one."

Vanessa said now, "How long will you be? They're coming round to-night."

"Oh, about an hour I should say. We'll just have a drink together and a natter . . . and do a little exchange."

"Why doesn't he transact the business in the office?"

"Not this kind of business, honey." He leant towards her and tickled her chin. "He's a very wise guy, is Mr. Andrew Fowler. He's got a secretary there and secretaries have ears and noses. As he said himself, the walls have ears. No, he's cunning and cute, yet likeable. You know, I like him. You can't help liking him because, in a way, he's sort of honest about it. 'Come for a walk along the river bank,' he'll say, and there we go out of the office and along the river bank, and he'll say to me something like he did a month ago, like this. 'Threadgill's are putting out a tender. They're opening up the land beyond Dark Town. It's just a sort of pilot scheme; your ten lorries could manage it. There's a fellow called Richardson there; he's got a lot of influence, but he's got a weakness for presents – a television, or a crate or two, or something like that. I said 'Wines?' and he said, 'No. His taste runs to something a bit stronger, whisky.' "

"But you got that contract, didn't you. I wrote—"

"Yes. Yes, I got the contract. O course I did. That's what's been pulling it in these past few weeks."

"And . . . and did you send him a . . . present?"

"Aye. Aye, I did. I didn't tell you about it at the time because I felt a bit chipped about doing it, sort of, well, half-ashamed like."

She came and stood close to him and looked into his face, "A television set?"

"No; nor whisky. You'd never believe in a month of Sundays what I sent him. Go on have a guess."

"A wrist watch?"

He shook his head.

"Gold cuff links?"

Again he shook his head.

"Was it something for himself?"

"Not exactly."

"I give up."

"A donkey."

"A what!" Her face was spread wide with laughter. "A donkey?"

"For his daughter; a very good donkey an' all. Now who would suspect anyone of doing graft through a donkey? Sixty-two quid it cost me, that donkey. And it's not a donkey really, it's a pony, and a spanker."

"Oh, Angus! Oh, Angus!" She leant against him sideways and they both began to laugh. "And you know something else?" They were still laughing. "I heard yesterday from Fowler that he's looking for a little go-cart, what they used to call a governess trap, you know. I haven't seen one in me life, and Fowler can't remember seeing one either, but that's what Mr. Richardson's looking for, so Mr. Angus Cotton is going to enquire if anybody's got a governess trap hanging about their back yard that they don't want." They were holding on to each other shaking. When he released her she wiped her eyes, then held her hands on her high stomach as she asked, "But what's the hundred pounds for?"

"I'm not sure meself yet." He turned his head slowly towards her again. "But if it means what I think it's going to mean that'll be the first of a few hundred I'll be dishing out . . . Now, now." He put his hand up to her cheek. "You don't have to worry; this is how business is done. Your big, ignorant slob of a man has learned a lot in the last few months, and he's got a lot to learn yet. But whatever he learns he's going to make it pay, because – because he's promised his wife something." He took her chin firmly in

327

the palm of his hand and squeezed it. "I'll never rest until I fulfil that promise."

"There's no need, Angus. Please, I've told you. I – I would rather you got the work in the ordinary way, I would, believe me, Angus, rather than run risks."

"Risks? Oh! Oh! Now you're on the wrong track. There's no risk. I told you. Fowler walks me along the river bank; I buy a donkey for Mr. Richardson's daughter. Why do I buy a donkey for Mr. Richardson's daughter? Because Mr. Richardson's daughter tells me that she is looking out for a donkey and I happen to see one going reasonable and I go and buy it. Does Mr. Richardson pay me for it? Of course he does . . . That would be the way it would go if anybody said anything. There's no risk." His face suddenly becoming straight, his jocular manner disappearing and his eyes hardening, he said, "No risk, only the feeling you want to kick somebody up the backside very time they give you a hint a backhander is required if you want the job. When I see tenders put out it makes me laugh – grimly."

There now came to them the sound of a door opening and Rosie's voice high and excited coming from the kitchen. The next minute both she and Emily were in the room, and Emily cried, "What do you think? Rosie says Old Davis has died at the corner."

"Aye?" Angus looked from one to the other. Then addressing Rosie, he said, "What do you expect me to do? Send him a wreath? I've hardly seen him for years."

"Don't be so daft, man." Rosie pushed her hand out towards him. "The house. He's been living there by himself since his wife died. The house; it'll be empty."

"Oh, aye, aye." He nodded at her. "You've got something there, our Rosie. You don't miss much, do you?"

They both flapped their hands at each other; then Vanessa, coming forward, said, "But there'll be a waiting list."

"Not for these places," said Rosie scornfully. "They're

all up for comin' down. Five years is the limit. Well, don't stand there, our Angus; go and do somethin'. If we hadn't got that place last month I'd have been after it like a shot."

"When did he die?" asked Angus, picking up his coat and going towards the door.

"About half-an-hour ago I should say. I saw Mrs. Green coming out of the house. She's just washed him."

"God! He's hardly cold."

"Warm or cold, it doesn't matter to him now," cried Emily. "Go on, get yourself away. It'll be a godsend, that house especially, 'cos there's a bath in it."

"Oh yes." Angus turned quickly towards Vanessa. "I forgot about the bath. There was quite a to-do in the street when he put it in. I'm off . . . Wait a minute." He went back into the room towards the small table and, opening a drawer, took out three pounds, saying, "I want more than this. Have you got any loose?"

Vanessa went to a chest of drawers to the right of the fire place and took her bag from the top, saying, "How much do you want?"

"Oh, give me what you've got. A fiver should help get me into that bath. If not, it can be doubled."

As he was passing Emily he gripped her wrinkled face tightly between his fists and, bending towards her, he quoted,

"Between the dark and the daylight,
When the night is beginning to lower,
Comes a pause in the day's occupation
That is known as the Children's Hour."

He ended on a deep note, thumbing towards Vanessa, "Hurry that Children's Hour up, will you, 'cos I can't stand much more. If I have another night like last night I'll never live to see him. I was twisted up with cramp."

Emily jerked her head from his grasp and pushed him through the kitchen, crying, "Go on. Go on, you great big gowk." But when they reached the front door the laughter went from his face and his bantering tone vanished as he said under his breath, "See to her, won't you? Don't leave her?"

"Look," said Emily, "bairns have been born afore, and they'll be born again. This is just one of millions."

"Aw, no, aw no." He jerked his head at her. "One in a million, that's what you mean. One in a million. Now do as I tell you, stay with her, don't leave her for a minute. You won't go out, will you?"

"I'm not barmy, lad, or in me dotage. Go on, get on with your job an' I'll get on with mine; and she'll get on with hers. What's the matter with you? Gone soft all of a sudden? Go on an' get that contract. An' get that house. And anything else you can lay hands on."

He nodded at her; then said slyly, "Will do, Mrs. Cotton. Will do." Then he stepped across the narrow pavement and into his car, a ten-year-old Rover, which he had chosen, because it was the remains of a good thing. That was to be his policy, he told himself, all the way up: he'd rather have the remains of a good thing until he could get the good thing. No shoddy tin-pot new stuff, not for him or his.

Vanessa, Rosie, Emily and Stan waited in the kitchen for him coming back. He had said to Vanessa he would be an hour, but taking into account his visit to the rent agent they gave him another hour. That should have brought him back into the house at eight o'clock. At nine, he hadn't returned, and at half-past nine Vanessa's pains began; and Emily began to swear. He was a thoughtless, ignorant swine, that's what he was. In some pub likely, or fancy hotel, stuffing himself. There was the supper spoilt and them all starving. He thought of nobody but himself. He was a selfish swine, he always had been and always would be. Damn him.

At ten o'clock they began to get worried. At half-past ten Vanessa was sitting in her coat with her bag packed waiting to be taken to the hospital in Angus's car.

"If he comes in sodden," said Emily, "I'll brain him. Before God, I'll brain him. We won't see him till closing time, you'll see. The night of all nights."

Rosie, pacing the kitchen, stopped at this point and looked at Stan and said, "If you did this to me, Stan, you'd have your eyeballs served up to you the next day, and I'm telling' you."

Stan grinned sheepishly at her, and then said, "Somethin's keepin' him. You know for a fact he's as worried as if he was going to have it himself."

Nobody said there could have been an accident, only the thought was constant in Vanessa's mind. Over the last half-hour she had resorted to prayer. It was as if she was back in the convent listening to the nuns: "Hail Mary, full of grace, the Lord is with thee . . . Blessed Michael, the Archangel, defend us in the day of battle; be our safe-guard against the wickedness and snares of the devil; rebuke him, we humbly pray . . . Angus, Angus, hurry up. Please come home. Hail Mary, full of grace, the Lord is with thee. Let him come now, please."

Her last prayer seemed to receive a lightning answer, for there came the sound of a car drawing up outside. The next minute Angus was in the room. He wasn't drunk, as they all expected, but he wasn't rightly sober. He stood in the doorway and raised his hands for silence, crying, "Now all of you, all of you don't say it. I'm telling you, don't say it." He didn't seem to take in the fact that Vanessa was sitting in her coat. "I've done it. A treble up . . . Mrs. Cotton Junior, Mrs. Cotton Senior, Mrs. Rosie Barrett, Mr. Stanley Barrett, you see before you a successful business man, a man who's going up and up. I've pulled off the Henson quarry deal, two years' work. I've got the whole contract. Twenty lorries I'll need. Twenty lorries and twenty men, Stan. And," he moved slowly towards Vanessa, "you're moving, Mrs. Cotton Junior, to a house with a bathroom. But it's only temporary; this is only the beginning." He wagged his finger down into her pale but smiling face. "And now for the last news, the top of the treble." He turned to his mother, where Emily was standing at the far end of the table, her fists thrust into her hips, her face grim. "Mrs. Cotton Senior, your son has had an honour bestowed on him. You always said it would happen. Give the lad a chance, you said and it'll happen. And it has." He leant across the table towards her. "I've been put forward as a member of the Round Table. Now what do you think of that?" He straightened up and looked from one to the other. There was both pride and scorn on his face. "Me, Angus Cotton, asked to represent the contractors of this town in the Round Table, because you know," he shook his head widely, "only one man can be in there representing one profession. Profession mind; I said, profession."

Whatever Emily felt at her son's success, at this moment what she said was, "You big, gormless gowk, shut up. Shut your trap a minute if you can. What do you think's been happenin' while you've been swillin' beer? She's had her pains all night since you left, an' we've been waitin' for you. She wouldn't let Stan get a taxi. She's a fool; she wanted her husband to take her, an' she's been hangin' on. Now, pick up that case, that's if you're able to carry it, an' get goin'."

Angus was deaf to Emily's bawling. He was looking down at Vanessa and she up at him, and he said softly "Aw, honey."

His voice was cut off by Rosie saying airily, "Well, you should have known what was happenin'. Didn't you have your pains?" On this, both she and Stan began to laugh heartily. Then their laughter was checked abruptly by Vanessa's body doubling forward.

"Look!" cried Emily. "Get her into the car as quick as you can."

"No . . . o. No . . .o." Vanessa refused to move from the

chair. She was gripping Angus's hands, her fingers digging into his flesh.

After a few minutes, when the pain didn't subside, Emily looked from one to the other and said, "God, no!"

But it was God, yes.

When Angus tried to get Vanessa to her feet she slumped down his legs on to the mat, saying between gasps, "Get . . . get the doctor."

While Stan flew for Doctor Carr they all tried in various ways to get Vanessa to her feet and into the bedroom, and when Angus put his arms under her to lift her up she cried out in agony, "No! No!"

It was Rosie who said, "Get·an eiderdown and sheets to put under her."

They managed to do this, and it was only fifteen minutes later when, on the mat in front of the fire, in the kitchen of the house where he himself had been born, Angus saw, to his horrified gaze, the head of his son coming into the world.

When Doctor Carr hurried into the room and took over, Angus went down the yard and was violently sick; and when he returned his mother was holding a screaming child in her arms. He did not look at it but went and knelt at Vanessa's side.

Vanessa looked at him. She was smiling. "It's – it's a boy," she said.

He nodded at her, unable to speak.

"It's been a day."

He nodded again.

"You know something?" Her voice was faint. "I want to laugh."

"You can laugh the morrow." His voice was shaking. "What you want to do now is to go to sleep. Here's the doctor." He moved aside and stood bewildered at what was going on around him. Rosie was gathering some pieces of linen from the floor and his mother was saying, "Put them in soak and get me a dish of hot water. And here," she turned to him, "this belongs to you, so hold him until I find some place to put him. Make yourself useful for once."

He took into his arms the thing he had created. It looked old and wrinkled, mummified, but it was his son, the beginnings of a man. He had been born on a mat in a condemned house. That shouldn't have happened; it was his fault. But he would remedy that. Oh aye, by God he would. His son would have education, the best money could buy, boarding school, public school, the lot. He'd have no memories of Ryder's Row, number twenty-four or number two. Angus Cotton's son would be a gentleman . . . He'd show them.

2

The Rover 2000 swerved expertly into the car park and to the corner opposite the side door of the club. Angus got out, and after adjusting his Aquascutum overcoat he went towards the building, not to the side door, but around to the main entrance of Ransome's Club.

Ransome's had first been established in 1864; it said so on a brass plate discreetly embedded in an alcove in the lobby. It was, supposedly, a non-political club, but it was rarely you found any well-known member of the Labour Party registered on its books. But there was one thing necessary to become a member of Ransome's . . . money.

The name of Mr. Angus Frederick Cotton had been on the books now for over six months now. He wasn't a frequent visitor, sometimes a fortnight would go by and he wouldn't look in, but whenever he did visit the club he came dressed in his best.

On the admission of Mr. Angus Frederick Cotton to Ransome's it had lost one distinguished member. Mr. Jonathan Ratcliffe had met Mr. Cotton in the lobby, and Mr. Ratcliffe's reactions had been apoplectic, and the town had something else to chuckle over.

The town was very interested in the situation that existed between the house of Angus Cotton – still after five years at the corner of Ryder's Row – and the house of Mr. Jonathan Ratcliffe of Bower Place, Brampton Hill.

It was said over both pints of beer and sherry before dinner that there was nothing against people getting on, but they shouldn't forget themselves and play God Almighty. The definition over the sherry might be reduced merely to God, but it meant the same thing: Jonathan Ratcliffe had become too high-handed, too uppish for the forthright, outspoken, down-to-earth citizens of Fellburn.

Now young Angus Cotton: there was a lad who had got on but who hadn't forgotten himself. This was almost entirely the view of the beer drinkers. He knew where he was going right from the start did Cotton. Not only did he take on Jonathan Ratcliffe's girl when she was going to have a bairn – and not by him mind, and that was the telling point, and it hadn't come out till after. Oh aye, that was a great telling point, to take on somebody else's bairn; it showed what a man was made of. Well, not only had he done that, but he had gone into business as a one-lorry man, and whether he had begged, borrowed or stolen the money, nobody knew, but in next to no time he had got two lorries, then four, then six, and seemingly overnight he had a fleet because you couldn't walk yards in the town without seeing one of Cotton's lorries. But he hadn't forgotten himself, had Angus Cotton.

At least, not yet, said the sherry drinkers. They were watching him very closely. He still lived in the same street as his mother, and although his wife was turned out in the best, as were his two bairns, Ryder's Row wasn't an address for a member of Ransome's.

Yes, both quarters of the town were very interested in the doings of Angus Cotton. And he knew it, and thrived on it.

He left his hat and coat in the cloakroom, looked at himself in the mirror above the wash-basin, rubbed his hands lightly over his discreetly oiled hair, opened his mouth wide and brought his fingers down tightly against each cheek to make sure there was no stubble, then straightened his tie and adjusted his coat and walked quietly out and into the hallway. Here he looked about him for a moment before saying to a passing waiter, "Mr. Fowler about?"

"Yes, sir; he went into the Brown Room just a minute ago."

"Thanks."

The Brown Room had an ornate high ceiling. Its walls were covered with faded red wallpaper on which was hung portraits of past distinguished members of the club. There were deep leather armchairs and down cushioned settees. In an armchair in a far corner sat Andrew Fowler. And he raised his hand as Angus entered the room.

"Hello, there." Angus took his seat opposite Fowler, then said, "I'm sorry I couldn't make it yesterday; I had to go down to Lessington; they are taking it too easy in that quarter."

Andrew Fowler smiled, nodded, then said, "What are you having?"

"Oh, a brandy." He would have preferred a beer, but beer wasn't drunk in this room; he had learned that early.

Andrew Fowler hailed a waiter who was bringing drinks to other occupants of the room. Having given his order, he settled back and said, still with a smile on his face, "Served you right if you had missed it."

"Missed what?"

"Oh." Fowler jerked his head to the side. "Just something I thought you should know about."

"Well, let's have it," said Angus. "You're just bursting at the seams . . . Don't tell me they're going to pull the new Town Hall down in Newcastle and they want me to salvage it?"

They both laughed a little; then Fowler said, "How would you like to live on Brampton Hill?"

"What!"

"You heard me. How would you like to live on Brampton Hill?"

Angus's face was straight, his eyes hard. "It all depends

which part. Brampton Hill's a long hill and there's all kinds of houses on it. I don't know whether I'd like to live there or not." He lay back in his chair and stretched his neck out of his collar. "It's not the place it was; a lot of the big houses are in flats now." He surveyed Fowler. He was giving nothing away to him, not about Brampton Hill, he wasn't. There were things about Fowler he couldn't understand. Sometimes he thought he was playing him like a puppet. He didn't like the idea.

"The Larches is to be put up for sale."

Angus felt a wave of heat cover him. It was as if he'd had an injection straight into an artery. His head seemed to be swelling and he knew his face was a deep red. The Larches. Brett's place. The house next to Jonathan Ratcliffe's. There was a tightness in his jaws that was painful. He drew in a long, steady breath. Was this it? Was this what he had been waiting for? Striving for? He had promised her he'd put her back where she belonged, even on the hill, but' he'd never dreamed of anything on the scale of The Larches. The Larches up for sale. And all that land. God, yes. He screwed his buttocks farther back against the soft leather of the chair. This was it. This was what he had been waiting for. He'd put her in The Larches.

"What are they asking?" he said.

"I don't rightly know; the bills aren't out yet. And then most likely it'll be put up for auction. But it'll fetch money, big money, because of the land. Six acres, all with river frontage; that'll bring money."

"Oh," Angus moved his head deprecatingly, "not as much as all that; it's controlled, isn't it? No building there."

"Not for a while. But they're pulling off the controls everywhere. Anybody getting it could hang on for a few years and then they'd be in clover, no matter what they had to pay for it now."

"Have you any idea what it will go for?"

Andrew Fowler pushed his head back into the chair and looked upwards for a moment before saying, "Well, the house needs a lot doing to it, both inside and out, I understand. I would say anything up to fifteen thousand. That's playing up the supposition that you'll never be able to do anything with the land, only as a garden. But if there's abreeze of a whisper that it could be used for building land in a few years' time when we have a change of Government," he pulled his nose at Angus, "the price will soar; it could go as far as thirty."

Angus gave a low whistle, then said, "Who's got the business?"

"Pearson."

"You know Pearson."

"Yes, I know Pearson."

"Could yo do anything?"

"I might."

Suddenly Angus tossed his head from one side to the other and gritted his teeth and muttered under his breath, "For God's sake, don't stall, Andrew. I hate this cat and mouse business. Could you?"

Andrew Fowler's expression took on a slightly cold look now and he said, "You get too agitated, Angus. That's your trouble. Play it cool; it pays off in the long run. I've got something else to tell you. It isn't only money you've got to worry about, Ratcliffe's after it. He's been at Pearson already; it could be sold privately before the sale."

Angus didn't ask why Ratcliffe didn't go next door to the Bretts and do a deal straight-away; he guessed there had likely been no interchange between those two houses since the day his mother had visited them both.

Do you know what he's offering?"

"Sixteen thousand. But here' another thing. He's not doing it himself, he's working through a third party. Crafty, very crafty."

Angus took a drink from his glass, then bent towards Fowler saying, "I'll go seventeen."

"Won't that be rocking your boat?"

"Aye, I supose it will. But if it means twenty-seven and it almost sinks me, I mean to get that house . . . And another thing, tell Pearson I'll see him all right."

"What would you suggest? It might be steep."

"Five hundred?"

"Five hundred, it is."

They both drew in deep breaths, and then Fowler said, "There's another thing I'd like to talk over with you, Angus, while we're on the subject."

"Aye, come on, let's have it; I thought we weren't finished."

"Well, you know me."

"Nobody better, Andrew." Angus's lip was up at the corner.

Fowler ignored the implication and went on: "As long as you buy the house and use it as a habitation, well and good, but should you sell the land for building . . . well, then I think there should be a little agreement on that."

Angus stared at his mentor for a moment before saying. "Fair enough, fair enough. Do you want it in writing?"

"Yes, I think that would be wise, Angus."

"What per cent?"

"Well, don't let's be greedy, say trade price." He smiled. "Thirty three and a third."

"Let's drink to it."

Andrew Fowler raised and glass, and after they had drunk he got to his feet and added, "Now we can have our dinner in peace. By the way, how's Vanessa and the children?"

"Fine, grand."

"What's she going to say when you tell her about this latest venture?"

"I'm not going to tell her."

"What! you're not . . . ?"

"No. At least until it's all signed and sealed. How long will it take?"

"Oh, don't gallop, Angus; I've got to put the wheels in motion first. And then it can be a slow business: solicitors, Land Registry, one thing and another, they take time. Once we get going two months should see it all cleared up."

"Two months! As long as that?" He bit on his lip and his step quickened unconsciously as he left the room, and he thought, "I'll not sleep for two months, I'll not know a minute's peace until it's mine, MINE . . ."

And Angus's sleep was fitful for the next eight days, during which time the price of The Larches rocketed from seventeen thousand to twenty-three thousand, but on the eighth day he wrote out a cheque for five per cent of twenty-three thousand pounds to be paid to James Pearson Esq., Estate Agents, being the deposit required to purchase The Larches from the joint owners, Colin, Paul and Michael Brett.

Now Angus was bursting to tell Vanessa, but a wariness in him warned him to keep quiet until the whole thing was legally settled. He believed if he were to tell her now she'd put a spanner in the smooth-running works, she'd bring up the excuse it was too close to her people. But once the thing was settled and he'd saddled himself with a liability of twenty-three thousand pounds she couldn't do much else but accept the house with a good grace, and oh, to see her ensconced next to the folks who had thrown her off as if she were a dirty clout. Parents or no parents, she was bound to feel one up on them, if only for his sake, because he had done as he said, and in a short time at that, and put her back where she belonged.

And he had no doubt in his own mind where Vanessa belonged. She didn't belong in Ryder's Row, and if she lived to be a thousand she would never fit in there. She stuck out like a sore thumb; she was as great an embarrassment to those around her as he would be, God helping him, to Jonathan Ratcliffe.

Although he constantly told himself he wanted the

341

house for Vanessa he knew that, with even more intensity, he wanted that house for Angus Cotton. Oh, to come out of that drive in the morning in a Bentley. Aye, the next car he would get would be a Bentley. And which Bentley would make way for which when they met in the road? He couldn't wait to find out. And another thing, he'd have his mother with him. Aye, that would be a feather in his cap, and in hers. She'd be going back to Brampton Hill, and not as a skivvy. No, she'd be going into the kitchen only to give her orders. He didn't conjure up what part Vanessa was going to play in this arrangement, but told himself he'd employ a couple of maids and a gardener; he'd have The Larches the show-place of the town. And one more thing, his bairns, they were going to be educated . . . Private school for Andrew, and then public school. God, aye, he'd see to that. There'd be no Ryder's Row for his family. He'd let Ratcliffe see how Angus Cotton did things. Angus Cotton, the contractor, who, but for being blamed for giving his daughter a bairn, might be still Angus Cotton the foreman. When he came to think of it he had something to thank God-Almighty Ratcliffe for after all, and he would thank him one day . . . Aye, by spitting in his eye. And the first spit would be when he moved into The Larches. Hurry up, hurry up, the days, the weeks; he couldn't wait.

Feeling as he did he had to tell somebody, so he told Emily.

Emily had just finished soaking her feet in a tin dish before the fire and he sat on his hunkers on the edge of the mat and told her, and she was so thunderstruck by his news that she let him go on talking. The water got cold and her legs began to turn blue and shiny, and when he said, "Well, say something, say something. Don't sit there looking like a stuffed duck with your feet in the water. Say something, woman," she closed her eyes, heaved a deep sigh, then, taking up a towel where it had been warming on the fender, she put it on the hearth rug and

342

lifted her feet on to it before she turned and looked at him and said, "You're bloody-well stark, staring mad, lad."

There was a short silence before he brought his body upwards in a bound, saying, "Aw, for crying out loud, Mam! Have you heard what I've been saying to you? I've bought The Larches. Me, Angus Cotton, I've bought The Larches in Brampton Hill, and all you can bloody well say is that I'm mad. Do you know what this means? We're all going to live on Brampton Hill."

"Who? Me?" She dug her thumb into the hollow of her neck. "Oh, no, lad. Now, you can count me out of your scheme. Me live on Brampton Hill? Now get this into that great, big, swollen head of yours, the only time you'll get me up Brampton Hill again is if they take the hearse up that way. But that's not even likely as it's the long way round to the cemetery."

"Well, we can't go and live up there and leave you down here, woman."

"Look. Look." She stood up now and walked to the edge of the towel, which brought her close to him. "You're not my keeper. You're married, you've got a wife and family. You see to them an' that'll take you all your time, but what I do is my business. This is my home and until they pull it down I'm stayin' here. And then I'll go into whatever they provide. But I'm not livin' with you and Van on Brampton Hill, or any any other bloody hill. Now get that . . . And here's somethin' else I'll give you to think about. You said you haven't told her, you're keepin' it a secret; well, if I'm any judge, you're in for one great, bloody, shock. And it wouldn't surprise me if you haven't got a twenty-three thousand-pound white elephant on your hands. What you still don't understand, lad, after five years is you've married somebody quite different to yoursel'."

"Oh, for God's sake, Mam, don't talk bloody tripe. I know what I married, nobody better."

"But you don't, lad, you don't. 'Cos if you think she's

343

goin' to go on livin' next door to her folks just like that, then you don't. She's a highly sensitive lass. Some folk call it breeding. Anyway, she's different, an' I can't see her lettin' you push her up there right on to their doorstep. She couldn't stand it. You know," she stabbed her finger at him and smiled a tight smile, "I know why you're doin' this. I know why you've bought Brett's place, an' I don't blame you. Oh, I don't blame you. And I'd be laughin' up me sleeve if you were takin' anybody else up there but his daughter. In fact, if your wife wasn't any connection of his I'd go up there on a Saturday night and have me knees up in the garden just to show him an' all." Her voice dropped to a sad note as she ended, "But you did marry his daughter, and if I know anythin' about your Van she's not going to like your little surprise, 'cos to say the least, it's sort of tactless like."

"Tactless be-buggered. Look, Mam, don't give me the jitters. Twenty-three thousand I've spent. Do you realize, twenty-three thousand! I'm going up fast, but twenty-three thousand takes some finding. And that's not all. With the side lines I've had to keep going to get the damned place I'll be lucky if I get away with twenty-five thousand when I'm finished."

Emily's voice was still quiet, but had a touch of laughter in it now and her smile was smirky as she said, "It should be a nice experiment for you playing with thousands. Now who would have thought that the snotty-nosed, shock-headed, ugly mug, Angus Cotton, whose mam was the Ratcliffe's daily for years, can now talk in thousands, twenty-five thousands, when up to a few years ago twenty-five shillings spare would have been a Godsend to him. It's a credit to you, lad, and it's your mother that's saying it. Go on, lash out with your thousands, but don't think," her voice rose sharply, "that you're goin' to push me around, or that you're goin' to make your wife do somethin' that will be against every grain in her body." She thrust out her hand and thumped him on the shoulder, her voice barking now as she finished, "If you want my advice, you'll spend the next few weeks preparing yourself for a disappointment, sort of building yourself up, if you get what I mean, 'cos your big-head is goin' to have a puncture."

"Aw, to hell with you!"

As he stalked out of the kitchen she bawled after him, "An' to hell with you. And if you see me there, don't you open your mouth to me because I'm particular about the company I keep. I've no room for upstarts. You're goin' the same road as the man you're fightin'."

When the door banged she quickly padded into the front room, and, standing to the side of the window, watched her son marching down the street. A big, well-dressed, prosperous-looking man, who had just been in this little box of a house talking about spending twenty-five thousand pounds as if they were shillings. Life was strange. Would he persuade Van to go and live in a house next to her parents? He persuaded her to do most things. It was always a mystery to her what Vanessa saw in her son; that she herself should know his worth was a different matter altogether. She knew him to be a good man, big-headed, bumptious, argumentative, all the qualities that went to make a rough northerner; he took after herself, and she knew what she was all right, nobody better, and him being the flesh of her flesh she could appreciate him; but how did it come that a girl like Vanessa could appreciate him? What did she see in him? She didn't talk much ever, never opened up, and she didn't seem to have any life of her own. She was his wife, the mother of his children; his secretary, aye, an' his teacher, she had been learning him for years to speak properly, grammer an' that. She had seen his efforts on his desk but she hadn't remarked on them; she knew better. She didn't want to spoil a good thing. Yet he showed no evidence of improvement when he was talking to her. No, he was the same old ha'penny dodger. But that lass; everything she did was for him, and what did she get out of it? Damn little that she could see. He could have got her into a decent house long afore this but he had put it off and put it off, partly, she had thought, because he didn't want to move away from herself. But now she saw the real reason for him staying put. He had been after big game all along, no modern bungalow or imitation Regency house for him; it had to be on Brampton Hill, and not only on Brampton Hill, it had to be one of the biggest houses; and not only one of the biggest, but the place that had the most land left. He was going too fast; he was rising too high; he'd blow himself up unless something, or somebody, put the brakes on him.

3

It was in the afternoon that she went down the street to the end house. She knew Vanessa's routine. It being after four o'clock Andrew and Annabella would be out with Mary Ridley in the park, and Vanessa would be preparing the evening meal.

She found her in the kitchen, a small, modern, well-equipped kitchen, and she said, "Oh, hello, lass. Isn't it close? And it's going to pour afore the day's out; I can tell by me feet."

"Aren't they any better?" Vanessa looked down at the swollen ankles bulging over the top of black-laced shoes.

"No, lass; an' they won't be until I'm in me coffin. And I bet you what you like, the swellin'll go down immediately then. Enough to make you kick yourself."

"Oh, Emily!" Vanessa was laughing. She always got a laugh and felt happy when Emily was about. It was a different kind of happiness from that which she experienced with Angus; that happiness was a taut, high-tensioned feeling. She said now, "Rosie popped in. She's just gone along to Stodart's; she'll be back in a short while. She was coming down to you."

"Stodart's! For more shoes? She's always buyin' shoes. How many pairs is that she's got?"

"At the last count," said Vanessa, breaking an egg into some flour, "eighteen."

"God above! Eighteen pairs of shoes. She would have to be a centipede to get her wear out of them."

Vanessa was laughing again. "She likes shoes."

"She likes too many things, that one. The money's gone to her head; she's never done spendin'. Have they got owt in the bank? She won't tell me; she says it's none of my business."

"Oh, I think they're all right, Emily. Stan's sensible where money is concerned."

"It would take him to be. She'd have him on the rocks else . . . Van."

"Yes, Emily?" Vanessa turned her head round, but still kept beating the egg and flour together.

"Can you stop a minute? I want a word with you, serious like."

Serious? Vanessa laid down the fork and wiped her hands and turned about, and Emily, going into the living-room, said, "Come an' sit down a minute; I want to get it over afore our Rosie comes in. This is atween you and me, understand?"

When they were seated Emily bent forward and repeated, "Mind, lass; this is just atween you and me. I want your word on it."

"Something's wrong, Emily . . . Angus?"

"Aye, Angus. Oh, it's all right. Don't look like that; it's not that kind of wrong." She reached out and roughly pulled Vanessa's hand away from her mouth and, holding on to it, she said, "Now listen, lass. Have you noticed any difference in him lately, the last week or so?"

Vanessa considered a minute, then said, "Well, yes. He's not sleeping. He seems excited about something; bursting out singing one minute, and gloomy the next. Yes. Yes, I've noticed it."

"But you didn't say nothing?"

"No, Emily."

"Well, I can tell you he is excited an' all, because he's keeping somethin' back from you. He's done somethin' an' he's not tellin' you until the matter is clinched. An' when it is it'll be too late to alter things; or so he thinks.

348

You know, he's your husband, Van, but I don't think he really knows you. I feel I know you a damn sight better than him; but then, of course, I've known you longer, haven't I?" she smiled.

"What's it all about, Emily?" Vanessa's voice was quiet; her whole demeanour was quiet. She had grown into a rather reserved young woman. She was very seldom gay, unless she was with her children, and then she had to be alone with them before she could let herself go. She added now, "Tell me. Tell me quickly, please, because Rosie might be back at any minute. And Angus himself will be in shortly."

"Well, hold on to your seat there, lass. Here it comes . . . He's buying the Bretts' place, The Larches."

Emily watched the colour drain completely from Vanessa's face. She thought for a moment she was going to collapse, and she said, "Now steady on, lass. Steady on. Don't let go. This is not the time for lettin' go; you've got to put your thinkin' cap on."

"The Larches? He's buying The Larches for us?" Vanessa's voice came as the smallest whisper.

"For you. He's goin' to give you the surprise of your life. He gave me the surprise of mine when he out with it. He was bustin' at the seams, like a bairn with a new toy. I've never stopped worryin' since. I told him he was mad . . . You don't want to go an' live in The Larches, do you?"

"Oh, Emily. Me! Live in the Larches? In Brett's house? O-Oh!" The last word came as a groan. "I couldn't. I couldn't live there even . . . even if it wasn't next door to home." She still thought of Bower Place as home. "And just think what it would do to mother and father. They wouldn't stand for it; they would leave."

"Aye, aye, I'd thought of that."

"And . . . and they love that place. Oh. Oh, how could he, Emily? How could he?"

"He could because he's barmy; he thinks that because

you came from there you want to go back there. It's no use tellin' him. But that's not the only reason he bought the place; the other is he's wantin' to get one back on your father. That's at the bottom of it; he wants to show him."

"I'll never go there, Emily."

"I know that, lass."

"He'll just have to sell it again."

"An' that'll knock the spunk out of him if anythin' will. And I'd hate to see it happen, 'cos he's mine, and I know how he'll feel. But as I see it there's nothing else for it. I thought I'd better tell you because if he sprung it on you and you hadn't time to think there might be a flare-up. And it's like this." She smiled now. "Him an' me, an' our lot, we can flare up and threaten to murder each other one minute, an' we'll be shakin' hands the next, but if you had a flare-up you wouldn't get over it easily. Would you now?"

Vanessa looked from the dyed-hair to the prematurely wrinkled face of her mother-in-law, and she thought: She's right. She's always right. But what was she going to do about this, this latest venture, which must appear to him as the summit of his aims? This is what he had been waiting for, working for, striving for, wearing himself out for, to give her this. Her refusal must be made in such a way that a flare-up, when it came, would not burn him out, burn them both out. Their marriage, as she saw it, was a precarious union, resting as it were on a knife's edge, and this in spite of love and two children.

At this moment they heard Rosie coming pitter-pattering up the stairs on her high heels and, after looking hard at each other, they went quickly out of the room, and Emily greeted her daughter with, "You want your lugs scudded, buying more shoes."

"Shoes are made for walking," Rosie sang, as she pranced round the table in her latest acquisition. Then stopping suddenly, she looked at Vanessa and said, "Oh, by the way. What's going with our Angus these days? Stan says he's like a dog with two tails."

Vanessa and Emily refrained from exchanging glances; then Rosie exclaimed, "You're not," she shook her head before adding, "again?"

"No, Rosie. I'm not again." Vanessa smiled.

"Well; what is it?"

"Oh," Vanessa turned towards the fireplace, "I suppose it's because things are going well."

"Oh, it isn't only that. Stan says they've been going well for a long time, and he wasn't like this. Stan says he's all keyed-up, just as if he was going to take off by parachute."

"Very likely is," said Emily now, going towards the door. "You never know what he's goin' to do next. The only thing is, I hope he doesn't forget to pull the strings afore he hits the ground."

On this enigmatic comment, enigmatic at least to Rosie, Emily left them.

Life seemed to follow the usual pattern until almost a week later. It was in the evening. Angus was late and Vanessa had just got the children to bed, promising them that their father would come and see them immediately he entered the house. But they were sound asleep by the time he did get in.

He looked tired to-night, and somewhat strained, and so she let him have his meal and cleared away before she said, "I want to talk to you, Angus."

"Talk?" He cast a sidelong glance at her. "Well, fire ahead."

She swallowed deeply and walked the length of the sitting-room and back to him before she said, "I understand you are buying me a house?"

She watched his head turn from her and swing from side to side, and when his fist crashed on to the table she said, "She had to tell me."

"The big-mouthed-old-bitch!" He spaced each word.

"That's all she is, a great, big, loose-mouthed, old bitch."
His head stopped its swinging, his fists relaxed, and then
slowly he turned and looked at her and asked in an entirely different voice, in which she detected a plea, "Well,
what do you think? Go on, tell me what you think?"

"I . . . I think it's wonderful that you could pay so much
money for the place."

"Is that all?" His shoulders stiffened. "Aren't you excited? You know what place I've bought, don't you?
Brett's. Now. Now." He thrust his hand swiftly out towards
her and jerked it back and forwards. "Don't get me wrong.
It isn't animosity; nothing like that; not against Brett; it's
just that I wanted you to be back on the Hill, where you
belong."

"I – I understand, Angus."

"Do you? Aw," his head was swinging again, "I don't
think you do really."

"Yes, yes, I do; and I think it's marvellous. There's only
one thing."

"Aye, one thing. Well, what is it?" His face looked grim
now, for he expected her answer to be, "I can't live there."
But it wasn't. What she said was, "Would you do something more for me?"

"Anything." His voice was full of relief. The tension
went out of his body; he grabbed her hands, saying softly,
"Anything in the wide world. You know that. I don't have
to tell you."

"But this is something big, different; you – mightn't
be able to understand why I'm asking it."

"Well, I won't," he smiled at her, "not until you tell
me."

She dropped her eyes down to their joined hands, and
then said softly, "Would you have the house put in my
name, not jointly, in – in my name?"

This request was the last thing in the world he imagined
her making. It sounded utterly preposterous. He wanted

to think he hadn't heard her alright, but he had. Put the house in her name? He wanted it for her but it was to be his property. He wanted to own The Larches, his name on the title deeds. That was one of the things he was living for, to see Angus Cotton written on the deeds of The Larches.

"Why? Tell me why?" he said flatly. "Jointly, aye; but why do you want it in your name?"

She raised her lashes but didn't look at him; she looked beyond him as she said, "It's – it's just a whim, I suppose."

He stared at her. Just a whim, she said. If he didn't satisfy her whim what then? She'd think him mean. All his life she'd consider him mean, and it would raise a barrier between them. Another one to be broken down. He spent his life breaking down barriers. The one that stood between Brampton Hill and Ryder's Row was about to fall, but if he didn't comply with her wish in this, even when the barrier was down, wouldn't she in some way, like a woman, hold it against him? He was always saying that everything he did was for her, now he'd have to prove it by giving her the house.

She was at the window looking down into the street. She was standing very still. She could do that, stand still with no muscle moving. He stared at her long, straight back. Even the lines of her could churn up his stomach any time of the day, and that after nearly six years. Aw, to hell! Who was to know whose name was on the deeds? The house would be known as Angus Cotton's place, and Van wasn't the kind of woman to go loud-mouthing it round the town that it was in her name. She wasn't like his mother. Wait till he got his tongue around that one. She had knocked all the guts out of his plans. The excitement of driving Van up there when the thing was signed and sealed and saying, "This is yours. I've bought it for you. Didn't I say I'd put you back where you belong?"

He said now, "Well, if that's how you want it, that's how you'll have it. It'll be in your name."

She turned round. "Thanks, Angus," she said. "Thanks."

That was all, just, "Thanks, Angus." No throwing her arms around his neck and hugging him and telling him that he was the most generous man on earth, that it was wonderful the things he had achieved in so short a time. Nothing like that. Just, "Thanks, Angus." Aye, well; that's how things went. Coolly. That was part of her make-up, coolness. If he ever could hate her it would be when she was cool.

"How long will it be before everything is settled?" She had her face averted as she asked the question, and he said, "Oh, a few weeks. The solicitor will have to make a few more alterations now, but the papers haven't gone up to the Land Registry yet. It won't be too long. A month; five weeks perhaps." His voice sounded flat as if he had lost interest in the whole project, and turning away, he added, "I think I'll go down to the club."

There was a pause before she answered, "Yes. Yes, I would do that; it will relax you."

"I don't need relaxing." His voice was brittle as he turned and faced her again, and there was about his face an explosive look, and she combated it by saying quietly, "All right, you don't need to relax. But you need a change. Go on; you'll feel better when you get back."

He stared at her. There was something here he couldn't get to the bottom of. She should be a bit elated that she was having a twenty-three thousand pound house as a gift. She should be acting differently, not sending him out casually to the club, as if it was an ordinary night in an ordinary week – as if he was an ordinary bloke ... Aye, as if he was just an ordinary bloke who hadn't one penny to rub against another. He had a feeling inside that things weren't right, the kind of feeling he had years ago when everything was going against him. He wanted to talk, to get to the bottom of it, but he couldn't do any probing with Van, not with the cool mood on her. But there was someone he could talk to, that loud-mouthed old bitch down there. He'd go down and blow her sky high.

He was in the street before he decided against visiting Emily; the mood he was in he'd want to bawl her down, and she didn't seem able these days to stand up to him as she used to. He cursed deep in his throat, got into his car and drove to the club. It was coming to something when he had to go to Ransome's to be appreciated.

When the house door banged Vanessa, sitting down suddenly on a chair, closed her eyes and thought, "This is just the beginning. He'll want to kill me when he finds out."

4

The day was dull and chilly. It had started with rain, which had slowed to a drizzle, and this in turn had developed into a wet mist. The streets were greasy. The town traffic bustled through the heavy greyness as if making for more pleasant scenes beyond.

Vanessa made her way down the main street to Tiller's Garage and asked for a taxi, and when she was seated in it she held her large handbag upright on her knees and tightly between her hands. In her handbag were the deeds of The Larches. She'd had them in her possession since eleven o'clock when the solicitor had smilingly handed them to her and she had surprised both him and Angus by saying, "I want to keep them with me for to-day."

"Look; what's up with you? They're yours," Angus had said. "Let Mr. Black hold them with all the other stuff."

"Just for to-day," she had repeated; and he had shaken his head and said, "All right, all right, have it your own way."

He had an appointment at half-past eleven but he was coming back about one for her and they were going up to . . . their house. It was a blind date, he said, because he had never seen inside The Larches. Fancy that, buying a place without looking it over. Had she ever heard of anyone doing that?"

When she said to the taxi-driver, "Brampton Hill, Bower Place, please," she shivered. She was going home. For the first time in years she was going home. Deep down in her there was a supressed longing to visit her old home, to see her mother and Susan, and . . . even her father. Knowing her father's temperament, she was well aware that if it lay with him she would never see the inside of her old home again, and that already, under the circumstances, he would be preparing to leave the house he had built, the house he loved; and this also he would have chalked up against her. She was aware that she was about to do something extraordinary, and something that would likely drive Angus mad, for the time being anyway. But as things stood, no word of hers would convince him that she would find it impossible to live next door to her people, and, in particular, in Brett's house. Angus wasn't insensitive, on the contrary, but he was totally blind in some instances to what was right and proper.

She was still shivering when the taxi drew up outside the gates of Bower Place. She had asked the driver not to go into the drive, and she paid him off for she did not know how long she would be.

She timed her visit. They would just be sitting down to lunch; they wouldn't be able to say he wasn't in.

It was strange to ring the doorbell. She could never remember ringing the doorbell. She wondered what kind of a maid they had at the moment.

When the door opened, Susan confronted her, a plumper, older Susan, Susan with her mouth open and her eyes popping out of her head.

"Hello, Susan."

Susan was unable to speak. She turned her head and cast a glance quickly back across the hall, then said on a high whisper, "Vanessa." She looked her up and down for a moment. Her younger sister was now a woman, a tall, beautiful woman, very well dressed. She knew a moment's keen envy of her. She didn't ask her to come in but stood staring at her, until Vanessa said, "Are they in?"

"Yes. At – at lunch."

"Will you tell them I'm here? I'd like to see them."

"Vanessa," Susan shook her head, "he's in a dreadful state. You've . . . your . . . ."

"I know, I know; me and mine. It's that I want to see him about. Things will be different from now on." She smiled reassuringly down on her sister. She felt older, oh so much older than Susan at this moment. Susan looked dowdy, harassed, surprisingly commonplace. This fact made her slightly more at ease, but it didn't stop her body trembling.

"I – I'll put you . . . I mean, you'd better go into the morning-room. I'll – I'll break it to them."

"All right, Susan." She looked about the hall for a moment before crossing to the morning-room door. It was as if the years had rolled away and all in them was but a dream and she was back home once more. The morning-room was the same, except that there was not so much silver dotted about. She stood looking out of the window waiting. And she waited . . . and waited. And then her mother came in alone.

They looked at each other across the length of the room until Vanessa moved slowly forward, saying, "Hello, Mother."

Jane Ratcliffe nipped at her lower lip and gulped gently in her throat before saying, "Hello, Vanessa." The words came out on a hoarse whisper as if she had a cold.

"How are you, Mother?"

"Quite – quite well, thank you." She did not ask her daughter to sit down; she just stared at her, because she was surpised at what she saw. She had caught a glimpse of her now and again in the town; once with her children; once a few years ago coming out of a store laden with shopping bags. But this woman before her was no relation to the girl she had known. She had never seen her before. This woman who had been associating with the common people for years was poised and dignified and looked sure of herself. She said stiffly now, "Why have you come? Haven't you wrought enough havoc on us?"

It was some seconds before Vanessa answered: "The reason for my visit is to try and rectify that in some small way. I would like to see Father."

Jane Ratcliffe closed her eyes and said, "That's impossible; he won't see you."

"But I mean to see him. I must see him. I don't suppose it's news to you that Angus has bought The Larches." She looked back into her mother's unblinking eyes, then went on, "He has given it to me. It's in my name and I can do entirely what I like with it. I – I propose to sell it to father for what it cost Angus. He's always wanted the land, and I know he would have bought it only Angus went over his head. Well, that's why I'm here."

Jane Ratcliffe blinked now. Then, after a moment, she exclaimed on a relieved note, "That's very kind of you, Vanessa, very kind. I'll go and tell him."

Again Vanessa waited, but not so long this time. And when the door opened again her father entered, and her mother was behind him.

She hadn't seen her father since that morning in the station yard. He had looked no different then from how he had always looked, but now there was a difference. Although he was only in his middle fifties he looked an old man, a bitter, tight-faced old man. She forced herself to speak, to break the tension-filled silence in the room. "Hello, Father," she said.

He did not answer for a moment, and then his thin lips scarcely moving he said thickly, "Feeling triumphant, aren't you? Having dragged yourself up from the gutter you come to show off, bearing a gift, I understand, from your husband. Well," his bony lower jaw jutted outwards, bringing his lower lip overlapping his upper one, and he went on in a spate of scarcely controlled fury, "you can take his gift back to him and tell him he's dealing with the same man that used to be his master. You can tell him that. I've never accepted gifts from menials and scum and I'm not starting now."

359

She choked as the words rushed from her, her anger almost matching his now. "He knows nothing about it. He didn't send me to you; he wouldn't because he loathes you. But I knew you couldn't stand us living next door. And what is more, I don't want to live next door to you. It was my own idea to offer you the house, because you've always coveted the land, but he knows nothing about it. As for being scum, don't you dare call him scum. He's worth more –"

His voice cracked at her like a whip, breaking off her words, "I didn't ask you into this house. If I'd had my way you wouldn't have been allowed through the door. Now get out! You made your choice years ago when you went to live in the gutter, and I repeat gutter, with your upstart." He moved two steps towards her, his head poked forward. "You think because he's making money that he can buy himself into decent society. Well, wherever he goes he'll be like a pig in a parlour and an object of derision."

"You would like to think so, wouldn't you?" She was glaring back at him. "You hate him; you've always hated him, and you wish that all the things you're saying were true. But they're not. He's getting on, rising fast, and he is accepted. Because he's himself, he's accepted. You called him an upstart. I – I wonder if you know what people call you."

"Vanessa!" It was her mother speaking. "Would you please go now."

"No. No, I won't until I've had my say." She kept her eyes on her father as she answered, "If there's anybody you should have hated it should have been Brett, but even knowing what he did you wouldn't have hated him, because you had felt guilty about him for so long. You had done him out of his job, his rightful job."

"Vanessa! Do you hear me? Leave the house this minute."

Vanessa now took three steps along the side of the breakfast table. It was a long way round to the door and she talked as she moved. "Brett never stood up to you. He hadn't the spunk to stand up to you, not as my Angus"— she stressed the "my" – "stood up to you when he was just Emily's son . . . and scum, as you have so kindly called him. And there's something I've learned over the years, and it's being proved at this moment, for even if he were still scum he'd be twice the man that you are, and he'll be a name in this town when you're forgotten, like you forgot your own people, my grandfather Ratcliffe."

"GET OUT!" Jonathan Ratcliffe's hand moved towards the sideboard and groped blindly for something to grip, to throw, to hurl, while his eyes remained fastened on his daughter; and Jane Ratcliffe, rushing in front of him, cried at Vanessa, "Go, will you! Go!"

It was Susan who, coming into the room, grabbed her sister's arm and pulled her into the hall and to the front door, and almost pushed her through it as she cried, "You were mad to come here. You know he'll never forgive you. You've only made things worse. And if you were actually aiming to get him to leave this house you've achieved it."

It was because she knew every inch of the curved drive that she could walk down it with her hand covering her eyes. It was as she turned out of the drive into the main road that a car raced towards her and pulled up with a skidding of brakes, and Angus shot out and stood confronting her, his face livid with an anger that had bleached his rugged complexion white and which had the power to frighten her as her father's anger had not done.

"YOU! YOU!" The spittle sprayed from his lips, and when she bent her head and fell against him, muttering his name, his body remained rigid, and he growled, "Don't you bloody-well 'Oh Angus' me. I'm going in there and getting that deed, if it means I do life for it."

She was gripping his coat as she sobbed, "He . . . he hasn't got it. It's here," She lifted her arm, from which hung the bag, and he snatched it from her and, tearing it

361

open, looked at the long, thick envelope that was wedged inside. He brought the air into his body so quickly that it sent him coughing and spluttering, and he turned from her and leant against the car.

He hadn't been able to take it in when his mother had told him where she had gone. She'd said she'd better tell him in order to break his fall. To break his fall! He had worked for years to get even with that bastard of a Ratcliffe and to see Vanessa installed in her rightful sphere, and what does she do? She takes all his efforts, his early strivings, his sixteen to eighteen hours a day, running, scurrying, planning, aye, and cheating, cheating other men out of contracts with the help of Andrew Fowler, and hands it to the one man he'd like to hang.

His mother had dared to tell him that Vanessa had asked to have the house in her name precisely in order to be able to go to her father and sell it to him, and at the same price. Not only had she tricked him but she had got his mother on to her side an' all, because the old bitch had bawled at him that no man in his right senses would expect his wife to go and live next door to her people after the way they had treated her, and that his wife wasn't out for revenge, only him. And he had bawled back at her that Vanessa would live in that house if he had to tie her in it, and let anybody get in his way to try and stop him getting that deed back from Ratcliffe, and they wouldn't live to tell the tale. And that went for her an' all!

And here he was within a few yards of his new home and his wife crying as if he had knocked her teeth in. And that's what he'd like to do at this very minute. He gripped her by the arm and pushed her into the car. Then, taking his seat, he turned the car swiftly about, drove down to the next gate and into the drive of The Larches.

Vanessa had been sobbing so much that she didn't realize where she was until the car stopped and she looked out of the window. Then she blinked upwards and turned to him and whimpered, "Oh, no! No, Angus."

"Get out!" He reached down and pulled her on to the gravel. Then taking firm hold of her, he mounted the steps, put the key in the lock, turned it, and pushed her before him into the house.

They stood in the hall, Vanessa with her head down, he with his up looking about him. He was in Arthur Brett's house. No, no; he was in Angus Cotton's house; but what he saw didn't please him. The hall was big and dark; the panelling browning to black; the twisted rails of the stairs gave them an old-fashioned appearance. This was an old house; it would take thousands to modernise it. He left her and moved towards a door and looked into a room with an ornate and very high ceiling and windows at the far end looking out on a tangle of undergrowth. He passed her once more and looked in another room. It was smaller and the walls looked as if they hadn't been papered or the woodwork painted since the place had been built, and his knowing eye detected the bulge of dry rot in the two-foot high skirting board to the side of the fireplace.

Vanessa stood perfectly still all the while he looked round the ground floor, and when he stood before her again he said quietly, "It'll be all right when it's done up."

Now she looked straight into his face. "I'll never live here, Angus," she said. "You can't make me."

"Then why did you let me go on and buy the bloody place?" He was bawling now in a restrained way.

"Because I knew I couldn't stop you. You had to buy it. You had to do something to get even with father. Well, now you've got even with him. When I asked you to put it in my name I saw it as a way of getting the hatred out of your system and making up for what I had done to them, because I don't hoodwink myself about that point, Angus. What I did shook the foundations of their life. It might be narrow; they might be mean-spirited, they are mean spirited; so what I did had a greater effect on them than it would have had it happened to parents more generous-minded. Their whole aim in life was social prestige, and I tore the foundations of it from under their feet. I . . . I might as well tell you now, I've wanted to go back for years; I've wanted to see them, not because I loved them, but, well, I can't really explain, ties, blood, kinship, what you will, but I've wanted to see them; I wanted to know if I was forgiven; and I've found out . . . They'll never forgive me. My father will live and die hating me. I knew he'd rather be crucified than be under the slightest obligation to either of us, and – and it saddens me to the very soul. I can't help it. That's how it is."

The mighty wind was being taken out of his sails. A deflating calm was settling on him. He fought it by saying, "We could pull it down and build."

"No, no, Angus; it wouldn't make any difference. You see, I couldn't bear to live near them. And anyway, they wouldn't allow it, they'd move."

"That's what I was hoping." There was iron in his voice again. "To put them on the move; to let them see that he isn't the only one that can crack a whip and see men jump."

"And what would that achieve? He would move to a bigger and better place. He could raise the money; his name is good."

"Meaning mine isn't?"

"You know I don't mean that."

"Look, I don't mind telling you now that I've had to do some twisting and bribing to get this piece of land. The house doesn't matter; it's the land. Yet all the while I've seen you here in this house, where you belong."

"I don't belong in this house, Angus. What is more, I've never liked this house. I belong," she paused, "I belong where you belong; but you don't belong here. Face it; you don't belong here."

He turned from her, the colour rushing into his face, and she said softly now, "I realized a long time ago that I never belonged here either. I was the odd one out. I couldn't help being born here no more than you could being born in Ryder's Row."

She watched him walk away from her and open the doors that led on to the overgrown terrace, and slowly she followed him. Her heart beating rapidly she followed him down the steps and along the narrow path that led into the wood, and all the while she knew what he was thinking. Somewhere in here they used to meet, him and her. She had known all along; at least since she had learned he had bought the place, that this moment would come, but she prayed now he wouldn't make his way down to the river and the summerhouse.

He stopped under an oak tree, almost on the spot where Brett had kissed her good-bye on that last night before he died, and standing dumbly before him she returned his look, his questioning, probing look; then, her voice breaking, she said, "Come away from here, Angus, please. Please. I'm asking you, begging you. Please."

He turned and walked silently up into the house, through it and to the car. His jaw was stiff and his eyes hard.

When they reached the bottom of Brampton Hill she broke the silence by saying, "Would . . . would you like to drive me out to the quarry, Angus?"

He cast a quick glance at her; then, his eyes on the road again, he growled, "Why the quarry?"

"I . . . I would like to show you something."

"At the quarry?" His mouth was square.

"Yes, YES, ANGUS." She shouted the last two words, and when again he glanced at her she was looking out through the windscreen and she said, quite loudly still, "You don't seem to take anything in unless it's bawled at you." Another time this would have made him smile, even laugh, but his expression didn't change; yet when they came to the roundabout he didn't go back into town but went straight ahead.

Fifteen minutes later he drew the car up in yellow

mud beside a great hole; and when he alighted he didn't open the door for her to get out but stood by the bonnet waiting, silent and tense. She came now and stood beside him, her hands resting on the bonnet as she asked, "How much would you have to pay for it, I mean the quarry itself and the bit of hill beyond?" She nodded into the distance.

"Pay for it? You mean buy it?" He screwed up his face at her.

"Yes."

"In the name of God what for? Why should I buy a hole? There's nothing more I can get out of it, it's finished."

She walked away from him on to flat ground, stepping on hard surfaces where she could find them, and made her way past stone outhouses that were the only remains of a country house that had once stood where the sandpit was now. She climbed a slope, not looking back to see if he was following, and at the top she stood and looked about her.

Angus stopped when he was a yard or so from her. He didn't want to go near her at the moment. If she had been May or someone like May he would have skelped her lugs long afore this, and likely given her a black eye into the bargain. Making a blasted fool of him. But she wasn't May, or someone like May. Funny, he should think of May now; she hadn't crossed his mind for years. He supposed he had thought of her, because she was the kind who wouldn't have thwarted him; his word would have been law to her. She wouldn't have wanted to have brought him down to pocket size.

Vanessa was pointing now. "Look," she said; "down there. There's the river. It's like a scaly snake going round the town, isn't it? And over there." She pointed to the right. "You can see for miles and miles, open country-side." She came towards him and put her hands on his thick, broad chest before she said, "I'd like you to build our house here, Angus."

He strained back from her, his face all creased up, his head moving slowly. Then with a jerk he was free from her hands, and he kicked the earth as he said, "Here! You must be bloody well barmy, woman."

"I'd – I'd like it built here, Angus." She was smiling now. "I can see it. I came out last week and measured."

"You what!" His shout resounded down the valley.

"That's it, shout." She nodded at him. "You'll hear the echo of it from up here."

He spoke a few tones lower now as he said, "You came up here and measured . . . ?"

She stared at him. She thought he was going to choke. She felt strangely calm now, at peace, and, more strangely still, in control of the situation . . . and him.

"Yes, I came up here and measured. I want it long and low, and spreading, with a paved terrace all about it. And that," she swung round and pointed to the quarry, "that'll be a lake with a boat on it. Two boats; and a diving board, just there." She pointed farther away to the side.

"Christ Almighty!" He had his head bowed now, holding his brow.

"How much land is there altogether, including . . . the hole?"

"You're not serious?"

"I was never more serious. That's a trite phrase." She smiled slightly. "What I should have said was, I'm doing something on my own for the first time in my life . . . besides having babies." Her smile widened. "How much land is there?" she repeated.

"About four acres."

"Very nice." She put her head on one side. "There used to be heather on this part of the fell at one time, and not so very long ago because I can remember it. We'll have heather again, a heather garden, and shrubs, rhododendrons and azaleas. And the house on the rise here." She spread an arm wide. "And the gardens running down to the road on that side, and down to the lake on that."

She was walking away from him now, down the slope towards the stone buildings. The door of the first one was half ajar and she went in and looked about her. The place had three rooms. One had been used as an office, the other two as a storage place for tools. She saw Emily living here, near Angus, yet still independent. She said so as soon as he came through the door.

He stood staring at her again. She looked different, more beautiful, more of a woman at this moment than she had ever been before; even after having the bairns. She was stately, mature, classy; aye, that was the word, classy. He was still furious inside at her, at the position she had put him in; at the way she had brought his castle tumbling down as if she had barraged it with a twelve-pounder, and now she was asking for favours . . . . No, she wasn't asking, she was demanding. She had her plans all made, and he knew that when he had time to simmer down and think he would realize that she was right about building above the hole. He knew that she had what he would never have, vision. And she had thought of his mother an' all. He would remember that, aye.

She had her back to him and she startled him now by saying, "You don't have to buy me anymore, Angus."

"WHAT!"

"You heard what I said. You still think you have to buy me; you've got to give me something to keep me with you. I've so many clothes I don't know where to put them, and jewellery that I never wear. You know, Angus, your imagination is limited, even to your own capabilities and attraction. Oh yes, you're always yelling about what you can do, but inside you're always fearful of not being able to accomplish it. It's true, isn't it?" She waited, and when he didn't answer she went on, "I've never really talked to you, shown you my real feelings, and you've been aware of this all the while, but I'd like you to know something now. It's just this, that whether I knew it or not I loved you when I married you, and now I can't love you any more . . . I mean," she moved her head hastily, "I can't love you any more than I do; I'll never be able to love you any more than I do at this moment. If you gave me everything in the world it wouldn't make any difference. As to yourself, I don't want you to change, no matter what you think. I know that only with you, and through you, can I be happy . . . . There's been a sort of vacant spot in me for a long time. You didn't fill it, and the children didn't fill it, so I thought it was the miss of my people, and my venture to-day was as much to see them and find out as to make things right in other ways. But now I know that we're cut off for good and all, the void, in a strange way, is filled, and . . . and I'm not unhappy about it now. One thing I know is that I want to start a life of my own, on my own plane, on our own plane, neither lower-class nor middle-class, but our class. Your mother and Rosie have ceased to stress how different I am from them by every look and word, yet they still look upon me in the same way as they did when I first came into their lives. Beneath the surface we haven't mixed. But you and I are different, Angus; we've rubbed off on each other." Her voice was trembling as she finished, "I love you, Angus; and – and not just out of gratitude, as you've always thought."

Her whole body trembled as he came towards her, and when he held her face between his rough hands she put hers up and cupped his. Slowly now he dropped his head forward on to her shoulder and muttered thickly, "Thanks, Van. Thanks." Then after a moment he added, haltingly, "I love you so much I'd go crazy without you. You know that, don't you?" Her heart beats were sending the blood flowing fast through her veins and she was about to answer, "You'll never have to be without me, darling, never." But that was a reply she could have made to Arthur Brett had she married him. It was a formal, acceptable, reply. What she wanted was a reply to fit the plane on which they were going to live from now on. If Emily had ever been called upon to reply to such a statement undoubtedly she would have said, "You might go crazy without me, lad, but there's an even chance you'll go bloody well stark staring mad with me." But she wasn't Emily, and she couldn't bring herself to swear to be amusing. Yet she wanted to make him laugh as Emily could; she wanted to bring him back to normality; she wanted to set the pattern for the future, and so she ventured, in a good imitation of her mother-in-law's voice, Aye, I do, an' I'll Emily Cotton well see that you never get the chance to be without me, lad."

The result was even more successful than she had anticipated. His head came up and he stared at her blankly for a moment; then he dropped it back on his shoulders and let out a roar of deep laughter, such laughter as she hadn't heard from him for a long time. It seemed to sweep away the obsession of his years of striving, and, as he picked her up, as if she were a child, and swung her around, she laughed loudly too.

When they were standing still again, he gathered her into his arms and he looked into her face before he said, with a self-conscious shyness that was new, "Remember Mam's bit of poetry? Well, I'm always saying it in me mind to you:

'I have you fast in my fortress,
And will not let you depart,
But put you down into the dungeon
In the round tower of my heart.

And there will I keep you for ever,
Yes, for ever and a day,
Till the walls shall crumble to ruin,
And moulder in dust away.'

"Oh, Angus. Angus." For the first time in their joint lives her mouth dropped fiercely on to his.

Bower Place and Ryder's Row were merging.